Linda Green is a journalist. She lives in West Yorkshire with her husband and son. I DID A BAD THING is her first novel.

I did a BAD thing

Linda Green

headline
review

First published in 2007
by HEADLINE REVIEW
An imprint of HEADLINE PUBLISHING GROUP
First published in paperback in 2007
by HEADLINE REVIEW
An imprint of HEADLINE PUBLISHING GROUP

3

Cataloguing in Publication Data is available

from the British Library

ISBN 978 0 7553 3341 7

Typeset in Clarendon by Avon DataSet Ltd,
Bidford on Avon, Warwickshire

Printed and bound in Great Britain by

Mackays of Chatham plc, Chatham, Kent Headline's policy is

to use papers that are natural, renewable and recyclable

products and made from wood grown in sustainable forests.

The logging and manufacturing processes are expected to

conform to the environmental regulations of the country of

origin. HEADLINE PUBLISHING GROUP
An Hachette Livre UK Company
338 Euston Road
London NW1 3BH

For Ian and Rohan

Acknowledgements

Warmest thanks to the following people: My brilliant editor Harriet Evans, for helping me get the words right; everyone at Headline; my agent Anthony Goff for his guidance and support and for making it happen; everyone at David Higham Associates; Martyn Bedford of Literary Intelligence for his critiques, invaluable advice and encouragement to persevere; my creative writing students for providing such a welcome break from the rejections; all the journalists I've ever worked with for providing me with inspiration and the odd anecdote to embellish; my friends and family for their support and encouragement; my gorgeous son Rohan for delaying his entrance into the world to allow me to finish the first draft and for finally going to sleep early enough to allow me to complete the final draft. And most importantly my husband Ian for his emotional and financial support, childcare and domestic services beyond the call of duty, never losing faith and waiting eight years (though not without complaint!) for the widescreen television I promised to buy when I got a book deal. May the portable TV rest in peace.

One

His name was fourth on the list. Coming after Flaherty, Rowbotham and Lees. It was his name but it didn't mean it was him. Only that after all this time, I still flinched at the sight of it.

'Is this it?' I said to Terry, waving the piece of paper in the air. 'No CVs or anything?'

'They're probably somewhere in Doreen's filing system,' he said, staring out from his goldfish bowl office across the newsroom.

'And where is Doreen today?'

'Shopping for shoes in Stratford-upon-Avon.'

'What's wrong with the shoe shops in Birmingham?'

'Not the same level of service, apparently.'

I shook my head. Doreen had filed Princess Diana's death under M for minor royal. Trying to find the CVs would involve probing the dark recesses of her mind as well as her filing cabinets. I didn't want to go there. To be honest, I didn't even want to be doing these interviews. But Phil was still off with stress (allegedly caused by the disappearance of his deputy editor clipboard) and Keith and Lisa were too busy presiding over the military junta on the news desk to be called upon. Besides, for some reason I had yet to work out, I was Terry's 'chosen one'. Which explained why I was sitting there staring at a list of names. One of which was causing the crisp white shirt I had put on that morning to stick to my back.

'Do you remember anything about them?' I said. 'First

names, male or female, where they're working?'

The permanent furrow in Terry's brow deepend. 'One's a woman, works on some magazine, one's shifted on the nationals, one's a lobby correspondent for the Press Association and one works for the *Western Mail* in Cardiff. Not sure which is which, though.'

It wasn't much help. A bit like playing the fifty-fifty card on *Who Wants to be a Millionaire*. I was left with two possible candidates, the middle ones. I was pretty sure he'd gone to London at some point as I'd seen his byline on political stories in various national newspapers. But my latest efforts to Google him had drawn a blank. He seemed to have gone off the radar. I managed a thin smile at Terry as I tapped my fingers repeatedly on the desk. Hating myself for being so pathetic, for getting worked up like this. I had to stop panicking, think rationally. Reassure myself that there was no reason on earth why he would apply for the job of political editor on the *Birmingham Evening Gazette*.

'Let's hope they're a bit more memorable in the flesh,' I said. Not the last one on the list, though. I didn't want that one to be memorable. Because, daft as it seemed, I didn't even want to work with someone with the same surname as him.

A robust knock interrupted my thoughts and the door opened to reveal a stern-faced woman dressed in a charcoal trouser suit with a fine white pinstripe.

'Marie Flaherty,' she said, only a trace of a Scouse accent remaining. Terry shook her hand, introduced himself and turned to me.

'This is Sarah Roberts, our chief reporter.'

Marie Flaherty nodded, shook hands like a man and sat down without being asked. I was impressed. The rest of the newsroom, it seemed, were not. On the other side of the glass, Cayte was holding up an ice-skating-style scorecard reading '3.5' followed by 'boots' as a way of explanation of her marking criteria which, she had already informed me, would concentrate on artistic impression rather than technical merit. As Marie detailed the qualities she could bring to the role, I allowed my gaze to drop to her feet, which were encased in black patent boots with kitten heels and splats of white fur all over them. It was weird how I never noticed these things myself.

'Anything you'd like to ask, Sarah?' Terry was looking at me, unaware that I hadn't been paying attention.

'Have you got any cuttings we can look at?' I said, hoping to fill in some career details from the missing CVs.

She unclasped her immaculate briefcase, which looked as if it had been bought especially for the occasion. As she pulled out a plastic folder a fluffy white toy dog with a red ribbon and a bell round its neck tumbled on to the floor. I waited for her to apologise, to blush, explain that it belonged to her daughter or something. She didn't. She simply giggled like a high-pitched machine gun and squeaked, 'Ooops, lucky mascot,' as she picked it up and sat it on her knee.

'Oh, God,' I groaned as I lowered my head into my hands. The warning sign was obvious now. Woman in unsuitable footwear. I should have guessed she'd be an emotional flake. She had a nerve to call herself a journalist. Come to think of it, she probably worked for *Dog World*. It would be on her CV, somewhere in the filing cabinet.

Terry couldn't suppress his laughter as Marie gathered her things and scuttled out of the office shortly afterwards.

'I wasn't sure who I should be interviewing,' he said. 'Her or the poodle.'

'I'm sorry,' I said.

'What for?'

'On behalf of the female species, I apologise for her existence.'

Terry laughed. 'Oh well, that's the token woman gone. Now we'll get on to the serious candidates.'

He said things like that to wind me up. He wasn't the only one. 'Sarah-baiting' it was called in the office.

Rowbotham looked like a Rowbotham should. Tall, sculpted hair like that stand-in newsreader on BBC1 at the weekends, creases in his trousers, perspiration on his upper lip. Cayte was holding up '2.1' before he'd even sat down.

He introduced himself as Rowbotham, as if he was a civil servant in the MOD. They pissed me off, people who pretended they didn't have a first name. I decided to go in hard.

'Can you tell me how you'd make politics relevant to the lives of our readers in Handsworth?' I asked.

Rowbotham raised his eyebrows slightly, shifted in his chair so he was facing Terry, and began. 'I don't believe in dumbing down, Mr Kay. I believe in encouraging working class people to embrace the complex political issues we face today, to recognise the implications that closer European union and the creation of a federal Europe would have on the sovereignty of this country . . .'

His voice droned on, directed exclusively in Terry's direction. As if I was some dumb secretary hired to relay the questions. I resisted the temptation to yank his head round to face me, deciding instead to let him continue talking himself out of a job. What he didn't realise was that Terry's instructions to the previous incumbent on the night of the local elections had been 'Don't make it too political.'

We were down to the last two. I could feel beads of sweat gathering on my forehead, belying my otherwise cool exterior. It was as if the old Sarah was seeping out of me. Telling me it was OK to lose control. It was fine that a tiny part of me wanted it to be him. Which it wasn't, I knew that. I had Jonathan now. I had a whole new life. The old one had nothing to offer me.

At some point in the proceedings Rowbotham had evidently stopped to draw breath and Terry managed to get him out of the office. Because a new man was sitting in the chair now. A man with a ridiculously small head for his body. Who was twiddling his thumbs, which sat on hands which were way too big for his arms. I imagined a new Mr Men book. *Mr Out of Proportion.* With a primary colour version of our man Mr Lees on the cover. Cayte had placed her scorecard on the top of her computer. '1.5 (ginger pinhead)'. I thought she was being a bit harsh. I didn't have a problem with red hair. I found the Welsh accent rather soothing after Rowbotham's clipped tones. And he seemed to be very knowledgeable about the Welsh Assembly.

'So, tell us about Cardiff.' Terry liked questions like that. Thought they opened people up.

Mr Lees took a deep breath, thought for a moment, his eyes glistening, and started to cry. Not a single tear trickling down his face but a torrent, enough to warrant a man-sized box of Kleenex. I noticed his crumpled jacket, the faint smell of alcohol which had drifted into the room with him, and wondered if he was going through some kind of personal crisis.

'I'm sorry,' said Mr Lees, eventually, his long fingers like windscreen wipers, brushing away the tears. 'I get very emotional talking about my birthplace.'

That was it. No family tragedy. No tale of death or destruction. The guy simply liked the place where he was born. I was quite fond of Leamington Spa myself but couldn't imagine ever bawling my eyes out at the mention of it.

I looked at Terry; he shrugged. I rolled my eyes. Three down, one to go. I wasn't going to be put out of my misery yet, though. I had to wait for Mr Lees to compose himself, to tell us how his great-grandfather came to work at Cardiff docks and how it was a joy to live and work with his fellow countrymen, before he finally left. Taking a look round the newsroom as he went, where Cayte's sign was still on prominent display.

'Imagine if I offered him the job,' said Terry, shaking his head. 'He wouldn't be able to tear himself away. Tiger Bay would be flooded during his leaving speech.'

I nodded and smiled. I wasn't thinking about Mr Lees though. I was thinking about the next person who was going to walk through the door. The one who, unless this was some kind of set-up for an 'interviewees from hell' TV show, was going to get the job.

'I reckon the next one will be smoking a spliff and suggest we run a feature on MPs' favourite porn websites,' said Terry, chuckling to himself. I wanted to remind him that he'd selected these people. It didn't say much for his judgement. Unless the rest of the applicants had been worse than this, which was hard to imagine.

We waited for fifteen minutes past his allotted time of midday. That was when I knew. He always used to be late for everything. It was simply a matter of waiting then, until I caught a glimpse of his head and shoulders bobbing along above the filing cabinets.

'I'll ring reception,' Terry said. 'See if he's left a message.'

'No need,' I said. 'He's here.'

'How do you know?'

'Female intuition,' I said.

The door opened and he walked in. Resplendent in his Burberry trench coat. Hair the colour of Bournville chocolate. Stubble caressing his chin. Shit. He looked even better than I remembered.

'Nick Hardwick,' he said. 'Sorry I'm late.'

His introduction was directed at Terry. But by the time he got to the apology he was, rather aptly, looking at me. Seven years too late, actually. That's what I should have said. I didn't though. I smiled politely at him. Waiting for him to react.

'Sarah.' He sounded surprised, unsure, nervous even.

I tried to hide the fact that I was disappointed he didn't sound pleased.

'Long time, no see,' I replied. It was a stupid thing to say. I'd tried to sound unimpressed but it had come out wrong. I stood up and steadied myself for a moment. I felt like one of those balloon animals, knotted and twisted in all the wrong places. I waited for him to come towards me, to hold out his hand, before I stepped forward and shook it.

'How are you?' he said, as if he cared.

'Fine, thanks,' I replied, as if I didn't.

'I take it you two know each other,' Terry said. I was trapped in some crap movie where everyone says stupid things.

I waited for Nick to answer but both he and Terry were looking at me.

'Nick was news editor on the *Rugby Chronicle* when I was a trainee there.'

I managed to make it sound as distant and fleeting as possible. Hardly worth a mention. Giving no inkling of what had really happened between us. I glanced at Nick to see if he looked hurt. He didn't.

'Small world, journalism,' said Terry. 'That's why I'm nice to Sarah, in case she ends up as my boss one day.'

My laugh sounded strained. Nick's wasn't much better. We all sat down. Nick took off his trench coat, looked round for a coat stand and, seeing there wasn't one, hung it over the back of his chair. He was immaculately dressed in a brown moleskin suit and cream shirt. It was weird seeing him like that; I remembered a much scruffier version. I could smell his aftershave on my hand. I didn't recall him wearing it before. I wondered what else had changed. He was older, for a start. Thirty-seven by my reckoning. But unfortunately he was one of those annoying people who got better-looking with age. The smile was still the same. I used to be a sucker for that smile. I tried to block out the memory of the last time I had seen it. In case I dislodged the cry of anguish which was still stuck somewhere in my throat.

Out of the corner of my eye I could see Cayte brandishing her scorecard: '6.0 (drop-dead gorgeous)'. I glanced around. Every pair of female eyes in the office were looking in his direction. And one pair of eyes belonging to a male sub-editor who was single and had a penchant for black polo-necks. Nick clearly hadn't lost his touch. Bastard.

'So, tell me about yourself, Nick. And why you want this job.'

Terry asked the question. I feigned indifference to the answer.

'Well, I've always had a keen interest in politics. I used to be politically active in my younger days. Bit of a hothead to tell you the truth.' He glanced at me and grinned. I didn't respond. 'I've spent several years shifting on the nationals in London and covered a lot of political stories in that time. But to be honest I've become disillusioned with national newspapers. I miss the contact with readers, the feeling of serving a community. And most of the stuff I was covering was tittle-tattle, nothing that affected real people's lives. This is a chance to do what I love doing, covering real politics about real people.'

It was as if he'd swallowed a book called *How to Impress Regional Newspaper Editors in Interviews* for breakfast that morning. I glanced at Terry: he had that expression on his face. Like a kid who'd found a Jammie Dodger in a box of Rich Tea biscuits.

He was going to get the job. I was going to have to see him, hear him, smell his aftershave, every working day. It was bad enough that he had the power to invade my dreams. Walking back into my life as well was such a bloody cheek. I sat on my hands to stop them shaking. Sarah Roberts didn't do shaking. Not the one everyone here knew, anyway. Nick only knew the old Sarah. I

8

wondered if I should tell him that she was no longer with us. Give him the chance to offer his condolences.

'Sarah?' It was Terry's voice. He and Nick were both looking at me. I guessed it was my turn to ask a question. Just one question, any question. Quickly.

'Who, what, why, when, where, how,' I blurted out.

That's what they taught you at journalism college. And they were the only questions I could think of. Nick and Terry were looking at me as if I'd lost the plot. Which I had. Ten minutes in his company and I was already a jibbering wreck. God knows what I'd be like after working with him for a month. But I wasn't going to let him do it to me again. Churn me up inside and then spit me out. I was stronger than before. The brittleness had been replaced by a Teflon coating. I took a deep breath.

'Nigel, sorry, Nick. Let me expand on that. Who are you trying to kid with this stuff? What went wrong for you in London? Why didn't you get a staff job? When did you decide you wanted to live in Birmingham? Where do you see yourself in five years' time and how seriously do you think we should take you?'

Terry finally broke the silence which followed with what sounded like a cross between a laugh and a snort.

'I think that was Sarah's way of finding out if you're up to the task of sparring with Clare Short,' he said.

Nick looked up. 'Actually,' he said, 'I think that was Sarah's way of getting past the bullshit. She was always very good at that.'

I wasn't sure if it was praise or sarcasm. I opted for what I hoped was a neutral expression.

'Right, moving swiftly on . . .' said Terry.

'I haven't answered yet,' said Nick.

'You don't have to.'

'I want to. OK, I admit it, I'm a sad failure of a hack. I didn't get a staff job because my face didn't fit. I didn't arse-lick as much as was required and I wasn't prepared to drop stories if they didn't fit the political line of whoever I was working for. Plus I was the wrong side of thirty-five. I never had any intention of living in Birmingham. I've no idea where I'll be in five years' time but if I'm still here it will be because I like it. And you should take me as seriously as anyone who comes in here telling you it's their lifetime's ambition to work for the *Birmingham Evening Gazette* and that if they get the job they'll never look at the ads in the *Press Gazette* again.'

Another pause followed. Terry sat scratching his head. He glanced across at me and raised his eyebrows. I shrugged. Terry nodded. I looked down at my foot just in time to see the bullet I'd fired blow it apart.

'Congratulations, Nick,' Terry said, standing up and grinning as he held his hand out across the desk. 'When can you start?'

Two

'So, did he get the job?'

I hadn't even sat down at my desk before Cayte started. I made a point of putting my notebook away in the drawer, clicking the lid back on my pen and shuffling some papers before I answered.

'Why the sudden interest in our political coverage?'

'Well, he's a damn sight better-looking than Andrew Marr, for a start. Did he get it or not?'

I realised the newsroom was eerily silent. I glanced around. Several people pretended to start typing.

'Come on,' I said. 'Your turn to buy lunch.' Cayte gave a toothy grin, picked up the heap of festering sackcloth which she claimed was a bag and headed for the door.

We made it to the swipe card barrier downstairs before her persistent questioning wore me down.

'Yes, he got it. But only because the others were all fruitloops.'

'Excellent.'

'You're a bit keen, aren't you? Forgive me if I'm wrong, but aren't you going out with someone called Jeremy?'

'His name's Jazz, actually.'

I'd forgotten the recent rebranding exercise. Apparently Jeremy was not a suitable name for a guitarist in a rap metal band called Septicaemia.

'Does the artist formerly known as Jeremy not do it for you any more, then?' I asked.

'I like to keep my options open, that's all.'

This was Cayte's euphemism for saying she didn't do monogamy. I gave her my disapproving look as we pushed through the front doors and hurried towards the subway, the October sunshine failing to take the chill out of the air.

'So, come on. Dish the dirt, then. What's the new guy like?'

'Well, sorry to disappoint you, but he's married, for a start.'

'Is he? Only he wasn't wearing a ring.'

I came to an abrupt halt on the bottom of the steps while I rewound the video in my head. It turned out I hadn't looked at his left hand during the interview. I tried to rewind further, to the last time I'd seen him. There'd been a wedding ring then. I could see it glinting in the sun. I couldn't see anything else.

'Are you sure?' I asked.

'Yeah. I clocked him as he walked past. You know me, never one to miss a detail.'

Cayte had all the *Prime Suspects* on video and could match any scrap of forensic evidence to a particular episode. They called her DI Thorneycroft at work.

'Did he say he was married then?'

'Not in so many words,' I said, struggling to get out of the hole I'd dug for myself. 'He just kind of gave that impression.'

I started moving again. Marching through the urine-stench of the subway and up the steps the other side, not wanting Cayte to see my face. Thinking about Nick Hardwick and the significance of the missing ring. It sounded like the next offering by J.K. Rowling.

'So what's his name?' Cayte caught up with me as I began threading my way between the human traffic in Colmore Row.

'Hardwick.'

'First name?'

'Nick.'

'Reason you don't like him?'

'What?'

'He obviously rubbed you up the wrong way.'

I wasn't making a very good job of this. I didn't usually lie to Cayte. But it felt wrong to be talking about Nick. He didn't belong in this world. He belonged to another time. Another place. Telling Cayte about him would make him real.

'I thought he was a bit of a prick, that's all.'

'Why, what did he say?'

'Nothing in particular, he was just, you know, full of himself.'

'So how come he got the job?'

'I told you, the others were crap. Anyway, it was Terry's decision.'

'You didn't want him to get it, then?'

I hesitated, unsure of the true answer and the answer I should give to Cayte.

'No, I didn't.'

It was the answer I thought I should give to Cayte.

The queue at Starbucks was longer than usual, probably because we were later than usual. Nick's fault. I gave the ritual glance over my shoulder before I went in, aware that if Jonathan's mum saw me I would have some serious explaining to do. I couldn't remember exactly what it was Starbucks was supposed to have done. Polystyrene containers, low wages, cruelty to coffee beans or just one of those non-specific globalisation things. Whatever it was it was bad and my patronage of their premises was telling them it was OK to be bad (I had resisted the temptation to point out that it was also telling them they made a particularly fine sun-dried tomato, mozzarella and pesto panini. I was already in her bad books, I didn't want to make it any worse).

I ordered a decaf skinny latte to go with my panini.

'And a tall latte, please,' said Cayte, who would have had my unwanted portion of caffeine and fat in hers if they'd do it. I led the way downstairs. It was easier to eat upstairs but Cayte had a thing about the comfy chairs, the aubergine ones in particular.

'So, what have you been working on?' I said, keen to steer the conversation away from Nick.

'Oh, the usual pile of crap from news desk. Though I am following up a call from some bloke who reckons an al-Qaida cell are running a minicab firm in Winson Green.'

'Cayte.'

'I know. Unlikely, but these things are always worth checking out.'

I shook my head. 'Never guess who I had in the back of my cab last week. Only that Osama Bin Laden.'

'You won't be taking the piss when I break the story.'

'I'm still waiting for the one about Elvis being alive and well and working for Cadbury's.'

'You always spoil it by wanting the proof.'

'I told you, when I unwrap a Flake with "Love Me Tender" running through the middle, I'll believe you.'

Cayte turned up her nose, slurped her latte and got stuck into her tuna melt. I needed our lunch breaks together. Without them the sanity became unbearable.

'They're repeating the best ever *Taggart* tonight,' Cayte said as we made our way back to the office. I'd never watched *Taggart*. Cayte knew this but it didn't seem to make any difference.

'I'm afraid I shall be busy writing letters to President Putin about the disappearance of a human rights activist in the Chechen Republic.'

Cayte looked at me blankly for a moment before the penny dropped. 'God, you get to write to some good people with this Amnesty lark. He's quite sexy, Putin. In a KGB kind of way.'

I smiled, imagining Jonathan's reaction if he'd heard Cayte's comment. 'Yep, that's what it's all about. Scoring with Russian presidents.'

'Come on, you know you wouldn't do all this worthy stuff if it wasn't for Jonathan,' said Cayte.

'Yes I would.'

'Bollocks. You only agreed to be their press officer because you didn't want to upset him.'

'I couldn't turn him down in front of everyone. He is the secretary.'

Cayte shrugged and wiped the last trace of tuna melt from her lips. Clearly being secretary of the Birmingham South branch didn't strike her as sexy. Not even in an Amnesty International kind of way.

I bought a bunch of flowers at the petrol station on the way home from work. Yellow spray chrysanthemums with two orange gerberas thrown in to justify the £4.99 price tag. They would brighten the flat up a bit. I only seemed to notice how drab it was when we were due to host an Amnesty meeting. Maybe it was the thought of all those grim faces reflecting the beige walls.

Meetings alternated between our flat and the branch chair Rachel's house. She lived in a four-bedroom town-house in Moseley. All antique furniture, stripped floor-boards, real wool rugs and high ceilings. You practically had to shout to make yourself heard on the other side of the drawing room. Rachel called it that. She was the only person I knew who had a drawing room.

Coming to our flat after that experience must be a little like visiting Ikea when you're used to Fired Earth. No one ever said that, of course. They were far too polite.

I turned into Melville Road. It wasn't a bad place to live. The postal address was Edgbaston, which made it sound deceptively posh. We had trees, granted: huge old sycamores dotted at regular intervals along both sides of the road like bodyguards for the lampposts. But we were on the wrong side of the tracks, in our case the A456 which split Edgbaston in two. It didn't bother me; we couldn't have afforded a flat on the 'right' side, and it was nearer to the school where Jonathan taught. But I was conscious of it when the Amnesty people came armed with their steering-wheel locks and immobilisers.

I reversed first time into a tight parking space, hoping the neighbour walking his Alsatian was suitably impressed. The fallen leaves from the sycamores had started to congeal, making the pavement slippery. I opened the gate, wincing as the bottom scraped along the concrete, and pushed my way past the shrubs which overhung the path. Once inside the main entrance I squeezed past Jonathan's bike before letting myself into the flat. The kitchen door was wide open, Jonathan was playing air guitar to Led Zeppelin in between stirring something which smelt very good and was bubbling away on the hob. He dropped the air guitar rather sheepishly as soon as he saw me.

'Oh, thanks, you shouldn't have.' He was looking at the flowers, his blue eyes fizzing, the ends of his mouth turning up, dimples showing. He never bought me flowers. Something to do with pesticides. I was waiting for the day they sold organic gerberas. Not that it bothered me, the flower thing. He made up for it in other ways.

He rested the wooden spoon on the side of the wok, bounded forward and grabbed me round the waist before kissing me on the lips. Almost a year we'd been living together. Yet he still greeted me with the same enthusiasm he'd shown the very first evening. His head nuzzled against mine. I resisted the temptation to ruffle his choppy hair, knowing how he hated it.

'Hello, you. Tough day?' he said, finally letting me go. I took it to mean I must look stressed.

'Frustrating. Didn't manage to get much done.'

'Did they want you on news desk again?'

I should have said yes. I don't know why I didn't.

'No. Terry asked me to sit in on the interviews for political editor.' I took the flowers over to the sink and started unwrapping the cellophane, conscious of the colour rising in my cheeks.

'I'd have thought you'd enjoy that.'

'Most of them were crap. The only woman was awful, really embarrassing.'

'Who got it then?'

'Oh, some guy from London.' I took the scissors out and started snipping the ends of the stalks. Diagonally, like you're supposed to.

'Any good?'

My stomach tightened. It was a simple, innocent question. So why did it feel like he knew something? He couldn't, of course. He didn't even know Nick existed. There had been no reason to tell. And lots of reasons not to.

'He was OK. Best of a bad bunch.' I carried on snipping.

'You'll have to introduce me at the Christmas do. I might be able to persuade him to do some stuff on the Green Party, or cover some human rights issues.'

I couldn't think of anything worse. Jonathan and Nick in the same room. Past and present colliding. Me, cringing in the middle.

'There won't be much left of those in a minute,' said Jonathan.

I looked down. I'd snipped away most of the stems.

'We've only got a small vase,' I said, hurrying into the lounge.

It was true. We only had a small most things. The portable TV was conspicuous by its lack of inches. The sofa was a close fit for two. The round table at the other end of the lounge took four at a push. Which was fine; we didn't need anything bigger.

I took the recycled glass vase (the bottom half of a wine bottle with a squiggle painted round the rim) back to the kitchen, filled it with water and plunged the flowers in. The gerberas barely poked over the rim.

Jonathan smiled at me. I wished he wouldn't, it made me feel guiltier than ever about Nick. For a second I considered telling him. At least mentioning that I'd worked with Nick before. But it would seem strange saying it now. It would be obvious that I was covering something up.

'How were the kids?' I said.

'A bit hyper this afternoon. Lewis thumped Bradley for calling him gay. I sat them all down and tried to do the "What's so bad about being homosexual?" thing.'

'And?'

'Lewis asked if I liked it up the arse.'

I gave Jonathan's shoulder a reassuring squeeze. He had spent most of his career waiting for that *Dead Poets Society* moment. A cry of 'Captain, my captain', and the sound of children scrambling on to their desks in a mark of unbridled respect. It wasn't going to happen at an inner city comprehensive in Birmingham. I'd realised that the first time I'd met him. Some worthy scheme he'd organised to get lads reading which I'd covered for the paper. But Jonathan had never stopped believing. And I didn't have the heart to take away the hope.

'Oh well, at least you try,' I said.

He shrugged. Nelson emerged from his basket, limped over and rubbed his smooth black body against Jonathan's legs.

'Hey,' said Jonathan, scooping him up in his arms, 'are you trying to console me, too?'

I suspected Nelson (named after Mandela, not Horatio) was actually just hungry. He'd sussed Jonathan out right from the beginning. Played the 'I'm homeless and have a leg missing' card, which had been guaranteed to work.

'Just give that a stir while I feed him,' said Jonathan, pointing to the wok. I swore I could hear Nelson purring 'sucker' under his breath. I picked up the spoon and moved it around in a figure of eight as Jonathan had taught me. It was about as far as my culinary skills went, stirring. But as Jonathan was such a whiz in the kitchen it didn't really matter.

'How long till it's ready?' I asked, peering into what appeared to be a vegetable chilli.

'Twenty minutes or so,' said Jonathan, carrying the tin of Whiskas at arm's length back to the fridge (the vet had advised against the vegetarian cat food Jonathan had found on the Internet, so Nelson was the only member of the household who ate meat. I didn't miss it that much, to be honest. And as Jonathan did all the cooking I didn't feel in a position to complain).

'Why don't you get a quick bath while I finish off and tidy up a bit before the gang descend on us?' he said.

I smiled at Jonathan as I brushed past on the way to the bathroom.

'You're too good to me,' I said.

'No such thing,' he replied with a grin.

Rachel and Richard were the first to arrive, both clutching piles of Amnesty newsletters, reports and magazines we already had. Rachel greeted us with kisses on both cheeks. Very continental but done with a distinctly British lack of warmth.

'All right, you two.' Richard had the sort of Brummie accent that comedians took the piss out of. Personally, I found it rather endearing. Jonathan shook his hand warmly and asked where he'd got his fleece jacket. It was one of his weaknesses, fleeces (the others being a passion for seventies rock music and Aston Villa).

'The Rohan shop in Sutton Coldfield,' said Richard.

Jonathan nodded, obviously calculating the likely price tag in his head, and said nothing. If he did ever wish he worked at a private girls' school, he never let it show.

They came through to the lounge and Rachel lowered herself on to a bean bag. She always did this, even when she arrived first and the sofa was empty. She looked uncomfortable but insisted she was fine. Maybe she felt the need to suffer a little.

'So, how's work, Sarah?'

She was being polite. I suspected that journalists came somewhere between tyrannical despots and brutal dictators in her estimation.

'Oh, you know. Busy as ever.'

'They're getting a new political editor,' chipped in Jonathan. 'Might be useful to us.'

'Oh, yes,' said Rachel. 'You'll have to use your charm on him, Sarah. Get him on message.'

Sex for column inches, that was what she was suggesting. I looked at Jonathan who was nodding enthusiastically. Having no idea.

By twenty-five past seven we had eight people squashed into our lounge, some perching on an assortment of chairs, others sitting cross-legged on the floor, seemingly enjoying the *Blue Peter*ness of it all. I was tempted to show them how to construct a human rights centre from a cereal box and a washing up liquid bottle.

'Right,' said Rachel. 'As we're all here, let's get started. I suggest we hear from Jonathan first then the individual campaign leaders. I'll give you a national update after that.'

Jonathan stood up. Not to be formal or authoritative but simply because he was incapable of sitting still while talking. He was the same when he was teaching. I remembered watching him that first time we met, pacing around the classroom, waving his arms about like Johnny Ball on acid. It was one of the reasons I'd fallen for him. That his passion was genuine, not something he could switch on and off at will.

'The good news is membership has increased. The bad news is attendance at branch meetings continues to fall. We need to find a way of encouraging more local members to get involved and come to meetings. Any ideas?' He looked at me, expectantly. I hated it when he did that.

'Maybe we could change the time,' I said. 'Make it six o'clock so people can come straight from work. It's difficult to get them out once they get home and put the TV on.'

'I'm not sure that would make any difference,' said Rachel. 'I can't imagine that Amnesty members would be bothered about missing *EastEnders*.'

The video whirred into life right on cue at seven-thirty. I could almost hear the drums at the start of the theme tune. I pretended to ignore it, hoping they would assume it was some worthy documentary on BBC2.

'I'll put the kettle on,' I said, hurriedly leaving the room. It wasn't supposed to be done like that. At Rachel's house, Richard would silently withdraw from the room at 8 p.m. and return five minutes later with a silver tea tray laden with bone-china mugs of Fairtrade tea and coffee and plates of organic, Fairtrade digestives. I returned after ten minutes with a plastic tray containing an overflowing teapot, a jug of coffee, an assortment of odd mugs and a plate of chocolate chip cookies.

'Mmm, these are lovely, said Rachel, taking a bite. 'What make are they?'

'Er, I can't remember the name,' I said. 'They're Fairtrade and organic, from that little health food shop in King's Heath.'

They weren't. They were pesticide-assisted, probably made by exploited Third World workers and bought half-price from Marks & Spencer. But they did taste good.

'Rachel's come up with a publicity idea, Sarah,' said Jonathan. 'For the campaign against the arms trade. She thought we could organise a photo call where we all had TV remote controls strapped to our arms. You know, to symbolise the need to control arms. Do you think the *Gazette* would go for that?'

I stood there wondering how long it would be before the howl of laughter brewing inside me made its way out of my mouth.

'Sugar,' I said. 'I've forgotten the sugar.' I ran to the kitchen and emptied my laugh into a kitchen cupboard. By the time I went back in they'd decided against the idea, in case it was seen as promoting the big electronics firms, who had some far-from-ethical practices.

'Never mind,' I said. 'I'm sure we can come up with something else.'

'Seemed to go well, didn't it?' said Jonathan.

We were lying in bed after the meeting. The light was still on. He had his arm round me and was nuzzling my neck, his body pushed up tight against the curves of my own, as if he couldn't bear for there to be any space between us.

'Yeah, I guess so.'

I found it hard, sometimes, to muster even a fraction of the enthusiasm he showed.

'You didn't like Rachel's idea, did you?'

'Was it that obvious?'

'Only to me.'

'They'd have pissed themselves laughing at work.'

'You've never really liked her, have you?' he said.

'She just gets a bit carried away sometimes. Forgets that we're not all as earnest about it as her.'

'How do you mean?'

'You know . . .' I searched around for a comparison and voiced the first one that came to mind. 'Bit like your mum, I guess.'

As soon as I'd said it, I realised it was a mistake. Jonathan's mum Dawn was beyond criticism. She had raised Jonathan single-handedly after his dad walked out when he was nine months old, informing her that he needed 'space' (which turned out to be a euphemism for a beach hut in Goa).

'Hey, come on, Mum's not that bad,' said Jonathan. 'She just gets frustrated that we can't all be like her.'

As far as I could understand, this meant being a social worker in the most deprived area in Birmingham, living with a bunch of fellow ex-hippies in some kind of eco-friendly housing co-operative and attending peace rallies even when it meant missing her only child's graduation ceremony. Jonathan insisted he hadn't been offended. Like he insisted that he hadn't minded spending most of his school summer holidays at Greenham Common. I suspected otherwise. Like I suspected that his own early activism (he'd joined Greenpeace with the money he'd received for his tenth birthday) had been prompted by a desire to please her rather than to change the world.

'I'm not having a go at her, Jonathan. I'm simply pointing out that it can be a bit relentless at times, this "I'm worthier than you" crap.'

'She's never said that.'

'She doesn't have to, does she? Just gives me one of her looks.'

'Don't, Sarah. You know I hate it that you two don't get on.'

'That she doesn't think I'm good enough for you, you mean.'

'Hey, come on. That's not true.'

We both knew it was. Jonathan tried to distract me by kissing my neck.

'Anyway,' he said, breaking off for a second. 'I've told you before, it doesn't matter what Mum thinks. I love you to bits and that's what counts.'

I smiled, knowing I should be grateful for the last part of the declaration but aware of the hollow ring to the first. Aware that Jonathan had spent his entire life trying to be a son worthy of her respect if not her affections. At least I didn't have to worry about her snubbing any future wedding for some anti-globalisation protest. Jonathan didn't believe in marriage. Which was fine by me.

I looked at Jonathan, who was wearing his anxious expression. I realised he was waiting for a response.

'And I love you, too. So stop fretting.'

'I worry, that's all. Don't want anything to spoil what we've got.'

'Nothing will.'

'The thing is,' he said, 'I'm so happy with you I get scared sometimes. Like it's too good to be true. I keep expecting someone to take it all away. To say, "Come in, Jonathan Beveridge, your time is up." '

I looked at Jonathan, laying himself open for me, baring his soul in a way I had still never managed with him, much as I wanted to. I kissed him on the lips.

'You're a daft bugger sometimes, you know,' I said. 'You're not on some sort of lease agreement. This is for keeps.'

Jonathan smiled, a real smile this time, and buried his head in the hollow of my shoulder, trying to hide the tears which were glistening in his eyes.

'I do love you,' he said.

'I know,' I whispered back. 'And now we've got that sorted out can you turn the light off and let me get some bloody sleep.'

We lay in the darkness together, Jonathan still not daring to let me go in case I somehow slipped away from him in the night. I stroked his back, conscious as ever of how fragile he was. How easy it would be to break him.

Sunday 26 January 1997

I wave to Mark, shut the front door and let out a long sigh as I trudge back upstairs to my flat. I am filled with an overwhelming sense that I will never see him again. Maybe it was the way he said goodbye with such an air of permanence. Or the way we had sex; that feeling of going through the motions, of not really connecting. Or the way he talked about the *Stockport Express* and all his friends up there, as if it was so detached from me. I suspect I am a leftover from his time at journalism college. I do not fit into his new life, which is why he had made so many excuses about not coming down to Rugby since I got back. No one should be too busy to see their girlfriend; it is not supposed to work like that. Not that I am blaming him entirely. I was the one who decided to go travelling for four months after college. Who left him behind when he said his new job came first and yet still expected him to be there on my return. Eager and faithful. He certainly hasn't seemed eager. Whether he was faithful I may never know.

I suspect it will simply fizzle out. More excuses for not meeting up. Longer gaps between phone calls. Until eventually he calls it a day. Says the relationship has run its course, has nowhere left to go. He will probably be right about that but it still makes me sad. It was never supposed to be serious. But that's just one of those things you say at the beginning so as not to frighten the other person off. You can't help getting more involved than you had intended. At least I can't, anyway.

I sigh again as I go through to the bathroom and turn on the taps, the hot on full, the cold little more than a trickle. It is not exactly the ideal preparation for your first day in your first proper job, spending the evening before worrying that you are about to be dumped by your boyfriend. I will try to push it to the back of my mind. To think about new beginnings, not something which may or may not be coming to an end. I feel the thrill surge through me again as I realise that this time tomorrow I will be able to call myself a journalist. A proper journalist, not a student one. A fully fledged member of the only profession I have ever wanted to be a part of. A smile spreads across my face as I undress and dip a toe tentatively into the water to test the temperature. It is hot but I like it that way. It means I will be able to stay in longer. It is mild for January but this bathroom is draughty: two sash windows which rattle in the breeze and a gap under the door which I haven't got round to doing anything about yet.

I have only lived here three weeks. I have a long list of things that need doing and a landlord who doesn't seem much bothered as long as I pay my rent on time. Not that I am complaining. I love it here. It is my own place. I spent four years in shared digs at university and journalism college, four months in noisy backpacker hostels in India and Nepal and four weeks in my old room at my parents' house in the run-up to Christmas. In comparison to all of them this is bliss. I can spend an hour in the bath without anyone hammering on the door, walk around with no clothes on and not have to worry about my aromatherapy oils leaving a mark on my mother's spotless white enamel bath. I sprinkle a few drops of lavender into the water and climb in, submerging myself until only my head is above the surface, my long dark curls pinned up high, only a few stray strands falling down my neck. That is the good thing about old baths. You can lose yourself in them, none of this half-reclining with your knees up round your ears business. I mentally scan the contents of my wardrobe, deciding what to wear tomorrow. I suspect it will be my interview outfit: black boots, long black skirt and fitted black jacket. I haven't bought any new work clothes as I've run out of cash. My parents are paying the rent on the flat until I get my first wage slip and I don't want to ask them for any more handouts. I want to stand on my own two feet, to break free financially as well as physically. Anyway, I may as well wait to see what sort of clothes the others wear. I can't remember from the interview. I only glanced in the newsroom on my way out, and I was on too much of a high to take in anything specific like mode of dress. It was the third interview I'd been for and the only one to offer me a job there and then. I'd almost snapped the editor's hand off, I was so excited. OK, the *Rugby Chronicle* may not be the *Guardian* but we've all got to start somewhere. And right now all I want to do is get started. I let myself sink down further and blew bubbles under water. Feeling like a big kid on Christmas Eve, barely able to contain herself.

I pause for a second outside the front door of the *Chronicle*, my knuckles clenched white round the handle of my briefcase. I can do this, I know I can. This is what I have been waiting for. My chance to shine. To make a difference. To be someone. A surge of adrenalin kicks in as I open the door and stride up to the reception desk, hoping I look more confident than I feel. Hoping I look the part.

'Hi,' I say to the receptionist, who is slumped over the counter as if she is leaning over a garden fence waiting for the chance of a good gossip. 'I'm Sarah Roberts. The new reporter.'

I have waited a long time to say that. It sounds good and so it should. I have practised it often enough.

'Oh, yes,' she says. 'Nick said you were starting today. I'll let him know you're here.'

She makes a quick call. I can hear the phone buzzing upstairs, not too far away, as I tap my fingers on the counter. Seconds later a man in his late twenties bounds down the open wooden staircase. He stops at the bottom, looks up and smiles at me. The sort of smile you should need a licence for. I am suitably dazzled.

'Hi, Sarah. I'm Nick, the news editor.' He has a warm voice and stubble. I am thrown. I was expecting someone stern and middle-aged in a suit.

'Pleased to meet you,' I say, holding out my hand, hoping my palm is not sweating.

'It's OK, we won't shake hands, too formal.' He grins, brushing his dark hair back out of his equally dark eyes. 'Come up and I'll show you round before you get started.'

I follow him up the stairs, conscious of my boots clomping noisily on the wooden treads. 'Simple Simon's out this morning,' says Nick, as we pass the editor's office. 'He's a bit of a prat but fortunately he's one of those hands-off editors, spends most of his time on some freebie or another. And don't worry if he doesn't remember your name. I've been here two years and he still calls me Neil sometimes.'

He leads me into the newsroom, which is smaller than I remember from the brief glimpse I had at the interview. The computers are relics of a bygone era, piles of newspapers, press releases and council agendas are scattered over the desks, paint is peeling off the walls. It is all rather shabby and messy. It pleases me, though. It looks the way a newspaper office should do.

Nick is watching me, one eyebrow slightly raised. I smile at him, indicating my approval of everything I see.

'Let me introduce you to everyone,' he says, leading me over to the far corner where an earnest-looking woman, not much older than me, is sitting behind a disturbingly tidy desk thrashing the computer keyboard for all it is worth.

'Karen, this is Sarah, our new trainee,' he says. Karen looks up.

'Hi, pleased to meet you,' I say.

She returns the greeting, smiles fleetingly and resumes the key-bashing.

'She was the trainee before you,' Nick whispers as we walk away. 'Just qualified with distinctions all round. Bit scary, if you ask me.'

I raise my eyebrows, not sure if he should be telling me this. Nick moves past an exceptionally messy desk, which I presume to be his. Behind it on the wall is the photo of Maggie Thatcher leaving Downing Street for the last time with tears in her eyes under the headline 'Maggie, Maggie, Maggie, Out, Out, Out'. It is surrounded by front pages from *Private Eye*, most of them at the expense of the Tories, and the face of the local Tory MP superimposed on to the body of an elderly woman in bondage gear. I smile but decide to pass no comment.

The man behind the next desk along sports a bulbous red nose which he is in the middle of blowing as we approach. Nick introduces him as Dave. He acknowledges me with a raised hand before unravelling a few more sheets of the loo roll sitting proudly on his desk and blowing again.

'Miserable sod,' whispers Nick as we move to the other end of the office. 'He's been here too long; it's not healthy. Get out before you get bored, that's my advice.'

I nod, although at the moment I can't imagine ever being bored here.

'And this lovely lady,' says Nick, proudly extending his arm like a game show host, 'is our Auntie Joan.'

A woman in her forties, whose desk is surrounded by an assortment of pot plants, shakes her head and pretends to slap Nick across the face.

'Hi, Sarah. Take no notice of him, he's a prize piss-taker. Anything you need to know, ask me.'

I nod and grin back at her.

'Here's your desk, Sarah,' says Nick, tapping the table opposite Joan. 'We've had it decontaminated since Paul left but if you do find anything in the drawers I wouldn't touch it without gloves. I'll quickly show you round upstairs while I get you a coffee.'

'Hey, what about the rest of us?' asks Joan.

'You can get your own,' says Nick. 'It's not your first day.' He winks and beckons me to follow him upstairs.

'She seems nice,' I say.

'She is. And you'll learn a lot from her. Best journalist I've ever worked with. Ex-Fleet Street, in fact.'

'Really? So what's she doing here?'

I realise this sounds rude but Nick doesn't seem to take offence.

'Wanted out,' he says. 'Fed up of working with a bunch of uptight wankers who rip off other people's stories. She should be news editor here by rights but she doesn't want the hassle. Prefers to take it easy and enjoy herself, which is fine by me.'

We reach the top of the stairs.

'This is the kitchen,' says Nick, showing me into what is essentially a broom cupboard with a butler's sink and a kettle. 'How do you like your coffee?'

'Er, white please, one sugar.'

'Thank God, someone else who takes sugar. We'll have to form a breakaway coffee circle.'

He fills the kettle up and flicks it on. I am conscious of being alone with him in a confined space as he brushes past me.

'You smell nice,' he says.

I blush, wishing I'd decided against the perfume.

'Sorry,' he says instantly. 'I didn't mean to sound creepy. I'm really sorry. It's just that Paul, the guy you replaced, had a serious body odour problem. Stunk the place out.'

I start laughing. It breaks the tension. Nick is laughing too.

'So when people tell you you're a breath of fresh air after him,' he says, 'you'll understand what they mean.'

'Thanks,' I say. 'I promise to pay particular attention to my personal hygiene while I'm here.'

'Good,' says Nick, smiling. 'And now we've got that one sorted, I'll show you photographic.'

He leads me into a large room at the far end of the landing. Two men in their fifties are slumped over their desks perusing the sports pages of the tabloids.

'Guys, meet Sarah, our new reporter. Sarah, this is Bill and Ted. No cracks about their excellent adventure, they've heard them all before.'

'Hello,' I say. Bill and Ted look up and nod their greetings.

'Blimey, I must be getting old,' says Bill. 'The bloody trainees are starting to look younger than my kids.'

I smile politely.

'Take no notice,' says Nick. 'He's bitter and twisted because Mike our trainee photographer won an award and he didn't.'

'Must have been your expert tuition that helped him,' I say.

'Hey, she's smart as well as pretty,' chips in Ted.

'Come on,' says Nick, rolling his eyes. 'We'll leave this pair to get back to their work.'

We return to the kitchen. 'They're the last two surviving examples of prehistoric man known to be living in Rugby,' Nick says as he hands me my coffee.

'Don't worry, I can handle them.'

'I'm sure you can,' says Nick, grinning at me. He leads me back downstairs to the newsroom.

'And there concludes your grand tour,' he says. 'Any questions?'

'Er, no, I don't think so.'

'Good. You'll pick it all up as you go along. Joan will show you the ropes this morning, and take you down to do the police calls later. I'll sort out some press releases and bits and pieces to get you started.'

'You haven't told Sarah yet, have you?' says Joan, looking up from her screen.

'Told her what?'

'About this afternoon. Her first assignment.'

I look at Nick. He is trying not to laugh.

'Go on,' I say.

'Tell me something,' says Nick. 'Are you the sort of woman who is prepared to tackle anything thrown her way? Who is willing to rise to any challenge that top-flight local newspaper journalism presents?'

'Yep, just tell me what it is,' I say.

Nick fixes me with a mischievous grin. 'Camel racing.'

I am not sure if he is serious or if this is some kind of bizarre initiation ceremony all trainee reporters have to go through.

'Fantastic,' I say. 'I've never ridden a camel but I can ride a horse if that helps.'

Nick is smiling broadly.

'I'm sure it will,' he says. 'A guy in Lutterworth is holding a charity camel race on his farm. I thought it sounded like fun which is why I've entered you. We just want a nice colour piece from it.'

I nod enthusiastically. Already working on the intro in my head.

'No problem. I just wish you'd warned me. I'm hardly dressed for camel racing,' I say, looking down at my long skirt and heeled boots.

'She's got a point,' says Joan. 'It is a bit much to expect the poor girl to do it on her first day.'

'It's fine,' I say quickly, not wanting to appear reluctant. 'All part of the job.'

'That's the spirit,' says Nick. 'Ted will be going with you. If no one's ever warned you about the way photographers drive, it might be worth putting some kind of hard hat on for the journey as well.'

I smile as I sit down at my new desk. The adventure

begins here. It is all I can do not to kick up my heels and spin round on the chair.

I am eating my lunchtime sandwich when Nick asks me to go downstairs to see a local councillor in the front office. Colin Leake his name is. Leader of the Labour group on Rugby Borough Council. Nick says he's a top contact, Labour candidate for the general election. Well worth keeping sweet. I wipe the crumbs from my mouth and hurry downstairs, desperate to do my first proper interview. To have some quotes in the pristine notebook I am clutching in my hand. For the second time that day I am confronted by someone who does not fit the image I had in my head. Councillor Leake is wearing a duffel coat. His glasses are wonky and need a good clean. He has mad, staring eyes.

'Hi, I'm Sarah Roberts, the new reporter,' I say.

He nods.

'Hope you're better than the last one,' he says. 'This is what I've got for you.'

He pulls a wad of letters from a satchel-type thing he is carrying and starts to talk to me about a family living with bad damp in a block of council flats. He speaks very quickly; my shorthand struggles to keep up. He explains every-thing: how long it's been going on, whose fault the delays to repairs are, the effect it is having on the little boy's health. He even gives me the phone number of the family.

'That's all you need,' he says, stuffing the letters back into his satchel. 'Do it well and I'll get something else for you.'

He turns and leaves the office without another word. I hurry back upstairs, my fingers tingling from all the scribbling.

'Good stuff?' asks Nick.

'Yeah, some kid getting sick because he's living in a damp flat. And the council have done bugger all about it. Sounds pretty bad.'

'Great, should make a page lead for us. Maybe even the splash. He's a top bloke, Leaky. You'll get on well with him.'

I wonder why Nick thinks that.

'Do you want me to go out there now?' I ask, keen to get started on the story.

'No, put in a call, arrange to go first thing in the morning with a photographer. You haven't got time now. I can hear the camels calling.'

I am sitting astride a bad-tempered camel called Humphrey, trying desperately to hang on as he lumbers across a field, seemingly intent on going in a different direction from everyone else. My skirt is riding up dangerously high on my thighs, my hair is blowing all over the place and it is beginning to rain. And all the while I can see Ted out of the corner of my eye, snapping away, capturing every bone-shaking second of it on film. The other competitors are so far ahead of me I have given up catching them. Not that I have any say in the matter. Humphrey is quite clearly the one in charge.

'I'm glad I didn't back you,' hollers Ted from below.

'Thanks for your support.'

'Give him some welly, girl,' urges Ted. 'A good kick in the ribs should get him going.'

I follow Ted's advice but Humphrey responds by digging his toes into the grass and stopping abruptly, sending me into the air only to arrive back down in the most uncomfortable part of the saddle possible. I wince, glare at Ted, who is chuckling behind his lens, and try a different tactic.

'Please, Humphrey, you gorgeous great camel you. Catch the others up, will you?'

The polite approach seems to strike a chord with Humphrey and he trots on up the field. And although I have come a resounding last, I whoop with delight as I cross the finishing line. Because I am loving this. Loving being alive. Loving being out there, experiencing new things, doing something a little crazy.

I arrive back at the office battered and bruised and smelling distinctly less fragrant than when I departed. I clatter up the stairs and walk straight up to Nick's desk.

'This is for you,' I say, handing him a package wrapped in several layers of newspaper.

He appears taken aback.

'What is it?' he says.

'My prize. Open it and see.'

Nick peels back the paper and peers inside at the small brown pellets, before throwing his head back to roar with laugher.

'What is it?' calls out Joan.

'It appears to be camel dung,' he says eventually.

'I came last,' I say. 'But it's the taking part that counts. And the owner says it makes very good fuel for a fire if you ever feel the need to join a Bedouin tribe.'

'Thank you,' says Nick, his eyes sparkling with amusement. 'I shall keep it and think of you always.'

I turn and walk back to my desk, a huge smile on my face. I am going to like it here.

It is a couple of hours after I return home that Mark rings. He asks me how my first day went. I begin to give him a rundown, babbling like a schoolkid recounting her first holiday.

'Great,' he says when I finally pause for breath. It is then I know. That he is being polite. That the real reason for this phone call is not to enquire how my day has been.

'What's up?'

'I need to talk to you,' he says.

I resist the temptation to point out that we have just spent the weekend together.

'Oh,' I say. 'What about?'

'Us. I need to be honest with you. I don't think it's going anywhere. I was going to suggest we give it a break for a while. See how we feel after a month or so.'

It hurts even though I have been half expecting it. Even though he is trying to soften the blow, make it sound like a joint decision when he is actually dumping me.

'Fine,' I say. 'You're probably right. A break might do us good.'

He agrees although we both know this is not the case. We will not get back together again. This is the end.

'At least it sounds like you'll have plenty of stuff to keep you busy at work,' says Mark. Maybe this is what he was waiting for, me starting work so he would not feel so guilty about dumping me. Though I still think he should have had the balls to do it face to face.

'Yeah. I'll drop you an e-mail sometime. Let you know how it's going.'

'That would be great,' says Mark, much too enthusiastically. I want to get off the phone now. I don't believe in prolonging the agony.

'Right, well. I'd better let you go.'

'Sure. Take care, Sarah,' he says. And with that he is gone. I put the phone down and am surprised to find myself crying. Little tears that hug the rims of my eyes. I am always the same with endings. I find it hard. We were together for ten months. Now, I will probably never see him again. If I'm lucky I will get an e-mail, maybe even a card next Christmas. Though probably not the one after that.

I go to the kitchen and pour myself a glass of wine, emptying the last dregs from the unfinished bottle in the fridge. The one I had shared with Mark only twenty-four hours ago. I take it back into the room and sit quietly on the bed, thinking how strange it is, the way things change so quickly. And wondering what tomorrow will bring.

Three

It was my last day of freedom. Physical freedom; mentally I'd never been free. I looked round the newsroom knowing that on Monday he'd be there, sitting a few yards away. Breathing the same air. Bastard. Why did he have to do this? Why did he have to spoil things for me?

I could always suggest moving the political desk. Have him excommunicated, or at least sent up to join sport. I wouldn't be able to see him then. It would be a bit obvious, though. I might as well suggest turning his desk round so he'd be up against the wall with his back to everyone. And hiring a firing squad.

He wouldn't always be there, I knew that. He'd spend most of his time at the Council House and sometimes he'd be down in London. But on Monday morning he'd be sitting two desks away, smiling at me. And I couldn't see past that.

I picked up my briefcase and went up to the news desk.

'I've sent you a page lead on domestic violence,' I said to Keith. He looked up at me from his Territorial Army magazine, a half-eaten pork pie in his hand.

'Is that still going on?'

I chose to ignore him. 'Our local refuge says a third of all cases they deal with are against pregnant women.'

'You know why that is, don't you?' he said. 'Their blokes have got more to aim for.'

He sat there chortling to himself. I resisted the urge to ram the rest of his pork pie down his throat. All I hoped was that when the call-up from the TA came it would be to somewhere within range of American friendly fire.

I glared at Keith, picked up my coat and walked out of the office. It was raining. The sort of rain you hardly notice but which actually drenches you within a few seconds. I put my umbrella up, my head down, and started walking towards New Street. I was going to grab a sandwich for lunch. Cayte had been at court all morning, which was OK because I fancied being on my own. I needed to sort my head out. To decide on a new strategy. I couldn't run any longer. He'd caught up with me.

The wind blew the bottom of my coat open, allowing the rain to spatter my trousers. I bit my lip. I was going to tough it out. To show him that he couldn't control me any more. That I was immune to the past.

I glanced up from under my umbrella as I reached the corner of New Street. I could see the lower half of a *Big Issue* seller. Frayed jeans and battered trainers which were clearly letting in water. His hands were pale and shaking, gripping a plastic bag containing a dozen or so copies of the magazine. The rain was running down the plastic on to his hand and disappearing inside the sleeve of his supposedly waterproof jacket. I stopped and rummaged in my briefcase for some change.

'There you go,' I said, holding out £1.20.

'Oh, cheers. Thanks very much.'

He delved into the plastic bag and produced a pristine *Big Issue*. In the time it took for me to take it and stuff it into my briefcase, the front cover turned soggy.

'Thanks,' I said. 'Hope it stops raining for you soon.' I raised my umbrella so I could actually see his face. The hood of his green waterproof was pulled in tight, leaving a crinkled cut-out of pasty flesh. The rain was running off his wonky, steel-rimmed glasses. His face was impersonating an exclamation mark.

'Colin?' I said.

He nodded reluctantly, as if he had been cornered by police and had no option but to turn himself in.

'Hello, Sarah.'

'What the hell are you doing here?'

I didn't mean to say it, but Colin Leake had just sold me a *Big Issue*. The last time I'd seen him he was leader of the Labour group on Rugby Borough Council. It was like some weird dream where people from my past turned up in unlikely new roles. Only it couldn't be because in my dreams it never actually occurred to me that I might be dreaming, no matter how ridiculous the scenario. Maybe I was in something like *The Truman Show* and the rest of the world was watching me now, waiting to see my face when I came across my old headmaster serving in Starbucks and Aunt Gladys in fishnet stockings touting for trade on the next corner.

Colin shrugged. 'It's a long story.'

'But I don't understand. Your job and your house and Sandra.'

'Gone. All of them.'

'Oh, Colin,' I said. 'I'm so sorry.'

He shrugged again.

'You're looking well,' he said.

I looked down at my faux suede coat and leather briefcase. The guilt bubbled up from the well inside me and gushed to the surface. I was rubbing his face in it. I may as well be waving a wad of notes in front of him. And to think that a few minutes earlier I'd felt smug about giving him £1.20. I ought to give him my coat and umbrella, not to mention my cash and credit cards. Because I was the one who'd put him here. Who'd made it all go wrong.

'Come on, I'm taking you for lunch,' I said.

'That's very nice of you but it's my first week and I don't want to lose this pitch. It's my busiest time, you see.'

'Of course, sorry. I should have thought. What about a

drink after work then, when we're both finished, about five? Give us the chance to catch up properly.'

'You don't want to bother with a sad old git like me.'

'Well, I don't know about you, but I haven't got any better offers.'

He grinned. 'OK, you're on.'

We arranged to meet at the Newt and Cucumber. I walked off up the road, shaking my head. I glanced back, checking I hadn't imagined it. Colin was shifting from one foot to the other, his shoulders hunched, the rain dripping relentlessly off his glasses. This was a man who'd stood as an MP, who'd got a standing ovation at the Winter Gardens at Blackpool the same year Tony Blair had made his first speech. Now standing on a street corner. It was all so awful. And it was my fault.

I stumbled into Pret A Manger and picked up a chargrilled vegetables on granary and a mango smoothie. I was about to pay for it when I realised how selfish I was being.

'Hang on a sec,' I said to the man serving. I dashed back and got another chargrilled veg, a carrot cake and an orange juice. Vitamin C, that's what he needed. I hurried back down New Street. The rain was harder now, drumming its fingers on my umbrella.

'Lunch,' I said to a startled Colin as I thrust the paper bag into his hand.

'You don't have to do this,' he said.

'You do like carrot cake, don't you? Only I can take it back and swap it for a chocolate brownie if you want.'

'Beggars can't be choosers,' he said, smiling.

'At least you haven't lost your sense of humour.'

'No,' he said. 'Not yet. Thanks very much.'

'No problem,' I said. 'See you later.'

I walked off, relieved to have won a few brownie points, or carrot cake points at least.

'Oi, Mother Teresa.'

The shout came from behind. I turned round. Cayte

was running towards me, her long fair hair slicked flat against her head by the rain, the ends flicking water at people as she ran. If she did own an umbrella, I'd never seen her use it.

'Have you gone all religious on me?' she said when she caught up with me. 'What is it, feeding the five thousand day?'

'Bloody hell, I can't do anything round here.'

'Or is it a mobile soup kitchen project you've launched?'

'I know him. He used to be a councillor in Rugby. He was my best contact. Anyway it wasn't soup, it was orange juice.'

'I'm sure he appreciated that. Just what you want when you're standing in the pissing rain in October, orange juice.'

She was right, of course. I hadn't thought.

'Do you think I should go back and get him something warm?'

'What, like a fortnight's holiday in the Seychelles?' Cayte grinned at me and sneaked under my umbrella as we walked back towards work. Somehow she always got away with it.

'Remind me not to help you out, if you ever fall on hard times,' I said.

'So how did he end up on the streets?'

'I don't know yet. He said it was a long story. I'm meeting him after work tonight to find out.'

Cayte started laughing.

'What?' I said.

'You going out with a *Big Issue* seller. The perfect way to cheat on Jonathan.'

The joke was meant to be on Jonathan, I knew that. I felt indignant on his behalf.

'It's only a drink, I haven't seen him for years. He was the guy who lost by one vote in the general election, the year Labour got in.'

'Fucking hell, I remember that. Saw him interviewed on telly. I've never seen anyone look so gutted.'

The guilt reared its ugly head again. 'Yeah well, the least I can do is buy the guy a drink and find out what happened.'

'Could make a story. Maybe Blair turned down his begging letters.'

I smiled at her as we arrived outside the *Gazette*. Actually that would be good. That would make it someone else's fault.

Terry was staring at his goldfish. This was a bad sign. He only did it after meetings with the MD or the bigwigs in London. I'd never known anyone able to look at a fish for so long. It was supposed to be therapeutic. For Terry, not the fish. The fish was probably suicidal by now. Being stared at by a mardy sod with huge bags under his eyes.

'I'd better go and see him,' I said to Cayte.

'I don't know why you bother,' she replied. 'He enjoys being that miserable. I'd worry more if he was sitting there chuckling to himself.'

I took my coat off, put my briefcase on my chair and picked up my sandwich. I suspected I was going to need sustenance to get through this one. I walked over and waved through the glass at Terry. Nothing. I knocked on the door. No reply. I went in anyway and coughed loudly. He looked up.

'Oh, thanks, Sarah. Just put it on my desk.'

I wondered if the news about me giving away sandwiches had somehow got back to the office.

'Er, it's mine, actually. Haven't you eaten?'

'I went down the cemetery.'

'Oh.' Did I need to explain to him that M&S would have been a better option for sandwiches?

'You're a long time dead, you know.'

I hated it when he went all profound on me.

'What's brought this on?' I said, taking a bite out of my sandwich.

'Look.' He gestured towards the newsroom. Keith was standing up zapping through Ceefax as if commanding a military operation. Lisa was eating a Pot Noodle in between laughing very loudly at Keith's jokes. Sport were busy as ever watching the one-thirty from Uttoxeter. And the sub-editors were conducting some kind of experiment with the up and down mechanism on their chairs.

'What about it?'

'It's my life, isn't it? It may not be much but it's all I've bloody got.'

'Apart from your wife and children, obviously.'

'You mean the woman who comes back to my house when the shops close and the baggy-trousered creatures who occasionally emerge from their bedrooms to ask me for money? Nah. This is what I live for. The reason I get up in the mornings.'

'You're not dying or anything, are you?'

Terry shook his head and sighed. 'I've had word from London. They're cutting the editorial budget again.'

'By how much?'

'Twenty per cent.'

'Fucking hell.'

'Yeah, that's what I said.'

'Before you told them they couldn't do it, you mean?'

Terry shrugged. 'What's the point? They're not going to listen to me, are they?'

His backbone slid, vertebra by vertebra, on to the floor and scuttled off to hide under the filing cabinet. I went to his bookcase, picked up the dictionary, flicked through it and slammed it on to his desk, my finger pointing to the offending word.

'Read it,' I instructed.

'Editor. Person in charge of the content of a newspaper.'

'Thank you,' I said, snapping it shut.

'And you know as well as I do that counts for nothing in London. It's the bean-counters there who run this place.'

'Lie down and let them walk all over you, then.'

Terry groaned and held his head in his hands. 'This newspaper means the world to me.'

'So fight dirty. Work out how much money they could save if they gave the ad reps Fiestas instead of Mondeos or took away their executive boxes at Villa Park and St Andrew's. And ask why they need five people in promotions to organise a half-price pasty offer every month.'

Terry looked up. A glimmer of hope in his eye. 'You're right, Sarah. You're always bloody right. Why didn't I make you my deputy?'

'Because I'm allergic to clipboards. Can I go and finish my sandwich in peace now?'

'Yeah. Not a word to anyone though. You know the score.'

I closed the door behind me.

'Well?' said Cayte.

'Just the usual domestic.'

'I don't know why we pay an agony aunt, you know. When we've got you in our midst.'

I made a mental note to raise this point with Terry.

It was gone five by the time I got away, having made the mistake of taking a call from a member of the public who wanted to know what the answer to eleven down had been in last Tuesday's crossword.

I hurried through the pavement rush hour. People were bursting out of offices in quick succession, like one of those speeded-up films, the buzz of Friday evening reverberating around them. The Newt and Cucumber was quiet in comparison. No more than a dozen after-work drinkers, their silhouettes just visible through the fog of smoke which never seemed to lift, no matter how quiet the pub was. Colin was standing at the far end of the bar.

His hood was down revealing a head of thinning sandy-coloured hair in the process of turning grey. He looked about fifteen years older than when I used to know him seven years ago. He smiled when he saw me. His teeth were wonkier than I remembered.

'Sorry, Colin. I got held up,' I said. 'What can I get you?'

'Oh, er, a lager, please. I can't afford to buy you one back, mind.'

'Doesn't matter. I'll get these on expenses. Like the old days.'

Colin grinned at me. I wouldn't really be able to put it on expenses. You couldn't claim anything back from this lot without a signed affidavit and a photocopy of the resulting story. But I wasn't going to tell him that. I ordered a Stella for Colin and a sparkling mineral water for me.

'Not drinking?' asked Colin.

'No. I'm driving. Anyway I don't actually. Not now.'

'Oh.' Colin looked as if he was about to ask why but obviously thought better of it.

We sat down at a little table in the corner, sipping our drinks and politely smiling at each other. I didn't know where to start. 'So, Colin. How did you manage to screw your life up?' sounded a bit harsh.

'Thanks for the sandwich,' said Colin.

'Oh, God, don't mention it. How did it go this afternoon?'

'OK,' he said. 'I sold them all in the end. Took a long while, mind.'

'So how many copies was that?'

'Twelve.' I did the maths in my head. Eight pounds forty wouldn't go very far.

'Do you want some crisps?' I said. 'Or something proper to eat. Something hot?'

'You don't have to do this, Sarah.'

'What?'

'Buy all my meals from now on. I appreciate what you're doing but . . .'

'I'm treating you like a charity case,' I said, finishing his sentence.

Colin smiled. We both looked down at our feet.

'Sorry,' I said. 'I just want to do something to help. Here I am with my nice flat to go home to. I feel so bloody guilty.'

'It's not your fault.'

I looked at Colin and grimaced. I should tell him now. It was the perfect opportunity. But still I couldn't quite get the words out. Once, when I was in infants' school, I'd wet myself while we were all sitting on the floor, listening to the teacher tell us a story. I'd wanted to say something then but I couldn't. I'd waited until the trickle of warm wee had reached one of the other kids. I'd let them shout out, 'Miss, Sarah's wet herself.' Anything to avoid holding my hand up and confessing.

I looked Colin in the eye. But I couldn't do it on my own. Not without a pool of piss to give me away. I decided to go into journalist mode. I was safe with that.

'Tell me what happened,' I said. 'From the beginning.'

Colin nodded slowly and took a slurp of his lager. It looked as if he was running through the story in his mind. Making sure he'd got all the salient facts in the right order. That he wasn't going to miss anything out. Very Colin.

'It all started with losing the general election in '97. One stupid vote. I've never known anyone lose an election by one vote.'

'Nor me,' I said. Every muscle in my body tensed. I ran my finger round the rim of my glass, pressing so hard I feared it could shatter at any moment.

'I took it very badly,' said Colin. 'You probably remember. But even months after you'd left, I still couldn't seem to shake the "man who lost by one vote" tag. There was a lot of manoeuvring in the local Labour party and next I knew I'd been ousted as group leader, and Hazelwood took over.'

'I never trusted that bloke,' I said. 'Eyes too close together.'

'Yeah, well. It didn't stop there. The following spring I was deselected to defend my ward seat in the local elections.'

'But that's outrageous. You'd done a brilliant job.'

'They didn't see it that way, said I wasn't New Labour enough for them. Didn't have the Blairite credentials.'

'Bastards.'

'Yep. Stabbed in the back, good and proper.'

'So what did you do?'

'I resigned from the Labour Party.'

'Good for you,' I said.

'And got depressed.'

'Ah, not so good.'

'Nope. But I had to blame some one so I figured I may as well blame myself.'

My finger slipped off the glass, which skidded to the left. Colin put out his hand and stopped it.

'Thanks,' I said as he put it back on my beer mat. He should have glassed me with it. If he'd known it was my fault he probably would have. No, that wasn't true. He was much too nice for that.

'It must have really hit you, not being in politics after all those years.'

'Yeah. My self-esteem had all been tied up with being a councillor. Plain old mister Colin Leake was a loser and everyone knew it. I started taking days off work. Ringing in sick. Sometimes I didn't even bother to ring. I'd never done that, you know. Never thrown a sickie in my life.'

I nodded. It was the old slippery slope syndrome. Very hard to get off once you're on the way down.

'Didn't Sandra help you?' I said.

'She tried to but I threw it all back in her face. I wasn't much fun to be around. Always moping about. Not even getting out of bed some days. And moaning the whole bloody time when I did. We made it through Christmas

'98 but on New Year's Day she said she couldn't hack it any more and walked out.'

I nodded in what I hoped was a sympathetic fashion. Usually I was good at this agony aunt stuff. But usually friends were telling me about stupid things. A guy who hadn't called when he said he would. Or a mother who couldn't stop interfering. Things that have always happened and always will. This was a whole different league.

'That's such a shame. You'd been together years, hadn't you?'

'Yeah, since school, practically. I guess the only good thing was that we'd never got round to having kids. So when the divorce came through all we had to worry about was who got the record collection. It was quite amicable really. I never did like Phil Collins.'

I took a sip of my water. It was like watching *EastEnders*. Unbearably grim but for some reason you felt compelled to go back for more.

'And after that?' I said.

'I was signed off work for six months with depression. The doctor gave me some pills but I didn't take them because I was worried about getting addicted. Eventually I got an appointment with some psychotherapist who told me that losing the election hadn't been the end of the world. I told him where to stick it so that was the end of that.'

'So what happened with your job?'

Colin had worked in the housing department at a neighbouring council. Some kind of housing welfare officer if I remembered rightly.

'They were OK at the beginning. Let me go back part time for a while. But when I went full time I started going a bit weird. Thought everyone was talking about me and laughing at me behind my back. I accused people of doing things they hadn't done. Stealing from me. Throwing my files away, that sort of thing. There was a hearing and I freaked out a bit and next I knew I was out of a job.'

'Bloody hell. Didn't they realise you weren't well? Couldn't they make allowances?'

'Not for calling my boss a fascist.'

'Oh.' I tried to suppress a smile. It wasn't funny. It was so awful I felt the need to do one of those hysterical laughs people do when they can't bear the onslaught of relentless bad any more.

'And what about the house?'

'I had to sell it as part of the divorce settlement. I bought a flat instead but I couldn't keep up the mortgage repayments after I lost my job so it was repossessed. I had to go and live with my mother, which made me worse. I got it into my head that she was plotting against me, trying to poison me, so I stopped eating her food. That's when I got sectioned.'

'Oh, Colin. I had no idea.'

I'd always wondered why he hadn't stood again in the next general election. But it had never occurred to me that he could be in a mental institution. I shook my head, unable to believe that the consequences of my actions were so far-reaching.

'It wasn't that bad,' Colin said. 'They put me on so much medication I was spaced out most of the time. Didn't really know what was going on. They said I had bipolar disorder. It means manic depression.'

'How long were you in there?'

'About a year, I think. I'm not really sure. When I came out I had to go back to live with my mum. Things were all right for a year or so. I took my pills and everything. Then I came back from an outpatients appointment one day and found my mum dead. Sitting bolt upright in her armchair. TV still blaring away. *Countdown*, it was.'

'That's terrible.'

'I know. I can't stand Carol Vorderman.'

'No, Colin. Your mum.'

He shook his head. 'It wasn't like we were close. She'd

been a real cow to me when I was a kid. Just came as a bit of a shock. A week after the funeral I got a letter from the council saying I couldn't stay there because my name wasn't on the tenancy agreement. So the next day I got up, packed a bag and left. Spent the first night on a park bench. Bit of a cliché I know but it was the only place I could think of at the time.'

'How long ago was this?'

'Nearly two years.'

'And you've been living rough all that time?'

'Not on the streets. In hostels mainly. Someone told me about one in Coventry so I went there. Then you kind of do the rounds. Go from one to another, trying to avoid the crackheads.'

I sat shaking my head, unable to look him in the eye. 'And what about now? Are you getting proper treatment?'

'I'm still on my medication. Don't really see any shrinks or anything. I'm staying in this hostel in Digbeth. A young lad in the next bed to me is a *Big Issue* seller, we got talking and here I am. That's it really. How about you? What have you been up to?'

I laughed. It was all so matter of fact. Like he'd just recounted details of a disappointing holiday rather than his entire life falling apart. And now he wanted my story.

'You don't want to hear about my life.'

Colin looked over his glasses at me. 'You can start by telling me why you buggered off without so much as a goodbye.'

'Ah, that.'

'I went in the office one day to ask for you and Nick said you'd gone to Scarborough. I thought he meant on holiday, asked when you'd be back. That's when he told me you'd gone for good.'

'Sorry. It all happened very quickly. Never even had time for a leaving do.'

'What made you leave? Nick didn't seem to know.'

I took another sip of water, playing for time as I worked out what to say.

'Oh, just fed up with the editor interfering. A good job came up in the same newspaper group, they needed someone to start quickly and that was it.'

Colin looked at me. I wished I wasn't so crap at lying.

'And what about since? How did you end up here?'

A potted history of the last seven years was required. Very matter of fact. In the style of Colin. I took a deep breath.

'Stayed at Scarborough for eighteen months. Moved to the *Sheffield Star* as health reporter. Stayed there two years. Came to Birmingham in 2000, also as health reporter, promoted to chief reporter last year. Live in a flat in Edgbaston with my partner Jonathan who's a teacher and a cat called Nelson. That's it. Not very interesting, I'm afraid.'

'You're happy, though?'

I put my glass down. I wasn't expecting that one. Colin never used to do emotions.

'Yeah,' I said. 'Of course I am.'

Colin nodded. His glass was nearly empty. I was about to ask if he wanted another when my mobile rang. It was Jonathan wondering where I'd got to. I told him I wouldn't be long.

'I'd better let you go,' said Colin, standing up.

'Sorry. I forgot to ring him. He's made dinner. You can come back with me if you like. He always does enough for three.'

'No, you go on. I'm fine.'

'Can I give you a lift home?' I realised as soon as I'd said it. We both laughed. 'Sorry. Back to the hostel, I mean.'

'No thanks. It's only a ten-minute walk from here. I'll be fine.'

I delved into my briefcase, pulled out my business card and handed it to him.

'If there's anything I can do to help, or you fancy meeting up again, call me, OK?'

'Thanks,' he said with a smile.

'Will you be on the same pitch next week?'

'Hope so.'

'I'll see you there, then. Save me a copy.'

'Will do.' Colin waved as I headed out the door. I wondered how long he'd stay there, enjoying the company and savouring the last few drops of his drink. I had to help him, I knew that. Had to make it my mission to get him back on his feet. I could never atone for what I'd done to him, but I could at least do everything within my power to make things better for him now.

I buttoned my coat and threw my scarf over my shoulder as I started to walk back towards the car park. That's what happens when you do something bad. You can run and hide for a while but in the end it always catches up with you. Colin was back in my life now, a living, breathing reminder of what the old Sarah had done. And on Monday Nick would be there too. Making sure I couldn't possibly forget how bad I'd been. Or why I'd gone away.

Friday 14 February 1997

I sit with my back to Nick but I am aware of his presence. He is looking at me, I know that. I always know. Sometimes I wish he wouldn't look, it makes things awkward, what with me being the new girl and him my boss. But today, Valentine's Day, I can't help being glad. I swivel my chair, a kind of coded acknowledgement. For some reason I assume he will understand the signal, although it is not something we have discussed.

Three weeks I have known him. And yet it feels like a lifetime. I do not make a habit of this. Falling for someone so quickly. It has never happened to me before. I do not even think I believed in it. Previous boyfriends have always grown on me. Friendships that drifted into relationships, fizzled out and drifted back again. Like with Mark. This is something entirely different. Though of course he is not my boyfriend. And almost certainly never will be. He is clearly out of my league.

I am aware that I may be on the rebound. And that Nick's was the first friendly face I saw after I was dumped by Mark. But it does not feel like a rebound thing. It does not feel like anything I have ever experienced before. I feel his eyes watching me as I twirl a long strand of my wild, dark hair round my finger. Winding it tight before releasing it and letting it spring back; an untamed gypsy curl. Nick has exactly the same colour hair as me. The deepest, darkest shade of brown imaginable. If we lay down with our heads touching it would be impossible to tell where his hair ended and mine began. I know this although we have never done it. And probably never will.

I am staring at my computer screen. My eyes are not focusing properly. I can't see the words, only the spaces in between. I stand up, pushing my chair away with the backs of my knees. I take the tray from the top of the cupboard and start collecting mugs.

'Thanks, Sarah,' says Joan. I haven't done anything yet. Just taken her mug. She is embarrassed because I do this more often than her. More often than all of them put together. But I am supposed to, I am the trainee reporter. Three weeks into her first job. And the truth is I like making the tea because it gives me the opportunity for contact.

Nick is on the phone. He sees me coming and picks up his mug, holding it out to me. He smiles and leaves his fingers there so that I touch them as I take it. The mug is still warm from his last coffee. Black, one sugar. Reluctantly I place it on the tray while I gather the remaining two and take them upstairs to the kitchen. I pop to the loo while I wait for the kettle to boil. Just the one tiny cubicle for women, with barely enough room to squeeze inside the door and the loo roll positioned in the most inconvenient place possible, so that you have to perform something resembling a yoga position to get to it. I glance in the mirror as I wash my hands. My skin looks brand new; there is practically dew on it. My eyes have opened wider, my hair has grown glossier since this morning. I am a calendar picture for Spring. Alive with the promise of good times to come. I smile at myself and hurry back to the kitchen.

There is no fridge. We buy a pint of milk in the morning and hope it lasts until the end of the day without going off. I lift the carton to my nose and sniff. A hint of sourness but not enough to warrant a trip to the shops. We can get away with it in February. By the summer, I suspect I too shall drink my coffee black in the afternoons.

I give the mugs a cursory rinse under the tap; we are out of washing-up liquid. Nick's mug has 'Smash the State' on it in big red letters. It also has a chip on the rim. Joan's mug has poppies. Dave's is Coventry City FC. Karen's has candyfloss stripes. Mine is black. Dark and mysterious or plain and uncomplicated. Whatever you care to think. I distribute the tea bags and coffee to the appropriate mugs and add boiling water, milk and sugar to taste. I have a colour chart in my head of how everyone likes it. That way I don't get any complaints. I descend the staircase gingerly with the tray, trying not to slop too much liquid over the sides and smiling as I think of the doddery waitress Julie Walters plays in the Victoria Wood thing. The one who says, 'Two soups.' I go to Nick's desk first. He is off the phone now.

'Thanks, Sarah.' He says it as if I have just given him a life-saving kidney transplant, not a mug of coffee. 'Are you coming over the road later?'

Someone in advertising whom I don't know is leaving today. He is having a do at O'Neill's.

'Yeah, I guess so.'

'Good,' he says, like he means it. 'You never know, I might even buy you a drink.'

His mouth is smiling, his eyes are smiling too. I am mesmerised. It is all I can do to move. As I walk away, some tea slops over the side of the fullest mug. I hand it to Dave who mutters something about half measures. I am used to him already, though, and take no notice. Karen thanks me without looking up from her computer screen. I am used to that as well. I turn and walk back to my end of the office. As I do so I hear Nick burst out laughing. Joan is pointing frantically and mouthing something to me. I cannot work out what she is trying to tell me. They are all laughing now, even Dave. I have no idea what the joke is but as I stand frozen to the spot with the tea tray I am suddenly aware of a draught on the back of my thighs. Before I can do anything Joan rushes up, pulls the back of my skirt out of my knickers and restores me to a proper state of decency. I groan inwardly, cursing the confines of the toilet cubicle and making a mental note to check myself before I leave in future.

I glance around at the others. Nick is trying hard to restore his face to neutral.

'It's funny, I never had you down as the bunny girl type,' he says.

'It made me a bit of extra cash while I was a student. I'll wear the ears tomorrow as well, if you like,' I say, hurriedly handing Joan her mug and returning to my desk.

'I shall look forward to it,' says Nick.

I type busily, allowing the colour to fade from my cheeks before glancing over my shoulder. Nick is still smiling. As I turn back to my computer I catch Joan's eye and realise that I am also smiling. I look down quickly and start typing again. A few minutes later Nick calls out that there is a Mrs Hurst in reception, asking to see a reporter.

'I'll go,' I say, welcoming the chance to hide my blushes and grabbing my notebook and heading for the door before anyone else has a chance to move. When I get downstairs, the receptionist points to a tall, dark-haired woman standing with her back to me, gazing out of the window across the street.

'Mrs Hurst?' I say, as I approach.

She turns round, revealing a grey streak in her hair and a large boil on her nose.

'I'm Sarah Roberts. How can I help you?'

She gestures for me to come closer.

'I have evidence,' she says. 'Of contact from beyond the grave.'

I nod, fearing the worst. Joan has warned me about people like her. Mrs Hurst delves into her capacious shopping bag and produces a candelabra which she proceeds to place on a pile of newspapers on the front counter. Fortunately she doesn't attempt to light it. I am well aware that naked flames in reception are against the fire regulations.

'Who is it you've been contacted by?' I ask.

She beckons me closer again. 'John Lennon,' she replies. I am pleasantly surprised. I was expecting it to be more C-list. Diana Dors, perhaps.

'And the evidence you mentioned?'

She shuts her eyes for a moment. I wonder if she is trying to make contact with him now.

'He left me his autograph,' she whispers. 'I was drawn to it by a force beyond this world. I knew exactly where to find it.'

'And where was that?'

'The bakery in Hillmorton High Street,' she says.

I nod. This is getting better all the time.

'You don't happen to have it with you, do you?' I ask.

'Oh yes,' she says. She delves again into her shopping bag and carefully removes a silver cake board upon which sits a round cake, about twenty centimetres across. It is covered in white icing, scalloped shells round the edge, a yellow ribbon tied round it. And in the middle, in pale yellow icing, is piped a single word in shaky lettering. 'Lemon'.

I look away, struggling to compose myself for a moment. And dying to share this with Nick.

'It's remarkable, isn't it?' says Mrs Hurst.

'Absolutely. I've never seen anything quite so remarkable in my life. In fact, do you mind if I call my news editor? I think he should see it.'

I ring upstairs for Nick. He bounds downstairs on the promise of a world exclusive, only to be confronted with the lemon cake.

'This lady has found a cake signed by John Lennon in the bakers in Hillmorton,' I tell him.

Nick looks at me, the cake, and back to me. I see his shoulders shaking as he looks down at the floor.

'You piss-taker, Roberts,' he says, as we walk back upstairs together after Mrs Hurst has departed, taking her autographed cake with her.

'Come on, you wouldn't have wanted to miss it,' I say.

'You're right. The *Sport* would love that, you know. I can see the headline already. "Lennon in Love Me Dough shock".'

I am still smiling as I sit down at my desk. I return to writing up the reports from police calls this morning. Two houses burgled in Brownsover, a man exposing himself to some ramblers in Newbold and several cars being broken into in the multi-storey car park in town. I ask Joan what constitutes a spate.

'Anything more than two,' she replies without hesitating.

I nod and start again on my intro. My phone rings. I pick it up.

'Hi, I'm calling from Sotheby's press office,' the male caller says. 'We've got an auction coming up and a couple of the items have got local interest for you.'

'Oh, great,' I say. 'Let me take down some details.'

'Well, we've got the boots worn by William Webb Ellis when he was at Rugby School and first picked up the ball and ran with it.'

'That's fantastic,' I say, aware this is shaping up into a good story.

'And the other item, the one I think you'll be really excited about, is the handwritten lyrics to "Imagine" by John Lennon. They were donated to us by a woman in Rugby and the interesting thing is that they were actually written in yellow icing.'

For a second I am unsure what to say. Then I glance over my shoulder. Nick is not at his desk.

'You bastard,' I say down the phone.

Joan looks up at me, startled. A second later Nick

sticks his head round the door, mobile phone still pressed to his ear, a huge grin across his face.

'I had you there,' he says.

'Yep, fell for it. Hook, line and sinker.'

'Is he bothering you, Sarah?' says Joan. 'I can have him thrown out if you want.'

'No, it's OK,' I say. 'Just a bit of harmless fun.'

At exactly five o'clock Nick turns off his computer. Everyone else does the same. I realise they are waiting for me. I'm halfway through a story. This is supposed to be a newspaper office. I want people to run around. I want to work through the night. I want to be Woodward or Bernstein.

'Come on, Sarah,' says Nick. 'That can wait till Monday.'

He is right, of course. Because this is the *Rugby Chronicle* not the *Washington Post*. I do as I am told and grab my jacket on the way out.

O'Neill's is quiet, only a couple of old boys and the advertising crowd who are already ensconced in the corner.

'What are you having?' asks Nick. He is looking at me. So is everyone else.

'Half a Stella, please.' I haven't socialised with them yet but I guess that's what they'll all be drinking.

'You don't strike me as a lager drinker.'

'I'm not normally.'

'So what's your usual?'

'Vodka and orange.'

'One screwdriver coming up.'

'No, there's no need. Lager's fine, honestly.'

He looks at me and turns on that smile. 'It's a pleasure.'

I wait with the others until the drinks come and follow them over to an empty table.

'Aren't we going to join them?' I say, nodding in the direction of the advertising people.

'Nah, bunch of bastards,' says Nick. I laugh and take a sip of the vodka. I shuffle along the bench seat into the corner.

'So, Sarah. Are you enjoying it?' he says, sitting down next to me. He makes me feel like the others aren't there. That it is just the two of us.

'Yeah, apart from the wind-up merchant in the office, I've loved every minute.'

'Even the camel racing?' he says with a grin.

'Especially the camel racing. It does you good to do something crazy every once in a while.'

'I'll remember that,' he says. He takes a swig from his bottle of Becks. His baggy, collarless shirt has the top two buttons undone. He goes to the gym four or five times a week. It shows. I wonder if he knows how good he looks. I suspect he does.

'So what journo college did you go to?' he asks.

'Stradbroke, Sheffield.'

'Ah, the People's Republic of South Yorkshire,' he says. 'I remember it well.'

'I loved it there,' I say. 'People are friendlier up north.'

'Yeah. The weather's crap though. You didn't get that tan in Sheffield.'

I smile and shake my head. 'I've been travelling since I left college. South-east Asia mainly. India, Nepal.'

'Ah, that explains it,' he says.

'What?'

'You have an exotic air about you. Not usually found in women hailing from Leamington Spa.'

I'm aware I am blushing. And that he has read my CV. I take a sip of my vodka. It gives me something to do with my hands.

'Rugby must be quite a comedown after Kathmandu,' he says.

'Yeah, I've had a lot of trouble finding a rickshaw.'

He laughs. His eyes haven't moved from my face since we sat down. He doesn't say anything. He wants me to continue. He wants to know more about me. I don't think the others are listening any more. We are in a world of our own.

'I was ready to come back,' I say. 'Couldn't wait to get started here, to be honest.'

'Always wanted to be a journalist?'

'Yep.'

'Never mind. You'll get over it.'

He opens a packet of peanuts which are on the table and offers them to me. I shake my head. He pours some into his cupped palm and tips his head back as he pops them into his mouth. I notice a couple of grains of salt, caught on his stubble. I want to reach out and brush them off. Like I want to sweep back that stray strand of hair which keeps falling into his eyes.

'So, how come you haven't got a hot date lined up for Valentine's night then?' he says.

'Because my boyfriend's just dumped me.'

'Oops, sorry. Put my foot in it there.'

'It's all right. You weren't to know.'

'What a bastard, dumping you just before Valentine's Day.'

'There's never a good time, is there?'

'I hope he had a good excuse.'

'He said it wasn't going anywhere. And that he was busy at work.'

'A mug as well as a bastard. I bet he's a journalist, isn't he?'

I nod. Deciding not to reveal any more details than that.

'Knew it. Steer clear of them, I tell you. Nasty swines. Not to be trusted.'

I laugh, hoping he isn't including himself in that sweeping generalisation. 'Thanks for the advice. I'll remember that.'

He smiles at me, opens his mouth to say something then thinks better of it. I'm aware that the others are talking amongst themselves. He is paying me too much attention. He leans back on the seat and stretches his arm out along the top of it behind me. I shuffle forward, knowing it would be wrong to allow contact.

'We're having a union meeting in here next Thursday after work,' he says.

'Right, I'll try to make it.'

'Actually, you've got no choice in the matter.'

'Closed shop, is it?' I joke.

'Yeah, good as. Those shits would suck the blood from us if they could.'

'And the union can save our souls.'

I am smiling as I say it. I know it is risky, to challenge him like this. It is not really my place. Nick turns and looks at me. A fire is dancing behind his eyes. A fire I have ignited.

'Do I detect a hint of sarcasm?'

'All the power's been taken away, hasn't it? Nothing we can do till Labour get back in.'

'You think Blair'd be any better? He's a closet Tory.'

'He's the only chance we've got.'

'There are other ways.'

'I know, come the revolution . . .'

'Hey, we have a sceptic in our midst,' he says. He is not annoyed, though. I can tell he is loving this.

'Let's just say I've yet to be convinced.'

'Fine,' he says, smiling. 'I like a challenge.'

He looks at me in a way that makes me feel uncomfortable. Like he can see right through me. Knows my most intimate secrets. If we were alone I think he would kiss me now. But we are not alone. The others have stopped talking. I look up and see a woman standing there, all legs, sophistication and immaculately applied lipstick. I don't know who she is but I hate her.

'Hey, great. You managed to get away early.' Nick slips his arm out from behind me so quickly I feel the air rush past my bare neck. He jumps up and kisses her on the lips.

I nearly choke on my vodka. I put the glass down heavily on the table, missing the beer mat. Joan looks across at me. I am aware that my eyes are bulging like a cartoon character's. Nick has a girlfriend. And I had no fucking idea.

'Sarah, this is Amanda.' Nick is looking at my left shoulder rather than my face. I smile lamely at her, unable to utter a word. 'Amanda, this is Sarah, our new reporter.' Amanda looks at me with no hint of a smile.

'Oh yes, the trainee,' she says. I feel about thirteen years old. Amanda sits down opposite me making no attempt at conversation. The others say hello to her. They don't seem very enthusiastic.

'Do you want a drink, Amanda?' asks Joan. 'It's my round next.'

'No, thanks, I'm not stopping. We're going for a meal before we catch a film.'

'Where are you taking her, Nick?' asks Joan. 'Somewhere nice, I hope.'

'Just for a curry at Titash across the road. They give all the women a free red rose, there. Saves me a fortune on flowers.'

'And they say romance is dead,' says Joan, shaking her head.

Nick is smiling. Amanda is smiling too. I suspect he sent her a dozen red roses this morning. Though he is not going to admit it in front of us.

He is hurriedly finishing his bottle of Becks. He hasn't made eye contact with me since Amanda arrived. My head is spinning. They will be leaving in a few minutes, walking off together hand in hand. The one thing I do know is that I do not want to watch it.

'Excuse me,' I say as I get up. Everyone shuffles along to let me out. I make my way to the ladies, shutting the door of the cubicle before letting my head fall back against it. I feel stupid for not realising he would have a girlfriend. Good-looking, nice guys generally do. And

there was I thinking he was coming on to me. How wrong
can you be? I feel the tears pricking. I hear my mother
telling me I am being ridiculous. I have only known him
three weeks, for goodness' sake. But she would say that.
She had known my father five years before they got
married. Five years of courting: fond goodnights, hand-
holding, waves across the street. Everything pleasant and
polite. She said there was no rush. What she means is no
passion. Not then or any point since. I suspect my
creation was considered a necessary chore. I am not
surprised I am an only child. Or that they have slept in
separate beds for as long as I can remember.

I hear the main door open. Someone enters the cubicle
next to me, pees and flushes. I hurriedly flush, needing to
make my extended absence sound plausible. When I come
out, Joan is at the sinks washing her hands.

'Are you OK?' she says.

I catch my reflection in the mirror and realise I don't
look OK.

'Yeah,' I say. 'Always feel crap, first day I'm on.'

Joan nods. She doesn't seem convinced.

'I don't suppose you knew Nick had a girlfriend, did
you?' she says, giving the soap dispenser a good squirt.

'Er, no. He hadn't mentioned her. Not that it matters.'

'He hardly ever talks about her. Plays his cards close
to his chest, I guess.'

'Have they been going out long?' I ask. Hoping it
sounds casual, as if I am just passing the time of day.

'About eighteen months, on and off. From what I can
gather she practically lives at his place. Every now and
then they have a big fall-out and she scuttles back to her
parents' house. Always goes back to him, though. Sucker
for that charm, she is. Most women are.'

I nod as I rinse my hands, deciding not to look up in
case Joan is looking at me. I sense she is doing this for
my benefit. The big sister routine.

'What does she do?' I ask.

'Lawyer. Works for the Crown Prosecution Service based at Warwick. You'll probably see her at court if you go to a big case sometime. Not that she'll bother to say hello. Bit of a cold fish, she is. I don't know what he sees in her, myself, apart from the obvious. And that's not enough to base a relationship on. Not really.' She shakes her hands and wipes them on her trousers. 'Anyway, none of our business, I suppose, is it? Best let them get on with it.'

She disappears out the door before I can say anything. I look at my hands under the dryer and realise they are still shaking.

As I leave the ladies I glance through the pub window and catch a glimpse of Nick and Amanda crossing the street. They are not holding hands. I watch as he opens the restaurant door for her and follows her inside. Out of sight, out of reach but not out of mind. I make my way slowly back to my seat and rejoin the others. I stay for another hour so as not to make it look obvious, before making my excuses and going back to my flat. To mourn the loss of what could have been.

Four

'You look nice.'

Shit. Jonathan had noticed. Which meant I had gone too far. It wasn't supposed to be obvious, the effort I had put into getting ready that morning. I looked down at my long black skirt. I was only showing a couple of inches of leg but it was a couple of inches more than normal.

'Oh, er, do I? Everything else needed ironing.' I hated lying to Jonathan like this. Hated the fact that the deceit had started already.

'These could do with a quick press really, but I haven't got time.' Jonathan brushed an imaginary speck of dust from his trousers. If you stared really hard you could just make out the hint of a crease about half an inch long. He was the only eco-warrior in the world with an ironing fixation.

'I'll see you later, then.' I said. 'After the gym.'

'What about breakfast?'

He was doing the caring bit again. It wasn't an act, it was genuine. Which only made it worse. I grabbed a banana from the bowl and shoved it into my briefcase. 'I'll have it when I get there,' I said, giving him a quick kiss before hurrying out of the door. I felt like I was cheating on him. Which was ridiculous. I was only going to work.

As I shut the door behind me I met Najma, our neighbour, coming down the stairs.

'Hi, Sarah. You look nice,' she said. I was starting to

think I must look a real mess most of the time. Najma was one of those women who always looked stunning without having to try. I suspected she looked great first thing in the morning without any make-up. She was dead nice as well, which made it even worse.

'Oh, thanks,' I said. 'How are things with Paul?'

'Great,' she said, an unfeasibly large grin on her face and a faraway look in her eyes. 'Still in those heady early days, I guess.'

She'd been going out with him just over a month now. They'd met at work. Najma was something big in accounts at the city council. He was the new guy, something equally big in human resources. I'd met him a few times in the hallway. Suitably dishy and very polite.

'I remember those days,' I said. 'Best make the most of it. Before you know it you'll be accusing him of stealing the duvet and wearing baggy grey pyjamas to bed instead of your best lingerie.'

Najma laughed. 'And Jonathan still worships the ground you walk on.'

I blushed, knowing it was true.

'So how is he?' she said as we walked down the garden path together. She'd been somewhat in awe of Jonathan ever since he'd taken her to the anti-war rally in Chamberlain Square, where he'd joined in the sit-down protest and had to be forcibly removed by a policeman.

'Fine, thanks,' I said as we reached our cars. 'Busy as usual with all his campaigning. We're just ticking along as ever. Nothing very exciting.'

Najma's faraway look returned for a second.

'Don't knock it,' she said. 'It must be lovely to be so settled like that. Have everything sorted.'

'Yeah,' I said as I opened the car door. 'I guess it is.'

'Say hi to him from me,' said Najma. 'And don't forget how lucky you are.'

I drove to work with her words ringing in my ears.

*

'Not you as well.' Cayte started laughing as soon as I set foot in the office.

'What?' I said stern-faced, as I sat down next to her.

'Notice anything?' she said, gesturing round the office. Every female in the newsroom was wearing a skirt, even those like me who had not previously been known to possess one. Several women who usually wore glasses were either typing blind or had resorted to contact lenses. You could practically smell the shampoo from the freshly styled hair. In fact, you would have been able to if it wasn't for the array of perfumes blocking it out. At least I hadn't sunk to the depths of Christian Dior.

'So we all made an effort this morning,' I said with a shrug.

'What a coincidence.' Cayte smirked.

'You can talk. That's one of your going out skirts. You wore that last Christmas.'

'Yep, but then I have no moral standards. You, I'm surprised at. I would have expected better from you.'

She sounded like Mrs Bell, one of my old school-teachers. After Philip Parkin had grassed on me and I was made to hand over the dirty joke I'd written on a scrap of paper and was passing round the class.

'OK, so I put a bloody skirt on. It doesn't mean I want to jump on him the second he arrives.'

'Good, because there's a long queue and I'm before you, anyway.'

I started laughing. Part of me was desperate to tell her. It was a long time since I'd been the subject of office gossip. Since I'd caused a bit of a stir. But then I remembered what that had led to. So I shut up and got on with my work.

Nick arrived five minutes late on his first day. Something of a record. He was wearing the same suit he'd worn to the interview. And the same look of self-assurance. The wedding ring was still absent. I noticed this time. There was a flurry of inactivity as he strolled up to the news desk. I heard him apologise to Keith, something about the parking. Keith wouldn't like him. I knew that already. Men who were good-looking, charming and intelligent had an unnerving effect on him. He would probably start a rumour that Nick was gay.

Nick turned and started walking towards me. I could tell, even though I wasn't looking. My eyes were fixed firmly on my computer screen.

'Hi, Sarah.' Two words. That was all it took. Two words and I was sucked into some massive time warp. I was twenty-three again. Not shaking hands with him on my first day. Because he said it was too formal.

I looked up. 'Oh, hi.' I tried to sound surprised. As if I hadn't realised it was him until that second.

'I don't think I've made a very good first impression,' he said, nodding towards Keith.

'You should have got here on time, then,' I said.

'Thanks for the sympathy.'

'No problem. Do you want me to show you to your desk? I can hold your hand if you like.'

Nick smiled. A smile of recognition. Not of me, the new Sarah. But of the old one, who had never quite mastered sarcasm.

'Thanks for the offer, but I think I'll be all right.' He bent down and whispered into my ear, 'Is the geeky lad at the end my underling?'

'His name is Andrew,' I whispered back. 'He may look like a pubescent computer nerd and have the charisma of a weasel but he's a shit-hot political reporter and he'll stab you in the back given half a chance.'

'Remind me not to ask you any more questions,' said Nick, still in hushed tones. 'Otherwise people will start to talk.'

He stood up and walked over to his desk. His smell lingered over me. The gaze of forty pairs of eyes lingered on my back. Cayte kicked me under the table.

'What was all that about?' she hissed.

'We were arranging to have sex later,' I said. She nodded before she realised.

'Piss off,' she said. 'Being witty doesn't suit you.'

Cayte went off on a job shortly afterwards, leaving only an empty desk between me and Nick. I was aware of him all morning, his presence as acute as his absence had been all these years. He appeared to be busy, although I had no idea what with. A few people went over and introduced themselves. Women mainly. A couple of times I heard him laugh and it made me start. I expected to look up and find myself back in the *Chronicle* offices. He was out of place or out of time. Or maybe both. I wasn't sure any more.

I busied myself phoning contacts. Making sure I didn't give him the chance to say anything. I had just finished a phone call when he put a cup of coffee from the machine down in front of me.

'What's this?' I said.

'It's called coffee, it's made from roasted and ground beans. You drink it. Gives you a bit of a buzz.'

'Don't try to be funny, Nick. It doesn't work with me.'

'It used to.'

I started typing. Not wanting to look at him for fear of what it would do to me.

'I didn't ask for a coffee,' I said.

'Call me spontaneous.'

'I don't take sugar any more.'

'I'll remember that for next time.'

'No need. I'll get my own, thank you.'

The smile faded from Nick's face. I could tell without looking.

'I'm trying to be civil, Sarah. I haven't seen you for seven years. I figured I could get you a coffee.'

'Keep your voice down, will you?' I glanced over my shoulder. A couple of people were looking at us.

'Oh, I get it,' he said. 'Nobody knows, do they?'

'No and I'd like to keep it that way.'

Nick was leaning closer. I could feel his breath, warm on my neck. His voice trickling into my ear. 'Fine. I'll just pretend you're some bitter, twisted hack who delights in being horrible to the new guy.'

'I didn't ask for this to happen, you know. I was doing perfectly well without you.'

'I'll go then, shall I? Hand my notice in today. Or better still do a runner. Disappear overnight. Leave you to explain away my sudden exit.'

I started typing the first few lines of my column. 'Writing Wrongs' it was called. Stupid title. I had no idea what I was writing. All I knew was that I couldn't stop. He stood there for a few seconds. Waiting for something that didn't come. Then he turned silently and walked back to his desk. I let the coffee go cold.

Nick went out on a job in the afternoon. The Council House, I presumed. I didn't ask. When the final edition of the paper came, I flicked through; just the usual crap, nothing unusual. Until I got to page five and saw his name above a story. Except it wasn't his name. It was 'Nic Hardwick'. A name I didn't recognise. I went up to the chief sub with the page in my hand.

'What happened to the k in the byline?' I asked.

'There isn't one. That's what he told us. Poncey southerner.'

I walked back to my desk. A lot had changed in seven years.

I drove straight to the gym after work. I needed a breathing space before I went home to Jonathan. Needed to get Nick out of my system. To sweat him out through my pores if necessary. I liked the anonymity here. Row upon row of cross trainers, steppers and exercise bikes facing the huge screens piping MTV. You didn't have to talk to anyone, you simply stared straight ahead like a blinkered racehorse, ready to jolt into action at the press of a button. The treadmills were even better, facing the huge window which ran along one side of the gym. You could jog along watching the Birmingham rush hour traffic grind to a halt below. Feeling suitably smug that you were working out while they were stuck in a traffic jam getting stressed, chain-smoking and eating any half-melted, out-of-date chocolate bar they could lay their hands on.

I changed into my gym clothes. Lycra shorts and vest tops were de rigueur here. It was a gym for fit people not fat people. For people who looked the part, wore the right trainers, carried the right water bottle. Jonathan, who had only been once, said it was like an experiment in human cloning by a dictator trying to create a master race. He declined to join on the grounds that he would rather be kept as a battery hen than lined up with a bunch of others on a treadmill. But then he was one of those annoying naturally fit people who didn't have to try.

The cool air hit me as I walked into the gym, made the hairs on my arms stand on end. I started doing my warm-up, stretching my hamstrings and my quads. It was important to do these things properly. I had a set routine, one that had been mapped out for me by a personal trainer. Not a personal trainer like Madonna has. One that spends thirty minutes with you every two months in order to assess your needs and devise a routine to target your 'problem areas' (a code for cellulite). They were invariably called Emma or Matt, had an NVQ in leisure something and had left to become a pilates instructor or go scuba diving in New Zealand by the next time you went.

I stuck to it, though. Whatever routine they gave me. And I went at least three times a week. So that when the instructor signed my card at the end of the session, I never had to think up excuses as to why I hadn't been for a month.

I started on the treadmill. I liked the sound of my feet pounding below me. Of the urgency it generated. The sense of being unable to stop, of having to keep up, to push yourself, to avoid being caught. I stared out of the window. Headlights snaked back up the road as far as I could see, plumes of exhaust fumes caught in their glare. I let my eyes unfocus, allowing everything to blur as I bounced up and down. I wanted to run for ever. To put real distance between us again. But it was no use. I was running at standstill. I knew that now.

The treadmill slowed down. I obliged obediently, dropping to a jog, then a brisk walk before gliding to a halt. I stepped off the back, took a swig from my water bottle and picked up my towel. I didn't need to check where I was going next: it was programmed into me, my route round the gym. The order of each piece of equipment, what programme number or weight, how long or how many repetitions. It was all in there; I was on automatic pilot. The troublesome, thinking side of my brain switched off.

I headed for the pull-down bar. The man on it was wearing a grey vest top. A dark circle of sweat was spreading from the centre of his back. The weights clinked each time he let the bar back up and I heard him inhale as he pulled it back down. He looked like Nick from the back. I glanced quickly round the gym. Half the men there looked like Nick from the back. Broad shoulders, dark hair, toned bodies. Came with the territory. I was being ridiculous.

The man got up, picked his towel off the seat and turned round. It was Nick. My freshly warmed-up muscles tensed again. I hadn't got used to the idea that I was working with him again yet, let alone the possibility of bumping into him around town. Though judging by the expression on his face, he was even more surprised to see me.

'Hello,' he said. 'I thought you hated gyms?'

'That was a long time ago. Before I hit thirty. I now consider them a necessary evil.'

He smiled, shook his head and rubbed himself down with the towel. I tried to keep looking at his face. But my gaze fell to his vest.

'How are you spelling Nike these days?' I said.

He looked at me, raising an eyebrow, waiting for me to continue.

'Only I wondered if you'd dropped the k from that as well. That's probably the trendy way of spelling it down in London.'

He smiled again. 'If you're not careful, Sarah, you could find that sense of humour you used to have.'

'So come on, why drop the k in your byline?'

Nick draped the towel round his neck and sighed. 'A sub on the *Express* did it by mistake. Someone said it looked better so I decided to stick with it.'

I wondered if the someone was Amanda but didn't like to ask.

'You've been branded a poncey southerner at work.'

Nick laughed. 'I don't give a fuck.'

He was taking everything I was throwing at him with a good-natured smile. Which made it worse, because I suspected my verbal tirade, brought on by seven years of pent-up anger, was intended to provoke a reaction.

'And are you still spelling fuck with the k or without?'

He smiled again, although it was a weak joke. 'So are you just going to stand there and abuse me or can we actually sit down and have a proper chat now we're not at work?'

He had me on the back foot now, not knowing what to say. I was torn. Part of me desperately wanted to satisfy my curiosity. But I also knew you shouldn't pick at old scabs. In case you made them bleed again.

'I'm in the middle of a workout,' I said, sitting down on the bench. It wasn't a refusal. At best it was non-committal.

'OK, when you're finished then. I'll see you in the bar in about forty minutes.' He went to walk away then turned back again. 'You're looking good, by the way. Shame about the curls though. I used to love your long hair.'

I took a deep breath and pulled the bar above me. Nothing happened. Nick stifled a laugh.

'I think you'll find that's a bit heavy for you,' he said. 'Might have to change the weights.'

It was a second or two before I realised I was laughing and managed to stop myself. I shouldn't encourage him. Or let him get to me. I devised a new gym routine based solely on maintaining the maximum distance between myself and Nick. I gave up after twenty minutes and went to have a shower.

Nick was already in the bar when I got there. Sitting on a stool with a bottle of Becks in his hand.

'I got one in for you,' he said, pointing at a glass of what I suspected was vodka and orange.

'I don't drink any more,' I said.

He turned to look at me. His hair was still wet from the shower. He smelt of something musky.

'Why not?'

'I just don't.'

'Can I get you something else?'

'No thanks. I can't stop long.'

'Got plans, have you?'

'Sort of.'

He nodded. I climbed up on to the stool beside him. We sat in silence for a moment. Neither of us seemed to know where to start.

'Why did you leave, Sarah?' he said eventually.

'You know why.'

'You could have said goodbye. Or left a note.'

'Yeah, I could have pinned it to your front door, couldn't I? Amanda would have liked that.'

He appeared taken aback by the bitterness in my voice. 'I thought we could still be friends.'

'Well you thought wrong.'

He shook his head. If I didn't know better I would have said he looked hurt.

'Please, Sarah. I thought we could catch up on each other's lives. Fill in the gaps of what we've missed.'

I shrugged, feigning indifference. I didn't want to let on. That I had thought about him every single day since. Wondered what he was doing. Who he was doing it with. I had to find a way round this.

'OK,' I said. 'Five questions each. Only who, what, why, where and whens allowed. You go first.'

Nick smiled. I knew it would appeal to the journalist in him. He took a swig from the bottle.

'Why Scarborough?' he said.

I hesitated before answering.

'I fancied walking home along the beach.'

'How often did you do that?'

'That's a waste of a question.'

'Answer please,' said Nick.

'Twice.'

He nodded, the edges of his mouth creeping into a smile. 'What else have you stopped doing since I last saw you? Apart from drinking and taking sugar in your coffee.'

I thought for a moment. It was hard to know where to begin. I decided to give an edited version.

'OK. I've stopped eating bacon butties, voting Labour and flying.'

'Why?'

'These really are stupid questions,' I said.

'My choice. You just answer. Why?'

'I don't eat meat because I've gone veggie, I don't vote Labour because of the Iraq war and I don't fly because of my boyfriend's concern for the environment.'

Nick hesitated and scratched his head. I wondered if it was the word boyfriend which had thrown him.

'So your boyfriend's one of those lentil-munching, sandal-wearing eco-warrior types.'

'That's your sixth question.'

'It wasn't a question. It was an observation. Your go.'

I was rattled. He'd found out more than I'd wanted him to. And he now had an image of Jonathan as some kind of Swampy figure. I wanted to point out that just because Jonathan was a fully paid-up member of the Green Party, it didn't mean he had a personal hygiene problem. I needed to score a few points of my own. I was desperate to ask about Amanda. But I didn't want to make it too obvious. Better to go in with something work related and build up to it.

'How long did you stay at the *Chronicle*?'

'Four months. Boring question.'

'Why did you leave?'

'It wasn't the same without you. It was like someone had switched off the lights.'

'Why can't you ever be serious?'

'I was being serious.'

I looked down. Anything to avoid looking at him. He didn't have any socks on. Just trainers. Jonathan said it was bad for your feet not to have socks on. Encouraged athlete's foot. I couldn't stop myself from asking the question any longer.

'Why don't you wear your wedding ring?'

Nick looked down at his feet. 'We got divorced a year ago.'

'Oh, sorry,' I said. I wasn't sure if I meant it or not. My insides were churning. It meant he was available. Unless he was seeing anyone else. I was trying to think of a way of asking without being too obvious when my mobile rang.

'Excuse me,' I said, pulling it out of the side pocket of my bag. It was Jonathan, asking what I wanted for tea. I told him fajitas. Then regretted it immediately.

'Is your boyfriend Jamie Oliver?' asked Nick.

'It's not your turn.'

'I know. You've got one left.'

'Why did you come to Birmingham? Really?'

Nick looked up for a second, swirled the last dregs of his Becks around in the bottle. 'The truth?'

'Preferably,' I said.

'To see you.'

I dropped my mobile on the floor. Nick bent down to pick it up. I stared at him as he handed it back to me. My brain was in danger of overheating.

'You knew I was here?' I said.

He nodded. 'I looked you up on Google. And I figured you were more likely to be a reporter on the *Birmingham Evening Gazette* than a professor of anthropology at Sussex University or a recently deceased classical guitarist.'

I was unsure whether to be flattered or horrified. I certainly wasn't going to admit that I'd trawled through most of the eighty-four thousand entries for Nick Hardwick.

'So why did you act surprised when you saw me at your interview?'

'I didn't know you were going to be in there with Terry, did I? I had no idea you were the Gordon Brown of the *Gazette*, the power behind the throne.'

I shook my head. 'It's not like that. Terry trusts my judgement, that's all.'

'So how come I got the job?' asked Nick with a smile.

I wasn't going to be drawn. I knew this was silly. I was ignoring the bigger question. The obvious one which was hanging in a speech bubble over my head, wondering how long it would be before I asked it.

'Why did you want to see me?' I said, relenting under the pressure.

Nick paused, took another swig from his bottle.

'Because I've missed you,' he said. 'And because I wanted to know if you were happy.'

I looked down, hoping Nick wouldn't see me swallowing hard, trying to remain composed. Realising that I wouldn't be able to answer without breaking down in tears.

'I've got to go,' I said. I slithered off the stool and hurried out of the bar. I sat in the car for several minutes before I started the engine. Taking deep breaths and waiting until the world stopped looking blurry.

Sunday 16 March 1997

I sit in the launderette watching my washing do an impression of the inside of my head, letting the noise of the machines lull me into a trancelike state. There are half a dozen other people in here. I recognise all of them. It is not surprising really. I ought to have some kind of loyalty card. My clothes have never been so clean.

I am marking time. It is what I do at the weekends. Count the days, hours, minutes until I can be with Nick again. I prefer it when it is my turn to do the weekend shift. It is easier to keep my mind occupied at work. Always places to go, people to see, stories to write. On weekends off it is more difficult to keep busy. To stop myself thinking about what he is doing because I know it will involve her. I try everything to block it out: shopping, going to the launderette, washing my car, even seeing my parents once a fortnight, I am that desperate. Anything to try to erase the picture I have in my head of the two of them together. It doesn't work, of course. I can still see the image reflected now, in the door of the washing machine.

I tell myself to stop it. This silliness, as my mother would call it. What I need to do is put a full stop at the end of the sentence. I have almost managed it a couple of times. Reminded myself he has a girlfriend. End of story. But always Nick manages to say or do something to start it all up again. This idea that there is something more there than friendship. That he is still interested in me. Despite being with her.

I realise the machine, unlike my head, has stopped spinning. I open the door and empty my washing into the laundry bag before lugging it across the street to where my bright orange Beetle is parked. I dump the bag on the back seat and turn the key in the ignition. Nothing. I try again, still nothing. I groan and bang my head on the steering wheel. I hadn't been able to afford breakdown cover. I get out and open the bonnet and stand there scratching my head. It could be the battery. Then again it could be a whole host of other things. The truth is I have no idea. It is Sunday morning, all the garages will be closed. I haven't even got enough money for a bus. It may be a long walk home.

I hear a car approaching and slowing down, then a familiar voice.

'Hi, Sarah.'

I realise I have finally lost it. Imagining I am hearing him now, as well as seeing his face everywhere. I choose to ignore it but the voice calls again.

'Can I give you a hand?'

I spin round. Nick is leaning out of the window of his car. Something inside me fires, setting my heart racing, the blood pumping round my body so loudly I fear Nick will hear it. Within a few seconds I am in serious danger of overheating. I only wish my car was as responsive. I realise my mouth is gaping open and I have yet to say anything.

'Nick, hi,' I manage eventually.

'I was on my way home from the gym. I don't usually stop for stranded female motorists, not since I watched *Thelma and Louise*. But as it was you I thought I'd make an exception.'

'Thank you. I'm very glad you did.'

'Don't get too excited,' says Nick. 'I haven't done anything yet. And you probably know more about cars than I do.'

He parks next to me, gets out and strolls over. He is the only person I know who can manage to look sexy in tracksuit bottoms and a polo shirt. He smells of soap and shampoo. I am suddenly conscious of my grubby clothes and lack of make-up. I wipe my brow and pull my hair back out of my eyes.

'Is this your pride and joy, then?' he says, tapping the bonnet.

'No, not really. I haven't had it long.'

'I bet it's got a name. Women always give their cars names.'

I start to laugh.

'Come on, out with it,' he says.

'Tango,' I say. 'Because of the colour. Not very original but it seemed better than satsuma at the time.'

'Not bad,' he says. 'Although I think I'd have called it Graham Taylor. You know, the former England manager, the one who said, "Do I not like orange?"'

I smile. I love the way he does that. Always brings a smile to my lips.

'So what's the problem?' he says, moving round to the engine.

'Won't start. Completely dead.'

'I've got some jump leads in the boot,' he says. 'At least it might get you home.'

'That would be great,' I say. He brings the leads over and I fix them on to my car. Glad I do at least know how to do that.

'If it starts, keep it running,' says Nick. 'I'll follow you home, just to make sure.'

The car starts first time. I do as Nick said. It is only as I pull up outside my flat that I realise I have no idea what to say or do now we are here. If he was just a friend, the obvious thing to do would be to invite him up for a coffee. But he is clearly much more than a friend, otherwise I wouldn't be hesitating. Or feeling guilty at the prospect of asking somebody else's boyfriend up to my flat. Nick parks behind me, gets out and walks over. I am frozen in my car seat, unable to do anything apart from wind the window down and smile pathetically.

'Thanks very much,' I say. 'What do I owe you?'

'A coffee would be nice. Unless you're planning to sit in there all day.'

I look at him, my eyes staring wide. Caught in the glare of the headlights. Unable to see an escape route to save me from the oncoming vehicle. Nick is looking at me. Still waiting for my reply.

'Yes, sorry, of course. Come on up.'

I get out of the car, hauling my laundry bag with me, trying not to let him see how flustered I am.

'Here, let me take that,' says Nick. He staggers exaggeratedly under the weight.

'Do you take in washing for the whole street?' he asks. 'Some kind of good neighbour initiative?'

I smile as I lead him to the front door, then up the flight of stairs to my flat. All the time, voices inside my head are hollering, 'Don't do it.' I tell them to shut up. It is just a coffee. Anyway, it is too late. He is here now. I open my door and he follows me through into the main room. It is weird having a bedsit, because essentially you are showing any visitors straight into your bedroom. I glance over at the bed, relieved to find I made it after I got up this morning and that I haven't left any dirty underwear lying around.

I turn back to Nick. I wonder if he feels as awkward as I do. If he does he is not showing it.

'So, this is where you hang out,' he says.

'Yeah. A bit on the poky side but I haven't got much stuff and it will do until I can get some cash together.'

Nick nods. I realise he is still holding the laundry bag.

'Here, let me take that,' I say. I dump the bag in the bathroom. When I get back Nick is looking at the photos on the wall.

'These from your travels?' he says.

'Yeah. Pokhara in Nepal. Beautiful place.'

'Who did you go with?' he asks.

'No one. I went on my own.'

He raises an eyebrow questioningly. I sense he is fishing.

'My ex-boyfriend couldn't get the time off work. Or maybe he just didn't want to come with me.'

'I wouldn't blame him,' he says. 'I wouldn't fancy it.'

'Thank you.' I say, smiling at him. 'And what makes me the world's worst travelling companion?'

'Well, you talk too much, for a start. You'd probably collect animal dung along the way. And judging by the state of you this morning, you let yourself go a bit outside work.'

I start laughing and dig him playfully in the ribs with my elbow.

'You're all charm, you are,' I say. He is looking at me, eyes twinkling, daring me to come back at him. I want him so much right now, it scares me.

'I'll put the kettle on,' I say. 'One spoon of arsenic or two?'

'Oh, go on, make it two. You spoil me.'

I go through to the kitchen, still laughing and shaking my head. When the two of us are together it is as if Amanda doesn't exist. And if she didn't exist we would be together. I am sure of that. I pour the coffees, take them back in and hand Nick his. He hasn't even taken a sip when the doorbell rings. Fuck. The interruption brings me back to the real world. The one where Amanda does exist and I am going out for lunch with my parents to try to forget that fact.

'Sorry,' I say. 'I completely forgot. My parents are coming round. And it sounds like they're early.'

Nick looks disappointed. Though not half as disappointed as I am. I consider not answering the door, pretending I am out. But my car is outside. And my mother is the sort who, despite my age, would ring the police if she thought anything was amiss.

'Do you want me to go?' he asks.

'No, finish your coffee. But I warn you my mother will probably jump to the wrong conclusion,' I say.

'And what would that be?' says Nick, the smile returning to his face.

The doorbell rings again.

'I'd better go and let them in,' I say.

My mother, who is dressed immaculately in a peacock blue linen two-piece, looks disapprovingly at my jeans and shirt, steps inside and greets me with a peck on the cheek. My father, who dresses like a banker, even at weekends, stoops to kiss me, though I suspect he would be more comfortable shaking my hand.

I try to tell them about my unexpected visitor but my mother is on a rant about the rudeness of the young man in the petrol station and they are up the stairs and into the flat before I have managed to get a word in edgeways. My mother stops in her tracks when she sees Nick standing there, coffee mug in hand.

'Oh. Sarah? You didn't say you had company,' she says, spinning round to me, her face and tone of voice suggesting she suspects he has stayed the night. I want to remind her that I am twenty-three now, no longer living under her roof, and do not owe her any kind of explanation. However, I am also aware of Nick's presence and do not want a scene. Especially when the truth is actually entirely innocent.

'Mum, this is Nick,' I say. 'My news editor at work. He stopped to help this morning when my car wouldn't start. Nick, these are my parents, Ruth and Norman.'

Nick puts his mug down, turns on that smile and offers his hand to my mother.

'Delighted to meet you, Mrs Roberts,' he says. My mother softens visibly. Nick continues his charm offensive by offering his hand to my father. 'Pleased to meet you, Mr Roberts. You must be very proud of your daughter.'

The look on my father's face suggests he has never considered such a possibility. We stand there awkwardly. All I can think about is what might have happened if my parents hadn't arrived.

'Right. Well, I'd better be off,' says Nick.

'Oh, but you haven't even finished your coffee yet,' says my mother. 'Do stay a little longer. It's not often we get the chance to meet one of Sarah's man friends.'

I groan inwardly. She has obviously decided Nick is son-in-law material. I glance at Nick who is clearly trying not to laugh.

'Well, maybe another five minutes, as long as I'm not intruding.'

'Not in the least,' says my mother, sitting down in one of the armchairs. 'Sarah can make us a coffee while you tell us a little about yourself.'

I cringe as I disappear into the kitchen. When I re-emerge a few minutes later my father is sitting in the other armchair and Nick is perched on the end of my bed. I put the cups down on the coffee table and look round, realising I have no option but to join Nick. As I sit down the bed sags in the middle, throwing us closer together than I had intended.

'Nick was just telling us he's a member of the local gym,' says my mother. 'You ought to join, Sarah. It would be nice for you to go together.'

I roll my eyes. This is rich coming from my mother who leads an entirely separate existence from my father, what with her tennis club and hospital league of friends and his bowls and bridge clubs.

'You know gyms aren't my thing,' I say.

'Sarah goes salsa dancing. Have you ever tried it, Nick?' she asks, seemingly intent on finding some hobby we can share.

'Can't say I have,' says Nick. 'I'll have to get Sarah to

give me a private lesson some time. Show me a few moves.'

I throw him a look. He is doing this on purpose. Trying to stir things up with my mother. I decide it's time to pull the plug before he gets me into any worse trouble than I am already in.

'Anyway,' I say. 'I'd better get changed if we're going out for lunch.'

'Where are you off to?' asks Nick.

'Just the Carlton. It's quite nice for Rugby,' says my mother, who would rather not leave Leamington Spa at all if she could help it.

'Right, well, I shall leave you to it,' says Nick, standing up. 'Lovely to meet you both,' he says to my parents. 'Enjoy your lunch.'

'Are you sure you won't join us?' asks my mother. 'We could easily fit an extra person at the table.'

I throw her a look this time, sensing she is enjoying this rare chance to meddle in my private life. She is not looking at me though. She is looking at Nick. Willing him to say yes. But he answers without hesitation.

'No thanks. I'd love to but I need to be getting home. Another time, perhaps.'

I breathe a sigh of relief. Much as I want to be with him I am not sure I could have coped with my mother trying to fix us up over three courses.

'We'll look forward to it,' says my mother. 'So many stories we could tell you about Sarah. I'm sure you'd like to hear them.'

'I would indeed,' says Nick, grinning at me. 'See you tomorrow, Sarah.' He leans over and gives me a peck on the cheek. Before I can get my breath back let alone say anything he is gone.

'Well,' says my mother the second the door is closed, 'you certainly kept that one quiet.'

'There's nothing to keep quiet, Mum. He's my news editor, my boss.'

'He seemed very familiar for a boss.'

'We get on really well, that's all there is to it.'

'As long as you know I approve of him. Very charming. And well spoken too. Such an improvement on your last one, that Mark chap. I never did like him, or that awful northern accent.'

I am getting exasperated now. 'Mum, I am not going out with him. If you must know, he has a girlfriend. He lives with her.'

My mother stares at me for a second, a look of horror on her face. 'But he seemed such a nice young man.'

'It just goes to show,' I say as I take a dress from my wardrobe and disappear into the bathroom, 'how looks can be deceptive.'

When I arrive at work the next morning Nick is on the phone. I sit down and turn my computer on, aware that he is looking at me. Aware that I have missed him in the twenty hours we have been apart. I hear him talking, his voice rising and falling, drifting over to me. Playing with my ears. I hear notes in it other people don't hear. It resonates deep within me. I take it home with me at nights. Because I can't take him. He goes home to Amanda. I don't know why because he doesn't love her. If he did he wouldn't look at me this way. It is as simple and as complicated as that. All I know is that if I can't have him I don't want anyone else. If it is not to be, I will lead a tortured, solitary existence. Like some modern-day Rapunzel, pining away in an isolated tower, with nothing more to do than brush my long tresses as I dream of my lost love.

Nick puts the phone down and walks over to me.

'Morning,' he says, smiling. 'Have a nice lunch?'

'Yes thanks. Despite your best efforts to stir things up.'

'I don't know what you mean,' says Nick. 'Anyway, it was good fun. Being your man friend.'

'You'll be pleased to know my mum approved of you.'

'Good stuff. I have a knack with the over forty-fives. I hope you let her down gently.'

'Not really. She thinks you're a cad and a bounder now I've told her the truth.'

'What's this?' says Joan, breezing past. 'Someone's rumbled Nick?'

'Yes, my mother unfortunately,' I say.

'Where did you meet Sarah's mother?' Joan asks Nick.

'At her flat. I was just having a quick coffee on my way home from the gym.'

Joan raises her eyebrows.

'There's a perfectly good café at the sports centre,' she says before walking off.

Nick looks down at his feet and returns to his desk. I shuffle some papers, feeling as if we have been caught snogging behind the bike sheds. I realise it sounded worse than it was. I want to tell Joan the full story, explain the bit about Nick jump-starting my car. Make it clear it was an accidental meeting, not premeditated. I decide to leave it, though. Aware that I might protest my innocence too much.

There is an uneasy silence in the office. A few minutes later Nick sends me down to Rugby Magistrates' Court. I'm not sure if he is trying to get rid of me or trying to do me a favour. It is my first murder case. A pensioner found battered to death in her flat after disturbing a burglar. It is only down for plea and directions today; it will be referred to crown court for the trial. But it is a big deal for Rugby and for me. When I arrive at court the big guns from the local TV and radio stations are there. Even a couple of news agencies covering it for the nationals. This is the real thing. I am the genuine article, the reporter from the local rag, the one with all the contacts, the inside information. My hands are clammy; I am worried someone will ask me a question I don't know the answer to. I hurry through the foyer

into court one and take my seat on the press bench.
I am rummaging through my bag for my notebook and
pen when I hear her voice. I look up to see Amanda
striding across the polished wooden floor, sophistication
oozing from her pores. Her long fair hair is cut into
a 'Rachel', every strand falling perfectly in place. Her
make-up is subtle but expertly applied, no trace of
mascara clumps in her feathery eyelashes. I catch myself
staring at her hands as she hugs a folder to her chest.
The nails on her long, elegant fingers are beautifully
manicured, the deep plum colour matching the silk
blouse beneath the well-cut black trouser suit which
shows off her wasp-waist.

Nick has done this on purpose. He must have known
she was trying the case for the CPS. So he sent
me here to remind me what I am up against. To stop me
getting carried away with any silly ideas about the
two of us. To force me to confront reality. He is with
her. And I can't begin to compete. Amanda looks across
at me and I do my best to smile. She nods in silent
acknowledgement.

The press bench is full now. The clerk opens the door
and asks the court to rise while the magistrates enter. We
nod and sit down again once they are seated. The
defendant is brought in handcuffed to a police officer. He
is young and scrawny with tiny startled eyes.

Amanda begins her performance. She glides purposefully up and down the courtroom, turning beautifully
poised on the balls of her feet when she gets to the far
end. Speaking clearly and deliberately in clipped, assured
tones. I am in awe of her. I am not the only one. The
defendant stutters a not guilty plea. He is remanded in
custody again, to be tried at Warwick Crown Court, where
any jury will no doubt hang on Amanda's every word and
find him guilty as hell. The defendant is marched away.
The other journalists file out of the courtroom. I remain
seated to hear the rest of the morning's cases. Amanda is

clearly still holding court. She is the queen, I a lowly pretender to the throne. Or perhaps the court jester. Making a fool of myself in public because I have allowed myself to become smitten. I need to put a stop to this. For everyone's sake. Starting from now.

Five

'He's a good operator, isn't he?' Terry looked up from the front page of last night's paper. 'School chief's own goal' by Nic Hardwick. Something about Councillor O'Connell's taxpayer-funded fact-finding mission to tour schools in Sweden. Which just happened to coincide with an Ireland football match in Stockholm. I hadn't read all of it. Just enough to know it was good.

'I guess so.'

Terry looked at me quizzically. 'You're not jealous, are you? Bit of competition for the splash.'

I gave Terry my look of utter contempt. 'It's not difficult, is it? Coming up with some dirt about that lot.'

'Parker never used to do it.'

'Yeah, well, I always told you he was a waste of space.'

'So what's Nick done to upset you?'

'Who said he had?'

'I just saw you walk straight past him without saying hello. I don't think you've said more than a dozen words to him in the past fortnight.'

I hadn't realised it was that obvious. The fact that I was avoiding Nick.

'We don't hit it off, that's all.'

'But he seems such a nice bloke. And he's got your sense of humour. I'd have thought you'd be great pals.'

'Well we're not. I talk to him if I need to. For work.'

Terry pulled a face and pushed the copy of the *Gazette*

to the far side of his desk. 'OK, suit yourself. As long as no one's upsetting my happy ship.'

Terry always talked like this. I supposed it was sweet of him really. Wanting us all to be blissfully contented. A bit weird though for a newspaper editor. Sometimes I felt like telling him he was supposed to be a ball-crunching bastard. But then again, it really wouldn't suit him.

'So, why did you want to see me?' I said, keen to change the subject.

Terry scratched his head. I could see bad news coming.

'The district offices,' he said. 'Reckon we could do without a couple of them?'

'I thought you were going to fight this?'

'Head office are putting a lot of pressure on. I've got to find some savings from editorial.'

'Well, you could get rid of Sonia, for a start.'

Sonia was our copy-taker. Unfortunately her spelling was atrocious, she was incredibly dense, had no knowledge of or interest in news or current affairs and gave a running commentary of nonsense as you filed your story over the phone. All the attributes needed for the job, really.

'She's not as bad as you make out,' Terry said. He had taken her on as part of the youth opportunities programme years ago and didn't have the heart to get rid of her despite a catalogue of blunders.

'I take it you haven't heard what she did yesterday, then?' I said.

Terry shook his head.

'Trevor filed a story from the press conference at Birmingham Eye Hospital? Only Sonia wrote Birmingham I Hospital. Fortunately news desk spotted it.'

Terry started chuckling.

'You won't be laughing when she costs you a lot of money one of these days,' I said. 'We'd be better off without her.'

'Sonia doesn't earn enough to make it worthwhile getting rid of her,' said Terry. 'I've got to do better than that.'

I was getting frustrated with him now. I got up and started pacing up and down. 'We can back you up if you want. As soon as this is out in the open the union can do a letter about protecting editorial quality. We could threaten to ballot on industrial action.'

'No. That'd make things worse.'

'And closing the district offices wouldn't? You know what they're like. They're doing this all over the country. We've only been saved so far because we're the flagship paper. Once they think they can get away with it here, they won't know when to stop.'

I realised I sounded like Nick. Or how he used to sound, at any rate. Terry shrugged. I threw up my arms and turned round to face the newsroom. Cayte was holding up my phone, gesturing wildly.

'I'd better go,' I said. 'But think about what I said.'

I hurried over to my desk. Cayte handed me the receiver.

'Who is it?'

'No one,' she said. 'Looked like you needed rescuing. Do you fancy lunch in a bit?'

'Haven't got time,' I said, pretending to talk for a moment in case Terry was watching, before putting the phone down. 'I'm nipping into town for a sandwich. I've got a job at one. Some guy who reckons he was thrown out of a psychiatric unit when he threatened to blow the whistle on their abuse.'

'How can you believe him, if he's wacko?'

Cayte still hadn't mastered the art of political correctness.

'He has mental health problems. It doesn't mean he can't tell the truth.'

I was thinking of *One Flew Over the Cuckoo's Nest*. Hoping to expose a modern-day Big Nurse and liberate the inmates. Hoping my source would turn out to be a McMurphy-type hero.

'Fine,' said Cayte. 'I shall dine on my own.'

'I'm up for lunch in about ten minutes, if you fancy it.'

It was Nick's voice. I hadn't even realised he was listening. I looked across at him. He was smiling at Cayte. I wondered if he was doing it to get to me.

'Great,' said Cayte. 'Give us a shout when you're ready, Nick.'

The freckles on her face rearranged themselves into the word 'smug'. I rolled my eyes and picked up my briefcase.

'See you later, then,' I said to Cayte, firing her a warning look which I suspected she would ignore.

I took deep breaths as I walked into town. I was sure Nick would pump her for information about me. And Cayte wasn't known for being discreet. I hated him for doing this to me. Putting me on edge. Making me feel I was losing control again. I told myself to think about something else. Something important. Colin, for instance. He hadn't been on his pitch last Friday. A young woman had been standing in his place. I'd asked where he was but she hadn't known. He could have caught a chill after the previous week. I hoped it wasn't anything more serious than that. A relapse of any kind.

I bowled down the road, peering to see between all the people. I could just make out a hunched figure on the corner. Then a glimpse of tufty hair and a glint of sunlight on glasses. It was Colin. He was all right. He wasn't, though. When I got up close I could see that. Purple and black circles under his left eye, a cut above the eyebrow and Sellotape round one arm of his glasses. I felt sick in the pit of my stomach. I wanted to lie him down on the pavement and tend his wounds, like some modern-day Florence Nightingale. I had put him on the streets. I was supposed to be trying to make things better. But it kept on getting worse.

'Colin, you poor thing.'

I watched him wince in pain as he turned towards me.

'Oh, Sarah. Hi.'

'Are you OK? What on earth's happened?'

'It's nothing. Got worse things in the school playground.'

'You went to a pretty tough school then. Those bruises look terrible. Have you seen a doctor?'

'There's no need. I'm fine.'

'What happened?'

'It doesn't matter. It's all done and dusted.'

'What happened, Colin?' I said again, my tone of voice demanding an answer this time.

'Are you Jeremy Paxman, or something?'

'You won't avoid the question by being funny, either.'

Colin gave a resigned sigh. 'Group of lads took exception to me. Called me a dirty beggar. Said I should climb back in my hole and stop messing up their streets. Then they laid into me and took my money. About nine quid.'

'Didn't anyone help you?'

'No one much about. Few that were walked past with their heads down. Didn't want to get involved. Can't say I blame them.'

'What did the police say?'

Colin raised his eyebrows above the rim of his glasses. 'Come on, they're not going to be interested in someone like me, are they? Probably accuse me of starting the whole thing, complain to the *Big Issue* and then I'd get my badge taken away.'

He had a point. I wanted to offer to sort it out for him. To run the story in the paper, expose the shocking level of violence against homeless people on our streets. But I knew most of our readers would probably think he deserved it. If the gang had kicked a stray cat, they'd be outraged. Inundate us with letters expressing their sympathy for the creature, offer to give it a home. But a homeless man with a history of mental illness? Not a chance.

'Oh, Colin. I'm so sorry. You really do deserve a break.'

He shrugged. I tried to think of something to say to cheer him up, make him feel human again.

'By the way, you're invited round for dinner tonight,' I said as I handed over my £1.20.

'Because you feel sorry for me?' he said.

'No. Because you're an old friend and you're more interesting company than most people I know.'

Colin smiled and handed me a copy of the *Big Issue* with Ms Dynamite on the front.

'Are you sure your boyfriend won't mind?'

'Of course not, it was his idea. He wants to meet you.'

This was a lie. I hadn't told Jonathan about Colin. Mainly because Colin was inextricably linked with Nick in my head. I was worried that if I tried to explain about Colin, Nick's name would slip out. Plus, talking about Colin made me feel guilty and Jonathan wasn't used to seeing me looking guilty. He wouldn't know it was guilt, he might even think it was indigestion, but he would definitely suspect something was wrong.

'Thanks, then. I'd love to come.'

I offered to pick him up after work but he wouldn't have it. Said he would come by bus. It would seem like a real night out. As soon as I was out of his sight, I rang Jonathan on my mobile.

'Hello?' I could hardly hear him above the hubbub of the staff room. Some sort of meeting appeared to be going on.

'Hi, it's me. I know this is very short notice but is it OK if I invite a couple of friends round for dinner tonight?'

'Yeah, I guess so. Anyone I know?'

'Cayte and a chap called Colin.'

'Is he her latest?' There was a disapproving tone in Jonathan's voice.

'No, he's an old friend of mine. Bumped into him in the

street, he's having a rough time. I'll explain later. Just a quick curry, don't go to any trouble. I'll get some bhajis or something from Tesco on the way home.'

'Sure, see you later,' he said. 'I'd better go.'

I felt bad after he hung up. Aware that I sometimes took Jonathan's good nature for granted.

I bought my sandwich and hurried back to meet our photographer Roger in the car park behind the *Gazette* as arranged.

'I hope this isn't another one of your time-wasters, Roberts,' he said as he edged his car gingerly between a line of newspaper delivery vans. Roger was the biggest whinger in photographic but for some inexplicable reason I had a soft spot for him.

'What do you mean?'

He pointed to the crumpled photo request slip on the dashboard. 'The name Mr Bear makes me a little suspicious,' he said, stroking his grey beard.

'The guy can't help having a funny name. You could have been born Mr Lillicrap, then you'd have had something to complain about.'

I ate my sandwich as Roger launched into his usual diatribe against the *Gazette*. The pay, the hours, the crap jobs, the arsehole on picture desk, the bloody digital cameras (never will be as good as using film), the stupid computers that don't do what you want them to do, the trainees who think they know it all, the ignorant security guard and the wanker from advertising who kept nicking his parking space.

I'd learnt not to say anything. Simply to nod and maybe offer the occasional supportive grunt. Once he was finished with that he moved on to the second half of his repertoire. The 'Of course, it used to be better in the old days, when I was working for real newspapers. Did I ever tell you about that time in Vietnam when . . .' He had told me, of course. But the story was embellished a little every time, so it was worth listening to. We were nearing the end of it now. The bit where he said, 'If I were you, Sarah, I'd get out while you can. Don't tell anyone, but I'm looking around. This time next year, I'll be gone, you know.'

I nodded as I always did. Knowing he'd been looking around for the past thirty years.

Mr Bear's flat was in a tatty road in Winson Green. Polystyrene fast food containers strewn over the pavement, a couple of dogs strutting down the street looking for trouble, bits of fridges and bicycles dumped in front gardens, trying desperately to look like an 'urban garden' exhibit at the Chelsea Flower Show.

I strode up to the door and rang the bell. Roger was cowering halfway down the path in case Mr Bear had a dog. He was scared of dogs, even little ones. He once legged it over a fence when yapped at by a one-eyed Yorkshire terrier.

Several minutes went past. I rang the bell again. I was about to leave when I heard a scuffling noise. A moment later the door opened a couple of inches and a man's face appeared above the door chain. He had dark, piggy eyes and a shock of reddish hair.

'You'd better come in,' he said.

I gestured to Roger, who followed me into the hallway. It was decorated in flock wallpaper which looked as if it had been up since the seventies. Mr Bear, who was wearing a red polo-neck jumper, looked at us expectantly.

'I need to interview you properly, go through exactly what happened,' I explained.

Mr Bear nodded and led us into a large room at the end of the hall. The carpet had purple and orange swirls on it. It smelt of the seventies. The room was full of chairs of every shape, size and colour imaginable, the sort of odd collection which would usually only be found in doctors' waiting rooms. They were arranged in five rows, each containing six or seven chairs, all facing in the same direction, like pews in a church. At the far end of the room was the object of worship. Dominating the wall, at least five foot high, was a portrait of Shirley Bassey.

I looked at Roger. Roger looked at me. It was too late now, we were here. We had to see it through. We sat down on the front row. Mr Bear did the same, bowing to Shirley as he did so.

'You're obviously a big fan,' I said, nodding towards the portrait.

'I write to her most weeks,' said Mr Bear. 'She's very appreciative of my support.'

'Good,' I said, hearing Roger groan behind me. 'Now, about your allegations. I need to take some details from you. Let's start at the beginning. What's your full name?'

'Rupert Bear,' he said.

I looked at him, hoping he was joking.

'I changed my name by deed poll ten years ago,' he said, by way of explanation. 'I can get you the letters if you'd like to see the proof.'

'No, it's OK, I believe you.'

Roger's head was now in his hands. Obviously he was remembering happier times in Vietnam.

It was gone two by the time we got away. I had about twenty pages of shorthand in my notebook. The story was a good one. Detailed descriptions of the abuse he and others had suffered in the psychiatric unit. Terrible things, people being tied up and left in cupboards, having excrement smeared on the walls of their room, forced to lap soup out of a bowl like a dog. He gave me dates and times when these things happened. Names and descriptions of all the staff involved. He even produced copies of letters he'd sent to the health authority and Clare Short, his local MP. But the spectre of Shirley loomed large over the whole thing. Should I believe a man called Rupert Bear who worshipped the woman who sang 'Goldfinger'?

When I got back to the office Cayte and Nick were sharing a joke. They seemed to be getting on exceptionally well, so well that Cayte didn't even look up as I sat down. I wanted to ask her how lunch had gone, find out what they'd talked about, but I couldn't in front of Nick. I didn't want to let on that I cared. I didn't even want to invite her to dinner within earshot of him, so I sent her an e-mail instead.

SUBJECT: Dinner tonight
Dear Cayte
You are formally invited to dinner at our place tonight, seven-thirty. If you value your health (which I doubt) or your Abba collection (I know where you live) you will not refuse. I want a full report on your lunchtime rendezvous with Mr Hardwick delivered to me discreetly at opportune moments during the evening. The other guest will be Colin, the Big Issue seller. You will be nice to him and not make jokes about standing on street corners or soup kitchens.
Regards
Sarah

She muttered a few expletives under her breath as she read it. The reply came back swiftly.

SUBJECT: Free grub
Saz
Will come only 4 Jonno's cooking. Will tell u f-all without bribes. You'd better not b fixing me up with beggar man.
Laters
C8
XX

She knew I hated the abbreviations. Texting took me for ever because I refused to miss out any letters. And as for Saz and Jonno, she really knew how to twist the knife.

I put a call in to Clare Short's office. I tried to speak in a very quiet voice. Said it was about a Mr Rupert Bear.

Cayte nearly choked on her coffee. Beyond her I could see Nick trying to stifle a laugh.

'Tell me that's not his real name,' said Cayte when I'd finished the call.

'Afraid it is. Changed it by deed poll.'

'I'll get some more coffees in.' Cayte was wiping the tears from her eyes. 'I've spilt most of this one laughing.' Halfway to the coffee machine she stopped and turned round.

'Sarah, you're wanted in reception,' she shouted. I picked up my notebook and stood up.

'A Mrs Jemima Puddleduck, for you,' she called out. 'I'd watch it, the floor's a bit wet down there.'

'Thank you, Cayte,' I called back, tossing my notebook on my desk as I sat down again. Nick was laughing out loud now. I shot him a look.

'What's the matter?' Nick said. 'You used to laugh at my wind-ups.'

'It's not that funny.'

'Maybe you've just lost your sense of humour,' he said.

I stared at my notebook for a long time. Thinking about what he'd said.

Jonathan was in the kitchen when I got home. The rasping voice of Ozzy Osbourne and the smell of burning onions rushed to greet me as I opened the door. Controlled burning, not my kind of burning. Jonathan said it was the key to getting the depth of flavour. He gave me a floury hug and a kiss which tasted of onions. I took off my coat and asked what I could do to help. Jonathan laughed.

'What you usually do,' he said. 'Stay out of my way.'

'At least let me start on the washing up,' I said, slipping on the Marigolds. 'I want to do something to help, they are my guests. Are you sure you're OK about this? I know I sprang it on you.'

'It's fine,' he said. 'I'm glad of the distraction, to be honest. It's been a difficult day.'

'Oh, why?'

'You know that year ten lad I told you about, Daniel, the sensitive one?'

I nodded as I scrubbed the chopping board, though I couldn't actually remember. Jonathan was always talking about various kids he taught.

'He came to see me at lunchtime. Said he's being bullied. Nothing physical, mostly name-calling, all the usual homophobic stuff.'

'What did you do?'

'Nothing. When I offered to have a word with the culprits he got really upset, said it would only make things worse. And that he'd only wanted to talk.'

'Not much you can do then, is there?'

'Not really. Makes it hard, though. By rights I should tell the head, get it on record. But he made me promise not to.'

I turned to face Jonathan. I would have given him a hug but I didn't want to get suds on him.

'Hey, at least he knows he can talk to you. Must be a big help for him, sharing it with someone.'

'I guess so,' he said.

'All you can do is keep an eye on things and be there if he wants to talk. With any luck it will all fizzle out by Christmas.'

'Yeah. You're right. Thanks.' He sounded brighter. Sometimes he simply needed reassurance that he was doing the right thing. The fact that he should seek it from me was ironic.

'So, who's this Colin guy?' asked Jonathan, understandably keen to change the subject. I sighed. There was only one way to explain.

'You don't happen to remember a story about a candidate who lost by one vote in the 1997 general election, do you?' I asked.

Jonathan thought for a moment. There was a hiss as he added some stock to the pan.

'Yeah, I think I do,' he said. 'A Labour guy, wasn't it?'

I nodded, the guilt prodding me from inside. 'That's him. That's who's coming to dinner. Only now he's a *Big Issue* seller.'

'Bloody hell,' said Jonathan, pouring the rest of the stock in. 'What happened to him?'

I related a carefully edited version of the story. Making sure to keep my own role in it hidden. And warning that Colin looked like he'd gone three rounds with Mike Tyson.

'Poor guy,' Jonathan said when I'd finished.

'Yeah, scary really. Could have been any one of us.'

'Well, no. Not really.'

'Why not?' I said, taking off the Marigolds and starting to dry.

'We'd never have got ourselves into that mess in the first place, would we?'

'Things can happen, Jonathan. Things that are out of your control.'

'Yeah, but you can always do something about it. Find a way to put things right.'

'It's not always as easy as that.'

'I don't see why not.'

I started to say something but stopped myself. Sometimes his innocence, his innate goodness, overwhelmed me.

Colin arrived first. He was wearing a moth-eaten jumper and crumpled trousers. Jonathan shook hands with him. 'I hear you're a *Big Issue* seller,' he said. 'That must be interesting.'

'It has its moments,' said Colin, turning to look at me.

I thought of showing Colin round the flat but decided against it, fearing it would be a bit like showing your baby photos to a childless couple undergoing IVF.

'If I remember rightly, I think you two have got something in common,' I said. 'Two Aston Villa supporters in the same room. Must be something of a record.'

'Ignore her,' said Jonathan, turning to Colin. 'She doesn't have claret and blue in her blood.'

'Not like me, then,' he replied. 'Lifelong fan, I am. Used to go to all the games. I was there in Rotterdam in '82 when our Dennis lifted the European Cup.'

A look of wonder spread across Jonathan's face. Dawn had let him go to a few home matches with a school friend and his father in a bid to encourage some male bonding, which she feared was missing from his life. But as soon as he'd got serious about the Villa she'd put a stop to it, saying the terraces were full of hooligans and racists. He'd had to go to his friend's house to watch the European Cup Final in secret. Telling her he'd been invited to stay the night. He'd whispered as he'd told me the story. As if he was still scared she might find out.

'Wow, that must have been fantastic,' he said, sounding like he was nine years old again. 'Seeing Withey, Sid Cowans, all those great players.'

'Yeah. Run rings round today's team, they would,' said Colin.

'You can say that again. Where do you sit these days, down the Holte end?' Jonathan asked.

'No. I, er, don't go any more,' said Colin diplomatically.

Jonathan clapped his hand over his mouth as he realised. 'Of course not, sorry, stupid question. The prices are ridiculous these days. Scandalous, really. I hardly ever go myself.'

This was true. But as much to do with home matches clashing with some protest meeting or another as the ticket prices. He still carried the fixture list around with him, though. Which was sweet but kind of sad.

There was a knock at the door.

'Hi, sorry I'm late,' said Cayte, peeling a very New Age multicoloured jacket off and draping it over the coat stand.

'Cayte, this is Colin,' I said.

'Hi,' she said. 'I remember you getting beaten by that fat Tory tosser in the '97 election. He didn't do that to you as well, did he?' She pointed at the bruises on his face.

There was a moment's silence before Colin started laughing. I breathed a sigh of relief. Her lack of diplomacy was made up for by her ability to break the tension in any room. I led them through to the living room. We all squashed round the table, knees touching, and tucked into the pile of bhajis and samosas.

'So,' said Cayte, turning to look at me as she wiped some yogurt and mint sauce from her chin. 'Have you told the others about the adventures of Rupert Bear?'

'What's this?' said Jonathan.

'Oh, just some guy I interviewed today. I'm investigating his claims about abuse at a psychiatric unit.'

'Only he's such a fruitloop that he changed his name to Rupert Bear,' chipped in Cayte.

I looked at Colin, who was eating his fourth onion bhaji, worried he might have taken offence, but he clearly hadn't.

'A few people I met when I was in the psychiatric unit had changed their names to something famous,' he said.

Cayte stopped eating for a second and looked at him, a trace of a blush in her cheeks. 'So why do you think they did that?' she asked.

'I guess it was a way of escaping from reality,' said Colin. 'They could pretend to be someone else.'

'What would you change yours to, then?' she asked. 'If you could be anyone you wanted.'

Colin thought for a moment as he munched a samosa. 'Sebastiao Salgado,' he said.

'Who's he?' asked Cayte.

'A photographer. An artist really. Paints pictures with light. Takes black and white photos of ordinary people doing ordinary things.'

'I never knew you were interested in photography,' I said.

'Yeah,' said Colin wistfully. 'Ever since I was a kid. I wanted to go to college and study it but my mum said I should get a proper job. I used to do bits and pieces as a hobby. Haven't done anything for years now.' He looked sad for a moment. It was obviously a big regret. Along with all the others he must have.

'Oh, but you must start taking photos again,' said Jonathan. 'It's great to have an interest like that.'

'I would, only I haven't got a camera.'

'No, no of course not,' said Jonathan.

I realised with a start that I could help there. I may not be able to get him back his home, his wife or his job but I could surely manage to get him a camera. I'd have a word with Roger at work on Monday.

'I'll go and dish up the curry,' said Jonathan.

'No, it's all right,' I said, jumping to my feet as I realised this was a good opportunity to grill Cayte. 'I'll do it and Cayte can give me a hand. You have a chat with Colin about the Villa. Get him to tell you some stories about the old days.'

I gathered the dirty plates, scraping them noisily as I stacked, and hurried out to the kitchen, Cayte trailing behind.

'So what exactly do you need me for? asked Cayte as I drained the rice and spread it between the four plates.

'The dirt on your lunch date,' I said.

'It wasn't a date.'

'You seemed to be getting on very well when I got back.'

'He's good company,' said Cayte. 'It's weird. Usually you pay for looks like that. Have to put up with a lousy personality. But he's witty and charming. He even insisted on paying.'

'So, did he come on to you?' I said as I scraped out the rice pan and started distributing the curry in even dollops, making sure everyone had enough chick peas.

'No, he was the perfect gentleman. Didn't lay a finger on me, not even a quick grope under the table. Very disappointing. Especially as he spent most of the time asking about you.'

I dropped a spoonful of curry on to the floor. I dashed to get a cloth, hoping Cayte wouldn't notice my trembling hands as I knelt to wipe the tiles. It was all spilling over, bubbling up and making a mess. The past I'd thought I'd put behind me. Colin was in my living room, battered and bruised physically and mentally as a result of what I'd done. And now Nick was back, asking questions. Perhaps already having given the game away.

'Oh,' I said, trying to sound surprised. 'What sort of questions?'

'Mainly about your love life. He wanted to know how long you'd been with Jonathan, what he did, what you got up to in your spare time.'

'So what did you say?'

'That you'd only known each other a month, you'd met on some Internet chatline, Jonathan worked for an escort agency and you enjoyed going to S and M parties together.'

I gave Cayte one of my looks.

'Well, what do you think I said?'

'I never know with you, that's the trouble.'

Cayte sighed. 'I told him the truth, that you enjoy saving the planet together in your spare time and that the pair of you are blissfully happy. Is that OK?'

I nodded. Although I wasn't at all sure it was. Maybe I'd wanted Cayte to leave some element of doubt. Say something to make him wonder if I was worth pursuing. Though if that was the case I was in trouble. Because I ought to have learnt my lesson. That I shouldn't play with fire. Or even be left alone with matches.

'And now perhaps you can tell me why Nick's so interested in you,' said Cayte.

I froze, a plate of curry in each hand. DI Thorneycroft had me cornered. I was her prime suspect. But I couldn't let her get anywhere near the truth. Because I was scared that if even a tiny bit of it came out, the whole thing would unravel.

'I don't know.' I shrugged. 'He's probably just trying to get some ammunition to wind me up with. He'll be taking the piss on Monday, you see.'

Cayte looked at me doubtfully. 'Nah. He fancies you. I can tell.'

'Whatever,' I said. 'I'm not interested. Now, come on, the curry's going cold.'

I walked back into the room and smiled at Jonathan as I handed him his plate. The smile was wrong, too big, even as a 'don't worry you're doing great' smile. He smiled back hesitantly. Not quite sure what to make of it. Colin was tucking into his curry. I kept my head down and ate. It seemed the safest thing to do. I was worried that if I spoke my voice would come out all squeaky. Fortunately Cayte and Colin kept up a constant chatter, mostly about her conspiracy theories. Colin seemed to find her entertaining. Either that or he was being polite. Though as far as I could remember Colin didn't do polite for the sake of it.

By the time Jonathan suggested coffee and we sat down, me on the beanbag, Colin and Cayte on the sofa, I was beginning to calm down. So Nick was asking questions about me. Big deal. It didn't mean he was going to do anything. And if he did I could handle it. Knock him back in an instant. Because he was chasing ghosts. The new Sarah wasn't interested. And wasn't going to let him screw up her life.

I smiled at Jonathan as he handed me my coffee. A proper smile, one I meant. Colin picked up the copy of the *Gazette* on the coffee table.

'Is this today's? Can I have a look?' he said.

'Yeah, of course,' I replied.

He started flicking through it, stopping on page five to read one of my stories. He turned the page and raised his glasses, squinting hard at something. I couldn't work out what he was looking at.

'That's not . . .'

I realised as he started the sentence. Nick's column was on page six, complete with a photo byline.

I leapt up from the beanbag but I was too late.

'It is, isn't it, Sarah? That's our Nick. Bloody hell, another blast from the past. Fancy you two ending up on the same paper again.'

Cayte and Jonathan turned to look at me. I stood hovering over Colin's shoulder. I needed time that I didn't have. I smiled lamely at them.

'You used to work with Nick?' said Cayte accusingly.

'Yeah, ages ago.' I tried to make it sound casual. I could tell by the look on Cayte's face that she was on to me.

'You never said.' Jonathan sounded like a child who was the only one in the class who hadn't been told a secret.

'It didn't seem worth mentioning,' I said, picking up my coffee from the table, hoping they couldn't hear the cup rattling in the saucer in my hand. 'I only worked with him for about six months.'

'Is that all it was?' said Colin. 'I thought it was longer, you two used to get on so well.'

I shrugged, trying to hide my exasperation as Colin dug me further into the hole. 'Like I said, it was a long time ago.'

Jonathan was looking at me, a bewildered expression on his face. He clearly wasn't going to let this one go.

'So you didn't keep in touch?' he said.

'God, no. Haven't seen or heard from him since I left Rugby.'

Jonathan nodded, seemingly accepting my explanation. Cayte was going to be more difficult. She was staring at me hard. Making mental notes of everything I said which I suspected would be used against me at a later date.

'So how is he?' asked Colin.

'Fine, I think. He seems fine. We haven't really talked much. We don't get the chance at work.'

Cayte's eyes were piercing my skin. I swore I heard her gasp out loud at my impudence.

'It would be great to see him again. Why don't the three of us meet up for a drink sometime?' said Colin. 'Give us all the chance to catch up properly, reminisce about the old days in Rugby. What do you say, Sarah?'

I hesitated, aware that refusing would sound even more suspicious.

'Yeah,' I said. 'Why not?'

'Just sort a date out between you two and let me know,' said Colin. 'It's not like I've got anything in my diary.'

'Sure,' I said, standing up. Desperate to end the agony of this conversation before I agreed to anything else I would regret.

'Anyone want another coffee?' I asked.

Thursday 17 April 1997

'Oh God, I've been summoned,' groans Nick, walking past my desk on his way into the editor's office. I keep my eyes fixed firmly on the computer screen. I have been watching Karen, trying to pick up tips on this blinkers thing she does. All I need now are the ear plugs and nose clip. Perhaps then I shall be oblivious of his existence.

It is not working, this pretence. I may feign indifference when he walks into the room. Or uninterest when he starts to talk. But I am fooling no one. Least of all myself. The truth is, the harder I try to cool it, the deeper I fall. Sometimes I do manage to avoid being alone with him, or even talking to him for a day. But it doesn't change the way I feel. If anything it makes it worse. The ache I have inside. I remain fired by his passion, amused by his humour and intrigued by his conversation. If there was something about him I didn't like, some annoying habit or objectionable aspect of his personality, it would give me a chance. Allow me to focus on the bad points. But I have yet to find anything to sway me from the view that I would be happy to spend the rest of my life with him. If only he wasn't with someone else. And that fact alone is not enough to put me off. It is like telling a child not to touch something shiny. It only makes them want it more.

'Fucking Tory puppet,' Nick says, slamming the door as he returns to the office and throwing his notebook down on his desk.

'What's up?' asks Joan, who is busy watering her pot

113

plants, being the only person who could get away with it on press day.

'Simple Simon's pulling the splash.'

'That's bang out of order,' Joan says.

I look up from my screen, hoping I am hearing this wrong. Nick turns to face me.

'I'm really sorry, Sarah,' he says. 'You worked so hard on this. And it's a bloody good story.'

It is my big Tory sleaze exclusive. One of Colin's tip-offs. The director of the company which has just won council approval for a controversial housing development turns out to be the son-in-law of George Pike, our Tory MP. It's the biggest story I've ever written. Nick went through the copy with me. Said it was watertight. Joked about me getting poached by the *Guardian*. And now it is being pulled. I do not understand.

'What's the matter with it?' I say.

'Nothing,' says Nick, walking over to me. 'He says it's too sensitive with the general election campaign going on. Reckons we could get accused of being biased.'

I am stunned into silence.

'That's bollocks,' says Joan.

'My words, exactly,' says Nick. 'The truth is he's had a call from Pike's election agent. Suggesting he holds it over until after the election.'

'He can't do that,' I say.

'I'm afraid he can,' says Nick. 'They're probably both members of the same funny handshake brigade. That's why Simon's decided to stick his oar in for once.'

My brow is creased and my mouth gaping incredulously. I thought journalism was supposed to be about exposing wrongdoing – not covering it up. About having the power to change things, not seeing your own editor trample over the truth.

'Can't we do something?' I say.

'I've tried. Threatened Simon with union action. He told me to go ahead. Said his decision was final. I'll raise it at the branch meeting tonight, though. See if we can kick up a fuss about it. Shame him into changing his mind.'

I nod. Nick is the branch chair, spends his spare time on picket lines fighting other people's battles. If anyone can kick up a fuss, he can. But I do not hold out much hope. It appears Simon is beyond shame. The disappointment must show on my face.

'Why don't you take an early lunch?' Nick says. 'Go and let off some steam. Call him every name under the sun. Buy a voodoo doll and stick pins in it. Anything to make you feel better.'

I nod and bend to pick up my bag.

'Don't let him get to you,' says Nick. 'You're worth a million of him.' He says it quietly. So quietly I don't think anyone else hears.

By the time I get back to the office, things seem to have simmered down a little, mainly because Simon has gone off to the printers. Everyone is slagging him off, saying what an arsehole he is. I am not sure if they are doing it for my benefit or if they are genuinely as appalled as I am. Nick smiles at me supportively, as if I have been bereaved. Which I suppose in a small way I have.

Our deadline has gone now. Joan worked up some road rage story she got from the cops into a stand-in splash. The usual Thursday afternoon lull descends on us. I busy myself bashing out some leftover bits and bobs from my notebook but my heart isn't really in it. For the first time since I started the job I feel as if I am just going through the motions. The bright, shiny bubble I have been living in has burst. Nick and Joan both make a few wisecracks about Simon. But I can't even raise a smile.

It is a good hour or so before my phone rings. I am aware as I answer it that I still sound pissed off. The male caller asks for me by name. His voice is deep and clipped but rather faint; I think he's on a mobile.

'Yes, speaking,' I say.

'Hello. It's Malcolm Freeman, George Pike's election agent. I don't think we've had the pleasure of speaking before.'

I feel my pulse quicken, my jaw tighten. I struggle to resist the temptation to tell him where to go. A rather curt 'hello' is all I manage.

'Simon told me that you won't be running the little story about the housing development and I just wanted to pass on Mr Pike's appreciation of your co-operation in this matter.'

My heart is beating so hard it is rattling my ribcage. A surge of indignation rises through me.

'The decision was taken by my editor. I didn't have any say in the matter.'

'Of course, I understand. You have to say that as a journalist. However, Mr Pike would like to show his appreciation in some small way. I have an envelope for you. I wondered if we could arrange to meet somewhere quiet. These things are always best done discreetly.'

I cannot believe what I am hearing. I start to scribble furiously in my notebook, making sure I have all this down in shorthand. Realising the implications of what he is saying. It is Neil Hamilton and Martin Bell all over again. All we need now is for Colin to don a white suit and declare a war on sleaze and we will be able to knock Tatton off the front pages. Sod the *Rugby Chronicle*, I am going to the nationals with this.

'Yes, yes, of course. And Mr Pike asked you to do this personally, did he?'

'That's right. As a token of his appreciation.'

'And I take it this, er, token, is not something he could send through the post?'

'Oh, goodness, no. That wouldn't be at all wise.'

I smile as I scribble. I have got him here. I am going to bring the bastard down. We arrange to meet at the Rupert Brooke statue in five minutes' time. He says he doesn't want to have the contents of the envelope hanging around in the office. And advises me to go straight to the bank afterwards. As I put the phone down I realise my hands are shaking. I am high on adrenalin. Finally I am Woodward or Bernstein. It is time to run about like a crazy person. To shout hold the front page. I turn to tell Nick but he is not at his desk. Dave says he has nipped out for a pint of milk. I haven't got time to hang around for him. I decide not to tell the others. I will wait until I have the evidence in my hand. And on film. I run up to photographic and grab Bill by the arm. I tell him it is a top secret mission. That all he needs to do is hide in the bushes and take a picture of the man with the brown envelope. He seems suitably intrigued. We hurry off together. The statue is in a little green triangle sandwiched between a church, a row of town houses and a street full of solicitors and estate agents. Bill disappears into the shrubbery at the far end. As I approach the statue I glance around me. An elderly woman sitting on a bench eating a sandwich. A man walking one of those yappy little dogs. Nothing out of the ordinary. Any second now Freeman will be here. I stroll up and down, trying hard to look inconspicuous. Several minutes pass. I worry he has got cold feet. That I have lost my exclusive. I wander nearer the statue. My eyes fix on a small brown object tucked behind Rupert Brooke's left foot. I go nearer still. It is definitely an envelope. Maybe he panicked and left it there. I edge ever nearer, glancing over my shoulder, making sure no one, apart from Bill in the bushes, is watching. I bend down and pick it up. The envelope is sealed. It has my name on it. The adrenalin kicks in again. I rip it open, looking furtively around me as I do so. Inside is a large packet of humbugs and a note. 'Just wanted to see you smile again.' Written unmistakably in Nick's handwriting.

For a split second I am angry, mad at myself for having been taken in so badly. But a moment later I am bent double with laughter, wiping the tears from my eyes.

I hear a rustle from the bushes. Bill emerges followed closely by Nick, who has a broad grin on his face.

'You bastard. You complete bastard.' I am laughing as I say it. Nick walks up to me and gives my shoulder a playful shove.

'Had you there,' he says.

'Yep, it was the posh voice that threw me,' I say, as I pretend to box him round the ears. 'I had it all worked out. I was going to flog it to the *Guardian*.'

'Sorry,' says Nick. 'Couldn't resist it.'

'You were in on this, weren't you?' I say, turning to Bill.

'Nick did warn me to expect a visit.'

'Dirty, rotten scoundrels, the pair of you.'

'Thanks, Nick. Made my day, that has,' Bill says before heading back to the office.

I am left standing there with Nick. He smiles and looks down at his feet. He feels it too. I know he does. I wonder if he and Amanda laugh together like this. Somehow I don't think so.

'Here, have a humbug,' I say, offering the packet to him. 'Anything to keep you quiet.'

We walk back to the office together. Nick sucking his humbug. Me still smiling and shaking my head. And wishing things were different.

I pull into the tiny car park off Spon Street in Coventry. It isn't even seven yet. I am running ridiculously early. It is less than two hours since I last saw Nick but already I am desperate to see him again. I know it is wrong. I am supposed to be weaning myself off him. Not increasing my fix. But although I tell myself that countless times, I still can't seem to break it.

At least I have a good excuse tonight. What with Nick planning to raise my pulled story at the meeting. Not that I need an excuse to spend more time with him. But it helps to ease my conscience.

I walk into the Windmill pub. I have never been here before. It is all low ceilings, beams and crooked doorways. There are a couple of separate rooms, not more than alcoves really. We are going to be in the one at the front. I poke my head round the corner: it is empty. I go to the bar to get a vodka and orange. I am served quickly. Too quickly, really. I am left standing there, drink in one hand, the fingers of my other hand tapping on the bar. My thoughts interrupted a few minutes later by Nick's voice in my left ear.

'I have a brown envelope for you.'

I am smiling before I even raise my head to look at him. 'I only accept humbugs, thank you.'

Nick smiles back. The ache inside me disappears again. I am surprised he is early. It is a standing joke that he is always late for meetings, even ones he is chairing. I allow myself to wonder if he came early to see me then think better of it. Probably just a fluke.

'Can I get you another drink?'

'No, I'm fine thanks.'

He gets a bottle of Becks for himself. I watch his fingers curl round the long neck as he takes it from the barman.

'The others not here yet?'

'No, couldn't see them.'

'May as well go through, anyway,' says Nick, ducking his head as he reaches the doorway. I follow him into the room, conscious that it is just the two of us. And that although I shouldn't, I like it that way. I sit on a stool opposite him. My knee brushes his accidentally under the table. I am not sure whether to apologise or whether that would only draw attention to it. I opt to say nothing and fiddle with my beer mat instead.

'Are you OK?' says Nick. 'It was a real blow about your story, wasn't it?'

I nod. I thought I'd managed to cover up my disappointment. Obviously not.

'I didn't think things like that happened on local papers. Thought it was only the Murdochs of this world who threw their weight around.'

Nick shakes his head. 'You know the saying, power corrupts and all that. And Simon is by no means the worst. Other papers around here have pulled things because one of their advertisers has complained. So basically their journalists can't write anything bad about any company which takes out a display ad.'

'That's outrageous. We're supposed to have a free press in this country.'

Nick smiles.

'What?' I say.

'You,' he says. 'Being so idealistic. You'll be saying we live in a democracy next.'

'Are you taking the piss?'

'Not at all,' he says. 'It's refreshing, finding someone who's not as jaded and cynical as the rest of us. Reminds me of what I used to be like when I started out.'

He lifts the bottle to his mouth and takes another swig. I watch his throat move as he swallows. I am mesmerised even by the way he drinks. I could sit here and watch him all night, take in every detail, and still I wouldn't know enough about him.

'I just hate the fact that Simon can get away with doing that,' I say. 'It's so wrong.'

'I know,' says Nick, brushing his fingers through his hair. 'I feel really bad about it. Maybe I should have called everyone out on strike there and then.'

'That wouldn't have been legal though, would it?'

'No, but why should that stop us?'

I raise my eyebrows, wondering what Amanda would make of his last comment.

'It's only Thatcher's union-bashing that's made it that way,' he continues. 'Made us so weak that some Tory MP comes along and offers to grease the editor's palm and he caves in, knowing he can get away with it.'

'What, you reckon Simon will get something out of this?'

'Of course he will. Might not be as obvious as a brown envelope but somewhere along the line a favour will be called in.'

'Like it was with the council granting Pike's son-in-law planning permission?' I say.

'Exactly. That's how it works. A nod and a wink in the right place and the old boys' network is still ruling the fucking country. That's why we need to fight dirty sometimes, show them they can't just trample all over the workers. That we can still find ways to hit them where it hurts, in their pockets.'

Nick puts his bottle down on the table with a thud. There are flashes of lightning in his eyes, thunder in his voice. I am electrified by it all. By the white heat burning away inside, at his very core.

'Sorry,' he says, looking across at me. 'Did I go off on a bit of a rant there?'

'It's OK,' I say. 'I enjoyed it. The students' union at Warwick uni was never this lively.'

'That'll be because they were a bunch of middle class worthies from—' His voice cuts off abruptly.

'You were going to say Leamington Spa then, weren't you?' I say, laughing.

Nick pulls a face. 'Er, yeah, but I thought better of it. Didn't want to offend you.'

'You wouldn't have,' I said. 'My mother yes, but not me. I just had the misfortune to be born there.'

Nick smiles. I realise I don't want any of the others to turn up. I like it like this, just the two of us. It makes me think about how good it could be. If he wasn't with someone else. I am out of luck, though. A bald-headed guy I recognise from the previous branch meeting walks in. He sits down and starts talking to Nick. For a second I feel aggrieved that he is breaking up our private party. But then a dose of reality floods in and I remind myself that there is nothing to break up.

The room fills rapidly; bodies, voices and cigarette smoke. We are surrounded by them but still I feel Nick's closeness. He introduces me to people I don't know, looks over at me every now and again, as if he is checking I am all right. Or maybe he is just looking. I don't know.

Joan arrives at the last minute and sits down next to me. She says Dave isn't coming, his sinuses are playing up, and that Karen will try to make it if the housing committee meeting she is covering finishes in time. I nod; I am not really listening. I am watching Nick. He is rising to his feet. People look up and stop talking. He kicks off the meeting, rattling through a list of union business; reporting back from other disputes across the country, picket lines he has visited, letters he has written on our behalf. He asks for updates from round the table, suggesting responses to various problems people are having, congratulating members from the evening newspaper on winning their fight for union recognition, rallying support for a big protest against regional cutbacks at the BBC. He eats, lives and breathes this stuff, that is obvious. The others are nearly as enthralled as I am. Nearly, but not quite.

'Moving on to any other business,' he says. 'We've had a problem today at the *Chronicle*. The editor has pulled an exclusive story written by Sarah Roberts, our new member, following a phone call from George Pike's election agent. It is blatant editorial censorship, designed purely to save the Tories' blushes during the election campaign. And as Sarah quite rightly says, he shouldn't be allowed to get away with it.'

I feel the colour rising in my cheeks. He is fighting my corner, leading the battle cry on my behalf. I will follow wherever he leads. Looking round the room, I suspect everyone else will too. That is the effect he has on people.

After much condemnation we agree to send a letter to the editor and the MD, complaining in the strongest possible terms, demanding that the story be run next week and stating that if not the branch will hold a public protest outside the *Chronicle* offices on Saturday morning. Nick wraps up the meeting. I feel enthused again, ready to take on the world. Most of the others get up and head to the bar, Joan leading the way. Nick sits down and looks across at me.

'That do you for now?' he says.

I nod. 'Yes, thanks. At least we're doing something, not taking it lying down.'

'I can see the placards now,' he says. 'Save Our Sarah's Story.'

'It's not about me,' I say. 'It's about the principle of a free press.'

'Watch it,' he says. 'You're starting to sound like me.'

I smile. It is no bad thing. Joan comes back in with the drinks.

'What are you two plotting now?' she says.

'Oh, just a revolution or two,' says Nick.

Joan shakes her head.

'Don't you go leading Sarah astray,' she says to Nick. 'She's a good girl.'

'Don't you believe it,' says Nick. 'I've seen that look in her eyes.'

I laugh and look down at my feet. I am sure now. That he knows.

Six

Nick wasn't at his desk first thing Monday morning. Which was probably just as well. I suspected I was going to be subjected to an inquisition when Cayte arrived and I was right. She came in, sat down with a thump and turned to me.

'Thanks for a lovely meal on Friday night. You probably don't remember it, mind. I know you've been suffering a lot with amnesia lately.'

She clearly wasn't about to forgive me for my 'oversight'. Nor was she satisfied with the limp explanation I'd offered.

'Like I said, it didn't seem important.'

'That's where your story falls apart,' said Cayte. 'If it wasn't important you would have mentioned it. The very fact that you didn't mention it is the giveaway.'

I blamed Miss Marple for encouraging Cayte. Giving her fancy ideas about her powers of deduction. Amateur sleuths were dangerous things, particularly when you had to sit next to one.

'Look, I didn't want to rake up the past, OK. Some things are best left there.'

Cayte turned to look at me. 'You had a thing with him, didn't you?'

I typed frantically, the pads of my fingers banging into each key. Racing to keep up with my heartbeat.

'I don't want to talk about it.'

'Is that why you don't like him, because of what he did

to you in the past? Did he cheat on you? Is that what this is all about?'

It was an understandable assumption to make. Especially from someone who only knew the new Sarah. The whiter than white version.

'Something like that,' I said. It was easier to keep up the lies than admit the truth. That was what happened, once you started lying. You got yourself into a deeper and deeper hole.

'Fucking hell, who'd have thought it. You and Nick.'

'Keep your voice down, will you?' I said, looking over my shoulder. To be honest, I didn't mind who heard at that precise moment. What I resented was the fact that she found it so implausible. She obviously didn't consider me worthy of the attentions of a man like Nick. Cayte had a theory that men sought a partner who was marginally less attractive than them. So David Beckham (a nine out of ten) had got Posh (a seven out of ten) which was acceptable. You could have a two-point gap between you; anything more and it wouldn't work. Nick probably came in at a nine on the Cayte scale. I, quite obviously, was a six or below.

'Don't worry, your secret's safe with me,' said Cayte, tapping her nose.

I smiled appreciatively. The detective had fallen for the red herring. The real secret was safe with me.

As I walked past Terry's office later I noticed he was acting weird. Even weirder than usual. Pacing up and down while opening and closing his mouth in quick succession, as if eating imaginary fish food. Sometimes I wondered if it got to him, sitting in there all day. If he was losing it, mentally. I decided to pay him a visit.

'What you eating?' I said, entering the office without knocking, as only I was allowed to do. Terry looked up at me blankly.

'Nothing. Why, you got something for me?'

'No. Why do you keep opening and closing your mouth?'

'I'm practising what to say.'

'When?'

'This afternoon.'

'What's happening this afternoon?' I said.

Terry looked down at his desk, shuffled his papers, held his head in his hands. He couldn't look me in the eye, it was that bad. I'd never seen him like this before. I decided to help him out.

'Redundancies?' I asked. He nodded.

'How many?'

He held both hands up in the air. I presumed he meant ten. Either that or he was surrendering. I had never been very good at those *Give Us a Clue*-style games.

'Fucking hell,' I said, sitting down on the chair opposite him. 'Are they compulsory?'

He shook his head and managed to speak. 'Voluntary if they get enough, compulsory if they don't. Last in first out.'

It wasn't hard to do the maths. Nick's head was the first on the chopping block. My heart stopped beating for a second. I glanced over at his empty desk, imagining it being permanently empty. I didn't want it to be. I was surprised how sure I was of that.

'How many will take voluntary, do you reckon?'

Terry shrugged. 'Hard to say. Phil, a couple of subs, maybe one or two from photographic.'

He was being optimistic. We both knew it was going to get nasty.

'When are you going to tell people?' I asked.

'Four-thirty. Figured I'd wait till the end of the day. Can't imagine anyone wanting to do much work afterwards.'

I nodded. 'Shitty job.'

'Yeah, but I'd rather it came from me than the MD.'

'If there's anything I can do to help.'

'Just have your counselling service available after-wards,' Terry said. 'I think it's going to be needed.'

I slunk out of his office and took the scenic route round the newsroom to allow myself to make a mental list of the last nine people to join before Nick. It was only as I got back to my desk that I realised Cayte was ninth in line to go. If two people took voluntary redundancy she'd be safe. But it was a big if. She'd gone out on a job, which was just as well. One look at my face and she'd have known something was up.

When Nick returned to the office ten minutes later I couldn't help myself. I smiled at him. The first time I'd acknowledged his existence in weeks. He looked over his shoulder and back towards me.

'I guess you misfired that one,' he said. 'It hit me by mistake. Do you want it back?'

I shook my head. If I'd been able to look him in the eye I'd have gone so far as to smile again.

Terry came out of his office on the dot at four-thirty and clapped his hands. People looked up and stared at him, wondering if he'd been on some motivational management course.

'If you could all stop whatever you're doing and gather round. I need to have a word.'

The expression on his face was painful to see. If he'd been about to knock on someone's door and tell them he'd just run over their only child, he wouldn't have looked any worse.

Cayte, who had only been back five minutes, looked at me, suspecting I knew what we were about to be told. I stood up and shuffled forward into the crowd which was gathering round Terry, wanting their cloak of anonym-ity. I glanced at Nick who was standing opposite me looking unfazed as he always did, confident in his ability to deal with any ball bowled at him. I wanted to warn him there was a bouncer coming. But it was too late.

Terry came straight out with it, no soft-soaping or

management bullshit about restructuring the operation to boost efficiency. I listened with a renewed sense of admiration as he spelt out the situation, talking to people, not down to them. As editors went, he really was one of the best.

I watched as people took it in, heard the cogs whirring in their heads as they did the same maths I'd done earlier and saw the expressions change on their face depending on the outcome.

Nick looked straight at me, realising that my smile earlier had been a knowing, sympathetic one. He was hurting, I could see that. It felt like we were the only two people in the room. I held his gaze and mouthed 'sorry'. I meant it. He blinked hard and looked away.

I caught sight of Cayte. She was trying to look cool about it. She was trying too hard. Terry stopped talking and asked if there were any questions. There were loads but no one said anything. People simply drifted away and reformed in small clusters in various parts of the newsroom. Sport started a book on who would take voluntary. Sonia the copy-taker started handing out business cards offering her dubious secretarial skills for a cut-price CV service. One of the subs told her where she could stick it. She fled back to her desk in shock.

Nick and I were left standing there. He didn't need to say anything. I knew. That this was about much more than him losing his job. It was about me, about us. An us that I had tried to pretend never existed. But just wouldn't go away. I couldn't bear to look at his face any longer. I went back to my desk.

Cayte was sitting very quietly. Too quietly.

'You'll be OK,' I said. 'Phil's probably got his name down already. And there's sure to be someone else who'll take it.' She nodded and started packing away her things.

People drifted off in the direction of the pub. Even those who never went to the pub, not even for leaving dos.

The newsroom emptied. Cayte and Nick left together, I said I'd be over soon and phoned Jonathan to tell him I was going to be late. Terry was still in his office, staring at the fish. I guessed he required my counselling services.

'Come on,' I said, popping my head round the door, 'come over the road with us.'

'They won't want me there.'

'No one blames you, Terry.'

I went in, shutting the door behind me, not that there was anyone left to listen.

'Maybe you're right. Maybe I'm not cut out for this job,' he said.

'I never said that.'

'You didn't have to. I've seen the look on your face.'

'It took balls to do what you just did. I know that. I guess I wish you'd show them more often. You're too nice for your own good sometimes. Too nice to work for a bunch of profiteering bastards who have no interest in newspapers.'

Terry gave a rueful smile. 'I was never as confident as you, you know. Not even when I started out.'

'Well you must have had something going for you. You wouldn't have got to be editor otherwise.'

'It's called staying in the same place all your working life, being a doormat and biding your time until the only people who've been here longer than you leave.'

'No one thinks you're a doormat.'

'My wife does for a start.'

'Don't let her walk all over you, then.'

'Bit difficult at the moment. He's living under my roof.'

'Who is?'

'The man she's having an affair with.'

It took a minute or so for the words to seep into my head, past the muddle of questions and concerns still spinning around from earlier. When they finally registered I sat down on the chair opposite Terry and stared at him. He always looked like he was carrying the world on his shoulders but this time I could actually see where it was making them sag.

'Tell me you're joking.'

'Believe me, it's not funny.'

'She can't do that.'

'Well she has. Didn't even have the decency to tell me first. I came out of the bathroom yesterday morning and there he was waiting to go in. Even had the nerve to introduce himself. Derek his name is.'

'I don't understand. Didn't you know about this?'

'I'd guessed she was having an affair. Expensive perfume and hair-dos, taking up exercise, all the clichéd things they tell you to look out for. Never confronted her about it, of course. Just took to sleeping in the spare bedroom. Seems like Sylvia took that to mean I was giving them my blessing. So she moved him into our old room with her.'

Terry ruffled his hair and laughed, as if it was some amusing anecdote he was relating about a story he'd once worked on.

'You're not going to let him stay?'

'Don't have much choice. She told me that if he goes, she goes with him.'

'Fine, let her go. No great loss. You haven't talked to each other for years, not properly.'

'She's the boys' mother.'

'Do they want her to stay?'

'I don't know. Haven't had the chance to talk to them. They've locked themselves in their rooms since. Sylvia says they're at an awkward age.'

'Fucking hell, Terry.'

The word 'dysfunctional' sprang to mind. Terry's domestic set-up had turned into some sort of limp farce that the local amateur dramatic society would put on. I didn't know whether to pity him or pluck the goldfish from his tank and slap him round the face with it.

'OK. Here's what you do. You go home now and tell her

he's got twenty-four hours to get out. If she doesn't like it, she can go with him and you'll start divorce proceedings.'

'That's a bit drastic, isn't it?'

'Fine, be a doormat. Make him a cup of cocoa tonight and offer to introduce him to the neighbours. And tomorrow you can come in and tell the MD he can get rid of the lot of us. Turn the paper into an advertising free sheet and offer to be an unpaid paper boy.' I got up and headed for the door.

'I know you're right, Sarah,' he said, his voice faltering. 'It's just not going to be easy.'

'The right things never are, Terry. Haven't you learnt that yet?'

By the time I got to the pub it had turned into a bit of a wake. The older subs and photographers were reminiscing about the 'good old days'. The ten who'd been the last ones in, including Nick and Cayte, were clustered round a table in deep conversation, like the immediate family whose loss is greater than everyone else's.

Not wanting to intrude on their private grief, I sat down next to Roger, who'd already got me an orange juice.

'Thanks, Rodge. Here's your chance to escape then. A nice little pay-off, set you up good and proper.'

'I'll have to see what they're offering, won't I?' he said.

'You won't get a better chance than this.'

'A chance to do what exactly?'

'Get out of this place which you've never stopped moaning about since I met you.'

He took a sip of beer, the head leaving a light, foamy moustache on his top lip.

'The thing is,' he said, 'it's like following the Villa. I moan about them all the time, they've got a chairman who doesn't give a toss about the fans, players who aren't worthy of cleaning the boots of the team that won the

European Cup, but I still go when I'm not working, don't I? Because it's what I've always done. I don't know any different.'

I nodded, beginning to understand.

'I know it's a big leap but think about it, won't you?' I said. 'And in the meantime I've got a favour to ask you. Are there any old cameras knocking about in photographic? Film ones that no one will miss.'

'Yeah, two or three, I think. Sitting in a cupboard.'

'You couldn't get me one, could you? And a lens or two if there are any going. They're not for me, they're for a friend.'

'Sure. Anything to stop this lot flogging them off.'

'Thanks,' I said. 'They'll go to a good home.'

Nobody seemed in a hurry to leave the pub. Content to sit and rake over the embers. The death row ten were still huddled together for comfort. I told them I'd arrange a union meeting. That we weren't going to take this lying down. Nick, Cayte and some of the others nodded. Though there didn't seem much stomach for a fight. I declined the offer of another drink and stood up to leave.

'Can I give anyone a lift?' I called out.

'Yes, please,' said a lone voice. Nick's.

I turned to face him, aware that people were looking at us. I hadn't meant to include him in the offer but I couldn't turn him down now. Not with everything that had just happened. I wasn't that mean.

'OK,' I said without actually looking at him. 'Let's go.'

The last thing I saw as I walked out of the pub was Cayte's 'I told you so' face.

We walked back to my car in silence. Our steps synchronised; we were even breathing in time with each other. I suspected our hearts were beating at the same rate too. I glanced sideways. He looked like a dead man walking. The hurt twisted inside me again. Nick got into the car without saying a word. I heard him fasten his seatbelt. I opened my mouth to say something but Nick got in first.

'I know,' he said. 'I'm sorry, too.'

I turned to face him.

'I only found out this morning,' I said. 'I'd never have let Terry take you on if I'd known.'

I pulled out on to the ring road, the glare of headlights dazzling me in the mirror.

'Who said I was blaming you?'

'I just thought . . .'

'Sometimes you think wrong,' said Nick.

I drove on in silence. I hadn't realised how late it was. Broad Street was getting busy. Young men in their shirtsleeves, braving the crisp November night air. Groups of young women tottering down the street, their arms folded against the cold.

'Why did you sell your Beetle?' asked Nick.

His words pricked my defences. Reminding me of a time before. A time when things were different.

'I needed something more reliable.'

He nodded slowly. 'I saw it once, you know. After you left. Pulled up at some traffic lights and it was in front of me. Two kids bobbing around in the back. It was weird, threw me for a bit.'

I kept my eyes on the road, not knowing what to say. I'd tried not to think about it. How difficult it must have been for him after I'd gone.

'So, are you happy with the Ford Focus?' he said, tapping the dashboard with his hand.

'It does the job.'

'They've got no character, though, have they?' he said.

'I don't need character. I need to get from A to B.'

Nick didn't reply. I drove on, under Five Ways and up the Hagley Road. We could still do it, have conservations on two levels. Knowing the real answers were in the subtext.

'How are your parents?' he said. He was taking me

back again. Reminding me of the time he met them. Of a time when it was still fun.

'Fine, thanks. Still in Leamington. Mum's busy as ever with her social life. Dad's only got a few more years before he retires from the bank.'

'Do they approve of your boyfriend?'

'I guess so. They get on OK.'

Nick was digging, probing. Getting too near the truth. But I wasn't going to reveal that my mum had once described Jonathan as 'nice enough, though rather odd'.

'Why did you run out from the bar at the gym?' he said.

He knew why. He wanted to see if I'd admit it.

'I told you, I had plans.'

'Nothing to do with what I said, then?'

'Why should it be?'

'Because you still care. I know you do. Despite this whole front you put on.'

He seemed to have all the best cards tonight. I could only try to bluff.

'I don't know what you're talking about.'

Nick laughed, seeing straight through me. 'Of course you do. You don't want me here because I complicate things. I remind you of a time when you used to live on the edge a little. Before you decided to become this super-cool woman who never lets her defences down. Who is too scared to laugh at jokes, in case she might start enjoying herself. Too scared to open up in case she gets hurt.

The character assassination took me by surprise. And got under my skin.

'Hey, if you don't like my company I can drop you off here,' I said. 'Go and abuse a cabbie and pay for the privilege.'

'I'm not having a go,' said Nick. 'I just want to get beyond this act of yours. This is me. I know you, remember.'

'Used to know me,' I said. 'People change, Nick. Things happen and people have to grow up. Sometimes very fast.'

It was far more measured than I felt. I wanted to let go of the wheel. To tear into him with my fists, beat him until he bled, scream pure fury at him, make him feel a tiny fraction of the hurt I had felt, that I could still feel now, at night when I lay next to Jonathan, safe, secure and loved but terribly wounded.

Nick fell silent again. I could hear him breathing: a deep sigh followed by short, sharp shallow breaths. Out of the corner of my eye I saw his face turn to look out of the window. Not that there was much of a view along the Hagley Road.

'How much further?' I asked at the next traffic lights.

'Third left,' he said. 'The first building you come to on the right. I'm on the ground floor.'

I pulled up outside. I didn't want to tell him about Colin. Didn't want to mention anything to do with the past. Anything that tied us together. But I had promised I'd arrange a get-together. And I didn't want to let Colin down.

'I've got something to ask you,' I said.

Nick looked at me. Hoping for something I wasn't going to say.

'Someone you know wants to meet up. Wants the three of us to get together for a drink.'

'Who?' said Nick.

'Colin Leake.'

'God, good old Leaky. I haven't seen him since I left Rugby. What's he up to these days? Still bashing his head against the wall on Rugby Borough Council?'

'Er, no. He's selling *Big Issues* actually.'

'You what?' Nick twisted round to look at me, his eyebrows caught between shock and bewilderment.

'I know. It was a bit of a surprise to me too.'

I told him the story, seeing his face go through the same range of expressions mine had. At the end of it

Nick's mouth was still gaping open. It was a few moments before he could say anything.

'Fucking hell. Poor bastard. And I was feeling bad about losing my job.'

'I know,' I said. 'It kind of puts things in perspective.'

'And makes you realise how it can happen to anyone. The old downward spiral thing. How easily everything can fall apart.'

I glanced over at him. Knowing full well what he meant. 'So shall I tell him you're up for it? To meet up, I mean.'

'Yes. Yes, of course. Monday or Tuesday evenings are good for me. If that suits you.'

'Fine. Let's say a week today. After work at the Newt and Cucumber. I'll let him know tomorrow.'

Nick nodded. He undid his seatbelt but didn't get out. 'Do you want to come in?'

'Nick, don't.'

'What are you scared of, Sarah?'

I turned to look at him, daring myself not to show a flicker of emotion.

'Myself,' I said. 'My old self.'

We sat for a while.

'If I thought you were happy,' he said, 'I'd leave it alone. I'd always hoped you were happy, wherever you were, whoever you were with.'

'What makes you think I'm not?' I said.

'Your eyes,' he replied. 'They used to sparkle with aliveness. Not any more.'

I turned my face to look straight ahead through the windscreen, determined not to let him see my trembling lip.

'I really am sorry about your job,' I said after a few moments.

'Hey, don't worry. I make a habit of this, remember. Crap decisions, lousy timing, big regrets.'

I knew exactly what he was referring to. Yet still I

wanted him to spell it out, to say the words out loud. So I could actually hear them, rather than imagine them in my head.

'You'd better go now,' I said.

'What about you?' he said. 'Any regrets?'

'Too few to mention.'

Nick smiled. 'Thank you, Frank. It only takes one though, doesn't it? To screw up your entire life.'

And with that he got out and slammed the door.

Thursday 1 May 1997

I am caught up in something beyond my control. It has been going on for months now. This feeling that we are meant to be. And that the only thing stopping us is circumstance. Or Amanda, to be more precise. I have tried to fight it, of course. Told myself all the right things about him being out of bounds, unavailable, already taken. But my feelings won't go away. It is impossible when I work with him every day. And when he gives me so many signals that he feels the same way. Things he says, things he does. The way he looks at me. It is all so intense. Sometimes I think I can hear a buzzing when he comes near me. If I can, it is inside my head. No one else hears it. Except maybe him. It is starting again now. He must be coming near.

'You can make a move if you want, Sarah,' he says. 'Pop home for a few hours to recharge your batteries. Long night ahead.'

It is general election night. My first as a reporter. Crap timing for us because we have gone to press for this week but it is still a big deal for me. I am covering the Rugby and Kenilworth count with Nick. His suggestion. Says it will be a useful part of my training. The others don't seem to mind; they have done it all before. I am elated at the prospect of spending time with Nick out of the office but wary of his motives.

'Are you sure?' I say.

'Yeah, I'm off home myself in a bit. I'm sure these guys can hold the fort until half five.'

He looks round the newsroom. Joan looks up.

'Yep, no problem,' she says. Dave sighs, Karen carries on typing.

'Thanks,' I say. 'I'll just finish this.'

I go back to my half-finished chemists' rota. I take my time over it, checking and double checking. I am in no rush to go home. I will wait until Nick leaves. As soon as he puts on his denim jacket I will log off. The jacket hangs on the coat stand behind my desk. It is the right sort of denim, worn and weathered, the right shade of blue. A rip in the side, frayed cuffs. Sometimes, when I cannot see Nick, I look at the jacket instead. Every now and then I think I can smell him on it. Not aftershave, he doesn't use aftershave. The scent is of him, unmistakably him. And once or twice, when I have been really bad, and I think I might collapse at any moment from the sheer exhaustion of wanting something that I can't have so much, I have gone over to the coat stand and rummaged for some lost thing in my jacket pocket. There is nothing there, of course. I am simply rubbing against his jacket, burying my head in his shoulder, brushing against his sleeve. It is sad and pathetic, I know this. But it is what I have been reduced to.

The jacket moves. Nick is behind me, taking it off the peg. I press send. It will be there for him to see tomorrow morning, the chemists' rota. A missive from me to him, it means nothing and everything at the same time. I switch off my computer.

'Right, see you guys tomorrow,' says Nick, looking round the office.

'Yep, have fun,' says Joan. 'Let's hope Pike gets stuffed. That'll teach him.'

My Tory sleaze story never did make it to the front page. We had our big union protest outside the office. Caused a bit of a stink. But Simon still refused to run it. Colin ended up going to the local radio station with the story instead. So at least Pike didn't get off scot-free. But it has left a bad taste all round. I am still fuming. I have hardly spoken to Simon since. And I am desperate for Colin to win. Though turning over a thirteen thousand majority is not going to be easy.

'See you at the town hall at ten, Sarah,' says Nick. 'And keep your eyes peeled for brown envelopes.'

He winks at me and walks out. Joan looks at me over the top of her glasses. I wonder if she saw the wink. Not that it means anything. It was just a joke. I gather my things together and pick up my jacket. The scent of Nick has rubbed off on it. I put it on, wanting it next to my skin.

'See you then,' I say to the others.

'Good luck,' says Joan. 'Keep Nick in order.'

I nod and walk downstairs. Nick is still in the front office, talking to Jill, the receptionist. If she corners you on the way out it is impossible to get away.

'Are you ready then, Nick?' I say.

He looks up gratefully. 'Yep, let's go. Bye, Jill, got to dash.'

We leave Jill in mid-sentence and hurry out the door and round the corner.

'You looked like you needed rescuing,' I say.

'Thanks,' says Nick. 'That woman should gossip for England.'

He smiles as he turns to look at me. And then he stops smiling. And just looks.

'Are you off home now?' he says.

'Yeah.'

'Got anything to eat in?' I shake my head.

'Me neither. Fancy going for a bite to eat? Build us up for tonight.'

My stomach clenches tight. I know I should not even contemplate saying yes. Should decline gracefully and go home to my empty flat. But it is hard when he is here and I want to be with him so much.

'Pizza Express, I was thinking,' says Nick,

unperturbed by my silence. 'Unless you've got a better idea.'

I tell myself it is no big deal. An innocent bite to eat after work. It gives me room to manoeuvre. And eases my conscience.

'OK. I can't be long though,' I say, weakening by the second. 'I need to pop home and vote at some point. I didn't have time this morning.'

'Pizza it is then. We'll take my car. I managed to get a space nearby.'

I follow him across the road to where his VW Golf is parked.

'Allow me,' he says, opening the passenger door.

Questions are swirling in my head. Why is he doing this? How come we're going by car when it is within walking distance? And what on earth am I getting myself into? I get in all the same. I have no choice. My legs pay no attention to my head. Nick shuts my door, jumps in and starts the engine. The Jam blare out of the stereo. 'Going Underground' at full volume. He says there is no other way to listen to it. And that he hates the Style Council.

I say nothing during the journey. He provides backing vocals to Paul Weller. He is a crap singer. Nick, not Paul Weller. When we get there Nick leaps out and opens the passenger door for me. He makes me feel special. He always has done. As we walk into Pizza Express together I realise I am loving this. The idea that we are a couple. That people will think I'm his girlfriend. Even though I'm not.

I order a Veneziana pizza. Twenty-five pence of it will be donated to preserving some old church in Venice. I think it's a church. I don't really care, to be honest. I just like pine nuts. Nick orders something with anchovies and sits gazing at me across the table.

'So,' he says. 'Who are you going to vote for?'

'Well, it's not George Pike. That's for certain.'

'Didn't think so,' says Nick. 'I spoke to Colin on the phone this morning. He sounded very upbeat.'

'Do you think he's got a chance?'

Nick shrugs.

'Hard to say. Depends if people are bothered about sleaze or not. And whether Blair's wooed enough of the blue rinse brigade.'

The waitress comes up with our drinks. She smiles at Nick. I wonder if she fancies him. If she is wondering what he is doing sitting here with me. Come to think of it, I'm not at all sure what he's doing sitting here with me, either.

'And has Blair wooed you?' I ask.

'I voted for Colin, not for Blair,' says Nick. 'To be honest it was an anti-Pike protest vote. If you'd done a Martin Bell and stood against him as an independent I'd have voted for you.'

'I'm not sure if that was a compliment or not,' I say.

'It was,' says Nick. 'I can just imagine you giving Pike a verbal pasting on Dunchurch village green. The woman in the orange Beetle, that's what the papers would call you.'

I laugh as I sip my white wine. Just the one small glass I am having. I need to keep a clear head. It's going to be a long night. We eat our pizzas quickly. I use my knife and fork, he cuts his into pieces and eats with his hands, licking his fingers clean afterwards, looking at me as he does so. Not taking his eyes off me the whole time.

'Can I tempt you with a dessert?' he says.

'No, thanks. I'm full.'

'We've still got a few hours to kill. How about coming back to my place for a coffee?'

My wine glass clinks noisily on the side of my plate as I put it down. I stare at Nick, unsure what to stay. Whether to treat it as a serious proposition, which I think it is, or laugh it off as a joke.

'And why would I do that?' I say eventually.

'Because you want to. And because I might be offended if you refuse.'

His eyes are glinting. But it is simply a veneer. Underneath they are deeper, darker than I have ever seen them before. He is being serious.

'What about Colin?' I say.

'You want him to come too? I didn't have you down as being into threesomes.'

I try to keep my composure, to think of all those things about being right and proper and decent. But a smile breaks out across my face and before I know it I am laughing. Throwing my head back, letting my hair dangle further down my shoulders. Nick leans over towards me. The buzzing in my head starts again.

'I'll take that as a yes,' he says.

He pays, says he will get it on expenses. Pizza with Councillor Leake. I tell him not to mention Colin. I feel bad enough already. Just being here with Nick is wrong. Going back to his place is indefensible. I hear my mother saying I am old enough to know better. That if I play with fire I will get my fingers burnt. He is worth the risk, though. He is everything I have ever wanted.

We let Paul Weller fill the silence in the car. Nick doesn't sing this time. He glances over at me a few times. I pretend not to notice and stare straight ahead. Hoping he can't hear my heart pumping at twice the speed of sound. Or see the sweat gathering in my palms.

His house is a few miles out of Rugby, a place called Dunchurch, complete with thatched roofs and a village green with ducks. Not exactly a left-wing stronghold. But it has links with the gunpowder plot. Guy Fawkes used to live there, or stopped there for afternoon tea once, something like that. That is why Nick chose it. He says it is a great place to plot the overthrow of the government without arousing suspicion. I assume no explosives will be involved. But I might be wrong.

I haven't been to his house before. None of us at work have ever been invited. I presume because of Amanda. She certainly wouldn't want me there. I know that. But I try to push it out of my mind.

We pull up outside a small terraced cottage, wonky-looking with lots of weeds in the front garden. I can't imagine Amanda likes the weeds but I don't suppose she can say anything. It is Nick's place. She moved in with him. Officially she still lives with her parents in an imposing five-bedroom townhouse near work. She is a lodger here, really. She has no right to ask the landlord to clear the garden. And she is certainly not going to get her own hands dirty.

Nick lets me in. Amanda isn't here. I know this already: he wouldn't have asked me back otherwise. But her things are everywhere and I think I can smell her. Nick leads me through to the kitchen and puts the kettle on, as if that is all we have come back for. A cup of coffee. It is only a matter of time now before he makes a move. The voices inside my head are getting louder. Telling me it is wrong. I shouldn't be here. I need a moment to think. To calm myself. I ask Nick where the bathroom is and follow his directions, top of the stairs, second door on the right. I switch the light on. Whoever tried tiling this bathroom must have been having a laugh. There isn't a straight line in the room. Consequently there are no full tiles round the edges, only bits of ones of various sizes, jostling for space. The grouting in between them is mouldy grey. Not recent enough to be Nick's handwork. Amanda's things are everywhere. A second toothbrush, red, new-looking. Cotton wool balls, L'Oreal cleanser, Max Factor face powder. I open the bathroom cabinet, a box of Tampax falls out. She is here all right. In everything but body. I go to the loo and wash my hands, quickly checking my teeth in the mirror for capers. I leave the bathroom. A crack of light is visible through the other door. I stop for a second and push it with an outstretched forefinger, as if I'm in some horror movie and fear what could be lurking behind it. The door opens enough to reveal the bottom end of the bed. The duvet is lying in a crumpled heap on the floor. Someone got up in a hurry this morning. Or maybe they made themselves late by whatever it was they were doing. A silk wrap is draped over a chair. Scarlet, same as her lipstick. I wonder if he bought it for her. If he kisses her neck as he takes it off. I shouldn't be here. It is wrong. I do not do this sort of thing.

I hear Nick moving about in the kitchen and hurry downstairs. Two mugs of steaming coffee are on the kitchen counter. He looks up at me. Eyes piercing and expectant. He isn't smiling any more. His breathing has quickened. That strand of hair is in his eyes again. I want to brush it back. But I am unable to move. Frozen on the spot. He walks towards me. I know what is going to happen. I reach out for the coffee mug but before I get there he pushes me back against the fridge.

The cold sears through my cotton top and prickles at the backs of my bare legs. He presses against me, the warmth of his body forcing back the cold, melting the last shred of resistance. His hands are on my head, delving into my hair, grasping and pulling urgently. His face is against mine now. I can hear the buzzing, louder than ever as he kisses me, long and hard and salty. It doesn't feel so wrong now it has started. The communication lines between my brain and body have been cut. The voices inside my head fall silent. There is nothing left to stop me doing what I want to do. What suddenly feels so right.

I tug at his shirt, pulling it out of his trousers, feeling him flinch as my cold hands slip on to his bare back. Finally touching skin. He undoes the top few buttons and pulls it over his head. Peeling back the layers between us.

'Your turn,' he whispers. I take off my top. He unfastens my bra and lets it drop to the floor. He bends down, kissing my breasts, using his tongue, circling, flicking. We are both breathing hard now. I run my finger down his spine; the small of his back is damp with sweat. He turns me round and presses me up against the cold metal of the fridge. I gasp and he laughs before turning me back and licking each erect nipple in turn.

'The next move is up to you,' he whispers. 'We can stay down here if you like, or we can go upstairs.'

I hesitate for a second.

'Upstairs,' I say.

He takes my hand and leads me up to the bedroom. I hover in the doorway. The hammering inside my head is getting louder. Connection is restored.

'Are you sure about this?' I say.

'It's good to do something crazy every once in a while,' he says.

'Is it?'

'Yeah. That's what you told me once, when I sent you camel racing.'

'That was a bit different,' I say. 'What about—' He puts a finger to my lips.

'Don't,' he says. 'Don't spoil it.'

He takes his trousers, socks and boxer shorts off and turns to face me. He is one of those rare men who look even better without clothes. The curtains are open and the light is on. He doesn't seem to care.

'Come here,' he says, beckoning with his finger.

I unzip my skirt and let it fall to floor. I step out of it and walk towards him in my knickers and heels.

'I want to fuck you,' he says.

His eyes tell me that he means it. I am flattered. I want to ask if that is all this is: a quick fuck. Because I don't want that. I want it to be so much more. I don't ask though. In case I don't like the answer. I allow him to slip off my knickers. He pulls me up close to him in front of the full length mirror. I see the reflection of his face, hungry and eager, feel his breath, warm and rapid, his fingers, deft and fast. I turn round to face him, kissing him roughly, stooping as I work my way down his body. Nick pulls me down on to the bed. I am lost to him. I pretend he is making love to me in an anonymous back street hotel room in Paris. Halfway through I lose it and tell him I love him. He smiles and mumbles something back. Either 'I know' or 'No you don't' or maybe even 'Love you too', though that is undoubtedly stretching it a bit. I hesitate and the moment has gone. It is too late to ask him to repeat it. And anyway, you don't ask people to repeat things like that. You believe you heard what you wanted to hear.

It is good. The best sex I have ever had. It is a long time before it is over. When it is we collapse down on to the bed, both of us wet with sweat. My head rests on Nick's shoulder, my tangled curls soft against his stubble. I look up at him, awash with love.

'I've wanted to do that for such a long time,' he whispers. His hand is stroking my arm. I am not sure he knows he is doing it.

'Me too,' I say.

'So why did you go cool on me?' says Nick. 'I thought I'd done something wrong.'

I am surprised. I hadn't realised it was that obvious.

'I was trying to fight it,' I say. 'Trying to be good. Anyway, I didn't know if it was all a game to you. A bit of harmless flirting.'

He hesitates before replying.

'I don't make a habit of this,' he says. 'I was trying to resist as well.'

The tone in his voice is serious. I am surprised and pleased.

'So what happened?' I say. 'What changed your mind?'

He doesn't hesitate this time.

'You turned out to be irresistible.'

He is smiling at me as he says it. For a moment I am dizzy with euphoria. Until the bubble bursts and the guilt rushes in. I don't want to spoil things but I have to ask. It is eating away at me.

'What about Amanda?' I say.

There is a long pause. His hand stops stroking my arm. I feel his body recoiling, pulling away from me.

'I don't know,' he says eventually. 'We've been together a long time. I thought we were sorted until you came along.'

I am no clearer. I don't want to push it but I need to know where I stand.

'So what happens now? With us, I mean.'

Another long silence.

'All I know,' he says, 'is that I don't regret what happened. And I don't want it to end there.'

I nod. I want more than that. But I don't want to scare him off by asking. I turn over, and catch sight of the alarm clock on Nick's bedside table. It is nine fifty-five.

'Shit. The time.'

'It's all right,' he says. 'She won't be back until tomorrow. Some legal conference in London.'

For once I hadn't been thinking about Amanda.

'The polls are about to close,' I say. 'I'm not going to make it in time. I won't be able to look Colin in the eye at the count.'

'Don't worry,' says Nick, brushing the hair from my eyes. 'No one ever loses by one vote.'

Seven

I went straight to court on Monday morning. Some date rape case Keith had picked out especially for me. 'These good-time girls have a few too many Hooches, wake up the next morning and don't like the look of the bloke next to them. That's all it is.'

As it turned out, Keith couldn't have been further from the truth. She was eighteen, still at school, hadn't even been drinking that night. He was twenty-five, loud and brash, had given her a lift home from a party and thought she owed him a quick one in return so locked the car doors and raped her before he let her out. I caught her eye once, poor cow. I turned the corners of my mouth up in what I hoped was a supportive smile. She looked straight down at her feet. Probably the first time she'd ever accepted a lift home. Probably the last as well. The prosecution did a decent enough job. But I knew the defence would play all the usual cards: make out she had slept around, claim she had consented and just panicked the next morning. And he'd get off, of course. Because it was mainly her word against his. And there were too many Keiths on the jury. I filed the story in over the phone. Sonia was her usual helpful self, muttering 'ooh's and 'aahh's as if it was some bloody pantomime. I headed back to the office still filled with frustration at the injustices of the world.

The union meeting was being held in the library at work. Terry had given us special permission, though I'd had to promise we wouldn't be burning effigies of the group chief executive, or anything sinister like that. As I had suspected, the spectre of redundancies drew a far bigger crowd than usual. The room was full by twelve-thirty, people who paid their subs but didn't usually bother coming to meetings marching into the room like strident activists.

'Wow,' said Cayte. 'I like it when people get angry. If we go out on strike do you think we'll get on telly? I might start designing a placard just in case.'

I gave her a look. Knowing it was her way of covering up her concern. Nick arrived as we were about to start and perched himself on a table to my left. It was weird standing up there facing him. Remembering a time when the roles had been reversed. When I'd watched in awe as he'd rallied his comrades into action. I hoped I wasn't going to mess things up. I'd never dealt with anything of this magnitude before. Nick caught my eye and winked, as if sensing I needed some support. I smiled. Knowing I could do this with him here.

'Thanks for coming, everyone,' I started. 'I'm going to outline everything I've been told about the redundancy situation and then run through the options we've got in terms of a response.' I looked from face to face as I talked, aware that Nick hadn't taken his eyes off me since he walked into the room.

'I suggest the first thing we do is write a strongly worded letter to the MD, copied to the group chief exec, requesting a meeting and asking him to withdraw the threat of compulsory redundancies and offer improved terms for the voluntary ones.'

'That'll put the fear of God into them,' said Keith. He didn't usually attend union meetings. Considered it incompatible with his management role. I wished he hadn't bothered to come to this one.

'And what do you suggest we do instead?' I asked.

'We need to catch the enemy by surprise. Attack them

when and where they least expect it. Not warn them of our battle plans.'

I groaned inwardly, wishing we didn't have General Norman Schwarzkopf in our midst. If he was armed he really would be dangerous.

'I'll bear that in mind. Any other suggestions?'

'I could get the local MPs and council leader on board,' said Nick. 'Ask them to write to the MD about fears over editorial quality.'

There were murmurings of support from other members. People respected Nick. As well as liking him.

'Thanks, Nick, that would be great. And if we don't get the required response from management we'll look at taking things further. Is that OK, folks?'

Everyone agreed, apart from Keith who walked out muttering under his breath something about giving the enemy time to regroup.

'Not bad for a former sceptic,' said Nick as he walked past. I smiled at him as I made my way back to the newsroom.

Nick went straight to the Council House. Which was just as well. I was aware I was starting to soften at the edges. To peel back a layer or two of the protective coating. I had to keep reminding myself of the hurt inside. Of the importance of keeping the wound clean, of not letting it get reinfected.

When the final edition came out, I flicked through it and read my court report.

'Oh no,' I groaned. 'Sonia's struck again.'

'What's she done this time?' asked Cayte.

'I told her the CPS woman was Anne with an e Dexter.'

'And what did she put?'

I pointed to the relevant line. 'Prosecuting, Ann Withany Dexter.'

Cayte roared with laughter. 'You have to hand it to her. She really can turn copy round.'

At four-thirty on the dot I logged off, took a battered

canvas bag containing Colin's camera from under my desk and slung it over my shoulder.

'What's this?' said Cayte. 'Are you working to rule already?'

'I've got an appointment to keep. With a certain *Big Issue* seller.'

'Oh yes, your cosy threesome. Where's Nick?'

'He's going straight from the Council House. Meeting us there.'

'Have fun,' said Cayte. 'Don't do anything I wouldn't.'

'That leaves pretty much everything, then,' I said with a grin.

Colin was hovering by the bar when I arrived at the pub. Tufts of hair were sticking out from under his baseball cap. He appeared uneasy in a social situation but then again he always had done. It was in the council chamber that he used to come into his own. That he grew in stature and confidence. But he had lost that arena. Thanks to me. His face brightened as soon as he saw me. Which made me feel even worse.

'Hi, Colin,' I said, patting him on the shoulder, trying my best to put him at ease. 'Your face is looking better. How was business today?'

'Bit slow,' he said, taking his cap off and scratching his forehead. 'People too cold to take their hands out of their pockets, I guess.'

I noticed he was still wearing a pair of fingerless gloves, the likes of which I hadn't seen since the eighties.

'What can I get you to drink?' I said.

'Oh, thanks. Half a lager, please.'

'Coming up. Now, prepare yourself, I've got a surprise for you,' I said, unable to keep it from him any longer. I handed him the canvas bag. He staggered exaggeratedly under the weight.

'Bloody hell, what is it?'

'Take a look,' I said. 'Though I wouldn't get it out in

here.' He unclipped the buckles and lifted the flap. It took a second to register before his face lit up.

'It's a Nikon FM2.'

'Yep. Old hat nowadays but top of the range in its time, I'm told. You'll find a couple of lenses in there as well. A wide angle and a two hundred.'

'What do you want me to do with them?'

'You could use them as doorstops or paperweights if you like but I'd try taking some photos.'

His face lit up. 'Are you sure they won't mind? When do you need them back?'

'I don't, Colin. They're yours to keep. Courtesy of those nice people at the *Evening Gazette*. Photographic have all got digitals now. You've saved them from gathering dust in a cupboard.'

The smile on Colin's face threatened to go full circle. It choked me up just seeing it.

'Thanks, Sarah,' he said. 'That's fantastic. Thanks very much.'

'I've put a few rolls of black and white film in there as well. I expect to see the results mind. And they'd better be good.'

I carried our drinks over to the table, Colin seemingly unwilling to let go of the bag, even for a second. We'd not been there long when Nick breezed in, trench coat swishing at his heels. He spotted us straight away and hurried over.

'Hello, Colin. Good to see you again,' he said, shaking Colin warmly by the hand.

'And you,' said Colin, smiling broadly. 'It's been a long time.'

'It certainly has,' said Nick. 'Now, can I get you guys a drink?' We both declined. Nick went up to the bar alone.

'He's looking well,' said Colin. 'Hardly changed at all, has he?'

'No,' I said. 'Just dresses a bit smarter.'

Nick returned with his bottle of Becks.

'Sarah was just complimenting you on your newfound sartorial elegance,' said Colin.

'Are you sure she wasn't taking the piss?' said Nick, grinning at me as I blushed.

'I had wondered what became of the denim jacket,' I said.

'Went to a charity shop a few years ago,' said Nick. 'Probably still there.' I smiled. I was slipping again. He made it hard not to. Nick turned to Colin. 'Sarah's filled me in on what happened,' he said, sitting down on a stool next to me. 'I'm really sorry you've had such a rough time of it.'

Colin shrugged and took a sip of his lager. 'Things haven't exactly gone to plan since I last saw you.'

'I remember looking for your name in the list of new MPs after Labour won again in 2001,' said Nick. 'I had no idea why it wasn't there.'

'I was in a bit of a state by then,' said Colin. 'Mind you, even if I had won in '97, I'd probably have only lasted one term under Blair. You were right, Nick. He did turn out to be a bloody Tory in disguise.'

Nick laughed and looked at me, as if suspecting I would blow the whistle on him at any moment.

'Watch it, Colin,' I said. 'Haven't you read Nick's column? He's turned into a Blairite in his old age.'

Colin nearly dropped his glass. He stared at Nick incredulously. 'You never have?'

Nick shook his head. 'I'm not exactly on message but I did vote for him last time.'

'What brought that on? You used to be further left than Karl Marx.'

Nick laughed. 'Realism, I guess. Growing old enough to see the value of appealing to middle England. Unfortunately it's the only way to win general elections.'

He said it with a note of resignation in his voice. It made me realise that Nick had changed too. Not only older but wiser and sadder. For all sorts of reasons.

Colin shook his head and turned to me. 'What about you, Sarah? Are you still voting Labour?'

'No, not since Iraq. I voted Green last time. Jonathan's a member.'

'Bit of a waste,' said Colin. 'You may as well not vote.'

'Oh no,' I said, my cheeks flushing. 'I couldn't do that.' I shifted in my seat. Nick looked at me and opened his mouth to say something. I shook my head firmly and he shut it again.

'He's a nice chap, Sarah's boyfriend,' Colin said to Nick. 'You'll have to get her to invite you round for a meal. He cooks a mean curry.'

Nick looked down. I fiddled with the stem of my glass. A silence descended on our table. It was Colin who broke it.

'How's Amanda, Nick?'

It had gone from being slightly uncomfortable to excruciatingly so. I cringed, realising I'd forgotten to fill Colin in.

'Er, she's fine,' said Nick. 'But we got divorced a year ago.'

'Oh, sorry,' said Colin.

'It's OK,' said Nick. 'You weren't to know. Anyway, it was all fairly amicable.'

'You're still on speaking terms, then?' said Colin. Nick glanced over at me. I took a sip of my orange juice and looked down at the table, trying not to appear interested.

'Yeah, we have to be.'

I looked up, unsure what he was getting at. Colin was looking at him too. Nick hesitated.

'We've got a little girl,' he said.

The music from the jukebox faded, the chatter from other tables became indistinct, the figures standing at the bar blurred into one. And I sat there staring at Nick. Hearing his words reverberating inside my head. Wondering why he hadn't told me before. And why I stupidly hadn't thought to ask. While all the time the knife twisted further, reopening old wounds.

'Oh, right,' said Colin. 'How old is she?'

'Just turned four,' said Nick, still avoiding eye contact with me. 'We tried staying together for her sake but it didn't work. I think children pick up on the bad atmosphere, even at that age.'

'What's her name?' I said, moved to speak by the sudden need to know.

'Jessica,' said Nick, turning to face me, seemingly pleased I had asked. 'We call her Jess.' The corners of his mouth turned up as he said it, his face noticeably softening. I nodded. She had a name now. She was real. I couldn't deny her existence.

'Do you get to see her much?' asked Colin.

'Yeah, most weekends. It's easier now I'm here actually. Amanda moved back to Rugby after the divorce.'

'Oh, right. Has the old place changed much?' said Colin.

'No, not really,' said Nick. 'The *Chronicle*'s gone downhill, mind, since Sarah and I left.' He looked at me as he said it. He was trying to be nice, to lighten the atmosphere. But I was still too busy trying to digest the news to smile.

'I haven't been back there myself. Too many memories,' said Colin, his eyes glazing over for a second. 'How about you, Sarah?'

I shook my head. Too many memories. Memories I couldn't even speak of. Memories I'd fought so hard to bury but which had now been unearthed. I blinked hard, struggling to hold myself together.

'Strange, isn't it?' said Colin. 'How everything worked out. Us three all ending up in Birmingham. What do you think of it, Nick?'

'Great place,' said Nick. 'Much better city to live in than London. It's a shame I might not be staying long.'

'What do you mean?' said Colin.

'I'm probably going to be made redundant,' said Nick. 'They're asking for ten people to take voluntary but if they don't get them I'm first for the chop.'

'Bloody hell,' said Colin. 'I'm sorry to hear that. What are you going to do?'

'I don't know yet,' said Nick. 'It depends on a lot of things.'

He glanced at me and looked away again before standing up. The knife twisted again. I couldn't stand this much longer.

'What can I get you, Colin?' he said.

'Oh, I'll have another half, if that's all right.'

'Of course. Sarah?'

'Not for me, thanks. I'd better be making a move.'

Nick nodded, as if he understood. I stood up slowly, feeling a little shaky on my feet.

'Of course. I keep forgetting that unlike us pair of sad bastards you've got someone to go home to,' said Colin, his face dropping for a moment.

'You know you're welcome to come round any time,' I said. It wasn't what he'd meant but it was the best I could do.

'Cheers. Thanks for coming,' said Colin. 'It's been great seeing you both again. Just like old times.'

'Yeah,' I said.

'See you tomorrow, Sarah,' said Nick. His liquid chocolate eyes were desperately trying to soothe away the pain. He didn't know, though, couldn't understand. How deep it went inside.

Eight

'Happy birthday, gorgeous,' said Jonathan. He had showered and dressed already and was standing beside the bed with a dimpled grin on his face, holding out a present neatly wrapped in recycled gift paper. He seemed far more excited than I was. Birthdays had never been a big thing for me, probably due to the fact that my parents had always seemed to mark rather than celebrate them. There would be a card from them in the post later with a Marks & Spencer gift voucher inside. So I could get myself something tasteful and sensible. And that would be it for another year.

'Thanks,' I said, blearily rubbing my eyes and propping myself up in bed with two pillows before taking the present. It was heavier than I had expected, almost a foot long and decidedly chunky. I was not hopeful; presents were not Jonathan's strong point. I blamed his mother for this. Dawn had always bought Christmas and birthday gifts from worthy charity catalogues, refusing to even set foot in a high street store for fear of buying something which was made with child labour in a Far East sweatshop. Consequently Jonathan limited his gift choices to those items on offer in the Amnesty International catalogue. For Christmas I'd dropped a hint about wanting something personal and received a towelling bath robe (page 12, organic Fairtrade cotton made on a disabled women's co-operative in India). Not quite what I'd had in mind but at least it was wearable.

I peeled off the Sellotape, a look of false excitement on my face, the same one I'd used for my great-aunt's inappropriate gifts as a teenager. The present fell out on to the bed, landing heavily on my thigh. I picked it up. It appeared to be a torch of some kind. If I recalled rightly, it featured on page 15.

'Oh, er, thanks,' I said, trying desperately to sound as if I meant it.

'It's an environmentally friendly self-sufficient flashlight,' explained Jonathan, rather too enthusiastically. 'It doesn't use batteries, there's a wind-up mechanism instead. Sixty seconds' winding gives up to five minutes' full beam. I thought it would be useful to have in your car, in case of an emergency.'

I tried to think of the type of night-time motoring emergency in which you would have a spare minute to spend winding up a torch before being able to see for certain that you really had lost your leg in the multiple pile-up.

Jonathan was still hovering expectantly. 'It's OK, isn't it?' he said. 'Only I never know what to get you.'

'Of course,' I lied. 'I'm sure it will be useful.' I stretched my neck up to kiss him. Our lips barely touched. It was enough for him, though. He was still on a high from the previous evening. It wasn't often we managed sex twice in one night but Jonathan had been in a particularly persistent mood.

'Eager to please and enthusiastic,' that's what I'd say about his performances if I were writing a school report. 'Jonathan is an active and willing participant in sexual intercourse, he demonstrates a thorough understanding of theory and always gives of his best.' Textbook stuff but it hadn't done the trick for me. Hadn't blotted the thoughts of Nick from my mind. Or purged me of the guilt about thinking I could use him in that way.

'I've got to dash, but don't be late home tonight,' said Jonathan, still wearing the expression of an anxious-to-please puppy.

'Oh, and why's that?' I said, feeling compelled to play along.

'I've booked a table for two for seven-thirty,' he said. 'Somewhere special.'

I smiled as he waved goodbye. I couldn't fault him for trying. But it was the fact that he did try which made it so hard.

I took a leisurely shower and did myself some toast for breakfast before gathering my things for work. As I opened the front door Najma was about to pop a card through the letter box.

'Hey, I can give it to the birthday girl in person,' she said.

'You should have knocked.'

'I didn't want to disturb you in case you were having a birthday morning love-in,' she said. Najma was still in the honeymoon period of her relationship with Paul.

'No such luck. Jonathan had to be in early this morning.'

'What did he get you?' asked Najma.

I hesitated, not sure I could muster the necessary enthusiasm.

'I don't know, I haven't opened it yet,' I lied. Unsure who I was protecting, Jonathan or myself.

'Oh, wow. I love surprises. I can't wait till Paul's birthday. It's great being so close you can get stuff you know they'll like without having to ask, isn't it?'

I nodded and smiled in agreement. Feeling the need to go on the defensive.

'He's taking me out for a meal tonight, as well. Though he won't tell me where.'

'Fantastic. He certainly knows how to treat you.'

'Yeah,' I said. 'He does.'

When I arrived at work, a brightly coloured notice was stuck to my computer screen. 'Happy 31st Birthday you old bird' it read, with a photo of a pensioner with a Zimmer frame under it. Two envelopes were propped up against my keyboard. Cayte sat staring stern-faced at her notebook, having failed yet again to master the art of looking innocent.

'Thanks,' I said. 'You know I'm going to get my own back next year when you're twenty-five.'

'If I'm still here,' said Cayte. No one had taken voluntary redundancy yet, not even Phil.

'The only reason you won't be here is if you've had a better offer. Some Hollywood celebrity news agency, perhaps.'

'I had a dream last night,' continued Cayte, disregarding my comment. 'I went for a pee in the ladies. Terry was on stilts, watching me over the top of the cubicle. When I'd finished, and it was a really long pee, he said, "If your copy flow was as good as your urine flow I wouldn't have to let you go." What do you suppose that means?'

'That you have some weird toilet fixation?'

'It means I'm on my way out.'

'If you believe that crap,' I said, ripping open the top envelope to reveal a picture of an old lady sitting on a lavatory with her considerably sized knickers round her ankles.

'I think I was right first time,' I said, shaking my head as I thanked Cayte for the thought, strange though it was.

I opened the next envelope. It was a Far Side card. I recognised it instantly: it was the same one I'd got Nick for his thirtieth. I opened it with trembling hands.

'Have a great birthday, love Nick.'

I felt like a thirteen-year-old who'd received her first Valentine's card. I stuffed it back into the envelope, trying not to appear ruffled. I glanced across at his empty seat. I hadn't told him and I didn't think anyone else had. Which meant he'd remembered.

Within minutes of my arrival the phones started ringing, the callers all ex-servicemen, complaining about our Remembrance Day report in yesterday's late edition.

Saying we'd got it wrong. That there was no such thing as the Kenneth Kohima Epitaph. That Kohima was a battle in India. One or two were irate, demanding to speak to the editor. I took their numbers and went to see Terry.

'Take cover, there's a storm brewing,' I said.

'I know. News desk have already put a couple through to me.'

'So what should it have said?'

'That there was a moving rendition of the famous Kohima Epitaph,' said Terry. 'You know the one: "For your tomorrow, we gave our today."'

'So where did the Kenneth come from?'

Terry started chuckling. 'Take a wild guess.'

I followed the direction of his gaze. 'Sonia.'

'Right in one. When Ravinder filed the copy in he spelt Kohima out for her. Told her it started with K for Kenneth. I suppose she got a bit confused. And neither Lisa nor the subs spotted it.'

I shook my head and groaned. Terry was still chuckling.

'You won't be laughing when they start getting the calls in London,' I said.

'What do you mean?'

'Our copy was syndicated to the nationals. Kenneth Kohima will be all over the country by now.'

Terry groaned and bashed his head on the desk.

'I did warn you,' I said. 'She'll start a bloody war one day.'

Nick didn't get back to the office until most people had left for the afternoon. Cayte had gone home. It was just the two of us on our desk.

'Hi, Sarah. Had a good day?' he said.

The warmth in his voice peeled another layer away. He was getting dangerously close now. To the inner core. I started hurriedly packing my things away.

'Yeah. Thanks for your card.' I mumbled. 'I've got to dash. I'm going out tonight.' I realised I'd got my excuse in before I'd been required to give it.

'Before you go, I've got a little something for you,' said Nick, reaching into his drawer and handing me a small box wrapped in tissue paper.

I looked at him.

'Oh, really, you shouldn't have.'

'Don't get too excited. You haven't opened it yet,' said Nick.

I tore open the paper, removed the lid of the box and peered inside at the brown, rather musty contents. It took a moment for me to realise what it was. My dried camel dung. I started laughing. Nick was laughing too. Just like we had seven years ago.

'You kept it?' I said.

'It was all I had to remember you by.'

I shook my head, the smile fading slightly.

'So why give it back?' I said.

'I don't need mementos any more. I've got the real thing sitting two desks away,' he said. 'At least for now.'

I picked up my briefcase. Trying not to let him see my face.

'So when are we going to celebrate your birthday?' he said.

I looked around, playing for time while I decided what to say.

'I don't know,' was all I managed to come up with.

'How are you fixed on Saturday evening?'

I opened my mouth to answer but nothing came out. The cleaner started hoovering at the far end of the office. She had almost reached us and I still hadn't said anything.

'Remind me if I ever get on to *Who Wants to be a Millionaire* not to put you down as a phone a friend,' said Nick. 'I'd hate to think what you're like with a tough question.'

'I'm busy,' I said finally. 'But thanks anyway.'

'Offer's still there if you change your mind,' said Nick. I nodded and strode off purposefully along the corridor, being careful not to slip on the wet floor.

I smiled at Jonathan as the waiter eased the chair in under me.

'This is nice,' I said.

We were in a restaurant called Mangos in Harborne. Very upmarket for us: we usually went to a glorified café run by a Fairtrade vegetarian co-operative in Digbeth. Apparently they were in the middle of a refurbishment, hence the new venue.

'It is your birthday,' he said. 'You deserve it.'

He reached across the table and squeezed my hand. I could forgive him the torch thing. It was, after all, the thought that counted. A sudden flare from the candle lit up his face. Capturing the look of love, bordering on adoration. Reminding me how lucky I was.

'Would you like to order some wine?' our waiter enquired, gesturing to a chalk board on the wall.

Jonathan scanned the list. 'Do you have anything vegetarian?'

The waiter looked at him quizzically.

'Fish bladders,' Jonathan explained. 'Most wines are filtered through fish bladders but there are vegetarian alternatives. I have a list on me, if it helps.' He pulled a crumpled piece of paper from his trouser pocket and handed it to the waiter. 'Red or white, I'm not fussy.'

I stared intently at the tablecloth. I had forgotten the downside of going to normal restaurants. We'd never had the pleasure of visiting one with Dawn but I suspected she would be far, far worse.

'Certainly, sir.' The waiter backed away and returned several minutes later with a bottle of white which Jonathan examined before allowing him to pour.

'Cheers, happy birthday,' said Jonathan. Our glasses met with a gentle clink. I returned his smile. According to the menu, Mangos offered 'A fusion of new world cuisine with a modern twist', which all sounded suitably impressive. Jonathan shifted in his seat and undid the top button of his collarless shirt.

'Everything OK?' I asked.

'Yeah. Not sure what to go for. There aren't as many veggie options as they said on the phone.'

'They sound good, though. And I'm starving,' I said.

The waiter returned and I placed my order. He looked at Jonathan with some trepidation.

'Er, I'll have the sweet potato soup for starters as long as it's made with vegetable stock; if it's not then I'll have the terrine. And for main course I'll go for the marinated tofu, aubergine and halloumi kebabs but could you just check with the chef that the soya isn't genetically modified. If it is you'd better come back and I'll have another look.' Jonathan smiled as he finished. I felt myself sink deeper into my seat as the waiter walked away, still scribbling furiously in his pad. I was surprised Jonathan hadn't asked whether the notebook was made from recycled paper.

I glanced round at the other diners, mostly couples, hoping no one had overheard. Jonathan looked at me.

'What?' he said.

'I just don't like having to make a fuss when we're out.'

'I was only checking. Loads of restaurants use chicken stock in the soups. You have to be careful.'

I nodded, deciding to leave it at that.

'So, did they spoil you rotten at work today, then?' he said.

'I got a couple of cards. And Cayte took me for lunch which was nice.'

'Who were they from?'

'Sorry?'

'The cards.'

I cursed myself for not thinking before opening my mouth. Or maybe I had thought. Maybe that was the problem. I knew I had to make a quick choice, the only options being to lie or to brush it off casually. I plumped for the latter.

'Oh, er, Cayte, of course. And Nick.'

'The guy you used to work with?'

'Yeah.'

'That was nice of him.'

If I hadn't known better I'd have sworn there was a hint of jealousy there. Maybe laced with a tiny drop of suspicion.

'Yeah, Cayte must have told him,' I said quickly. 'You know what she's like, always trying to turn things into a party.'

Jonathan nodded. The silence was broken by the waiter returning with our starters.

'Is your terrine good?' asked Jonathan.

'Mmmm,' I said in between mouthfuls. 'And your soup?'

'Sorry?'

'Your soup, is it OK?'

'Oh, yeah. Fine thanks.'

It was said without his customary enthusiasm. I wasn't sure if he suspected the chef had lied about the stock or whether there was something else bothering him.

'Are you sure you're OK?' I asked. 'Only you seem a bit distracted.'

'Sorry. I've got things on my mind.'

'Like what?' I said, praying Nick wasn't one of them.

'It's only work stuff, it can wait. This is supposed to be your night.'

'Come on, we can still talk,' I said, relieved I was off the hook. 'What is it?'

Jonathan sighed. 'That lad, Daniel, the one who's getting bullied. He came to see me again today. Turns out he is gay. Or at least he thinks he is. Asked me whether I thought he should come out to the other kids. If it would get them off his back.'

'I hope you told him no.'

'Er, no. Not exactly.'

'You know what they're like, Jonathan. They're bad enough without any encouragement. I can't imagine they'd respect his honesty and leave the poor kid alone.'

'No, I guess not.'

'So what did you tell him?'

'That it was up to him to do whatever he thought was right. And that I'd be there to support him if he needed it.'

I nodded while cringing inside. Sometimes the real world seemed too harsh a place for Jonathan.

'I wouldn't worry,' I said. 'Hopefully he'll decide to keep it to himself.'

The main courses arrived. Jonathan tucked into his tofu without any further questions. He seemed to relax a little now he'd got the Daniel thing off his chest. He even related an amusing tale about Ozzy Osbourne one of the kids had told him. It made me laugh out loud. I liked it when he did that.

After a suitable pause, we were given the dessert menus to peruse. When our waiter returned a few minutes later he was looking understandably anxious.

'I'll have the lemon and coconut cheesecake,' I said.

'Make that two,' said Jonathan. 'But could you check there's no gelatine in the topping, please.'

The waiter disappeared scratching his head. I gave Jonathan another look.

'Sorry, shouldn't I have asked?'

'Um, sometimes it can be a bit much,' I heard myself say.

'I am trying,' said Jonathan anxiously. 'I didn't ask if there was palm oil in the base.'

'What's wrong with palm oil?' I asked.

'Mum told me about it. They're cutting down half the

rainforests in Borneo to make way for palm oil plantations. Sometimes they kill baby orang-utans in the process.'

'Right,' I said, wondering if this would be added to our list of boycotted products.

The waiter returned with the grim news that the chef had confirmed the presence of gelatine in the cheesecake.

'Oh, I'll have the ice cream then,' Jonathan said.

'And does madam still want the cheesecake?' the waiter asked.

'Er, no. I'm fine, thanks. Nothing for me.'

'You could have had it if you wanted,' said Jonathan as soon as the waiter had gone. 'I wouldn't have minded.' He didn't understand that once he'd refused something on moral grounds it was difficult for me not to do the same.

A dish of mango ice cream appeared for Jonathan.

'Are you sure you don't want to share this?' he said.

'No, thanks. You tuck in.'

We sat in silence while Jonathan ate the ice cream. I wondered what Nick was doing, what he'd been planning for Saturday evening.

'Would you like coffee?' the waiter enquired. I bit my lip, willing Jonathan not to say anything.

'Have you got anything Fairtrade?' he asked. The waiter rolled his eyes. I stood up sharply.

'We don't want any coffee, thank you,' I said. 'Just the bill please and could you order a cab.' I turned to Jonathan who remained sitting, a startled expression on his face. 'I'll see you outside,' I said, taking my jacket from the back of my chair and marching out of the restaurant.

I stood for a moment, gulping the damp night air, trying to stop my body from shaking. Jonathan emerged a few minutes later.

'I'm sorry,' he said. 'I didn't mean to upset you.'

'Well you have. It was supposed to be a quiet birthday meal, not a party political broadcast on behalf of Friends of the Earth.'

I lowered my arm, conscious that I was jabbing a finger at him. Jonathan stood staring at me.

'But I thought you agreed with all that stuff.'

'I do, but I don't want it rammed down my throat and everyone else's. Sometimes you sound just like your mother.'

The cab pulled up outside. I opened the rear door and got in. Jonathan was a few steps behind.

'Sorry,' I said, turning round and slamming the door behind me, 'the cab driver filled up at Esso. I'm afraid you'll have to walk.'

I hated doing it. But it was the only way he'd learn.

Friday 2 May 1997

I wake up. I am in my own bed. It is eleven-thirty in the morning. I have had less than four hours' sleep. It was indeed a long night. I feel as if I had the best dream ever followed by the worst nightmare. I didn't though. They were both real. They happened to me.

A mass of images are swirling in my head; I see Nick gazing longingly into my eyes as we make love, before the picture fades and is replaced by Amanda's face smiling in blissful ignorance. The image blurs into Colin's stricken expression as the returning officer reads out the results and he realises he has lost by one vote. Followed by Pike's smug grin as he acknowledges his narrowest of victories. And finally, my bemused and bewildered reflection as I stare into the bathroom mirror, struggling to comprehend that I set off that whole chain of events. And that I must now face the consequences.

My head aches as if I have a hangover, which I don't, of course. It would be easier if I did. All I would have to do then is drink lots of fluids, go back to bed and sleep it off. Unfortunately this ache is not going to go away so easily.

I get out of bed and draw back the curtains. The sun comes streaming in. A new day and a whole new era has dawned. Tony Blair is our shiny new leader, John Major nothing but a fading grey has-been, retreating into the distance with his defeated troops, a shell-shocked Michael

Portillo lying mortally wounded among the battlefield casualties.

I should feel elated. I have waited for this moment a long time. But my own maelstrom has overshadowed it all. I haven't got time to celebrate the liberation of our country. I am too busy surveying the devastation around me.

I walk into the bathroom and look again at my face in the mirror. Guilt is seeping from my pores and running down my cheeks. I slept with another woman's boyfriend. I have never done that before. I didn't think I was capable of it; I am not that kind of person. Or at least I wasn't – until last night. The awful thing is that although I know it was wrong, and although I feel terrible about Amanda, I do not regret it. Because it proved what I have always known. That Nick and I are meant to be together. And that I have never loved anyone as much as I love him.

I turn on the shower attachment and step into the bath. I can still smell Nick on me. Part of me wants to leave it that way, to never wash again. But I know I have to be mature about this. To retain some degree of common sense. I lean my head back and let the water cascade over my hair. I wonder if Amanda is home yet. And whether Nick has changed his mind about regretting last night having seen her. Having lied to her, or at the very least been economical with the truth. Things look different in the morning, in the cold light of day. He may well have decided it was a mistake. That he got carried away. Let his heart rule his head. And that it will not happen again.

Do I want it to happen again? Of course I do. Bad as I feel and wrong as it was I cannot bear the thought of never touching skin with him again. It was too good to be a one-night stand. It was too right.

I drop the shower gel in the bath. As I pick it up I realise my hands are shaking. The mere thought of seeing Nick again is doing this to me. We are both due in work at twelve-thirty. A half day off in lieu of the night shift. I can't imagine sitting at the far end of the office from him. Being so close but unable to touch him. Last night at the count the atmosphere in the town hall was so charged anyway, no one noticed what was going on between us. The looks, the sparks of energy, the sense of intimacy. Today it will be different. We will have to sit in the same office pretending nothing has happened, nothing has changed. And I don't want to do that. Because it did and it has.

I get dressed quickly and skip breakfast, or brunch, or whatever it would be by now. I don't think my stomach could deal with food at the moment. I grab my bag and hurry down to the car, turning the radio on as I drive off.

Five Live are rounding up their election coverage with a look at quirky stories from across the regions.

'Colin Leake must be the unluckiest man in Britain today,' is how they start the report. I slam the brakes on to avoid crashing into the car in front. 'Leake, the Labour candidate for Rugby and Kenilworth, failed to oust sitting Tory MP George Pike by just one vote, making it the narrowest general election defeat in post-war Britain.'

They cut to an interview with Colin, which I vaguely remember him giving to BBC local radio last night.

'It is bitterly disappointing to lose by such a narrow margin. I knew it was going to be close but had no idea just how close. I have no complaints about the result: there were three recounts and I'm satisfied they got it right. I'm only sorry for the people of Rugby and Kenilworth who voted for me and who deserve a Labour MP to represent them.'

The presenter is clearly taken with Colin's plight. He launches a phone-in on the back of it: 'Are you an unlucky loser? What have you narrowly missed out on?'

My knuckles have turned white, I am gripping the steering wheel so hard. I fear my heart palpitations may soon lead to some kind of coronary. I am half expecting the presenter to ask listeners to hunt down the person who didn't vote for Colin. To turn them in so they can receive a deserved public flogging. Other drivers are looking at me, I am not sure if it is because of my erratic driving or whether I have a neon sign on the top of my Beetle: 'I'm the one who didn't vote for Colin.' It is worse than that, though, because I don't even have a good reason. It's not as if I was tending an ageing aunt on her deathbed or working on some voluntary charity project overseas. I was shagging somebody else's boyfriend, for goodness' sake. The belief that he is 'the one', the absolute love of my life, can be submitted as mitigating circumstances but it does not change the fact that I committed the crime. I sink down low in the driver's seat and put my sunglasses on even though it is not sunny. The first person rings up Five Live with their unlucky loser story. I turn off the radio.

Nick is already at his desk, reading the morning papers. He looks as if he has had even less sleep than me. The palpitations start again. He glances up as I walk into the office, makes momentary eye contact then looks straight back down again.

He regrets it. I am sure of it. Considers it a terrible mistake. He is probably wondering how he can get out of it without hurting my feelings.

'Hi, what a night you had,' says Joan, peering over her glasses as I sit down. For a second I think she knows, that Nick has spilled the beans, boasted of his conquest and it is all over town. Then I realise that she is talking about Colin.

'I know, it was awful,' I say. 'He could barely speak last night, he was so cut up.'

'Poor bastard's been on Sky and the BBC this morning,' says Joan.

I groan as I shake my head.

'Shame we can't find a mislaid ballot paper or two and wipe the smug grin off Pike's face,' says Joan.

'Yeah, that would be good,' I say, feeling my cheeks reddening.

'Still, at least the Tories are out,' says Joan. 'Did you see Portillo's face? What a picture. I bet Nick's going to get that blown up for his wall.'

Nicks looks up, his eyes meeting Joan's, not mine.

'I'm going one better than that,' he says. 'I'm getting it framed.'

I burst out laughing then stop myself. Not even sure it is right to laugh at his jokes any more. I turn on my computer and start leafing through my shorthand notes from last night. Quotes from Colin and Pike. I hardly need my notebook, I can remember most of them verbatim, they are so ingrained in my mind. Nearly an hour passes before Nick says anything. He waits until Joan has nipped to the loo before venturing over to my side of the office.

'Are you OK?' he asks quietly.

I look up at him, struggling to keep my emotions under control.

'Yeah, I guess so,' I say. 'What about you?'

'Yeah, fine.' He doesn't sound fine. He sounds like someone whose internal organs are in a torture chamber. I want to talk to him. Really talk to him. But before I can say anything else Joan comes back into the room.

'So, keep it fairly tight, about two hundred and fifty words from each candidate should do,' says Nick, retreating into safe news editor mode.

'Sure,' I say, nodding rather too enthusiastically. Nick walks away. I can see Joan giving me a funny look out of the corner of my eye.

'So what time did you get to bed this morning?' she says.

'Oh, about seven, I think, by the time they'd finished all the recounts.'

'You must be knackered,' she says. 'I'm surprised you

didn't get your head down for a few hours before the count last night.'

I wonder how she knows I didn't. I decide not to reply in the hope she will leave it alone.

'Only I saw your Beetle in the car park when I left work,' she continues.

Shit. I can't believe I didn't think of that. Serves me right for having such a distinctive car. Joan is looking at me, waiting for a reply. I am not going to get away with ignoring her.

'I went for a bite to eat with Nick,' I say. 'Didn't have much in at home. Anyway, I was too hyped up about it all to be able to sleep.'

She nods. I have done nothing to ease her suspicions. I wonder if she knows more than she is letting on. My phone rings and I pick it up, relieved at the interruption. It is the front office downstairs.

'Sarah, Colin Leake's here to see you,' says Jill, the receptionist.

My day is getting worse. It was bad enough interviewing him last night but at least then we were both still in shock. Enough time has elapsed now for him to be utterly miserable. And for me to feel utterly responsible.

I pick up my notebook, though I suspect Colin has come for a chat rather than to be interviewed, and go downstairs. He is standing by the front window, staring out blankly across the street. He has clearly had no sleep, and from the look of his ruffled hair and what I am sure are the same clothes as last night, I suspect he has not even been home. I take a deep breath.

'Hello, Colin,' I say, the guilt squelching in my shoes as I walk over to him. 'How are you bearing up?'

Colin shrugs. 'It hadn't really sunk in last night but this morning when everyone's going on about the Labour landslide . . .'

I nod. He looks like he needs a good hug but I'm not

sure I'm the person to give it. Being the one who didn't vote for him.

'I heard you on the radio,' I say. 'And Joan saw you on TV.'

He rolls his eyes. 'My fifteen minutes of fame as the man who lost by one vote. That's what I'll always be known as, you know. A loser.'

He is staring disconsolately out of the window. I fear he is about to cry.

'Hey, come on,' I say. 'Where's that fighting spirit gone? You reduced a thirteen thousand majority to one single vote. That's a hell of an achievement. And in four or five years' time you'll trounce Pike at the polls.'

He shrugs again.

'Maybe,' he says. His heart is clearly not in it any more.

'Why don't you come up for a coffee,' I say. 'Nick's here, and all the others.'

Colin shakes his head. 'No thanks, I'm not very good company at the moment. I just wanted to pop in to thank you for all your efforts during the campaign. I do appreciate it, Sarah. And please pass my thanks on to Nick. You've both been a great help.'

This is the point where I should confess. Hold my hand up and reveal my role in his defeat. I open my mouth but the right words don't come out.

'Yes, of course. I'm just sorry we couldn't do more.'

I cringe as I say it. I am quite clearly a coward now as well as the sort of woman who sleeps with someone else's boyfriend. Colin opens the door to leave.

'See you around,' he says and trudges off down the street.

I let out the mother of all sighs and go back up to the office, walking over to Nick's desk, a pained expression on my face.

'Colin's just been in. Says to say thank you for all we've done to help him.'

Nick grimaces. 'Oh, God. How was he?'

'Not good. Take a look for yourself,' I say, pointing out of the window. 'He's the suicidal-looking guy, wandering aimlessly along.'

Nick swivels round in his chair, watches Colin disappear round the corner and turns back to me.

'Sorry,' he says.

My hands are clammy. I am not sure what he is talking about.

'What for?'

'Telling you no one ever loses by one vote.'

'It's all right,' I say. 'I'll just never listen to another word you say.'

I smile. He smiles back. I wonder if that means we are OK.

I go out on a feature later. Something I'd arranged days ago, having no idea of the state I would be in at this point in time. I am glad of the opportunity to get out of the office, though. To breathe properly again.

The woman I'm interviewing is anorexic. Deborah Saunders her name is. Nineteen years old and weighing barely five stone. She contacted us to ask if the *Chronicle* could do a feature about the lack of specialist treatment available for people with eating disorders. She lives with her parents in a small terraced house in Newton on the outskirts of Rugby. I pull up outside and knock on the door, my head still full of other things. Deborah's mother greets me. A tall, gaunt woman with worry lines threatening to turn into crevices. She shows me into the front room where Deborah is sitting on the sofa, propped up by cushions as if she might fall over and snap in half without them. It is all I can do not to gasp out loud. I have never seen anyone so thin in the flesh – or should I say the bones – before. Her eyes appear huge in their sunken sockets; the hollows of her cheeks look as if they must almost touch inside her mouth. It is only the photos on the window sill which prove she was once a very pretty young teenager.

'Hi, I'm Sarah from the *Chronicle*. Thanks for getting in touch.'

She gets up and offers her hand. I shake it lightly, fearing I may snap her wrist. She is wearing a loose long-sleeved top and baggy jogging bottoms. Somewhere underneath there is what is left of her body. She sits back down again and I settle myself in the armchair opposite. Her mother leaves the room, perhaps unable to bear hearing what she is about to say. I ask Deborah about her family, giving her the opportunity to relax a little before I have to enquire about more sensitive matters. She is quietly spoken but articulate. Very clear about what she wants to say. She starts talking about her anorexia without any prompting from me. Says she was fourteen when it started. She was getting bullied at school and her first boyfriend dumped her for a skinnier girl so she figured she should lose her 'puppy fat'. But when she had, her ex-boyfriend still didn't want her back and the bullying continued, so she decided to lose some more. And then found that she couldn't stop. And hasn't been able to since. She has been in and out of hospital more times than she cares to remember. Each time they stabilise her weight, send her back home without any support or therapy, and only when she gets dangerously ill do they admit her again. Her family have paid for her to have some private counselling but although it has helped she is desperate for specialist treatment. She mentions an eating disorders clinic in Leicestershire but says there is a long waiting list. And then burst into tears.

'I'm sorry,' I say, fishing in my bag for a tissue and handing it to her. 'Do you want to take a break? Say if you want me to go, I'll understand.'

Deborah blows her nose and shakes her head. 'No. Sometimes it gets to me, that's all. Talking helps though. My counsellor says so. Stops me bottling things up.'

'As long as you're sure.'

She nods her head, takes a few moments to compose herself and carries on. Going into more detail this time. About the constant weighing, the vomiting, the obsessive exercising, all the hidden parts of an anorexic's daily life. By the time I leave, well over an hour later, I am emotionally drained but full of admiration for her. Deborah hugs me on the front doorstep.

'Thank you for coming,' she says. 'Maybe your article will force them to do something.'

'Let's hope so,' I say. 'You take care.'

I get back in the car, feeling unworthy to even have been in the same room as her. I look at my watch. It is five-thirty. The others will have left the office by now. I have missed Nick. Missed the chance of talking to him. Of the comfort of being in his presence. I need to go back there anyway, to get my things. I hadn't planned on being this long.

I let myself in the side door and climb the back stairs to the newsroom. The tears are massing at the corners of my eyes, waiting impatiently for the chance to escape. The newsroom door is open, silence pours from within. And light. Someone has left the light on. I walk through. Nick is sitting at his desk, staring up at me. The tears begin their descent.

'Are you OK?' Nick asks. I shake my head, looking at him through blurry eyes. He stands up and comes over to me. Pulling me close to him. Enveloping me in his arms. I feel a release valve open, letting the tears and the tension drain away. I am comforted by the smell of him. The feel of his body next to me. I raise my head.

'Sorry,' I say. 'The anorexic woman. She looked terrible, it was awful. Kind of got to me.'

Nick nods although we both know that is only a small part of it. That the source of these tears goes back beyond this afternoon.

'Poor you,' he says. 'You've had a tough day.'

He holds me for a long time. Until I am finally able to prise myself from his body. Only a couple of inches away, that is as far as I am going.

'Sorry,' I say when I see the damp patch I have left on the shoulder of his shirt. He glances down.

'It doesn't matter, it'll dry.'

I nod, feeling the warmth, the softness in his voice.

'It's been so hard,' I say. 'Not being able to talk to you properly.'

'I know,' he says. 'That's why I waited for you.'

I smile. Relieved he feels the same.

'I was worried you were going to say it was a mistake.'

He shakes his head. 'The only thing I regret is the situation.'

I know what he means. I want to ask about Amanda. Whether she is back yet. Whether he will be having sex with her tonight. But I can't put any pressure on. In case I scare him away.

'I've never . . . I feel really bad about what we did,' I say.

'Well don't,' he says, squeezing my shoulder. 'Believe me, I feel bad enough for both of us.'

I hesitate, unsure where we go from here.

'So what happens now?' I ask.

Nick shrugs. 'I'll tell you what should happen. We should both go home and get a good night's sleep.'

I try not to show how disappointed I am.

'If that's what you want,' I say.

'It isn't,' he says. 'It's you I want.'

He leans forward and kisses me. One kiss, one touch of his lips on mine is all it takes. The world is all right again.

Nine

I woke at six the next morning. Jonathan was fast asleep next to me. I didn't even remember hearing him come home. Normally I'd have tried to get back to sleep. But today I knew it wasn't worth it. I slipped out of bed and into the bathroom. Jonathan's wet clothes were hanging over the radiator. I felt a twinge of guilt. Maybe I'd been a bit harsh on him. But maybe it was the only way. I took a shower but as I crept back into the darkness of the bedroom to dress, I noticed Jonathan's eyes were open.

'You're up early,' he said, voice croaking slightly.

'Yeah, got a lot on at work,' I mumbled, trying to avoid eye contact by rummaging in the drawers for some underwear.

'Look, about last night,' he started.

'I'm sorry you got wet,' I said, hoping to head off a row.

Jonathan leant up in bed, switched the bedside lamp on and rubbed his eyes awake. Clearly the subject was far from finished.

'I'm sorry I upset you,' he said, his face suitably apologetic. 'I guess I was a bit distracted with the stuff at work. And wanting you to enjoy it made me a bit anxious and when I get anxious I tend to babble and, well, you know what happened.' He threw his hands out wide as he said it. His way of begging for forgiveness.

'It's OK,' I said with my back to him as I fastened my

bra. 'I understand. It's just that occasionally I need a night off from making the world a better place. A nice quiet meal without any hassle.'

I pulled a top over my head, hoping I'd managed to end the conversation. But the look on Jonathan's face as my head poked through suggested otherwise.

'What you said about me sounding like Mum. Did you mean that?'

I paused for a second, going back to the wardrobe to find some trousers to give myself more time.

'All I meant was that sometimes it's like you're trying to impress her when she's not even there.'

'I wasn't. It's how I am.' The hands were out again, his voice indignant.

'No, Jonathan, it's how she brought you up. You're a big boy now, you don't have to follow her teachings to the letter. Or impose them on everyone else.'

He scratched his head as he tried to digest what I'd said. His face as crumpled as last night's clothes.

'So what are you saying? That I'm an irritating bastard who rubs everyone up the wrong way?'

I sat down on the corner of the bed and touched his leg through the duvet.

'Of course not. What I'm asking you to do is to stop and think before you say things. And once in a while, if it's not the right time or the right place, bite your lip and let it go.'

He sighed heavily and nodded. 'OK. I'll give it a try. Anything's better than having to walk home in the rain.' He smiled an uncertain smile. It was the best I was going to get.

'Anyway,' I said, slipping on my shoes. 'I'd better get to work. See you later.' I leant over and kissed him.

'Love you,' he said.

And I knew he meant it.

*

It was still only six forty-five. Too early for Starbucks and though the gym opened at seven it would be filled with thrusting early morning types, the sort who would have a power breakfast afterwards. I didn't fancy it. I drove straight to work.

I liked being at the *Gazette* at this hour. Only a handful of people in, the office still slumbering before the chaos of the day ahead. Even Keith was comparatively quiet this early, as if his loud, obnoxious self hadn't woken up yet. I wandered over to the coffee machine, got a number four and a number seven and took them into Terry's office, the strong, sweet smell prompting him to lift his head from his copy of *The Times*.

'Oh, thanks, Sarah,' he said as I put the number seven down in front of him. Terry would never think to ask why I was in so early. He found it odd that other people weren't as keen to get to work as he was. The bags under his eyes looked larger than usual, as if carrying two weeks' shopping instead of one. I noticed how gaunt his face was as well. Clearly the situation hadn't improved at home.

'How's things?' I said.

'Oh, you know.' He shrugged and raised his eyebrows.

'I don't, Terry, that's why I'm asking.'

'Phil's taking voluntary redundancy,' he said.

'Good. No great loss. Anyone else?'

'A couple have been in to discuss terms, nothing definite.'

Terry went back to staring at the paper, though I could tell his eyes weren't focusing.

'And what about at home?' I asked, determined to drag it out of him.

Terry let go of a long sigh and shrugged again. His face was empty, expressionless. As if he'd given up all hope.

'I take it that means Sylvia's still there,' I said, taking a sip of my coffee.

'And that Derek. Makes things awkward. It's not that I don't like him. He seems a decent enough sort of chap.'

'Terry, he's shagging your wife under your roof,' I said, throwing my hands up in the air.

'I know, I can hear them some nights.'

'Fucking hell.' I got up from the chair and started pacing about. 'Why didn't you throw her out like I said?'

'I tried to but she laughed in my face. Said I'd have to throw all her stuff out in the street and change the locks.'

'And what's wrong with that?'

Terry pulled a face. 'People don't do things like that, not in Solihull.'

'I don't suppose many people shack up with someone else's wife in Solihull either.'

Terry shrugged again. I wanted to rip his arms from his shoulders and use them to prop his pride up.

'I'm not going to drag her out kicking and screaming. I couldn't do that to the boys.'

'How are they?'

'Hard to say. Their PlayStation games seem to be getting more violent. But maybe that's a stage they're going through.'

I shook my head. He was a brilliant newspaper editor but he seemed to find the domestic front mind-bogglingly difficult.

'So how long are you going to go on living like this?' I said, sitting down again to finish my coffee.

'I don't know. She might get bored with him by Christmas. Depends what he gets her for a present. I never seem to get the right thing. Women can be very odd about presents, you know.'

I smiled weakly, wondering if Terry could find a use for a wind-up torch.

'Drink your coffee,' I said as I headed for the door. 'Before it gets cold.'

Cayte announced her arrival at ten past eight by kicking over a waste paper bin and knocking the business editor's coffee off his desk. I'd briefed her before

on the art of slipping in quietly if you were late but
somehow she never managed it. She collapsed on to her
chair looking as if she'd scaled Everest and swum the
Channel on her way in.

'I've got some good news for you,' I said.

Cayte took a brush from her bag and scraped her
matted hair back into a pony tail. 'Don't tell me, Kurt
Cobain is back from the dead and wants my phone
number,' she said.

'No. But Phil's taken voluntary redundancy. Only one
more to go and you're safe.'

'Great,' she said, fishing in her bag again and
producing a purple scrunchy which she tied round her
hair.

'I thought you'd be pleased,' I said, frowning at her.

'I'm ecstatic. I'm just tired. Didn't get much sleep last
night.'

I remembered she'd told me she was going to some
club in Digbeth with Jazz.

'Was it an all-nighter then?' I said.

'We didn't go in the end. Had a change of plan,' she
said, switching on her computer and pulling her
notebook out from under a pile of papers.

'Oh, why was that?'

'Jazz had to go somewhere with Davina.'

'Who's she?' I said. It wasn't like Cayte to be so reticent.

'The new singer in his band. They had to go and see
some guy about a gig.'

I noticed the red rims round Cayte's eyes as she
glanced up. And the quivering tone in her voice.

'Ladies' loos. Now,' I said.

I stood up and waited for Cayte to stumble to her feet
before marshalling her out of the office and along the
corridor. The loos smelt of Elnett hairspray (the one in
the gold can that they use in hairdressers which haven't
been refitted since the seventies). Terry's secretary Doreen
used it on her hair approximately every fifteen minutes,

presumably concerned that the fanning of a few sheets of A4 could spoil her immaculate coiffeur. The haze coupled with our breathing difficulties indicated that we had not long missed her.

'I don't know why you're fussing. I'm fine,' said Cayte.

'You said you didn't get much sleep.'

'I'm a bit stressed, that's all.'

'What does she look like, this Davina?'

Cayte walked up to the sinks and stared in the mirror at a spot on her chin.

'A younger version of Courtney Love,' she said.

'How young?'

She was squeezing the spot now. I had to look away.

'Straight out of sixth form young,' she said.

'And is it her you don't trust or Jeremy?'

'It's not a matter of trust,' said Cayte, rinsing her hands under the tap. 'Me and Jazz have an open relationship.'

I raised my eyebrows. I didn't buy this at all.

'And does it swing both ways, the door on your open relationship?'

'If I want it to,' said Cayte, drying her hands on a paper towel.

'Except you don't, do you? You'd rather the door was firmly closed.'

'I'm fine with things as they are, thank you,' she said, stuffing the towel into the overflowing bin. 'We're not like you and Jonathan.'

My back stiffened as she turned to face me.

'What's that supposed to mean?' I said.

'You know, all cosy and coupley, quiet nights in and home-cooked lentil pie.'

'Are you taking the piss?'

'No,' she said. 'Simply stating the facts.'

I felt the indignation rising. My skin beginning to prickle.

'Jonathan took me out last night, actually. For a surprise birthday meal.'

'OK, chill out,' she said. 'I believe you.'

'You make us sound like some boring old farts.'

Cayte sighed and shook her head. 'I wasn't saying that at all. Have I stepped on a raw nerve or something?'

'Jonathan and I are fine as we are, thank you.'

'I didn't say you weren't. Honestly, Sarah. What's got into you this morning?'

Before I had a chance to reply, Doreen entered, brandishing her can of hairspray.

'Hello, ladies,' she tweeted before giving Cayte's tangles a disapproving stare. Cayte hurried out before Doreen could offer her grooming advice. I followed a few seconds later, troubled by my reaction. I was supposed to be listening to Cayte's problems and yet somehow mine had got in the way. I should have told her about my row with Jonathan. But I hadn't wanted to reveal the chink in my armour. Or her to guess who had chipped it away.

I popped out for a sandwich at lunchtime, stopping off to see my favourite *Big Issue* seller on the way back. He was standing in his usual spot, stamping his feet to keep warm, the pink tips of his fingers poking out from his fingerless gloves. The bruises had almost gone from his face; in fact he was looking decidedly chipper.

'Hi, Colin. How's the photography going?'

'Great, thanks,' he said, greeting me with a huge smile. 'I'm really enjoying it. I was just telling Nick.'

I looked at him quizzically.

'He popped by to see me on his way back to the Council House,' said Colin.

'Oh, right,' I replied.

'He told me it was your birthday yesterday,' said Colin. 'You should have said.'

'Don't be daft. It's no big deal.'

'Well, happy thirty-first birthday, anyway.'

'Thanks,' I said, aware that Nick must have told him how old I was.

'I suppose it's a bit of a comedown after last year. Did you have a big party for your thirtieth?' asked Colin.

'Er, no. I didn't actually.'

'I remember Nick's thirtieth birthday party,' continued Colin, disregarding my reply. 'You and him dancing together, all in black you were, like that pair from *Grease*.'

I smiled politely, wondering if they'd talked about anything else apart from me. 'That was a long time ago, Colin.'

'I know. Nick remembered it, though. Even told me what song you were dancing to. "Brown Eyed Girl" by Van Morrison he said it was.'

'Um, probably. I can't remember.'

'Too many parties since, eh?'

'Yeah, something like that. Anyway,' I said, trying not to sound flustered. 'I'd better be getting back.'

'Of course,' said Colin. 'See you soon.'

I made my way back to the office, singing the song in my head. A lightness in my step. Remembering Nick's touch. Realising I was losing control again.

'Where are you off to?' asked Jonathan. It was early Saturday evening, we hadn't made any plans but he still looked disappointed as I put my shoes on.

'Out,' I said, feeling at once like a truculent teenager. Things had been rather strained since Thursday evening but I knew I should at least aim to be grown-up about this. I tried again.

'I'm going round to see Cayte. She's having problems with Jeremy, could do with a shoulder to cry on and a video and a pizza to cheer her up. I might stay over, I'll text you to let you know.'

Jonathan looked at me hard. Obviously not wanting me to go but deciding not to say so.

'No problem, I've got loads of marking to do,' he said. 'You have a good time.'

It felt like he was reading from the script of *How to*

make up after a row. What he didn't realise was how difficult he was making things by being so reasonable. I opened the door.

'Sarah,' he called after me. I turned round. 'You look really nice,' he said. I smiled weakly, for once wishing he hadn't paid the compliment.

I stepped outside, my black linen trousers flapping in the breeze, and made it to the car before I started hyperventilating. I looked at the reflection in the rear-view mirror. I wasn't sure whom I saw any more. Or who was in control.

The car started second time. I set off, switching in my head to automatic pilot, feeling less culpable that way. The Hagley Road was busy, people heading out for the night. I waited in the filter lane for the traffic lights to turn green, giving me permission to carry on. To cross to the other side. I remembered exactly where to go. I pulled up outside. I didn't have to go any further. I could turn round now and go home, make some excuse to Jonathan, no one need ever know. I wasn't going to do that though. Not now I was within touching distance.

I stepped out of the car, feeling as unsteady on my feet as if I was wearing a pair of stilettos. I wasn't. I'd dug a pair out of the depths of the wardrobe but had put them back because they looked far too obvious. FF shoes, Cayte called them. Follow me, fuck me. Not that Cayte was the fount of all wisdom. But on some things she was spot on.

I made my way up the short path and rang the bell to the ground floor flat, two short, sharp bursts. I waited for what seemed like a lifetime before the door opened and a scruffy Pooh bear glove puppet appeared round the edge accompanied by a squeaky voice asking, 'Did you forget someone?'

For a second it occurred to me that I might have got the wrong place. But I knew I hadn't because despite the Disney tones I recognised the voice.

'Er, no. I don't think so,' I said.

Pooh disappeared and Nick's head poked round the door frame, surprise etched in his face and his voice.

'Sarah. I thought you were . . .'

'Eeyore or Piglet?' I enquired.

Nick grinned. 'My daughter's not long left. She forgot Pooh.'

I nodded, trying to conceal the hurt clawing at my insides. We stood a moment longer, neither of us saying anything.

'So, is the offer still open?' I asked eventually.

'What offer?'

I froze for a second, worried it had been a joke.

'You wanted to help me celebrate my birthday.'

'Yes, of course. You said you were busy, though. I thought I'd been snubbed. That's why the flat's a mess and I haven't got any food in. I was going to order a takeaway but if you fancy going out . . .'

'It's OK,' I said. 'A takeaway will be fine.'

Nick smiled and held the door open. I stepped inside, straight into the main room, which was furnished as I'd imagined. Two small leather sofas, a round glass table and four high-backed chairs at the far end. Laminated wood floor, a couple of rugs, blinds at the windows. It could almost have been one of the show-rooms at Ikea, purchased as a job lot and reassembled at home. Almost but not quite. Because spread all over the floor were an assortment of plastic toys in bright primary colours, left where they'd been dropped in favour of something more exciting. A trail of havoc and happiness. They didn't do that at Ikea. It didn't come in flat-pack.

My eyes took it all in, registering it and having to readjust the mental image I had of Nick in my mind. And my gaze finally rested on the photograph on the coffee table. A smooth, flawless pixie-face beaming out of a mess of soft dark curls, eyes sparkling, lips smeared with what looked like chocolate ice cream. She was unmistakably Nick's daughter. I swallowed hard.

'Is that Jess?' I asked. Stupid question, said to buy me more time to compose myself.

'Yeah. I've got a proper studio one somewhere but I prefer that, it's more her.'

I nodded as if I was well versed on the posed versus natural child portrait issue.

'She's gorgeous.'

'Thank you. She's very bright for her age, too. Takes after her dad.'

He was smiling as he said it. The word 'dad' rankled. As did the pride in Nick's voice.

'I never had you down as the family type,' I said.

Nick looked as awkward as I felt.

'It was Amanda's idea, having a baby. I went along with it, stupidly hoping it might bring us closer together. It didn't work, of course. But at least we've got Jess. Wouldn't be without her for the world. I love her to bits. We both do.'

His eyes were glistening. Mine were too. Trying to put the images of him with his newborn daughter to the back of my mind.

'So you said you see her most weekends?'

'Yeah. I pick her up first thing Saturday morning and Amanda doesn't collect her until six. Sometimes she lets her stay over, if she wants a night out. She's seeing someone else, some hotshot corporate lawyer. Robert his name is. Jess calls him Rob.'

Nick said it through gritted teeth. It was obviously a sore point.

'Anyway,' he said, seemingly keen to change the subject, 'sit down and let me get you a coffee.'

I perched on the edge of the sofa as he disappeared into the kitchen, shutting the door behind him. Perhaps he needed a moment. I certainly did. This wasn't how it used to be at all. We were awkwardly tiptoeing around each other's feelings, trying not to trip over Tweenies tea sets in the process. Maybe I'd got it all horribly wrong. Made a complete fool of myself by turning up here. Maybe I should go. I stood up as the kitchen door swung open and Nick came back in carrying two mugs of coffee. Plain white mugs, no complications. I wondered if he usually used a 'Best Dad in the World' mug but had thought better of it.

'Look, if you want me to go I won't be offended,' I said. 'I should have rung first. I probably shouldn't have come at all.'

Nick put the mugs down on the coffee table, turned to me, placed his hands on my shoulders and pushed me back down on to the sofa.

'Sit down, shut up for a second and listen. I'm glad you came. I wasn't expecting it, that's all. I was thrown for a minute, maybe even a little nervous. But the one thing I'm sure of is that I don't want you to go.'

I nodded, reached for my coffee and went to take a sip, only I couldn't because it was still too hot. I pretended anyway before putting it down again.

'Right,' said Nick. 'Now we've got that sorted out, let's order some food. I don't know about you but I'm starving. What do you fancy, pizza, curry or Chinese?'

'Chinese, please,' I said. It was the one thing Jonathan didn't cook. And I felt the need to be different.

'Sure. Hang on a sec, I'll get the menu.'

He rang the order over while I drank my coffee, trying to stop my eyes from wandering back to the photo of Jess.

'It'll be here in fifteen minutes,' he said as he put the phone down. I nodded, hoping my stomach would have stopped turning somersaults by then.

'It was good to see Colin again,' said Nick. 'I was with him in the pub until closing time, you know, after you left on Monday evening.'

'Really? What did you talk about?'

'A lot of council chit-chat; he misses all that stuff. And

about how much we've all changed. Especially you. About how much older you seem, how serious you've become.'

'Yeah, well. That's what life does to you.'

'Or what you do to punish yourself,' said Nick.

I looked at him, floored by the accusation and the tone in his voice.

'What do you mean?' I said.

'You, going all worthy. Stopping doing all the things you used to enjoy.'

'No I haven't,' I said, putting my empty mug down with a clatter on the coffee table.

'You as good as admitted it, that night in the gym.'

'Three things I said I didn't do any more. That was all.'

'On top of the two I'd already found out about,' said Nick, his voice firm and measured compared to my squeak. I shifted on the sofa, feeling under an unwarranted attack.

'There's plenty of other stuff I still do.'

'Good. How's the salsa dancing going?' said Nick.

'Er, I don't go any more,' I said, my cheeks reddening. 'I don't really have the time.'

'Too busy helping Jonathan save the planet.'

'It's not like that.'

'It sure looks it to me.'

I got up from the sofa and walked over to the patio doors, staring out into the darkness. I didn't want to hear this. I'd put a lot of effort into creating the new Sarah. To make sure she was beyond criticism.

'So what do you want me to do?' I said, turning back to him. 'Start going to raves, take up rollerblading, join a circus?'

Nick looked at me reproachfully and shook his head. 'I'd simply like to see you enjoying yourself again. Having fun.'

I snorted a laugh.

'Remember what happened when I had fun?' I said. 'You were sitting next to him in the pub on Monday night.'

Nick got up from the sofa and walked over to me. He put one hand lightly on my shoulder.

'You can't hold yourself responsible for Colin's downfall, Sarah.'

'Why not? I'm the one who didn't vote for him. Because I was with you.'

He turned me round to face him, holding both of my shoulders now.

'Why don't you tell him? Come clean. It might ease that conscience of yours. I'm sure he wouldn't have a problem with it.'

'I will do,' I said, looking down. 'I'm just waiting for the right time.'

'I bet you've voted at every election since,' said Nick.

'Yep. Learnt my lesson. Not to listen to people who say no one ever loses by one vote.'

Nick managed a wry smile.

'I didn't mean to have a go, Sarah. I just want you to be happy. To stop beating yourself up about what happened in the past. Believe me, it doesn't do any good.'

'I know,' I said, looking him in the eye, feeling the warmth of his touch. We stood there a moment, both of us unsure about what to do next.

'I'd better get the table ready. The food will be here soon,' said Nick, letting go and disappearing into the kitchen.

He emerged a few minutes later with a bottle of red wine for himself, some sparkling water for me and a couple of candles in black metal holders.

'If we're going to do this, we may as well do it properly,' he said, placing the candles centrally on the table and lighting them.

I wasn't sure exactly what he was referring to. Or why I was here, having dinner in his flat. All I knew was that by the time the food arrived I had that familiar churning feeling in my stomach again.

'Cheers,' Nick said, raising his glass as we sat down at

the table. 'Happy birthday.' My hand was shaking as our glasses clinked together. I wondered if he noticed. Nick had only taken one bite of his spring roll when the doorbell rang.

'Sorry,' he said, jumping up from his seat. 'Better see who it is.'

I knew what he was thinking. That it could be Jess returning for Pooh. And if it was, Amanda would see me and would want to know what I was doing here and it could all get horribly messy and uncomfortable.

I peered round the corner as Nick opened the front door. It wasn't Jess and Amanda but a young woman, barely out of her teens, small and sinewy as she stood there in a black leather jacket, miniskirt and stilettos, holding a bottle of wine in her hand. She looked straight past Nick to me, her face dropping and her cheeks flushing.

'Oh, you've got company. I'm really sorry, I had no idea.'

'Hello, Charmaine,' said Nick. 'I'm not used to seeing you without your gardening overalls. What can I do for you?'

The young woman looked floored. Presumably she'd thought she had his exclusive attention. Had decided that tonight was the night she would make her move.

'Er, the lawn,' she stuttered eventually. 'I'm here to mow the lawn.'

It was a Saturday evening and pitch black outside. People didn't mow lawns in the dark in November, even I knew that. I suspected Nick knew it too, but he obviously decided to spare her blushes.

'Right,' he said, looking down at her stilettos. 'Are you sure you're going to be OK in those shoes?'

'Yeah, no problem. It won't take long, I promise. Sorry to have disturbed you.'

She disappeared from view and Nick came back into the room with a grin on his face.

'Before you say anything, I should point out that she's the gardener. And that the landlord hired her, not me.'

'And you had no idea?' I asked as he sat back down at the table.

'What, that she's got a crush on me? It's no big deal.'

'It obviously is to her. The poor girl was mortified. Imagine it, she's probably spent weeks working up the courage to do this. Her big seduction scene. And I go and screw it up by being here with you.'

'I'd have blown her out anyway,' said Nick with a twinkle in his eye.

'I hope so. She only looks about twenty-one.'

'You weren't much older, when I met you.'

'That was different,' I said. 'And a long time ago.'

We were interrupted by the whirr of an electric lawnmower. A few seconds later the outside security light flicked on to reveal Charmaine sinking into the ground in her stilettos as she defiantly pushed the Flymo across Nick's grass.

We both burst out laughing. 'Maybe she thinks the heels will aerate the lawn,' Nick said. 'Like those big spiky shoes they used to advertise in the Innovations catalogue.'

He raised his wine glass to Charmaine through the window before I pulled his arm down.

'Don't be a bastard,' I said. 'This will probably screw her up for life. It'll be her cross to bear for falling for you.'

'Honestly, I haven't done anything to encourage her,' said Nick as Charmaine disappeared into the darkness at the far end of the garden.

'You don't have to, do you? It's your magnetic charm. Women are suckers for it.'

Nick smiled and looked down at his plate.

'Is that what it was for you?' he said.

'Something like that.'

'And what about now?'

I pushed my bean sprouts around the plate. The truth was I didn't know why I was there. I knew I shouldn't be.

That it was wrong. And I didn't do bad things. Not any more. But I could hear the old Sarah calling, screaming to be let out. Hammering on the door of her tower as her prince prepared to ride off into the sunset alone.

'Nostalgia maybe,' I said. 'Or curiosity about what could have been.'

'Or still could be?' asked Nick, as the light flicked on again for Charmaine's return leg.

I wiped a trace of sweet and sour sauce from my lips and looked down at my plate, unable to answer.

'We were good together, Sarah. You know that.'

'So good you married someone else.'

Nick looked away, hurt pouring from his face. He took a few moments to gather himself.

'And why do you think it didn't work out?' he said.

'You drifted apart, you said so.'

'Because every time we made love I used to shut my eyes and see you.'

I dropped my fork on the plate and put my trembling hand under the table where he couldn't see it. He didn't mean that. He was saying it to make me feel better. To get me to lower my defences. To ease his way back into my life. I couldn't allow that to happen. However much I wanted it to.

'I'm with Jonathan now,' I said.

'No you're not,' Nick said, reaching out across the table to take my hand. 'You're here with me.'

I watched as his fingers closed round mine. Felt the connection restored between us. The buzz pulsing through my body, awakening something deep inside. I tried to pull my hand away but it didn't move. I didn't have the strength to resist any longer.

We waited until after the meal. Until after Charmaine had trudged away, her feet coated with mud. It seemed only decent. I didn't want to rub her face in it. I knew how that felt. We even waited until after our coffee. It wasn't self-control that made us wait. Certainly not on my part. It was guilt. The guilt of knowing Jonathan was sitting at home marking English essays, thinking I was doing my Good Samaritan bit with Cayte. I'd lied. I was about to cheat. But for the first time in years I'd found something which outweighed my guilt. My love for the man who was sitting next to me on the sofa. About to lean over and kiss me. And I knew he was going to. I remembered the taste of those kisses. The way you remember the taste of your first alcoholic drink.

'I've missed you,' he said. 'The real you.'

He kissed me on the lips. I started unbuttoning his shirt. That was the thing with the taste of your first drink. It inevitably left you wanting more.

It was gone midnight when Nick finally drifted off to sleep with me in his arms. I slithered out of bed, being careful not to wake him, and tiptoed into the living room, fumbling in the dark for my handbag. I turned my mobile on and started to text Jonathan that I was staying over. Before I had the chance to finish the phone beeped with a message. I called it up. 'Figure you're needed there. See you in the morning. Love you x'

I turned it off and crept back into bed with Nick. Hating myself as I did so.

Ten

I slipped out of Nick's bed before he woke the next morning. Which was strange really. All those times I'd dreamt of waking up next to him in the morning, having breakfast together. Yet when the opportunity finally came along I couldn't go through with it. In some ways I felt it would be worse than having sex with him. A bigger deceit. Sex you could blame on lust, primal forces beyond your control. Breakfasting in bed together, that was sheer selfish indulgence. There was no need for that.

I gathered my clothes from where they had fallen on the bedroom floor the night before and turned to look at Nick. He was lying with his arm draped over the hollow in the duvet where I had been until a few moments ago, his breathing deep and contented. Unaware I had left the warmth of his body. Had stepped out into the cold.

'Goodbye,' I whispered as I pulled the bedroom door shut behind me. Exhaling as I did so. I wanted a shower, to wash away the evidence before I went home, but I was too scared of waking him. So I dressed quickly and let myself out of the flat.

A small, unshaven man with a West Highland terrier emerged from the flat next door at the same time. He smiled at me, presumably thinking I lived there. Or maybe guessing that I didn't and therefore realising what I'd been up to. I hurried to my car, the guilt snapping at my heels.

I was still not entirely sure why I'd done it. Apart from

the fact that I loved him, obviously. All I did know was that somewhere along the line I had lost control. I remembered how it felt. The buzz you got at first. What I had not remembered, probably because I'd buried it so deep inside me, was how lousy it made me feel afterwards.

Jonathan was still asleep when I got in. I opened the bedroom door a crack to look at him. Curled up in the duvet, a picture of innocence, blissfully unaware of the betrayal which had taken place while he'd been sleeping.

I took my bathrobe silently from the back of the door, undressed in the lounge and padded into the bathroom, the tiles cold against my bare feet. I could feel the tension in my neck and searing down my back. I stepped under the shower, turning it on full power, allowing the heat to penetrate deep beneath my shoulder blades. I screwed my eyes up tight to try to relieve the pounding in my head, my body and brain telling me what I'd known all along. I wasn't cut out for affairs. Not then, not now. I'd suffered a relapse. And the important thing with relapses was not to make a habit of them.

I made breakfast for both of us. Nothing special, just cereal, toast and coffee. When Jonathan emerged from the bedroom, bleary-eyed, the look on his face made me want to cry.

'What's this?' he said.

'A crap way of saying sorry.'

'It's OK, I've dried out now.'

'No, I mean for last night.'

'Not a problem,' he said, running his fingers through his hair. 'Cayte needed you. How's she doing?'

'Oh, you know.'

It was tearing me apart inside, having to lie to him like this. Pretending I'd been doing something good. When actually I'd been bad again. Very bad.

'Have they split up, then? Her and what's his name?'

'Jeremy. No, not exactly. He's been seeing someone else.'

'Bastard,' said Jonathan. 'She may do my head in at times but she doesn't deserve to be treated like that.'

'No,' I said, 'she doesn't.'

I walked up to him and gave him a kiss on the lips. Then held him. Tighter than I'd held him for a long time.

'Are we OK now, then?' he asked when I eventually came up for air.

'Yeah,' I said, 'we're good. Now drink your coffee before it goes cold.'

When I got to the office on Monday morning, Nick was already there. I walked straight past him with my head down, scared that if I so much as acknowledged his existence I would suffer another relapse. I turned on my computer to find an e-mail from him. 'We need to talk.' I deleted it. I could do the cold shoulder thing pretty well.

If I didn't allow myself to look at him, speak to him or go within a few feet of him I figured I'd be OK. I could resist. I did have willpower, after all. And if I slipped back momentarily, all I would need to do was think of Jonathan's face the previous morning.

I managed to avoid all contact with Nick until mid-morning. I dropped my guard for a moment, venturing to the coffee machine. Not expecting to be ambushed.

'Was I that bad?' Nick said.

He was standing behind me, jingling change in his hand. I decided not to respond. Nick seemed unperturbed.

'First you creep out without saying goodbye, then you ignore me all morning. I must have committed some kind of sexual faux pas. Something women snigger at in *Cosmo*.'

I took my steaming cup of coffee and turned to walk away. Nick abandoned any pretext of wanting a drink and followed me.

'Only I didn't hear you complain at the time,' he said. 'Maybe I read the signs wrong but you gave a very good impression of someone who was enjoying herself.'

'Keep your voice down,' I said.

'I'm wondering if that's the problem,' continued Nick. 'That you enjoyed yourself too much. Which is why you are punishing yourself now. And punishing me as well.'

I carried on walking, Nick a couple of steps behind.

'The thing is,' said Nick, 'I'm not going to give up that easily. If you want I can chase you round the office but sooner or later you're going to have to talk to me.'

'OK,' I hissed, corralling him into the corner by the coat rack. 'Let's talk. It was a mistake, a big one. Nothing personal but it won't happen again. I suggest we both forget all about it and go back to being work colleagues.'

He stared at me and shook his head. He could see straight through me. I knew that.

'Don't do this, Sarah.'

'What?' I said, determined to keep up the pretence.

'Deny yourself any chance of happiness. You saw a glimpse of how good it could be and now you're slamming the door in its face.'

I looked away. Ravinder came in from a job and squeezed past us to hang his coat up.

'Morning, guys,' he said.

We both smiled and returned the greeting. I waited until he was out of earshot before replying.

'All I'm doing is putting a stop to this before Jonathan gets hurt. He doesn't deserve that. He's helped me pick up the pieces that you left shattered on the floor. I can't throw that back in his face, simply because you've turned up again. We made a mistake, Nick. One not to be repeated.'

I turned to walk away. Nick grabbed my arm.

'The only mistake I made was letting you go first time around,' he said.

The old Sarah sprouted wings and rose up to the ceiling, circling the newsroom in laps of delirious joy. Nick had declared his undying love for her. This was what she had waited for all these years. But within seconds Jonathan's face materialised in front of me and I found the strength to regain control. Sending her crashing back down to earth. Landing in a heap amongst a pile of coats and umbrellas. Dazed and bewildered.

'You walked away from me to stop someone you cared about getting hurt,' I said. 'I'm doing exactly the same thing.'

'I hope you don't end up regretting it as much as I do.' said Nick.

He let go of my arm and walked away, his touch fading with every step. I stood perfectly still for a moment, waiting until I felt steady enough on my feet to move. Before turning and burying my head in the coats, pretending I was looking for something in my pocket. While I wiped my tears on the sleeve of Nick's coat. Comforted by the smell of him on it.

I was not in the right frame of mind for our meeting with the MD. But having fought so hard to get it I could hardly ask him to postpone because I was having some kind of personal crisis. Jobs were at stake here. I had to be professional about this.

We gathered in the newsroom at three-thirty. Everyone had returned from their jobs, a pensive-looking Cayte included. The phones were put on divert. For the first time I could remember everything ground to a halt. People stood stony-faced as Terry emerged from his office with the MD by his side. They both looked decidedly uncomfortable.

'Right, everyone,' said Terry. 'For those of you who haven't met him, this is Mike Winters, our MD. He's kindly agreed to your request for a meeting. Please do him the courtesy of listening while he speaks. There will be a chance for you to put questions to him afterwards.'

Winters stepped forward. He looked like my old headmaster at school. Tall and severe with a grey moustache which had been clipped into shape with some precision.

He fixed his gaze on a point on the wall while he spoke. Not lowering himself to make eye contact with the proletariat. The script was pretty much as I'd expected. Lots of stuff about these being tough times for regional newspapers, figures detailing how the bottom had fallen out of the display advertising market and a call to be realistic about the need to downsize in order to survive. Predictable management bollocks, as Nick would have said once. Maybe he was thinking it now. I glanced over at him. He looked serious, sad even. Justifiably so. His was the first head on the block. And I'd already kicked him in the teeth that morning.

'Thank you, Mike,' said Terry, when Winters finally stopped talking. 'Now, any questions?'

Terry was looking at me as he said it. Knowing I'd be first in the queue but willing me not to go in too hard. He'd told me he didn't want a big confrontation. And I'd told him I didn't want my friends to lose their jobs.

'Mr Winters, how can you justify making ten people redundant when you received such a large bonus last year? Forty thousand pounds, according to the company accounts. That would pay two of these journalists' wages for a year.'

I could see the veins in Winters's neck bulging.

'I find your remarks rather inflammatory, young lady,' he said. 'I'm here to discuss your concerns about editorial. Not to be drawn into a debate about the rewards necessary to ensure this company retains its top executives.'

'Fine,' I said. 'Perhaps you could explain how decimating our editorial department is going to address the problem of falling circulation?'

Winters was rattled. His eyes locked in on me.

'I don't think you fully understand the seriousness of the financial situation we are in. Or of the need to react swiftly to changing market forces.'

He had gone into patronising, authoritarian mode. I

knew I had him now. And I was not going to let him off
the hook.

'I don't think you understand the impact these
redundancies would have on this department,' I retorted.
'And on the credibility of this newspaper.'

Winters gritted his teeth. 'We have had auditors and
management consultants in to look at this and they are in
agreement that this department can withstand a
significant reduction in staffing levels.'

The anger rose inside me. My pressure valve was close
to blowing.

'They aren't numbers, Mr Winters. It's people you are
making redundant. People who are standing here
listening to you now. I'll point some of them out to you,
shall I?'

'I don't think that will be necessary.'

'Oh, I think it is. That's Nick over there,' I said,
pointing. 'The best political editor we've ever had, worked
on the nationals. Tina on his left is a multi-award-
winning photographer. Ravinder at the back there,
fantastic contacts in the Muslim community, Cayte
standing next to me won the scoop of the year award
from the Birmingham Press Club last year. Would you
like me to continue?'

'I'd like you to show some respect,' he said sternly. 'I
came here to answer questions not to be verbally
attacked. You really are the rudest woman I've ever met.'

I was aware that everyone in the room was staring at
me. And that I was on the verge of losing it.

'All I'm trying to do is to save these people's jobs. These
are my colleagues, Mr Winters, my friends. It's their lives
you are about to mess up.'

My voice broke as the tears started trickling down my
face. Cayte put her hand on my shoulder. Terry looked
down at his feet. Winters reverted to staring at the spot
on the wall. It was Nick who broke the silence.

'I think Sarah has put our case forward very clearly,

Mr Winters. What we want is an assurance that if you don't get the voluntary redundancies you are looking for, there will be no compulsories.'

'That's not an assurance I can give you.'

'Can you improve the terms on offer for voluntary redundancies?'

'No. That's company policy. I think that's the end of our meeting.'

Winters strode out of the newsroom with a sly grimace on his face. I wiped my eyes, conscious that everyone was still looking at me. And that my reputation as the unflappable, cool-headed one of the office was in tatters.

'Well done, Sarah,' said Keith, giving a mocking handclap. 'Always a good move, showing the enemy how weak you are. How easily you can be destroyed.'

'Fuck off, Keith,' snapped Nick. 'This isn't the Gulf War, you know. At least Sarah had the guts to speak up for everyone. And to show that unlike you she's a member of the human race.'

A few people nodded; there was a muffled 'Hear, hear' from someone at the back. Keith sneered at Nick and retreated to his desk, no doubt already planning his retaliation. I fled the newsroom, heading for the relative safety of the ladies' loos. I slumped on to the floor next to the sinks, holding my head in my hands, and sobbed. The main door swung open behind me as Cayte burst in.

'Hey,' she said, sitting down next to me. 'Take no notice of Keith, everyone knows he's an arsehole.'

'He's right though, isn't he? I let you all down. Blubbing like that.'

'Don't be daft. You were brilliant. All you did was show you care. Don't go apologising for that.'

Cayte wrapped her arms round me and squeezed hard. I let her hold me for a minute while I waited for the tears to subside.

'Nick was good, speaking up for you like that,' she said when I eventually raised my head.

I started crying again. She got up from the floor, tore off several sheets of toilet paper and handed them to me as she sat back down again.

'What's the matter, Sarah? You wouldn't normally let things get to you like this.'

I hesitated. Part of me wanted to tell her about Nick, the other part was so twisted up with guilt I couldn't bring myself to admit what I'd done. I decided to reveal some of the story.

'Me and Jonathan,' I said. 'We're going through a bit of a rocky patch.'

Cayte frowned at me. 'But you two never even row.'

'We do now.'

'What about?'

'Oh, stupid stuff. He went into worthy mode, the night of my birthday. We had a big scene in the restaurant. I made him walk home on his own.'

'So that's why you snapped at me,' said Cayte.

'Yeah, I'm sorry. I guess you did hit a raw nerve.' I took a deep breath. 'The thing is I'm not sure if he's the right one for me any more.'

'What's brought this on?'

'Nothing specific. We just seem to be in a bit of a rut.'

'But he adores you,' said Cayte.

'I know. That makes it worse.'

'And he hasn't done or said anything to upset you? Apart from some little rant about coffee beans in a restaurant?'

'No. I'm sorry, Cayte. It must sound pathetic. There's you worried sick about Jazz and I'm getting in a state about nothing.'

'Exactly,' she said. 'So go home and put things right. It's nothing that can't be mended. You probably just need a holiday.'

I wiped my eyes and nodded. Cayte stood up and hauled me off the floor.

'Thanks,' I said. 'You go on home. I'll be fine now.'

She hugged me again before leaving. As soon as the door closed I sat back down on the floor. I stayed there for another ten minutes or so. Until I was sure Nick would have left.

When I got home I knew instantly that something was wrong. There was no smell of cooking drifting from the kitchen. No Black Sabbath or Led Zeppelin blaring away. A jacket and two scarves which had been casualties of my rush that morning were still lying on the floor where I'd left them. Jonathan was sitting on the sofa in the lounge, staring intently at the wall. As I walked up to him I noticed the red rims round his eyes. My first thought was that he knew. He must have found out somehow. I'd left some telltale sign. I was already bracing myself, starting to formulate my defence, as I asked the dreaded question.

'What's the matter?'

Jonathan turned to look at me, as if he hadn't noticed me come in until I'd spoken.

'That kid Daniel's in hospital,' he said. 'And I as good as put him there.'

I hesitated for a second, allowing the relief to surge through me and simmer down a little before I attempted to speak.

'What do you mean?'

'He told them he was gay, didn't he? Came out and admitted it, all grown up and responsible. A gang of them beat him up on his way home from school. Punched him, kicked in the stomach, the works. He's got a couple of fractured ribs and a busted jaw.'

'Poor kid,' I said. 'But you mustn't blame yourself.'

'I'm the one who told him it was OK to do it, aren't I? I let him down, Sarah. Could have got him killed.'

I sat down next to him on the sofa, put an arm round his shoulder. It was like trying to comfort a piece of driftwood.

'You did what you thought was best. You weren't to

know what would happen.'

'You did, though, didn't you? You said straight away it was a stupid idea, that it would only make things worse. I should have listened to you.'

I shook my head. 'It sounds like his mind was already made up. It probably wouldn't have made any difference.'

'It might have, though. He trusted me. That's why he confided in me. All that stuff I came out with about me being there to support him. I was on fucking gate duty, you know, and I still didn't hear or see anything. Fat lot of good I did him.'

Jonathan started to cry. Silently, though that didn't diminish the pain in the tears. I took my coat off and sank down on to my knees in front of him, gathering him to me. Feeling like a fraud on two counts, for trying to ease his pain when I could have caused him so much, and for allowing him to think I was the good one, that I had never made the wrong choice, the wrong judgement.

We stayed like that for a long time, Jonathan trembling in my arms, me stroking him, telling him it would be OK. Eventually he lifted his head.

'Thank you,' he said.

'It's what partners do.'

'No, I mean for putting up with me. I know I can be hard work sometimes. Especially when I'm feeling insecure. That's when I start coming out with all that stuff.'

'What, like in the restaurant?'

'Yeah. I get anxious in unfamiliar surroundings. So I revert to what I know best. What I feel safest with. It helps to disguise my lack of confidence.'

'You don't need to hide behind anything. Not with me.'

'I know. I must really piss you off sometimes.'

'Don't be silly,' I said. 'I'm lucky to have you. I know that.'

I buried my head in his shoulder. To cry my own silent tears.

Tuesday 27 May 1997

I am not very good at this. Being the other woman. It has been going on for nearly a month now and it is making me ill. Most of the time I feel sick with guilt. Scarlet woman, cheat, bitch. That is what I say to myself when I look in the bathroom mirror. I used to hate people like me, who trample over other women to steal their men. But now I am one of them. I have crossed to the other side. The only way I have found to stop the self-loathing is to tell myself that my behaviour is somehow virtuous. That Amanda and Nick are incompatible. That if he really loved her he wouldn't be doing this and I am therefore doing her a favour by encouraging him to see sense and break up with her sooner rather than later. I even have references for my 'why it's sometimes right to sleep with someone else's boyfriend' thesis. I cite the divorce statistics. Point out that people often find out too late that the person they thought was 'the one' isn't. And if they discovered it earlier, perhaps by having an affair with someone else whom they suspected might actually be the right one, Britain's divorce statistics would plummet. It is bollocks, of course. My desperate, flawed logic. But it is all I have to cling on to. This idea that he is the right one for me, that once we get this minor complication of his girlfriend sorted out we will be together for life. And that makes it all OK.

But for now we are not together. Not publicly at least. So we have to pretend. We tiptoe around each other trying to get the balance right. Between not smiling, lingering, speaking too much, in case we give the game away, or avoiding each other so much that the others guess there is something going on. I scream inside while we do it. Because I cannot scream out loud.

Nick walks past me on the way to the photocopier. My arms try to pull away from me and touch him. I have to drag them back, put myself in an imaginary straitjacket. It is the only way I can control myself. A month ago he would have said something, made some wisecrack or wound me up about a story I had written. But today he says nothing. Head down, blinkers on, to the photocopier and back in record time. No one would guess that in a few hours' time we will be having sex, desperately reacquainting ourselves with each other's bodies.

It has been three days. Three days too long. I exist for the time I spend with him. Alone. Away from the others, away from her. Mostly at my flat but occasionally, if she is away, at his. He is coming to mine this evening. Seven-thirty. He has told her he is going to the gym. But he will be working up a sweat with me instead. I shouldn't say that because it is not funny. I know that.

I busy myself for the rest of the afternoon. The phone tucked under my ear, banging the computer keys, scribbling furiously in my notebook. I am counting the seconds, filling time. Until I can be me. Because it is only when I am alone with him that I come alive. The rest of the time I am taking in air but not breathing. There is an umbilical cord between us that the others cannot see. He gives me nourishment, oxygen. I take it all in greedily. And me? I offer the promise of a better future, if he would only choose it.

I leave before him; he says goodbye as I walk out. Although it is not goodbye, more au revoir. I run a bath as soon as I get home. Sinking into the warm water, letting the smell of lavender waft over me. A sense of anticipation fills me, gently easing out the guilt. Telling me it is OK. Because he is the one. When I eventually haul myself out and get dressed, I do not put any underwear on. He likes it like that. And I like to please him. I pour myself a vodka, knowing it will help to chase the last of the guilt away. The aching inside me deepens, now that the time is near. I put the kettle on. It is all part of the ritual. Sometimes I actually get as far as making us mugs of coffee. Though we never drink it. It is always stone cold by the time we have finished.

The bell in my flat rings. I always worry it could be the last time. But he keeps on coming back. I don't hurry. I figure he will need a moment or two to compose himself. To switch whatever button it is he switches when he moves between Amanda and me.

I open the door without showing my face; as if I'm a celebrity, afraid of being snapped by the paparazzi outside. He steps inside, gym bag slung over his shoulder. The deceit entering with him. Neither of us says anything. He follows me upstairs, always I lead the way. We go through to my flat, shut the door and it starts. In a flurry, a panic, as if we might never get the chance to do this again. Because maybe we won't. Maybe every time he sees me he intends to tell me this is the last time, it is over. Maybe that's why it feels so desperate, so passionate, so much like the first time and the last time all rolled into one.

I can smell her perfume on him. It clogs up my throat and threatens to suffocate me but I have to suffer in silence. To even cough would be to acknowledge her existence. And he has left her now, he is in a kind of no man's land. It is my job to see him safely across to my side.

We don't even undress properly today. As soon as he realises I haven't got any knickers on I am up against the wall, my long, flowing skirt hitched up, my legs wrapped round him as he supports my weight. I have to undo his trousers for him. I cling on to his shirt, feeling the cotton creak under the strain. I hope it will rip, a sign of how powerful this is, how it is tearing me apart.

I am conscious of how thin the walls are in these flats but there is nothing I can do. If any of my neighbours are in they will have to turn the TV up louder, put a CD on at full volume, anything to block out the sound of someone having a better time than them.

Afterwards we sink down together on to the floor, me sitting astride him, picking the damp strands of hair from his face. It is only now he speaks.

'I hope you weren't walking round like that all day.'

'Why? Afraid I'll get a bit too close to one of the fans?'

'Just not sure I can control myself at work if I know what state you're in.'

'Don't worry, I save this for you.'

He smiles and kisses me on the nose. It is unmistakable. A fond kiss. It means more than all the passionate, sexual ones put together. Every now and then he slips up and says or does something like that. Always it makes him uncomfortable, perhaps realising he has crossed the line again. He gets round it this time by taking my top off, starting to fondle my breasts. If in doubt go back to the sex. Then we can kid ourselves that there is no more to it than that. When we both know that is not the case. Because we are not in this for laughs, for some cheap thrill. This isn't some seedy little office affair. It is something far deeper, far scarier. Because neither of us knows how to stop it. Even if we wanted to.

We end up lying on my bed, naked, breathing hard. My body entwined with his. We talk about all sorts of stuff. Not us, of course, that is strictly off limits. But we chat about other stuff: what, in Nick's words, 'this whole Cool Britannia bollocks' is about, whether Di and Dodi will get hitched and why Tony Blair is fast disappearing up his own arse. Idle speculation, all of it, but it passes the time. And I welcome anything that will give me a moment or two longer with him. I can't deal with him leaving straight after sex, before I've even got my breath back. It is cheap and nasty. Talk isn't cheap, talk is what real couples do. It makes it acceptable. Allows me to pretend it is a proper relationship. And that he isn't about to run back home to his girlfriend.

I trace my finger down his spine, wondering if she does this. And if it makes his flesh tingle in the same way. I tell myself it can't do. Otherwise he wouldn't be here, would he? It's always at this point I start to wobble. Knowing that any second now he is going to utter those three little words, 'I'd better go.'

I think of distraction techniques. We could have sex again, he has the stamina for it, but that is not really what I want. I could ask him to do some job for me, fix the dripping tap. But that would make me sound like a drag, some nagging wife. My role is to provide something different, whatever it is that is missing from his relationship. He never talks about her. I guess he thinks I don't want to hear it and mostly he is right. But occasionally curiosity gets the better of me. I want to peek into their private world, get some inkling of what it is that keeps him going back to her. Instead of staying with me.

I feel my jaw tighten. It will start clicking soon, though normally not until he is getting dressed. My pulse quickens, my breaths become shallow. It is fight or flight time. Though I feel incapable of uttering a word of resistance and I haven't got anywhere to run to. He is the one who does the running. I pretend it is fine, him leaving me like this. Keen not to appear desperate or clingy in case he does not find it attractive. I may hate his going but I have to ensure he keeps coming back.

'Anyway,' he says. I know the words which are coming next. I think he realises this because he doesn't even bother to say them. Just swings his legs over the side of the bed, starts prowling around the flat collecting his clothes. I watch his naked figure disappear into the bathroom and hear him peeing loudly. Sometimes I wish he would piss against the wall, mark his territory like some male tiger, fiercely protective of its mate. Any signal that this is his patch, that he is here to stay, not simply passing through.

Nick comes back into the room fully clothed. I am still lying on the bed naked, unable to bring myself to move. The last desperate act of a desperate woman. It doesn't work though. Mentally he has pulled the shutters down. He bends down to kiss me.

'I'll see you tomorrow.'

It is meant to sound casual while at the same time giving me the reassurance which he knows I want. It is easy for him though. Because what he means is that he will see me at work. It's not a commitment to me he is offering but to his job. The resistance weakens and something inside me cracks.

'Can't you stay a bit longer?' I say.

I know instantly from Nick's expression that I have done wrong, overstepped the mark.

'Please don't, Sarah,' he says. 'This is hard enough as it is.' And before I can think of what to say in reply he picks up his holdall and leaves, pulling the door to behind him.

I turn over in bed and bury my head in the pillow, seeking some kind of comfort, or perhaps to block it all out. I have done it now. I have upset him. Started wanting more than he can give. It has tipped the balance, changed the chemistry. We have both seen *Fatal Attraction*. It is a slippery slope from here; I am only a few moves away from becoming a bunny boiler.

I had to do it, didn't I? Had to go and spoil things. Except that is not really true. Things were already spoilt. They have been from the beginning. I simply pointed it out instead of carrying on ignoring it. I try to go to sleep but my head won't let me. It is in overdrive now, paranoia gear. What if that is it? What if he doesn't want to see me again? What if he is cursing me now as he drives back home? Looking forward to seeing Amanda, to fucking her tonight?

I get up and start busying myself, tidying, washing up. When there is nothing left to tidy I cook myself some dinner, nothing fancy, a pasta dish with sauce from a jar. It isn't worth going to any more trouble because I know I won't eat much. It has been the same for weeks now. Ever since I started sleeping with Nick. I sometimes manage a slice of toast in the morning but several times I have even thrown that back up. It is my body's way of punishing me. Of making me suffer for my sins.

I sit at the table, winding the spaghetti round my fork. It is good, spaghetti. Takes a lot of concentration. Several times it slips off my fork as I raise it, splashing blood-red tomato sauce against my white shirt. Stupid. I should have thought. Put a grubby old sweatshirt on instead. I kind of like it though. Seeing the red splattered down my front. It makes it tangible somehow. The hurt inside.

I manage about two mouthfuls. My stomach won't allow any more, although I was hungry an hour ago. My body no longer allows me to eat. No longer allows me to do lots of things, like breathe properly, sleep, function at anything like a normal level. It is making me ill, I know that. But I find a strange comfort in it. Because this wretched feeling inside is one thing she can't take away from me.

The night passes in the normal mixture of sleeplessness, as I taunt myself with images of the two of them together, and, when I do eventually drop off, the usual vivid dream. The one where we are making love in his bedroom when Amanda walks in, tears streaming down her face, and I stop to offer her a tissue. Before going straight back to the sex. Because that is the sort of woman I am now.

I wake with a start and haul myself out of bed,

deciding to skip breakfast. It is a different sensation that overpowers the hunger now. The one I get before I am due to see him. Like the leaving sensation but turned inside out, so that the excitement comes after the gut-wrenching hurt. It twists tighter as I climb the steps to the office, exploding inside me as I catch my first glimpse of him, bent over the office copy of the *Guardian*, the strands of dark hair like fingers caressing his face.

'Morning,' I say. It is directed at him but applies to everyone.

He looks up and returns the greeting with a smile. He has to smile, it would seem weird to the others if he didn't because he smiles at everyone. Usually the smile he saves for me is subtly different. Not to anyone else's eyes but apparent to mine. Today I am not so sure.

I sit down heavily in my chair. I feel like a mouse who is being toyed with by a cat. Unsure whether I am about to be finished off or whether I will have to endure another painful mauling first.

Joan buzzes past.

'Morning, Sarah,' she says, then stops to take a second look. 'Are you OK?'

'Yeah, fine.'

'Only you look a bit pale.'

'I'm fine,' I say again.

But I am not fine. My hands are clammy, my legs weak. Something is draining from my head and running out the end of my toes. The room starts spinning. I realise what is going to happen but not in enough time to stop it.

I come to as Joan wafts a handkerchief in front of my nose. I am sitting on the floor, my legs astride – like I was last night. Only this time Nick is standing above me looking concerned. 'Fuck' his eyes are saying.

'She's back with us,' Joan says. 'Give the girl some space, she needs to get some air.'

Dave and Karen go back to their desks.

'I'm OK,' I say. Joan hands me a glass of water.

'You had us worried there,' she says. 'Do you want me to call a doctor?'

'No, I'll be fine. Didn't have time for breakfast this morning, that's all.'

Joan looks at me and then at Nick who is hovering above us. I think she knows more than she is letting on. They help me back up on to my chair.

'Give me ten minutes, I'll be fine,' I say. 'Nothing a bacon buttie can't put right.'

'You're not staying here,' says Joan. 'You're going home. Nick will take you, you're not fit to drive.' She fixes Nick with a look, making it clear he doesn't have a say in the matter.

'Joan's right,' he says. 'You're best off at home.'

I don't argue. The chance of ten minutes alone with Nick is too good an opportunity to miss. Nick picks up my bag and the two of them help me down the back stairs. It is only once we are out of earshot of the others that Joan speaks.

'I don't know what's going on between you two but I suggest you put an end to it right away. Before someone gets hurt. Seriously hurt.'

We nod solemnly. Joan turns and goes back upstairs. We set off for the car park, Nick holding my arm like I am some old lady he is escorting across the road. I get into the passenger seat, feeling the colour start to return to my cheeks.

'Why aren't you eating?' he says.

Nick doesn't usually ask dumb questions. I struggle to find an answer he might want to hear as he pulls away.

'I was in a rush.'

'When was the last time you weren't in a rush?'

'Yesterday lunchtime. I had a sandwich.'

I see him shake his head. I'm not sure who he is mad at, me or himself. I assume it is me.

I know this is my chance. I have probably already

blown it so I have nothing left to lose. And he can't leave for at least a few minutes.

'I'm not cut out for this,' I say. 'I can't turn my feelings on and off depending when you're available. I don't work like that.'

'I know,' says Nick. 'I know.'

'I can't go on like this. It's making me ill. I want you to choose. Me or her.'

The ultimatum startles me probably as much as it does Nick. He is staring straight ahead at the road but I can see the muscles in his neck tense, his eyebrows rise. We sit in awkward silence until he pulls up outside my flat. I wonder if he is thinking about what to say or if he is simply pretending he didn't hear. He sees me up the stairs and in the front door.

'Have you got food in?' he says.

I nod.

'Then please eat something,' he says. 'I can't bear seeing you like this.'

'I meant what I said, Nick. I need a decision. Soon.'

He nods, turns and leaves. The stomach-churning starts again.

Eleven

'You're off early,' said Jonathan as I reached for my coat.

'Yeah, I'm going to the hostel where Colin lives.'

'Why?'

'He wasn't on his pitch all last week. I want to make sure he's OK.'

'Are you sure it's safe?'

'The mobs of marauding vagabonds, you mean?'

'I can't imagine they're very nice places,' Jonathan said. He'd been like this since the Daniel thing. As if having failed him it was now his duty to protect me.

'I can look after myself, remember. I'll be fine. Are you going to be OK at this meeting today?'

Jonathan nodded. He had owned up, of course. About knowing that Daniel was being bullied. The school had launched some kind of internal investigation. The head had told him she needed to show the governors she'd taken action.

'I can't say I'm looking forward to it,' said Jonathan. 'But I've got to stand up and take anything that's coming to me.'

It had hit him very hard. He'd been to visit Daniel in hospital and even written to the boy's parents to apologise. I was beginning to see that I didn't have the monopoly on feeling guilty.

'Well, good luck. I hope it goes OK. I'll be thinking of you.'

I gave him a kiss and a hug before leaving. I

was trying. Trying very hard. But somehow not hard enough.

The Digbeth Hostel for the Homeless was actually an old bingo hall. There was a headline in there somewhere about people who didn't have a 'house'. I was still trying to think of it as I pushed the buzzer.

'Hi, Sarah Roberts here to see Colin Leake,' I said. Silence at the other end. Maybe they didn't allow people in who turned up to see their mates. For all they knew I could be a drugs mule.

'I'm his social worker,' I added.

'Wait in the foyer,' a male voice said. The door clicked open and I went in. A musty smell greeted me. An intoxicating combination of dust, sweat and stale urine. The foyer was faded grand, way past its prime, much like many of its temporary occupants. A cleaner shuffled past me, metal bucket clanking, fag hanging out of the corner of her mouth, a clear winner in a stereotypical charlady audition. After a few minutes a bemused-looking Colin emerged from behind the double doors at the end of the corridor and walked in an odd crab-like fashion towards me.

'Social workers never call before nine,' he said.

I gasped as I caught sight of the two-inch scar on his left cheek.

'Oh, Colin. What's happened now?'

'I'm OK. A minor altercation. Comes with the territory.'

'That's all right then. As long as you're happy getting beaten up every few weeks.'

'Twice, Sarah. It's only happened twice.'

'Is that why you weren't on your pitch last week?'

'Yeah. Wasn't feeling up to it. And I didn't want to frighten my regulars away.'

'Was it the same lads? Did they take your money again?'

Colin shook his head. 'The camera. He took the camera.'
'Who did?'
'A chap in here called Razor. Named so for obvious reasons. Took exception to me taking photos. Decided to rough me up a bit.'
I groaned out loud. Every time I tried to help him I ended up making things worse.
'What did he do with it? The camera.'
'Sold it, probably. You could buy a nice bit of gear with the proceeds from that.' Colin looked down at his feet and sighed deeply. 'It's a shame, I'd taken some nice stuff. Two rolls of thirty-six. People in here, people sleeping rough on the streets, other sellers. They were in the camera bag, he took the whole thing.'
'Can't you get the films back?'
'And how exactly would that work? "Excuse me, mate. That stuff you nicked after slashing my face. Couldn't give me some of it back, could you?"'
'Didn't you report it to the staff here?'
'I don't want to get a reputation as a grass.'
I shook my head. There was only one thing for it.
'OK, where is he?'
'Who?'
'This Razor guy.'
'Still up in the dorm. You don't want to get involved, Sarah.'
'Ah but I do, that's the whole point.'
I marched up to the security man sitting in what appeared to be a broom cupboard. 'Is it OK if I go up to the dorm with Mr Leake? I need to go through some forms with him, somewhere we can sit down.'
He shrugged and turned back to his copy of the *Sun*. I took it as a yes. A reluctant Colin led the way up a narrow flight of stairs to a dingy dormitory with three rows of beds.
'Seriously, Sarah. He's a nasty piece of work. Got a bit of a temper on him.'

'So have I.'

'You could make things worse.'

'Or I could make them better. Which one is he?'

Colin sighed and, sensing I wasn't going to let it drop, pointed to a middle-aged man with short-cropped hair who was sitting on a bed in the far corner. I strode over to him, trying to give off an air of confidence even if I didn't feel it.

'Excuse me,' I said, having been unable to decide whether to address him as Razor or Mr Razor. Razor looked up from the cigarette paper he was rolling. 'I understand you took something that belonged to a friend of mine. A camera.'

'What's it to you?'

'It was a gift from me. I'd like to know what you've done with it.'

Razor laughed in my face. 'Sold it to David fucking Bailey.'

'Have you still got the films? They were in the bag.'

'Why? You wanna buy them off me?'

'I thought you might like to give them to me, actually. As a gesture of goodwill.'

Razor laughed again, tipping his head back so I could count the numerous fillings which adorned his teeth. I was aware of Colin standing behind me, groaning quietly.

'Who do you think I am, Father fucking Christmas?'

'I know Colin would be very grateful. He's been very good about the whole business, considering.'

'Considering what?'

'It's his dream, you know. To be a photographer. Do you have any dreams?'

'Only ones where that girl from the film is running along the beach, tits bouncing all over the place. You know her, short, funny name.'

'Bo fucking Derek,' I replied.

'That's the one.'

'Tell you what,' I said. 'You give me back those films,

I'll get you more photos of Bo than you know what to do with.'

Razor's eyes lit up. 'Topless ones?'

'Er, yeah. The works. Make your eyes pop they will.'

'Hang on a sec.'

Razor got up, went round to the other side of his bed and started rummaging in a large cardboard box.

'This what you're after?' he enquired, holding up two film canisters.

'Yep. Keep the cases, they're good for tobacco. I only need the films.'

Razor took them out and handed them to me.

'Thanks very much. I'll have the Bo photos to you by the end of the week. Delivered in a brown envelope. Discretion guaranteed.'

Razor winked at me and nodded at Colin before turning his attention back to his roll-up. I walked away, allowing my heart to begin to return to its normal rate. Colin was grinning at me.

'Where you going to get pictures like that?'

'No idea,' I said. 'But I'm a journalist. I'll find out.'

'What are you going to do with those?' he said, pointing at the films.

'Get them developed at work,' I said. 'They'd better be good, mind.' Colin smiled. 'Thanks, Sarah.'

'No problem,' I said. 'I owed you one. A big one.'

I made my way down the stairs, wondering if Nick was right. If I'd only done it to ease my guilt. In the hope my good deed would help to cleanse my soul. And take my mind off the bigger issue. Of why I'd let Nick go again. When I still wanted him.

Roger was on his own in photographic, staring gloomily at his laptop and smoothing his bald spot as if he still possessed hair.

'What's up?' I said.

'Stupid things. Never do what you want them to do.

Waste of time if you ask me. I could have printed these
out by hand in half the time.'

'You miss it, don't you, Rodge? The old black and
whites in the dark room, creating a little bit of magic in
there.'

Roger's eyes glazed over for a second before he looked
up at me.

'What do you want, Roberts?'

'Just a couple of films printed up. Black and whites,
nice stuff. Taken by that friend of mine I was telling you
about. On your old camera.'

'And what's in it for me?'

'Nostalgia value, the chance to get your hands dirty.'

Roger was still looking at me. He drove a hard
bargain.

'And I'll get one of the computer nerds over to have a
look at your laptop.'

Roger's face brightened and he took the films from my
outstretched hand.

'I'll do them for you at the weekend, when it's quiet,' he
said. 'Heard any more from your friend Rupert Bear?'

'I have actually. Clare Short's taken up his case. The
health authority is carrying out an investigation into his
claims.'

'That lot must be as gullible as you are,' he said.

'Rupert will come through for me. You'll see.'

Roger shook his head and went back to bashing his
laptop. I alerted one of the IT guys of the urgent need of
his expertise and went back to my desk. Nick looked up.
I'd hardly spoken to him since the morning after.
Relations were strained to say the least. But I knew I
should tell him. He'd want to know. And he might be able
to help.

'Colin's OK,' I said. 'But he's been slashed with a razor
by some guy in the hostel.'

Nick winced. 'Bloody hell. His luck doesn't get any
better, does it?'

'No. The guy took his camera. He's already flogged it but I managed to get the films back.'

'Well done you. Birmingham's very own Robocop. I take it you used brute force?'

I smiled at him. Surprised how easily we had slipped back into the banter.

'Er, no. Bribery actually. Told him I'd get some mucky photos of Bo Derek in return. She's probably never done any. Someone who looks like her would do. Got any ideas?'

'Of course. You don't spend the best part of seven years shifting for the nationals without learning a trick or two. Hang on a minute. I'll find something on the web.'

By the time Cayte returned to the office and glanced over my shoulder half an hour later I had a picture of a Bo Derek lookalike with cornrow hair and an ample chest on my screen.

'What the hell are you doing?' Cayte asked.

'Researching porn on the Internet.'

'That's what they all say when they get caught.'

'Nick found it. It's a favour for Colin, or not for him exactly, for one of his mates. Well, not a mate exactly. Oh, it's a long story.'

Cayte looked from me to Nick and shook her head. 'For once I don't think I want to know.'

My phone rang. It was Terry. I knew this even though he didn't say anything. I could tell by the sighs on the other end of the line. I felt like a Samaritan, waiting for the caller to pluck up the courage to speak. I tried to peer into the goldfish bowl but Terry had his back to me, slumped over his desk.

'Are you OK?' I asked eventually.

'You'd better come in,' he said. That was the good thing about working for the Samaritans. You never had to come face to face with the person on the other end of the line.

I entered Terry's office. When he turned to face me I wished I'd brought a syringe with me, filled with something that would put him out of his misery. The deadline for voluntary redundancies had passed at noon. I guessed it was more bad news.

'So how many took it?' I said.

'Just Phil.'

'I thought you said you'd had others in to discuss terms.'

'I did. None of them took it though.'

I looked over to Cayte's desk. She was tapping away on her keyboard, breaking off every now and again to take a sip from her ridiculously large bottle of mineral water, oblivious of the fact that her appeal for clemency had been refused.

'Cayte's going to be gutted.'

'I don't want to lose her either. Or any of the others for that matter.'

'Well do something about it then.'

I didn't mean to lose it. It just slipped out. The way everything did at the moment. Terry threw his hands up in the air and let them fall with a thud on to his desk. The nearest he could get to thumping it.

'We've been though all this. I don't have an option. You heard what Winters said.'

I wasn't used to seeing him react like that.

'Sorry,' I said. 'I didn't mean to have a go. I'm upset, that's all.'

'You and me both,' said Terry.

'So when are you going to give them their notice?'

'Tomorrow, I guess. Soon as Doreen's done the letters.'

'We'll have to call a union meeting afterwards.'

'I know. You're not going to go on strike or anything daft are you?'

I rolled my eyes. 'The only person doing anything daft in this place is the tall guy upstairs who drives a Mercedes.'

'You mean the one who won't set foot in editorial ever again, thanks to you.' The corners of Terry's mouth were almost turning up as he said it.

'Yeah,' I said. 'That's him.'

I walked out of Terry's office and went back to my desk. Cayte and Nick were sharing a joke together. I sat down and started typing. Knowing they wouldn't be laughing tomorrow.

Najma was getting out of her car when I pulled up outside our flat that evening.

'Hi,' she said. 'Haven't seen you for a while. How's things?'

'Fine,' I said, locking the car door and walking over to her. 'Just been busy with work stuff. All a bit hectic at the moment.'

'You look like you could do with a break,' she said, pulling her coat collar up against the cold. Perhaps Cayte was right. Maybe all Jonathan and I needed was a good holiday to rejuvenate our relationship.

'Chance would be a fine thing.'

'Why don't you go away for Christmas?' Najma said. 'Book some cosy old hotel in the middle of nowhere. Just the two of you. It would do you the power of good.'

I wondered for a moment if she suspected that something was wrong. Maybe she'd spoken to Jonathan, maybe he'd said something.

'Jonathan's mum is coming to us on Christmas Day,' I explained. 'It's all been arranged. Can't really back out now. And I'm working on Boxing Day.'

'That's a shame,' said Najma. 'Maybe you'll have a chance to get away for a few days over New Year. Before the schools go back.'

'Yeah,' I said, though I knew we wouldn't. 'So what are you and Paul doing for Christmas?'

'We're going to stay with his parents in Brighton. Should be very romantic, strolling along the beach on Christmas morning.'

I nodded. Not really wanting to think about what I'd be missing out on while Dawn was berating turkey farming.

'Will that be the first time you've met his parents?'

'Yeah,' she said. 'I'm a bit nervous about it but Paul says not to worry. Reckons they'll love me. I hope he's right. We're staying for a week.'

She smiled. A big, head-over-heels-in-love kind of smile. I wished I had one of those in my repertoire.

'So don't your family mind?' I said. 'About not seeing you?'

Najma glanced down and fiddled with the tassels on the end of her scarf.

'No. They don't really celebrate Christmas. As long as I put in an appearance at Eid, I'm all right.'

'Have they met Paul yet?' I asked.

'No,' she said. 'Not yet. Anyway I'd better let you get in. It's freezing out here. Say hi to Jonathan for me.'

She hurried up the path, her long black coat almost trailing on the ground. I wondered what Nick would be doing for Christmas. Whether he'd be on his own.

I let myself in. Jonathan had at least made it to the kitchen. Though Ozzy Osbourne was still noticeable by his absence and whatever it was he was cooking looked unusually limp and pathetic as it was stirred into submission in the pot.

'Hi, how did it go?' I asked.

He leant over to kiss me, though even his kiss tasted lifeless.

'OK, I guess. I got a written warning for not following the anti-bullying guidelines. It'll be on my records, of course. Make it difficult if I want to move schools.'

'I'm sure you'd be able to explain,' I said, rubbing his shoulder.

Jonathan shrugged.

'At least Daniel's making some progress,' he said. 'Should be back at school after Christmas. He's going to be allowed to leave fifteen minutes early every afternoon so he can get home in one piece.'

'That's big of them. What about the bullies?'

'Oh, the head's washed her hands of it. Said that because it happened outside the school premises it's a police matter. And as Daniel won't grass them up, they're going to get away with it.'

I raised an eyebrow, unused to the tone of resignation in his voice. He looked a broken man. Daniel's injuries were at least healing. I sensed Jonathan's were going to take a while longer.

'Well, at least it's over with now. You've got to try to put it behind you.'

Jonathan snorted and turned back to the pot of whatever it was I was going to be eating shortly.

'There won't be any rice with it, I'm afraid,' he said. 'They were out of organic.'

I managed to stop myself mentioning that a packet of Uncle Ben's would have done. He was going through a tough time. I was going to have to make allowances.

Saturday 7 June 1997

I am not going. I have changed my mind five times since I woke this morning but as I stare at yet another untouched lunch, I know the decision is final. Nick's thirtieth birthday party will happen without me. I desperately want to be there with him, to share in the celebration. Especially on the actual day of his birthday. But I cannot bear the thought of seeing him with her. Properly with her. Dancing and smooching and kissing and being all over each other. That is what it will be like. And I can either stand there and watch or stay home and play some loud music to drown out the hurt. I am opting for solitude over torture. It is not much of a choice.

The party is in the function room at O'Neill's. Everyone else is going. All the gang from work, loads of his union mates, even some contacts, people like Colin Leake. Nick thinks I am going too. 'See you tomorrow,' he said. I nodded. Unable to tell him of the turmoil going on inside me. He still hasn't given me an answer to my ultimatum. But we haven't seen each other since. Not properly. Not outside work. I take it that means he is still making his mind up. Though maybe it means he has chosen her and simply hasn't been able to face telling me yet. I should end it myself, of course. You don't give ultimatums unless you are prepared to carry them through. But I love him so much I am not strong enough to do it. This relationship, if you can call it that, has sapped every ounce of strength from me. I am tired.

Emotionally drained. I will simply have to wait to be put out of my misery.

I will make up some excuse about why I didn't go on Monday. Say I had a stomach bug, some twenty-four-hour thing. Nick will know the real reason but hopefully the others will buy it. They will all be talking about the party, of course, but I think I can cope with that. It is the being there I have a problem with.

I scrape the contents of my plate into the bin. I hear my mother telling me that wasting good food is sinful. Although no doubt that would pale into insignificance on my mother's sin scale compared with having an affair with someone else's boyfriend.

The phone rings. It is Joan.

'Hi, Sarah. Wondered if you wanted a lift to Nick's do tonight.'

The offer takes me by surprise.

'Er, I don't think I'm going.'

My reply does not come out as certain as I had intended. Nor do I sound at all poorly.

'Oh. Why's that?' asks Joan.

'I'm not feeling brilliant. Think I'm going down with something. I should probably get an early night.'

'Nonsense. Don't be a party pooper. What you need is a good night out, blow the cobwebs away.'

I suspect Joan knows the real reason I don't want to go. But neither of us is going to say it.

'I'm not sure I'm up to it.'

'I'll do you a deal,' says Joan. 'I'll pick you up at eight. If you feel rough later I'll ferry you home. You can't say fairer than that.'

'I don't want to spoil your night.'

'The only way you'll spoil it is by not turning up. None of the other buggers will dance with me. Reckon I show them up.'

I manage a faint laugh. 'I probably won't stay long.'

'No problem. See you at eight.'

Joan puts the phone down before I get the chance to protest any further. Cinderella will go to the ball. A tiny part of me is excited, mentally scanning my wardrobe to decide what to wear. The rest of me is already regretting changing my mind.

We are among the first to arrive. The function room still feels like a function room rather than a party venue. Empty chairs arranged neatly round tables, the air free of cigarette smoke, the floor squeaky clean. Nick is deep in conversation with the DJ, both with their heads bowed, rummaging in boxes. I scan the room but can't see Amanda, though she must be here somewhere.

'I'll get the drinks in,' says Joan. 'You grab a table before everyone else arrives. One near the disco. I like my music loud.'

I do as I am told. As I sit down I notice Colin standing on his own in the corner. He hasn't been into the office much since the general election. I see him at council meetings but it is not the same. I suspect he is still struggling to come to terms with the defeat. He is wearing jeans and a crumpled stripy shirt. He doesn't appear to have shaved for a couple of days. I beckon him over. He seems pleased to see a familiar face.

'Come and join us,' I say. 'Joan's at the bar. Can we get you one in?'

'I'm OK, thanks, Sarah,' he says, raising a half full pint glass. 'I'm pacing myself. Nick tells me they've got a licence extension until midnight. Bloody ridiculous, if you ask me. What with this being in a residential area.'

I smile. Clearly he is more at home at council committee meetings than parties. Joan comes back from the bar with our drinks.

'Hello, Colin,' she says. 'I expect to see you up on the dance floor later. Always had you down as a bit of a secret groover.'

Colin shakes his head.

'I don't think so,' he says. 'Dancing's not really my thing. No sense of rhythm and two left feet, I'm afraid.'

I nod distractedly. Nick has stopped talking to the DJ and is walking towards us. He is wearing black jeans and a black T-shirt. He looks good enough to eat.

'Hey, three of my favourite people,' he says. 'Glad you could all make it.'

He kisses Joan, shakes Colin's hand warmly then bends down and kisses me on the cheek. His hand squeezes my bare shoulder as he does so. It is over in a second. But the spark leaves a tingling sensation all the way down my arm.

'Happy birthday,' I say, handing him a card. I wanted to get him a present as well but decided the others would think it inappropriate. It is a Far Side card. I laughed when I read it in the shop. Nick opens the envelope and laughs too.

'Thanks, Sarah,' he says. 'All the others have been jokes about my age. Anyone would think I was turning forty or something ancient like that, eh, Joan?'

'Piss off, Hardwick. I can still outlast you on the dance floor,' says Joan.

'We'll see about that later,' Nick says. 'What about you, Colin? How long till you hit the big four-zero?'

'Er, three more years, if I remember rightly.'

I try not to look surprised. Colin looks at least fifteen years older than Nick.

'Mind you, it's OK for a politician,' says Nick. 'Maturity will get you more votes. Lets you play the experience card.'

'I don't know,' says Colin with a shrug. 'They all seem to be getting younger these days. Look at Blair and all his babes, or whatever they call them. Sandra reckons I'll be past my prime after the next general election.'

'Don't you believe her,' says Nick. 'Anyway, where is Sandra tonight?'

Colin hesitates.

'She's, er, having a quiet night in. Parties aren't her thing.' He looks down and shuffles his feet. I sense all is not well at home.

'And where's Amanda?' Joan asks Nick, in an apparent effort to change the subject.

'Oh, she's coming later with her sister. I left her getting ready. Didn't want to be late for my own party. I'd never hear the end of it.'

He is avoiding eye contact with me, maybe because he is talking about Amanda. Maybe because he still hasn't decided. Or maybe because he has.

'Anyway, I'd better go and mingle with my other guests,' he says. 'I'll catch up with you later.'

I watch him walk off, my card still in his hand. His touch still on my shoulder. The ache still deep inside. The DJ puts on 'Love Shack' by the B52s.

'Come on, Sarah,' says Joan. 'If you'll excuse us, Colin. I think it's our duty to start off the dancing.'

I allow Joan to drag me up with her. She is indeed an enthusiastic dancer, whooping with delight as she struts her stuff. But she is having far too much of a laugh to be embarrassing. Nick is chatting to someone at the bar but every now and again he glances over at us and smiles. I am not sure if he is smiling at me or Joan's dancing.

Half an hour or so later Colin gestures that he is getting another round in. We mouth our requests to him. Neither of us wants to stop dancing. The music is good. The Stones, the Clash, the Jam and some Motown, soul and eighties stuff thrown in. All clearly Nick's choices. I have lost sight of him for the moment. It doesn't matter though. I can still see him inside my head. And feel his presence in the room. The dance floor is getting crowded. I become separated from Joan, hemmed into a corner by a couple with flailing arms and legs. The air is getting heavy: a heady mix of alcohol, sweat and smoke. Van Morrison's 'Brown Eyed Girl' comes on. I love this track. I shut my eyes for a second, losing myself in the music. I feel a hand fall lightly on my hip, a second later another hand the other side. I know who it is without looking. He is singing in my ear, 'Sha, la, la, la, la, la, la, la, la, la, la, te, da.' I allow my eyes to open, half scared it might be a dream. He is here though, right behind me, our bodies moving together as if they have been programmed by computer. I glance over my shoulder. For once he is not smiling. He is looking at me with hunger in his eyes.

'I've missed you,' Nick says.

I smile at him as I toss back my hair. Allowing myself to get carried away. To think that means he has chosen me. I don't push it. I'll wait for him to tell me when the moment is right.

'Good. I've missed you too,' I say.

'You look fantastic,' says Nick.

I am wearing an off-the-shoulder top and tight-fitting black trousers. I figured it wasn't a little black dress kind of do.

'Thanks.' He pulls me in closer, our hips gyrating to the music. I have a theory that you can tell how good people are in bed by how they dance. Nick proves the theory. And right now I want to go to bed with him. I know I shouldn't be doing this. Even dancing with him, let alone anything else. But I am oblivious of everyone around us. This is about me and Nick. About how good we are together. Van the man merges into Simple Minds' 'Don't You Forget About Me'. Somehow the moment is lost. A handful of people leave the dance floor. I am aware we are suddenly conspicuous. Nick lets go of my hips and moves away slightly. I see her at the same moment Nick does. A vision in red entering the room. The only woman I've ever known who can carry off a little red strapless number without even bordering on tacky. Amanda is here. The pendulum swings again.

'I'll catch you later,' Nick says. And with that he has gone. I realise my legs have stopped moving. I decide to sit down.

'Thanks,' I say to Colin as I pick up my drink.

'I bet you need it after all that dancing,' he says. 'You and Nick reminded me of that scene in *Grease*.'

'Oh,' I say. I hadn't realised Colin could see us.

'The one at the end where they're both dressed in black and dancing together. What's the song they sing again?'

' "You're the One That I Want",' I say, still with one eye on Nick and Amanda.

'That's it. Sandra loves that film. Must have watched it dozens of times.'

I nod. Amanda has her arm round Nick's waist. He can't take his eyes off her. I am thinking of the other scene in *Grease*. The one where Danny and Sandy are doing really well in the dancing competition until Cha Cha steams in and steals him from her. I gulp my drink down, depositing the empty glass on the table with a thud.

'Can I get you another, Colin?'

'Er, no. I'm fine, thank you,' he says. 'Haven't really started this one yet.'

I make my way to the bar. Nick is chatting to Amanda and her sister. The sister is pretty without being a head turner. It is Amanda who is getting noticed. Nick has his arm draped round her shoulders now. It is starting to hurt. Starting to seem like a bad idea to be here.

Karen and Dave from work both arrive while I am at the bar. Karen with her boyfriend in tow, tall and equally earnest-looking, and Dave clutching his roll of toilet paper.

'Sinuses playing up again,' he says. I nod. Even less interested than usual. They help me back to the table with the drinks. Joan is still dancing, the Duracell batteries showing no sign of running out. The DJ fades out Frankie Goes To Hollywood.

'A few announcements to make, folks,' he says. 'The first is that the buffet is now open.' Somebody at the back cheers. 'And your host Nick would like a quick word.'

The dance floor clears. Joan sits down and takes a swig of her Diet Coke. Nick hurries up to the mike, Amanda trailing a few steps behind.

'Just wanted to thank you all for coming to my birthday bash,' Nick says. 'And for all the rude cards and not so rude presents. And to say I expect to see some serious partying from now until midnight.'

He steps back and goes to walk away. The DJ stops him.

'Hang on a minute, Nick. Someone else would like a word.'

Amanda steps forward. She is smiling one of those nervous-looking smiles. I notice that her hand is shaking as she holds the mike.

'Nick has no idea what this is about,' she says.

He shakes his head. He appears anxious. I wonder if she's got him a stripogram girl. I can't imagine he'd like it if she has. Though he would probably go through with it, simply so she didn't lose face.

'But I wanted to take this opportunity to ask him a question,' continues Amanda. 'A very important question. And I want you all to be my witnesses in case he can't remember what he said in the morning.'

She does the nervous laugh again and turns to face Nick. She hasn't got him a stripper at all. I didn't think it was her style. I know what she is going to ask him. I mouth the words as she says them. In a strong, unfaltering voice.

'Nick, will you marry me?'

A hush descends on the room. Nick's features rearrange into the phrase 'oh fuck'. He really did have no idea this was going to happen. Amanda is smiling at him. A confident smile, now. Sure she is going to get her man. Nick looks at her, then allows his gaze to lengthen to me. I find myself shaking my head. Shaking it so vigorously my hair flies from side to side. Our eyes meet for only a millisecond. He looks away again, back to Amanda. Then stares out at his assembled guests, all of them waiting with bated breath. Every one of them bar me willing him to say yes. He is taking a long time. Too long really. It is starting to get embarrassing. He needs to give her an answer. Now. He opens his mouth. It seems to take an age for the word to come out.

'Yes.'

The bullet punctures my lungs, forcing me to gasp for air. I did not expect my life to be over so quickly. I am only twenty-three years old. I am supposed to have it all before me. Not feel it ebbing away. I feel sick and light-headed. The room spins a little. I hear Rapunzel calling.

The guests start clapping and cheering. Amanda throws her arms round Nick in delight. His eyes are shut. He does not open them for a long time. When he does he looks momentarily stunned, before he realises everyone is watching him and he breaks into a smile. Amanda kisses him on the lips, pulling him in closer, her grip on him tightening.

The cheering subsides a little and the DJ takes over again.

'Congratulations to the happy couple,' he says. 'There's a free glass of champagne for everyone at the bar, courtesy of the bride-to-be's father. Amanda tells me Nick's allergic to Cliff Richard, so I'm going to play this one instead.' Billy Idol's 'White Wedding' comes on. People head off to the bar or buffet. Amanda's sister rushes up to give her a huge hug. Nick is left standing awkwardly a few yards from our table.

'Congratulations,' calls out Joan.

There is a mumbled chorus of congratulations from the others. Nick nods in acknowledgement. I try to catch his eye but he is avoiding me. He has forgotten to stop smiling. I am still struggling for breath. I need to get some air.

'Excuse me,' I say, getting up quickly and stumbling over the table leg as I grab my bag.

'Eh, Sarah's off to get her free champagne while she can still stand,' says Dave. I ignore him and carry on walking. Through the crowds of champagne-quaffing partygoers, out of the room, down the stairs and out the front door. The fresh air hits me hard. I sit down on a low wall and hold my head in my hands. It was the one thing I hadn't expected when I gave him the ultimatum. That someone else would make the decision for him. I wonder if Amanda suspected. If she had picked up on something about Nick's behaviour. Decided to tie him down quickly before he slipped through the net. I have always said it is a sign of insecurity – people who propose in public. There is no reason to do it unless you are worried the person might say no. Maybe I should have shouted out my proposal as well. Turned it into some sort of game show. See if I could outbid Amanda. Not with money. She would win that hands down. With love.

'Are you OK?' Joan sits down beside me on the wall.

'Yeah,' I say, looking up. 'Just feeling a bit rough.'

'You don't have to pretend, Sarah. I've seen the way you two look at each other. I know there's been something going on.'

I burst into tears. Huge, hot tears, cascading down my cheeks. Joan produces a tissue from her jeans pocket and hands it to me as she puts an arm round my shoulder.

'Hey, I'm sorry,' she says. 'Had you two . . .'

I nod my head quickly. Not wanting her to say it out loud.

'I know I shouldn't have,' I say. 'I feel awful about it. But I do really love him. And I genuinely thought he was going to finish with her.'

'That's what they always say, love,' says Joan.

I shake my head, desperate for her to understand that it wasn't like that.

'No, I'd given him an ultimatum. I actually think he'd chosen me, something he said earlier. And then she went and blew it.'

'You poor cow,' says Joan, giving me another hug. 'For what it's worth I think he made the wrong choice.'

I start to sob uncontrollably. 'I can't believe that's it. That it could end so cruelly.'

'Life's a bitch,' says Joan. 'Just ask Colin.'

I wince with pain at the reminder and shake my head. 'But Nick and I are so good together. He's the one. I can't just let it go, like it's no big deal.'

'I'm afraid you're going to have to,' says Joan, stroking my arm. 'He's going to marry her, Sarah. It's over.'

She holds me while I cry some more. Then lifts up my chin and wipes the tears from my face. For the first time I am aware of the people walking past staring at me as if I am some drunken wreck who's had a lovers' tiff.

'So what do I do now?' I say, clutching the crumpled tissue in my hand.

'You pop to the ladies, clean your face up and go back in there and show him what he's missing. It won't change anything but it will make you feel a tiny bit better.'

I manage a watery semblance of a smile. 'It's not going to be easy.'

'I know. But it's the only way to go. I work with both of you, remember. I don't want some horrible atmosphere. There's no reason why you can't still be friends.'

I nod although I don't think it will be possible. Not for me anyway. Joan gives me a hug.

'That's the spirit. See you on the dance floor,' she says.

I sit there for a few minutes after she has gone, gathering my thoughts. My strength. Eventually I stand up, steady myself a second and go back inside. I make it to the ladies' loos without anyone seeing me. I shut the cubicle door and let the rest of the tears out. No point in cleaning up until the flood has subsided. Eventually I make it to the sinks and splash cold water on my face, making my hot eyes sting. I glance in the mirror. I look awful. I'm not sure there is anything in my make-up bag capable of repairing the damage but I figure I should at least have a go. My hand is shaking as I apply the eye-liner. All I am doing is papering over the cracks. I do not intend to stay long. It only needs to last until I get home.

I leave the harsh lights of the ladies behind and emerge into the welcome hazy darkness. I head straight for the dance floor. Joan is somewhere in the thick of it. I don't see her, though. I see Nick and Amanda dancing together. Nick looks up, catches my eye and looks straight back down again. Alanis Morissette is playing. I understand why she is so angry now. Why she has to swish her hair like that. I spit the words out with her as I shut my eyes and dance like crazy. It is only when the song has finished I realise I am crying again. I stumble over to the table, pick up my bag without saying a word to the others and head for the exit. Before I get there, someone grabs my arm.

'Sarah, wait,' Nick says.

I turn to face him. His eyes burning with confusion. His face begging for forgiveness. He gestures towards the corridor outside. I nod and follow him to the far end, away from the noise and anyone who might overhear.

'I'm sorry,' he says. 'I had no idea.'

'I know,' I say, fighting to keep the tears from spilling over again. 'But that doesn't make it any easier.'

Nick sighs. A long, drawn-out sigh. 'I didn't see what else I could say in the circumstances.'

I shake my head. 'That's a lousy reason for agreeing to marry someone.'

He looks taken aback. 'She's my girlfriend, Sarah. I do love her.'

'So much that you were having an affair with me.'

He is visibly wounded this time. 'Please don't, Sarah. I didn't want it to turn out this way.'

'So how did you want it to turn out? Only I never got a proper answer.'

Nick shrugs. 'It doesn't matter now, does it?'

'You said you'd missed me. Tonight, when we were dancing.'

He shuts his eyes for a second, as if reliving the conversation. 'And I meant it.'

'So doesn't that count for anything?'

He runs his fingers through his hair. 'It was an impossible situation, Sarah. At least this way it gets sorted out. At least you've got your answer.'

I look at him, unable to believe that he means that. And that he thinks it will satisfy me.

'And what about us?' My voice is high-pitched and wobbly. I am struggling to hold it together.

'There can't be an us, Sarah. Not any more. I'm sorry. Really I am.'

He looks away. I swear I see a tear in his eye. We stand in silence for a minute or two. Neither of us seeming able to speak but also unwilling to walk away.

'I'd better go back in,' he says after a while. 'Will you be all right? Shall I ask Joan to run you home?'

'No, she's enjoying herself. I don't want to ruin anyone else's party.'

'Can I call you a cab then?'

I shake my head. 'No, it's OK. I could do with the walk. And to be on my own.'

He nods. Still neither of us have moved.

'What shall I tell the others?' he says.

'Say I didn't feel well. I'd had one too many. Whatever, I don't care.'

He reaches out his hand to clasp mine. I look down, fearing my paper-thin mask is about to crack.

'I'll see you Monday,' he says, squeezing my hand.

I pull away, screaming inside as he slips through my fingers.

Twelve

I could tell by the expression on Cayte's face when I arrived back at work from court the following lunchtime that the redundancy notices had already been handed out. She was staring solemnly at a blank screen, a faraway look in her eyes.

'I'm really sorry,' I said as I sat down next to her. 'We'll have a union meeting later, see what we can do.'

Cayte nodded. I hated seeing her like this. The life force sucked out of her. I glanced across at Nick. He shrugged, as if resigned to his fate. It was real now. He was leaving. No sooner had he come back into my life than he was going to disappear again. I didn't want that. But I wasn't sure if it was within my power to stop it.

The atmosphere was horrible all afternoon, the newsroom eerily silent apart from the ringing phones and the sound of the racing commentaries drifting down from the radio in sport. I caught Terry's eye once as he gazed out from his goldfish bowl. I could swear there was a tear in it.

We held the union meeting in the Turk's Head pub straight after work. Nobody wanted to stay at the office a moment longer than they had to. The mood was sombre, though there was a strange sense of camaraderie, photographers talking to sub-editors they probably hadn't said more than two words to previously. A kind of 'backs to the wall, we're all in this together' spirit. I was

half expecting Vera Lynn to come in and sing a number
or two to rally the troops.

I explained that our options were limited. The local
MPs and council leaders had sent their letters and
received bog-standard 'thank you for your concern but
there's no need to worry' replies from the MD.

'It's up to you now,' I said. 'If you want to we can go
ahead and ballot on strike action. How do people feel?'

I looked round the room. Nick remained silent, as did
the others who had been given their notice. Waiting to see
if their more fortunate colleagues were going to back
their cause.

'If we don't do anything, they'll get rid of ten more of
us next year,' said Brian, one of the subs.

'He's right,' said Naomi from features, who had only
previously been known to speak out against the price of
sandwiches at Marks & Spencer, 'it's time to make a
stand.'

'OK,' I said, feeling suitably heartened, 'let's put it to
the vote. All those in favour of balloting on industrial
action.'

A show of hands greeted me, Nick's amongst them.

'Against.'

A dozen or so hands went up.

'Carried,' I said. 'I'll speak to the union bigwigs at
Acorn House about arranging the ballot. Make sure we do
everything by the book.'

Most people stayed where they were, keen to talk over
the day's events. A few came up to ask questions about the
ballot. By the time I looked up, Nick had gone.

I didn't like works Christmas dos at the best of times. All
that false jollity and being nice to people you couldn't
stand. And the fact that they invariably took place in the
first week of December, when any glimmer of festive
spirit was so far in the distance you couldn't see it with
the naked eye.

But it had to be said that the timing of this year's was particularly unfortunate. The day after a sixth of editorial had been given their notice, we were supposed to whoop it up at a massive party. The only redeeming factor for me was that it happened to fall on the same night as Jonathan's staff Christmas party, conveniently getting me out of the terrifying prospect of him and Nick meeting.

I pulled up outside the Eden Gardens, Doreen's choice of venue. She claimed it would be 'cultured' but I suspected it was because she had a thing about Alan Titchmarsh.

My insides were playing the accordion. Because it was so much more than a works Christmas do. It was an evening with Nick. And I remembered only too well how the last evening I'd spent with him had ended up. Because hard as I'd tried to erase them, I could still feel the tingling sensation in my skin as he touched me, taste his kisses, smell him on my fingers. It was bad of me, I knew that. Almost as bad as the act itself. But the memories refused to leave me, even at nights as I lay next to Jonathan. The guilt spilling through my pores. All I could do was chase them from my mind each time, in the hope that one day they would not come back to haunt me.

I stepped out of the car and crunched across the gravel car park to the main entrance. I looked good, I knew that. I'd made an effort, despite trying not to. Most of the others were already there, mingling in the foyer, a sea of dark suits and little black dresses, removed from their polythene wrappings at the back of the wardrobe for the occasion. My dress was a rich golden velvet, with a strapless bodice and a long skirt which clung to my hips as I walked in to join them.

'Wow. You look amazing.'

I heard Nick's voice before I even realised he was next to me. It had the same effect as a double shot of spirits used to. No one else heard what he said. They weren't supposed to.

'Thanks,' I mumbled, fiddling with my earrings, knowing it was wrong even to accept compliments from him.

'There's only one problem with turning up looking like that,' said Nick.

'And what's that?' I said.

'Every other woman in the room now hates you.'

I tried hard not to smile. I knew I shouldn't encourage him. But a smile crept out anyway.

'I'll wear leggings and a T-shirt next time, shall I, then?'

'Only if you want to look like some lowlife off the Castle Vale estate,' said Nick.

I laughed again. This wasn't going to plan. I had intended to be aloof, give him the cold shoulder. I needed to try harder.

'No Jonathan tonight?' asked Nick.

My laugh cut off abruptly as reality came flooding back in on a tide of guilt.

'It's his school's Christmas do,' I said. 'What about you? I thought you might bring someone.'

'The only person I wanted to invite was already coming,' he said.

I looked down at my feet, not wanting him to see how good that had made me feel.

'Shame you didn't make the effort to impress her then,' I said, looking him up and down. He was wearing black jeans, a black moleskin jacket and a charcoal grey shirt open at the neck. He looked better than any other man in the room without even trying. But I wasn't going to tell him that.

'No point. She's not interested. Anyway, I figured I should dress down, look the part, if I'm going to be unemployed soon.'

I wished he hadn't said it. I didn't want to be reminded. He was making it even harder for me now.

'I'm really sorry, Nick. You know I'll do everything I

can to fight it.'

'I hope you don't have to go on strike,' he said.

I frowned at him. Trying to equate his comment with the Nick I used to know.

'But you voted for the ballot,' I said.

'In case that's enough to get some concessions out of management. But an all-out strike could go on for ages and turn nasty. It will affect people's livelihoods long after I've disappeared. I don't think it's fair of me to ask people to make those sorts of sacrifices. Not when I've only been here five minutes.'

I looked at him, seeing him in a new light. It struck me as a very grown-up view to take.

'But you will come out with us, if we do vote to strike?'

'Of course. I'll do a banner with "Save the Birmingham Nine" on it. I could get a fair few people up here on the picket line, you know. Old lefties never die.'

'They just roll over and let New Labour tickle their bellies.'

'Ouch. That hurt.'

'You can take it,' I said, smiling at him. Aware of a dripping sound inside my head as the resistance drained from me, drop by drop. And of the need to plug the leak before it all washed away.

People started making their way into the Frobisher suite where dinner was about to be served. I scanned the room for Cayte. She wasn't hard to spot, being the only one sporting purple tights with her black miniskirt.

'Hey, Thorneycroft. Don't leave me to sit in the empty seat next to Keith,' I said as I slid in next to her in the queue, leaving Nick behind in the process.

Cayte looked up. I saw her do a double take.

'God, you scrubbed up well,' she said.

'It's Christmas. Thought I'd make an effort.'

'You'd better watch it,' she said. 'Someone might try to stick you on top of the Christmas tree.'

I pulled a face at her as we shuffled forward in the

queue.

'I take it you're on your own,' I said.

'Yeah, Jazz is at a band rehearsal tonight. What about Jonathan?'

'Works do,' I said. Knowing it sounded no more convincing.

'So are you two all right now?' asked Cayte.

I hesitated. I wasn't sure what to tell her because I didn't know myself.

'We're getting there,' I said. 'What about you? Is that Davina still on the scene?'

'I guess so. Jazz is spending a lot of time with the band.'

'And you still say it doesn't bother you?'

'It's up to him, isn't it? Anyway there's no point getting stressed out about it if I'm going to be leaving soon.'

'You wouldn't want to go too far away, would you?'

'I don't know. There's an advert for a reporter on the *Shetland Times* in the *Press Gazette.*'

'You're not thinking of applying?'

'Haven't got much choice. There's not much else about at the moment. Anyway, it could be fun. I fancy covering a good sheep-shagging court case.'

She said it with a smile on her face, but I could see the reluctance underneath. I decided to let it drop for now. It was neither the time nor the place for big discussions. The Frobisher suite was decorated with garish green and red tinsel, a huge Christmas tree at the far end towering over the proceedings. We sat down in the last available seats on one of the two long tables which ran down the centre of the room. Nick had to sit on the other table, safely out of view.

I noticed Terry had come on his own. It wasn't surprising. His wife would probably have insisted on bringing her live-in lover as well.

The world's naffest Christmas compilation CD played in the background, at least masking the silence as we ate our lukewarm leek and potato soup. The Christmas crackers remained unpulled. No one even suggested putting a paper hat on. I'd been to more lively funerals. And all the time I was aware of Nick's presence, of his eyes boring into my back. Willing me to let down my defences. To stop fighting it. To submit.

My main course was served first. That happened when you were a vegetarian. It gave everyone else a chance to stare at your food and ask what on earth it was. On this occasion I wasn't at all sure. Even the waitress looked embarrassed as she lowered the plate containing a round brownish object down before me. I looked up at her questioningly.

'Stuffed onion,' she said.

'What's it stuffed with?'

'Er, Stilton,' she replied. 'And it's dressed in a vegetable gravy.'

'And what about the other eighteen pounds I paid?'

'Sorry?' said the waitress.

'Well, that and the soup must have cost less than a couple of quid to throw together. I wondered what had happened to the rest of the money I paid for my meal.'

'There are some roast potatoes coming,' she muttered apologetically.

'Fantastic. What's everyone else having?'

'Roast turkey with all the trimmings or poached salmon.'

'I'll have the salmon then.'

'Are you sure?'

'Positive.'

The bemused waitress removed the offending onion and scuttled away. Cayte looked at me, a barely concealed smirk on her face.

'Whatever would Jonathan say?'

'He'll never know, will he?' I said, fixing Cayte with a threatening look.

The salmon arrived. It tasted good. Better than I

remembered. Some things were worth breaking the rules for.

I waited until the meal was over, until the disco had begun and Cayte and the others were busy slagging off management, before I approached Nick. He was standing on his own at the edge of the dance floor.

'Having fun?' I said.

He turned to look at me and smiled. 'Let's just say I won't be sorry to miss next year's.'

I would miss him, though. I knew that. Would wish he was there. Wish I could turn the clock back to this point in time. To do what I wanted to do, rather than what I thought was right. I watched as he took a sip of wine. My body ached for him. The final drop of resistance evaporated.

'Fancy going somewhere else?' I said.

Nick raised an eyebrow. 'Where did you have in mind?'

'My place. Jonathan won't be back till late.'

He frowned hard at me.

'Have you been drinking?' he said.

'Only mineral water. Are you coming or not?'

I started walking towards the rear exit, through the conservatory with its wild sprawl of tropical plants. I didn't need to turn round to check that Nick was following. I could hear his footsteps on the tiles behind me. Quick and eager.

I didn't say a word on the five-minute drive back to my flat. Neither did Nick, who appeared too taken aback to be capable of speech. I let us in and led him straight through to the kitchen. Nelson got up from his basket and rubbed around my ankles before moving across to sniff Nick's shoes. I wobbled for a second, wondering if he was capable of passing information back to Jonathan. Of somehow communicating the fact that a strange man had been on his territory. I dismissed the thought and started kissing Nick. Slowly and deeply. Savouring the taste, the feel of him on my mouth. His hands on my face, touching me, cherishing me.

I tried to block off the thoughts which were crowding my mind. The voices in my head telling me not to do it. That it was wrong. Very wrong indeed. Every time I heard them I responded by kissing Nick harder. Trying to defy the guilt, to meet it head on.

'You look beautiful tonight,' he said as we broke for a second. 'Really beautiful.'

I smiled and started unbuttoning his shirt. Nick took his shoes and socks off and helped me wriggle out of my dress.

'Come with me,' I said. I led Nick into the bedroom and turned on the lamp. I regretted it instantly. Jonathan was everywhere. In each direction my eyes looked I was confronted by things which were unmistakably his. He might as well have been in there watching. I caught sight of our reflection in the mirror. Me in my matching push-up bra and hot pants, Nick's bare back as he bent down to take off his trousers. Preparing for our deceit.

'I'm sorry,' I blurted out. 'I can't do this.'

Nick stopped, one leg in his trousers, one leg out, and looked at me.

'I don't understand. This was your idea.'

I sat down on the end of the bed.

'I know. Because it's what I want and I thought I could do it but I can't. Not here.'

Nick sighed, put his trousers back on and sat down next to me.

'The guilt getting to you?'

I nodded. 'I've felt awful since we . . . I haven't been able to look Jonathan in the eye.'

'I know,' he said. 'I've been there, remember.'

'Why is it never the right time for us?' I said, throwing my hands up in the air. 'Why does there always have to be someone else involved?'

'Because life's complicated,' Nick said. 'And sometimes you think you're with the right person, until someone else comes along.'

'Are you saying Jonathan isn't right for me?'

'I don't know. That's up to you to decide.'

I buried my face in my hands. I wanted Nick, I knew that. But I also knew it was wrong to hurt Jonathan.

'Can I ask you something?' Nick said with a sigh.

I uncovered my face to look at him.

'What?'

'If we're not going to do anything would you mind putting some clothes on? It's doing me in, having to look at you like that.'

I started laughing. Grateful for anything that would break the tension.

'I'll go and put my dress back on,' I said.

I was in the kitchen, struggling to do up the zip, when I heard the car pull up outside. And the unmistakable sound of Jonathan's voice thanking the cab driver. I ran back to the bedroom.

'Jonathan. Home. Shit. Fan. Hit. Run. Now.' I screamed the last word and bolted to the kitchen, dragging a startled Nick behind me. I hurriedly pulled my shoes back on as Nick hopped around, doing up his shirt while trying to find his socks. I heard the gate click and a minute later Jonathan's key in the lock.

'You've got ten seconds,' I said. 'Go along with whatever I say.'

I pulled the kitchen door shut behind me as Jonathan entered the hall.

'Hi,' I said breezily. 'You're back early. Was your do crap too?'

He shrugged, looking despondent. The guilt stabbed and twisted inside.

'I guess I wasn't in the party mood,' he said. 'I don't suppose most of your lot were, either.'

'No, more like a wake. That's why we left early.'

'You and Cayte?'

'Er, yeah. And a few of the others. I invited them back

here. Didn't think you'd be home yet. You don't mind, do
you?'

'No, course not,' Jonathan said. 'Where are they?'

'In here,' I said, throwing open the kitchen door to
reveal Nick standing by the sink, fully clothed apart from
one missing sock, casually holding an empty coffee mug
as if he'd been there for hours.

'Hi,' he said, nodding at Jonathan.

'Er, this is Nick,' I said, 'Nick, Jonathan . . .'

My voice trailed off as they shook hands. I expected a
buzzer to go off at any second, signalling that the game
was up.

'Pleased to meet you,' said Jonathan. 'You must be the
politics guy, the one who used to work with Sarah.'

'That's right,' said Nick. 'Long time ago now.' He
laughed, much too heartily. I joined in to try to cover it
but only made it sound worse. Jonathan looked around.

'So where are Cayte and the others?' he said.

'Oh, they stopped at the off-licence,' I said. 'I'd better
give her a ring actually, in case she's got lost. You know
what she's like when she's had a few.' The false laugh
came again. I fished my mobile out of my handbag and
called Cayte.

'Hi. Where have you got to?'

'I was going to ask you the same question.'

'Only we're waiting back here at the flat. Can't start
the party without you and the booze.'

'Are you with Nick?'

'Yeah. Jonathan's here as well. You and the other guys
hurry up in that offy.'

I hung up before she had a chance to argue.

'They're on their way,' I announced. 'Sounded a bit
worse for wear, mind.'

Jonathan was looking at me quizzically. I wondered if
he suspected. Any moment now he could confront me.
Force me to confess.

'Is that dress new?' he said. He'd left before me that

evening so hadn't seen it.

'Er, yeah.'

'You look fantastic in it,' he said.

'She does, doesn't she?' said Nick. I glared at him. 'So did everyone else,' he added. 'Look good in their dresses, I mean. Apart from the men, of course . . .'

'Do you want another coffee, Nick?' I interrupted before he could dig the hole any deeper.

'Oh. Yes, please.'

'I'll get them,' said Jonathan. 'Go through to the lounge, Nick. Make yourself at home.'

I winced. The fact he was being so nice made me feel so much worse.

'Where's your sock?' I whispered to Nick as we shuffled out of the kitchen.

'Don't know. Can't find it. Your zip's not done up properly at the back. Here, let me.'

Nick fiddled with the zip and we sat down on the sofa, looking like two naughty schoolchildren waiting outside the headmaster's office. Jonathan came through with the coffee and perched on the beanbag. I noticed him staring at Nick's sockless left ankle.

I looked at Nick, gesturing with my eyes to make something up, help me out here.

'It's the latest trend, just wearing one sock,' Nick explained hurriedly. 'Beckham started it.'

Jonathan nodded. 'Wonder I haven't seen any of the kids doing it yet.'

'Oh, you will,' said Nick. 'Only a matter of time. Has to be the left one missing, though.'

'Music,' I said to Jonathan, deciding to change the subject before Nick dug us in any deeper. 'Why don't you put some music on?'

Jonathan buried his head in the CD rack as I heard a cab pull up outside.

'That'll be the others,' I said, leaping up from the sofa and rushing to open the door. Cayte staggered in with three bottles of wine.

'Where are the rest?' I asked.

'This was all I could carry.'

'No,' I said, staring at her hard. 'The crowd from work.'

'Oh,' she said, watching my face carefully to make sure she got it right, 'they changed their minds. Decided to go home. Bloody party poopers.'

'Never mind,' said Jonathan. 'Quality not quantity, eh?'

'Absolutely,' said Cayte, giving me a perplexed look as she sat down on the floor next to me. 'And this is obviously where all the action is, eh Sarah?'

Friday 13 June 1997

'So, have you set a date for the wedding yet, Nick?' asks Karen. The words slap me round the face, leaving me red-cheeked. It's not her fault. She has no idea. We are sitting in the pub, the way work colleagues do on a Friday lunchtime, making small talk as we eat our jacket potatoes. And it is a perfectly reasonable question to ask, given that he got engaged six days ago. It is just that for me, it is still too soon. The cut too fresh. The pain too intense. The wound gaping open, unable to heal when I see him, hear him, smell him, feel his presence and taste him in the air I breathe every day.

Nick looks at me then away again quickly. The others are waiting.

'Yeah, we have,' he says, putting another forkful into his mouth as if he wants to end the conversation there.

'Go on, then,' says Karen. 'When's the big day?'

I have to wait until he finishes chewing and swallows. Whatever he is going to say, I don't want to hear it. But I do not have any choice.

'July the nineteenth,' he says.

'What, next year?' asks Karen.

'No,' he says, picking up his bottle of Becks. 'Next month.'

It hits me like a punch in the stomach. Below the belt. I am winded for a second, reeling on the canvas, unsure if I will be able to get up again. I thought I would at least have some time to get my head round the idea. Or maybe even to try to talk him out of it. Persuade him that he's chosen the wrong woman. But no. In five weeks' time they will be married. It is all too soon. Too much. Too final. The hammering inside my chest starts again. I look at Nick for an explanation but he is staring intently at his beer mat.

'Bloody hell, that's a bit quick isn't it?' says Karen. 'Are you sure there's nothing else you want to tell us?'

'Eh, yeah. It's not one of those shotgun weddings, is it?' says Dave.

'No,' snaps Nick. Clearly he wants to leave it at that. But Karen isn't about to let it drop. We don't call her the Rottweiler for nothing.

'So what's with the big rush then?' she says.

Nick sighs. 'Amanda rang St Andrew's and they'd just had a cancellation. We were lucky enough to be offered it so we figured we may as well go for it. No point in hanging around.'

He looks up and glances sideways at me. I keep my eyes fixed firmly on the table. Their luck, someone else's misfortune. Amanda must be delighted, whizzing him up the aisle before he's even had a chance to catch his breath from the proposal, let alone get cold feet about the wedding.

I push my barely touched jacket potato away. My insides are too contorted to even contemplate allowing food down. I down the rest of my vodka and orange in one. I wish Joan was here, instead of on a job. She would be able to put a stop to this, manage to change the subject. Karen and Dave, however, have no such inclination.

'So how are you going to get everything organised in time?' asks Karen. 'Aren't all the reception venues booked up?'

'We're having a marquee in Amanda's parents' garden,' says Nick.

'Is it going to be a big do then?' asks Dave. 'One of those top hat and tails jobs?'

263

'Probably,' says Nick. 'You'll have to ask Amanda for the details. She's handling all the arrangements.'

'That's not very gallant of you,' says Karen. 'Letting her do all the work.'

Nick shrugs, still avoiding eye contact with me. 'She enjoys it. Besides, I'd only get in the way.'

'Trouble is,' says Dave, 'you could turn up on the day and find she's had the church decked out in pink ribbons and ordered some poncey horse and carriage lark to take you to the reception.'

'Whatever, it's up to her,' says Nick. 'It's her day.'

My hand is squeezing my empty glass so hard I fear it could shatter at any moment. I want to shout at the top of my voice, the way you do when you're a kid and you're trying to drown out something you don't want to hear.

'And you don't mind looking a prat?' asks Dave.

'You'd be disappointed if I didn't.'

'I can't wait to see you in a penguin suit,' says Dave.

'You'd better give me a break then. Otherwise I might not invite you.' He says it jokingly but I detect a serious undertone. I hadn't even thought of that. We are all going to be invited to this wedding. Me included. I am going to be expected to stand there and watch him pledge himself to another woman for life. To remain silent when the vicar asks people to speak now or for ever hold their peace. To raise my glass and toast their future happiness. I won't go, of course. It would be like volunteering for an afternoon in a torture chamber. Though I can't imagine sitting at home picturing it will be much better.

'What date did you say it was again?' asks Dave.

'July nineteenth,' mumbles Nick as he finishes the last mouthful and puts his knife and fork down.

'Eh, that's the same date as Rugby carnival,' says Dave. 'You'll be able to hitch a lift to and from church on one of the carnival floats. Save her old man a few bob or two.'

Nick manages a strained smile.

'Still don't know why you're bothering,' says Karen, who has just moved in with her boyfriend. 'It's a damn sight cheaper to live in sin.'

Nick is starting to look rattled.

'Anyway, we'd better be getting back,' he says, putting his unfinished bottle of Becks down on the table and standing up. Karen and Dave are visibly taken aback. Usually Nick is the one advocating an extended lunch hour. And he always finishes his drinks. I stand up and follow Nick to the door, relieved for the chance to escape.

'Sorry about that, couldn't shut them up. Are you OK?' asks Nick as soon as we get outside.

I nod. Unable to manage any words. This is only the beginning. It will get worse as the day draws nearer. Until the point where it becomes unbearable. When I shall need something to numb the pain. We walk back to work side by side, Karen and Dave a few steps behind. Neither of us says a word. We don't even look at each other. I keep my eyes firmly on the pavement. But all I see are the images of him and Amanda in their wedding outfits swirling around in my head.

We get back to the newsroom at the same time as Joan.

'Have a good lunch?' she asks.

Nick shrugs. I look down at my feet.

'You'd better buy a hat, Joan,' says Karen. 'Nick's getting married in five weeks.'

Joan raises her eyebrows, glances at me then back to Nick. 'Well, you don't hang about, do you?'

'No,' says Nick. 'And before you ask, no, she isn't.'

He sits down at his desk and starts typing. Joan turns to look at me for an explanation.

'Not now,' I say.

An uneasy atmosphere descends on the newsroom. I sit in the gloom for half an hour or so before deciding to escape up to photographic with a picture order. Ted is busy scribbling on a piece of paper. He looks up and fires a question at me.

'How long do you give it?'

'What?'

'Nick's marriage. I've started a book.'

'That's nice of you.'

'Karen's gone for three years. I think she's being optimistic. Bill's gone for one year and Dave reckons they won't even make it to the altar.'

I slap the photo order down on the desk.

'So what shall I put you down for?' he says.

'You can say I'm a conscientious objector.'

'Ooohh, get you. It's only a bit of fun.'

'I'm sorry, but I don't find it amusing.'

I walk away, my own words bouncing off the walls and coming back to me, the laughter echoing. I have no place on this moral high ground. I am a fallen woman.

Back at my desk I wonder who will win. Dave's money is essentially on me, although he doesn't realise it. He has backed a horse which is no longer running. That fell at the first fence and is yet to get back up again. It should probably be shot, put out of its misery. It would be the kindest thing to do in the circumstances. And as for the only other horse running, I am buoyed by the knowledge that no one seems to think it will last the distance. I shouldn't be, I know. But I am.

I do not look at Nick for the rest of the afternoon, I find it too painful. I used to hate having my back to him. Now I am glad of it. Not that I can forget he is there. Because when you block out one sense the others simply become more acute.

It is gone four o'clock when Jill on reception buzzes up to say there is a Mrs Saunders in the front office to see me. The name doesn't mean anything at first. It is only when I see the gaunt figure standing in the corner that I realise who she is. Deborah's mother. I haven't seen her since I visited their house. But I know from Deborah that she was pleased with the article. Just disappointed, as I was, by the lack of response from the health authority.

She turns to look at me. Her body is hunched, her hands anxiously clasp a shopping bag, and the worry lines on her face are deeper still. But it is her eyes that tell me something has happened. Dull and lifeless and surrounded by layers of puffy red skin.

'Hello,' I say as I approach her. 'Is everything all right?'

She shakes her head, closing her eyes for a second before dragging her lids open again.

'I'm afraid Deborah passed away on Tuesday night.'

I stand there staring, open-mouthed, wanting her to take the words back. Desperate for it not to be true. Although I know from the moist coating on her eyes that it is.

'I'm so sorry. I only spoke to her a few weeks ago. I had no idea she was so ill.'

'She went downhill very quickly this time,' says Mrs Saunders. 'They admitted her to hospital at the weekend but it was too late. She had a lung infection and a blood infection. The doctors said she was too weak to fight them. Less than four and a half stone, she was at the end.'

Mrs Saunders gets a tissue from her handbag and dabs at her eyes.

'I really am sorry,' I say again, unable to find the words I need. 'Do you want to come through and sit down? Can I get you a cup of tea?'

'No, thanks. I just wanted to let you know. And to ask if you could put this in the paper.'

She reaches into her handbag again and produces a crumpled piece of paper which she hands to me. It is a death notice, complete with a short poem. I have read dozens like it, unfortunately usually bad enough to make me cringe. But this one is beautiful. This one leaves me swallowing hard.

'Deborah wrote it,' says Mrs Saunders. 'I think she knew, you know. That there was no way back this time.'

I nod slowly.

'Of course we'll use it,' I say. 'We'll do a story as well, more of a tribute to her really, if that's OK with you.'

'Yes,' she says, having taken a moment to think about it. 'Yes, I'd like that. How much do I owe you for the notice?'

'Nothing,' I say. 'It's the least we can do. She was very special, your Deborah.'

'Thank you,' she says. 'At least she's at peace now. In a strange way it's almost a relief. I couldn't bear to see her suffer any more.' She starts to walk away but turns back before she gets to the door.

'If you use a photo with the story,' she says, 'can you use the one of her when she was younger, before it all started? It's how I want people to remember her.'

'Of course,' I say. 'And if there's anything else we can do . . .'

She nods before turning and walking out the door.

I am left standing there, holding the death notice in my shaking hand. I have broken the golden rule of journalism. I have got involved. I thought I was becoming hardened to it, the way Nick said you do. I have covered two murder cases, written stories about people who have died in accidents or through illness, and have always managed to remain detached. But this is different. Someone I have met and interviewed has died. Someone who was young and beautiful. Someone I was going to phone next week to see how she was.

'Poor woman,' says Jill, who has a habit of overhearing conversations. 'I remember that article you did on her daughter. Such a shame about these silly girls. I don't know why they can't just eat something.'

I resist the urge to throttle her. And I am not in the right frame of mind to try to explain. I simply shake my head and walk back upstairs to the newsroom, biting my trembling lip. I should tell Nick. The story will make at least a page three lead for us next week. But I know that if I so much as look at him I will burst into tears. And I do not want to do that. Not in front of the others. I sit down at my desk and stare at a blank screen, unable to start an intro I do not want to write. After fifteen minutes I give up and start gathering my things together.

'What's this, knocking off early?' says Joan, looking up. As soon as she sees my face her expression and tone of voice change. 'Sarah? Are you all right?'

I shake my head and walk over to her, so the others don't hear.

'Not really. Deborah Saunders, the anorexic woman, died on Tuesday. Her mother's just been in.'

'Oh, Sarah.' Joan's face crumples in sympathy.

'I'm not going to be much use here so I may as well go home. Just tell Nick I'm not feeling well. I'll make up the time in the morning.'

I slip out without the others noticing and tread quietly down the back stairs. It is only when I reach the sanctuary of my car that I allow the tears to fall.

I haven't bothered cooking at home since Nick got engaged. It is a lot of effort to go to just to scrape most of the food into the bin an hour later. I have laid the table every night as if I was having a meal. Not that you need a knife and fork for a vodka and orange, but it has kept some sense of normality. Tonight, however, it feels wrong not to be eating. Tonight I feel I should make the effort – for Deborah's sake.

I do a quick stir-fry with some bits I have in the fridge and a packet of noodles and a jar of sauce from the cupboard. Not exactly cordon bleu but it is better than nothing. I manage to eat about a third of it before my stomach reminds me that it is not used to this and clenches and churns so much that I decide to leave the rest. My body is still in mourning for Nick. And I feel bad about that because I should be in mourning for Deborah now. Deborah who is really dead, not Nick who is still here but has simply chosen to be with someone else. I am selfish as well as bad. The guilt compounds the guilt. I pour myself another vodka. I don't bother to put any orange juice in it this time. When I have finished it I pour another. I am about to down that as well when the doorbell rings. I am not expecting anyone. It will probably be someone trying to sell me something I don't want or telling me that Jesus is my saviour. I decide to go anyway, suspecting it will make me feel better to slam the door in someone's face. I pad down the stairs in my bare feet and open the door. It is Nick. His body silhouetted against the late evening sunshine. His eyes mournfully dark and open so wide I fear I shall fall into them.

My stomach lurches violently as the roller coaster starts up again, propelling me to the first peak and leaving me hanging there, teetering on the edge, unsure whether I am going all the way to the top or am about to plummet back down to the depths again.

I do not say anything. I shield my eyes from the sun, trying not to squint as I wait for him to speak.

'Joan told me,' he says. 'About the anorexic woman. I wanted to make sure you were all right.'

I want to collapse sobbing into his arms. Ask him to hold me, stroke my hair, make everything all right again. But I am not allowed to do that any more. We are over. There is an invisible barrier between us, which I must not penetrate.

'I'm OK, thanks,' I say.

'You don't have to pretend, Sarah. Not with me.'

He is pushing against the barrier; if I give it a shove from my side it could topple. But I am scared of what I may do if it falls.

'It came as a shock, that's all. Normally I'd have been OK but it's been a tough . . . well, you know . . .' My voice tails off as I decide to stop talking before it cracks completely. I blink back the tears and look down, hoping Nick will think it is the sun in my eyes.

'Can I come in?' he says.

I look up at him. Not daring to believe there is anything more to it than friendly concern but feeling the ground shifting, the awkwardness starting to recede. I nod, still biting my bottom lip, and turn to walk up the stairs. I hear Nick shut the door behind him and follow me, his footsteps familiar, the situation foreign. I lead him through to the main room. We have been here together so many times. But this evening I am unsure what to do or say. Because it is different; everything has changed. Even offering him a coffee could be wrongly construed. I turn to face him. His eyes are reaching out to me. It is impossible – simply looking at him kills me inside. My body is screaming out for him. He is the person I am closest to in the world. But I am only allowed to look, not touch. I can't bear it any longer. The bottom lip goes.

'Come here,' Nick says. I take a step towards him, then another. Before I know it my head is buried against him, his arms close about me. I shut my eyes and drink it in. The feeling of safety, of belonging, of being home. It is a long time before the tears ease. Before I am able to speak.

'It's all so sad. I don't think she wanted to die. I think it just got out of control, so she couldn't stop it.'

Nick nods and strokes my hair. Like I wanted him to. Like I didn't think he could do any more. I'm not sure what is happening. Or how long it will last. All I know is that I need him now, more than ever.

'The funeral's next Wednesday afternoon,' I say, wiping my eyes. 'I'd like to go, if it's OK with you.'

'Of course it is,' he says, still stroking my hair. 'What did I tell you about getting involved?'

'I know, I know. You must think I'm so pathetic. Maybe I need to toughen up a bit.'

He shakes his head. 'I like the fact that you care. That you give a toss. It's one of the things I love about you.'

He stops short, as if realising he is not supposed to say things like that any more. I want to ask what the other things are. To have him list them, put them in writing if necessary. Anything to help me remember that it wasn't some cheap fling. That he had real feelings for me. When I am sitting here alone in my flat at nights. And he is at home with his wife. I start crying again. Though these tears are for my loss. For Nick. He holds me tighter still. As if trying to squeeze the hurt out of me. When I eventually look up he is gazing fondly at me.

'What?' I say.

'You're the only woman I've ever known who still manages to look beautiful when she cries,' he says.

I blink in appreciation. He is too polite to say what the others look like. An image of Amanda resembling a bulldog chewing a wasp as she bawls her eyes out comes into my mind. I chase it away. I am being unkind. I still don't understand, though. How he can say that to me when he is marrying her in five weeks' time. I don't want to spoil the moment but I have to know.

'I didn't think it would be so soon,' I say. 'The wedding.'

Nick pulls away a little, as if startled into reality. Remembering that he shouldn't be here, holding me. That it is not me he is marrying.

'I thought it would be for the best,' he says with a shrug.

'For who?' I ask.

He lets go of me and walks to the window, running his fingers through his hair.

'For all of us,' he says. 'I didn't see the point of dragging things out once the decision had been made. At least this way it will be done and dusted and we'll all have the chance to move on.'

I stand there shaking my head. Nick is staring out of the window. Unable to look me in the eye.

'And that's what you want, is it?' I ask. 'To move on?'

He hesitates before answering.

'I don't know what I want. All I know is that I've made

a mess of everything. And hurt you, which is the one thing I never wanted to do.'

He holds his head in his hands, covering his eyes, stopping me from seeing his pain. It is my turn to do the comforting. I reach out for his hand and lead him over towards the bed. He looks at me, his eyebrows raised questioningly, about to tell me to stop.

'It's OK,' I say. 'I just want to hold you. No funny business.'

I sit down on the floor with my legs outstretched and my back propped up against the bed. He hesitates before lying down next to me, resting his head on my lap. I brush a few strands of hair back from his face, my fingertips skimming softly across his forehead. Touching skin again, if only for a few precious seconds. Nick reaches up a hand to lightly cup my face. I kiss his palm. The tiniest kiss imaginable. He closes his eyes. He is hurting every bit as much as me. I know I shouldn't say it but I have to try. And this could be my only chance.

'You can't go into a marriage feeling like this, Nick. It's not fair on either of you.'

He takes his hand away from my face and opens his eyes.

'And would it be fair to Amanda to call it off? She cried at the end of the party, you know. Cried all the way home in the taxi. Said I'd made her so happy by saying yes. And I sat there without saying a word, thinking about how I've cheated on her. About what a bastard I've been.'

I stop stroking his forehead. I don't want to know this. He has told me too much. I don't want to hear about her tears. I want to tell him about mine. All the tears I have cried over the past months when he has gone home to her, leaving me with just the smell of him lingering on my fingers. The times I have lain awake at night imagining them together, the times I have wished that just once I could wake up with him next to me in the morning. But I know if I say it it will sound as if I am bitter and twisted. And I don't want to come over like that. Even if I am.

'You don't have to call the whole thing off. Just tell her you want to put it back until next year. Give yourself a chance to think things through properly.'

He sighs and shakes his head. 'All that would do is prolong the agony for you. I'm not going to change my mind, Sarah. I made her a promise, in front of all my friends and family. She's wearing my ring on her finger. I'm not going to back down now. It wouldn't be right.'

It is my turn to shut my eyes. He reaches up and strokes my face again.

'Believe me, you'll be better off without me. And before you know it some lucky bastard will come along and sweep you off your feet. I only hope he'll treat you better than I have.'

I open my eyes, letting a solitary tear out as I do so.

'I don't want anyone else,' I say. 'I only want you.'

Nick reaches up and pulls my head down to him. We stay like that for a long time. Our foreheads touching, feeling each other's breath warm on our faces. Both of us knowing this is the last time we will do this. It is our long goodbye.

It is getting dark outside by the time he lets go of me, and stretches out his creaking limbs.

'I've got to go now,' he whispers. He clambers stiffly up to his feet and offers his hand to help me up. I take it, wanting to feel his touch one last time. As he walks towards the door he glances at the table, where the remains of my stir-fry and my untouched glass of vodka are standing. I don't think he noticed them when he came in.

'Are you going to be OK?' he says.

'I guess so.'

'I'll see you on Monday.'

'Yeah.' I nod my head. The words I want to say stuck in my throat. I watch him walk out of the room, hear him close the front door behind him. Quietly. As if he doesn't want to disturb me in my grief. And I am grieving. For him as well as Deborah. The tears carve deep chasms in my cheeks. I pick up the glass from the table and drink it straight down, stopping to refill it before settling back on to the carpet in exactly the same spot. Only this time it is uncomfortable, this time I feel the wiry fibres digging into the soft flesh of my thighs through my skirt. This time there is no one here to take the pain away.

He will be going home to her now feeling unburdened. Free from the pressure which has blighted his life these past few months. I hear my mother saying 'I told you so'. Maybe I shouldn't have played with fire in the first place. Maybe I shouldn't even be let near matches.

I reach for my glass. The alcohol slips easily down my throat, soothing everything it comes into contact with. It is my medicine. It will not make me better but it will dull the pain.

Thirteen

Cayte passed me a polystyrene cup of coffee through the open car window, hurried round the front, slipped into the passenger seat next to me and took a noisy slurp of her own latte. I closed my window. I felt I should check the car for bugging devices, or expect a tap on the glass and a brown envelope to be offered by a man in a trench coat and trilby. I'd always wanted a Deep Throat-style encounter in a dingy, foreboding location. However, I hadn't expected to be the one imparting previously top secret information. The venue had been Cayte's idea: I think it appealed to the private investigator in her. I'd been so relieved that she had played along with my story to Jonathan that I would have agreed to meet anywhere. Seven-thirty on a Monday morning in a multi-storey car park seemed a small price to pay. Especially as she'd agreed to get the coffees in on her way.

'So,' said Cayte, still bleary-eyed and devoid of her usual vibrant pink lipstick. 'The dirt, please. What were you and Nick up to on Saturday night?'

'I know you won't believe me,' I said, staring straight ahead through the windscreen, 'but nothing happened. Nothing much, anyway. I got cold feet.'

'So why did you need me to cover you?' said Cayte.

'Because it looked bad. And because it had already happened. Weeks ago.'

Cayte's eyes bulged as she let go of an audible gasp. 'What, you and Nick have—'

'Yes,' I said quickly. 'Just the once.'

'Fucking hell. I thought you didn't like him.'

'I had to pretend not to. To myself as much as anything.'

Cayte shook her head, obviously struggling to digest the news.

'You'd better fill me in then,' she said. 'From the beginning.'

I found myself surprisingly keen to talk. It was only as I explained what had been going on that I realised what a strain it had been to keep things to myself. Cayte listened, transfixed, her jaw crunching up and down as she shovelled a packet of cheesy Wotsits down her throat in record-breaking time. I'd seen the same behaviour traits from her when watching daytime confession shows like *Trisha*. 'I'm having an affair with an old flame and my live-in partner is too trusting to realise' could have been the title of this one. When I finished my potted version of events she turned to me and shook her head.

'I can't believe it. Best bit of office gossip for years, happens under my nose, and I have to force it out of you under interrogation,' she said, turning the crisp packet upside down and emptying the remaining crumbs into her gaping mouth.

'I'm not proud of it. I didn't want to broadcast it to the world,' I said.

'I'm not the world. I'm supposed to be your best friend.' She sounded hurt.

'I know. But I didn't want you to think badly of me,' I replied.

Cayte burst out laughing.

'What?' I said, brushing the spilt crisp crumbs from my seat.

'Were you under the misguided impression that I look up to you as some sort of paragon of virtue?' she said.

'Well, I seem to have built myself a certain reputation. She who never does wrong. The wise woman of the office who can be relied upon to do the sensible thing at all times.'

'Is that what you think?'

'Why else does everyone come to me for advice?'

'They don't. They start talking about their lives, you, unlike most people, bother to listen, and then you tell them what you think they should do.'

I sat quietly for a moment. I'd never thought of it like that.

'Am I that bad?'

Cayte grinned. 'Most of the time you're spot on. But sometimes people don't want to hear the truth, do they?'

'Like when I tried to talk to you about Jazz, you mean.'

It was Cayte's turn to fall silent.

'You always seemed so sure of yourself,' she said at last. 'So sorted and secure with Jonathan. He worships the bloody ground you walk on. I guess it was that much worse coming from you.'

'And now you've found out that I'm in a worse mess than you, you don't mind telling me about what's going on with you and Jazz?'

She took a deep breath.

'The thing is I actually love him,' she said. 'All this crap I come out with about chasing after other men. The fact is I wouldn't want them if they offered themselves on a plate. I only want him.'

'And what does Jazz want?'

Cayte shrugged. 'He wants it all, I guess. Me on twenty-four-hour call whenever he feels like it and some posh eighteen-year-old bird getting down and grungy with him in between times.'

'Is he shagging this Davina, then?'

'It doesn't take all night to rehearse a couple of songs, does it?'

'And what does he say in his defence?'

'Don't know, I haven't asked. Too scared of driving him away.'

I nodded, remembering how I'd once played by the same rules. Except I'd been the one Nick had escaped to, not the one he'd run home to.

'And now,' continued Cayte, 'with all this redundancy lark, I'll probably have to move to the fucking Shetland Islands or something to get a job and I can't exactly see him bothering to keep it going. Not when Davina's on his doorstep.'

Cayte sighed. The cheesy Wotsit crumbs on her lips began to tremble. She reached into her bag for her lipstick and started to apply it, more to stop herself crying than anything else. I gave her shoulder a squeeze, careful not to jolt her enough to smudge the lipstick.

'My advice – and I realise you haven't asked for it but I'm going to give it to you anyway – is to stop letting him have it both ways. Make sure you're busy sometimes when he wants to see you. Stay out yourself one night. You can kip at our place if you want.'

'He probably won't give a toss.'

'Maybe not. But maybe he'll realise what he's got to lose. You could try telling him how you feel, as well. Believe it or not he might be insecure himself. He might want to hear how much he means to you.'

'And what about you?' said Cayte. 'Are you going to tell Jonathan how you feel about Nick?' It was my turn to sigh. 'How can I? He's going through a really tough time at work right now. I feel such a bitch for having cheated on him. He's always been so good to me.'

'So why did you let things start up again? If you know it's so wrong?'

I looked away for a moment, gazing out of the window as I wondered how to explain it.

'It's like Charles and Camilla,' I said. 'You know how everyone slagged them off for carrying on while he was still married to Di? But they did it because they couldn't stop themselves. Because they knew they were right for each other. That they were meant to be together. And they

were proved right, weren't they? In the end. Theirs
turned out to be the real love story.'

Cayte had a worried look on her face.

'You're not going to get Jonathan bumped off in a
Paris underpass, are you?' she said.

I shook my head. I'd forgotten she was one of the
conspiracy theorists.

'What I'm saying is that I don't seem to be able to stop
it. Even though I know it's wrong. Because I also know
that Nick's the one for me. That we are meant to be
together. No matter what.'

I started crying. Cayte leant over to give me a huge
cheesy-Wotsit-flavoured hug. I let her hold me. Feel my
vulnerability. Relieved at last to be able to share it with
someone. When I eventually let go I glanced at the
dashboard clock. It was nearly eight o'clock.

'Come on,' I said. 'We'd better get to work.'

'I should warn you,' said Cayte, 'there might be a bit of
gossip going around. People noticed you and Nick going
AWOL at the same time. Some of them are starting to
wonder. Tongues are wagging.'

'And what will you tell them?' I said, wiping my eyes.

'That it's the wise agony aunts you have to watch,' she
said with a toothy grin.

Cayte was right. People looked up as I walked to my desk.
I wasn't imagining it, I saw their heads turn and their
lips start moving as they alerted the person sitting next
to them of my arrival. I'd managed to put a seed of doubt
in their heads. That maybe I wasn't who they thought I
was, after all. A tiny part of me wanted to climb up on my
desk, shout so the whole office could hear, 'I'm shagging
Nick Hardwick, you know. He lusts after me, can't get
enough, I drive him wild in bed.' Wanted to see the
expression on their faces, see Lisa choke on her coffee.
People look at me in a whole new light. Think of me as the
tousle-haired temptress of the office. I would never do it,

of course. But it didn't stop me thinking about it.

No one said anything to me directly. That wasn't how it was done. But I could feel them watching me as Nick walked in ten minutes later, studying me for some kind of reaction. A reddening of the cheeks, a guilty smile. Anything they could put down as a sign, some fuel to keep the fire burning.

Nick must have been aware of it as well, because he made no attempt to converse with me, or to even make eye contact, simply got stuck straight into a pile of council agendas.

Roger was the only person who came up to speak to me. And as he was oblivious of office gossip and hadn't been to the Christmas do I knew I wasn't about to be confronted with an accusation.

'I've got something to show you,' he said, looking surprisingly cheery for a Monday morning.

'What?' I said.

'Walk this way.'

He led me into the darkroom. It was known as the tardis. Wholly unimpressive from the outside but once through the small swing door you were transported to another world, another time. It took my eyes a moment to adjust to the low lights and my nose several more to stop sniffing in lungfuls of chemicals which I was convinced would spark an American invasion if George Bush ever got wind of them. Only then did I see the row of black and white prints laid out on the bench at the far end of the darkroom. I shuffled towards them, turning my head to one side as I walked along the line. Grainy shots of a man slumped in a doorway, sleeping bag pulled up tight against the cold, a young woman clutching a pile of *Big Issues* to her chest as a businessman walked past in a blur of umbrella and briefcase, shots of a man, whom I instantly recognised as Razor, showing off his fillings as he roared with laughter, presumably a few seconds before he'd taken exception to Colin's paparazzi techniques, and one of Colin himself, a self-portrait showing the rain chiselling its way down his face, his lips cracked at the edges with the cold.

I looked at Roger. 'They're brilliant.'

Roger nodded. 'Best stuff I've seen for a long time. The lighting is fantastic. They've got a great feel about them.'

'Good enough to publish?'

'They're a damn sight better than the pile of crap we get in most days.'

'I'll take some to show Terry. Help me pick out the best ones.'

A few minutes later I arrived in Terry's office clutching an armful of Colin's photos.

'Take a look at these,' I said, spreading them out on the carpet around his desk.

'Yeah, nice stuff,' said Terry, nodding. 'Bit arty for us, mind.'

'Would you rather we got a few cheque presentations in or did a spread on kiddies rehearsing their nativity plays?'

'The grannies always buy at least twenty copies.'

I groaned. 'Terry, this is proper photography. Taken by a homeless *Big Issue* seller who loads of our readers walk past every day. It's a great story. We should print them. Do a big spread.'

'He's not on drugs or anything, is he?'

I rolled my eyes. 'Do you remember the guy who lost by one vote in the general election the year Labour got in?'

'Yeah,' said Terry, scratching his head. 'I think I do.'

'Well, it's him. He got depressed, fell on hard times. And now he's hauling himself back up again. Doing what he's always wanted to do.'

'Blimey, that is a good story,' said Terry. 'And it would fill the hole on page three today.'

I grinned at him.

'Thanks, Terry,' I said as I gathered the photos up and hurried off to see the picture editor.

When the lunchtime edition landed on my desk I turned immediately to page three. 'Life on the streets, through homeless Colin's lens' read the headline above five of his photos, with the strapline 'Man who lost by one vote bounces back' underneath.

'Hey, Leaky's photos, they're fantastic.' It was the first thing Nick had said to me all day. He was standing directly behind me, looking over my shoulder. Tension instantly crackling between us. The office was quiet, most people being out for lunch, but still a few heads turned to look. I was aware that not replying to Nick would be tantamount to admitting my guilt.

'I know. They're great, aren't they? I'll take a few copies down for him later. He's got no idea. He's going to be so chuffed.'

'Say well done from me,' said Nick. 'Tell him the *Gazette* would take him on if they weren't getting rid of half the staff.'

It was only when Nick went back to his desk that I noticed the piece of paper he'd left on my keyboard. I turned it over.

'Dinner, six-thirty Thursday, my place. We need to talk. Please bring lost sock.'

I felt the ache grip me again. Mixed with a fresh shot of guilt. I didn't bother sending a note back. I didn't need to. He knew I would come. That was the power he had over me. The reason I had veered so violently out of control.

It was getting dark by the time I made it into town later that afternoon. The first thing I saw was the reflective armband round Colin's parka. It made me think of road safety lessons at school. And how uncool it had been to wear one.

'Anyone recognised you yet?' I asked, striding up to him with a big grin on my face. He looked at me nonplussed. 'I mean, now that you've got your face in the paper and your name in lights, thought you might get pestered by fans in the street.'

Still the same expression. Clearly Colin hadn't seen the *Gazette*. I unfurled one of the half a dozen copies under my arm, turned to page three and held it up for him to see.

Colin looked at it, then back to me, a mixture of disbelief and excitement in his eyes. 'My photos. I don't understand.'

'You know how it is, Colin. These bloody journalists come along and next thing you know, you're splashed all over the papers. Headline news.'

'You didn't say you were going to publish them.'

'I didn't know if they'd be any good, did I?'

'Thanks for the vote of confidence.'

'You don't mind, do you? Only everyone agreed they were brilliant. I wanted to surprise you.'

'Who's everyone?'

'Roger, ex-Vietnam war photographer, Terry our editor, and Nick. He said to congratulate you.'

Colin nodded. His eyes had glazed over.

'I don't know what to say,' he said eventually.

'That's fine. Take a vow of silence. Creative types are allowed to be distant and aloof. I bet your mate Salgado doesn't give interviews.'

But a second later he let out a whoop, punched the air and picked me up and kissed me in the middle of the street, his lips cold and crusty on my cheek.

'Thanks, Sarah. Thank you so much. You don't know what this means to me.'

'You've just given me a small inkling,' I said. 'Don't let it go to your head, mind. This new-found fame and fortune.'

As soon as I said it I realised and snapped my mouth shut. The words, however, could not be retracted. My gaze slid from Colin's face down to the ground.

'Sorry,' I said. 'I'll ask the editor if we can pay you for

them. It won't be much, though. Things are a bit tight at the moment.'

'Sarah,' Colin said. 'I don't care about the money. Seeing them in print is enough. That's what I've always dreamt about.'

I looked up admiringly at Colin. The word 'humbled' did not begin to explain how I felt.

'Well, the other good news is Roger is going to try to sort you out another camera. He wants you to come in later in the week to pick it up. Said he'll show you round, let you have a play in the darkroom. Friday afternoon.'

He nodded.

'And are you free tomorrow morning about nine for me to interview you? Terry wants us to run your life story.'

'People won't want to read about me,' he said.

'Of course they will. It's an inspiring story. We've already had calls from our readers this afternoon, saying how much they liked your photos.'

Colin appeared incredulous.

'Good things can happen to you, too, Colin. There is some justice in this world after all.' I handed him the bundle of newspapers under my arm. 'You can show these to the other guys at the hostel. Put them up in your dorm,' I said.

'No room left,' said Colin. 'Razor's got your Bo Derek pics plastered over the whole bloody place. Keeps asking me if you can get him any more like that.'

'I'll see what I can do,' I said, turning to leave. 'Anything to keep him sweet for you.'

I was still on a high when I got home. The flat was silent. Jonathan was in the lounge, bent over a pile of school books. He was spending more time than ever on marking these days. Probably as a way of trying to redeem himself.

'Look at these,' I said, laying a copy of the paper out on

the coffee table. He gave them a cursory glance, nodded, and turned back to the book he was marking.

'They're Colin's,' I said. 'Aren't they fantastic?'

'Yeah, great,' he said.

'Don't sound so enthusiastic.'

'I'm sorry, Sarah,' he said, running his fingers through his hair. 'I'm up to my ears in marking and it's parents' evening next week and I haven't prepared anything yet. I guess it's all getting on top of me.'

He gave a big sigh. He looked done in. He'd been through a lot lately.

'Why don't I cook tonight?' I said, stroking his hair. 'Won't be up to your standard, of course, but I can throw something together.'

'Thanks, Sarah,' he said, a glimmer of a smile returning to his face. 'I'll look at Colin's photos properly later, when I'm done.'

I wandered out into the kitchen, got out the spaghetti and a jar of pasta sauce and began to look for Nick's sock.

Saturday 19 July 1997

I do not wake up. I simply drift from not sleeping to being awake. I have nothing to get up for today. And I am feeling sick already. Pre-wedding nerves. That is what it is. I wonder if the bride-to-be is suffering as well. As for the groom, I do not know what I wish for him. The pain receptors in my head go into overdrive if I so much as picture his face. I guess I hope he is thinking of me, maybe even having second thoughts. Not that they will make any difference. He has made his choice. It is over. For him, at least.

The invite is still on the table where I left it last night. I tell myself that it is helping me confront the truth, a kind of self-help therapy to kick-start the healing process. Though in reality there is no possibility of healing when the wound reopens every time I see him. I could still go, I know that. I bought an outfit just in case. A black dress with white polka dots and a huge black wide-brimmed hat. It is a bit much for a wedding, black. The polka dots are my concession to convention. They can appear jolly, even if I am not. Nick will be wearing a charcoal-grey morning suit. Or a mourning suit as I prefer to think of it. I don't know what she will be wearing. White, I suppose. Probably sleek and simple. Nick let slip to Joan a few weeks ago that she still had a couple of pounds to lose to fit into her gown. I could help her out there, pass on some dieting tips. The vomiting one in particular.

I turn over in bed, still unwilling to get up. I can see my wedding hat now on top of the wardrobe. It was bought with the intention of giving me somewhere to hide, so I could be there without actually having to watch. But I couldn't find anything to block out the sound. Sometimes when it is very quiet at nights, I can hear them saying their vows. I scream to try to drown it out but they simply speak louder. I wonder if they will both get the words right. I have this dream, more of a fantasy really, where he says my name instead of hers and she calls the whole thing off in a fit of pique.

But the reality is, that is not going to happen. Nick is marrying Amanda today. I am not going because I cannot bear it. There is no place left to hide. The only option now is to run.

I have applied for a job at the *Scarborough Evening News*. I've got no idea if I will get it. Or even whether I will go if I do. All I know is that I need an escape route. The prospect of sitting at work welcoming Nick back from his three-week honeymoon in the Caribbean is looming ominously closer. He wants us to be friends. But I am not sure I can do that. Not sure the wound will ever heal while I still breathe the same air as him.

I look at the clock. Just gone nine. Three hours to go. Amanda will probably be having a bath, pampering herself in readiness for her big day. She is staying at her parents' house. It is bad luck to see the groom on the morning of the wedding. It is also bad luck for the groom to have been having an affair a couple of months before the wedding. But she doesn't know that. And what she doesn't know won't hurt her. I could spoil it all and go round and tell her. I know where she lives. But I am not that low. Not quite.

I toss back the duvet and swing my legs out of bed. My body follows reluctantly. I pad bare-foot to the bathroom, all cheery yellow and green. I sit and pee but halfway through I realise that I am about to throw up. I lean over towards the bath and retch into it. The vomit spatters loudly on the plastic. It is mostly liquid, vodka I suspect. I am surprised to see some remnants of food there. I can't remember the last time I managed a proper meal. I sit on the loo, my legs feeling too weak to support me. My body can't stomach what is happening. That much is clear. I wonder how long it will go on punishing me like this. Eventually I summon the strength to wipe myself. As I fumble for the loo roll the box of Tampax topples from the top of the cistern. I stoop to pick them up, realising that I still haven't come on. It will be the stress. It made me miss my period entirely last month. I didn't think that could happen when you were on the pill. My body is pushing the boundaries of science and nature. But that is stupid. Not even my body is capable of that.

With a rising feeling of unease I stagger to the bathroom cabinet and take out the box containing my pills. I pull the leaflet out. I haven't read it for years; you don't bother after the first couple of months. I skip to the part I am vaguely starting to remember. The warning bit which tells you the circumstances when the pill may not work properly – such as when you have been sick – and advises you to use alternative forms of contraception during those times.

I spin round and survey the contents of the bath again. The unease is turning to panic now, my brain trying to make sense of it all. I turn the shower attachment on, swishing the vomit down the plughole. It is not as easy as that, though. The real evidence is inside me. Now the thought is in my head I can't shake it. I am gripped by a sudden need to know.

I get dressed quickly, not bothering to shower. I make do with washing my face and swilling my mouth out until I get rid of the taste. I take the key off the hook, pick up my purse and pull on my jacket. I switch to automatic pilot for the walk to the chemist's. All sorts of thoughts are going through my head. Above all I feel stupid.

Fifteen-year-old-girl-stupid for not even thinking of it before. The chemist is in the process of opening up as I get there. I walk past, pretending I have other things to do, places to go. A few minutes later I turn and walk back again. Inside it is cool and feels suitably clinical.

I find the pregnancy testing kits in the far corner. They are sold in packs of two. I wonder if this is a cynical marketing ploy to rip off the desperate or whether the manufacturers think that if you have got yourself into this mess once you will probably do so again. I pick up a box that promises ninety-nine per cent accurate results in two minutes. I consider whether to buy something else to try to disguise my purchase but decide I would be fooling no one. The chemist smiles politely at me as he takes my money and wraps the box discreetly in a paper bag. Presumably he is past judging people. I am grateful.

I walk home twice as quickly, my legs seemingly anxious to know even if my head is not so sure. I dash upstairs straight into the bathroom, which still smells of sick. I open a window, tear open the box and fumble with the cellophane wrapper. I scan the instructions for anything that looks important, take the stick from out of the case and hold it under me. I am shaking as I start to pee; more urine seems to go on my hand than on the stick. When I have finished I put it back in its case, deciding I will wait two minutes before looking rather than watch second by second.

I sit on the lavatory tapping my fingers on my legs as I count in my head. I don't want to be pregnant. Pregnant with a baby whose father is about to marry someone else. I used to read about people like that in women's magazines. Think how stupid they were. And now it could be me. I would have to lie about who the father was, make up some story about a drunken one night stand to tell them at work. Or else get rid of it. Like Nick got rid of me.

The time is up. I open the case. Two thick blue lines stare back at me. One in each window. I am pregnant. I start to cry. Unable to believe what is happening to me, on this of all days. I sit staring at the blue lines through my tears, watching them blur into one then expand into a line of a dozen or so. Eventually I put the stick back in the case and throw it in the pedal bin. Out of sight, out of mind. If only.

I start cleaning the bathroom. Frantically, desperately, manically. I scrub at the bath first, rubbing at the plastic until I fear I will rub it away. I can see my face in the taps now, not that I want to, but I can. The toilet cleaner has dust on it, that is how little I use it. I squirt it violently round the rim, wanting to flush everything away. The smell is overpowering, making me feel sick again. I retch into the toilet bowl. My sparkling clean toilet bowl. Covering it with whatever combination of liquid, bile and alcohol is left in my stomach. The alcohol, I had forgotten the alcohol. This thing inside me has been growing in it. Forty per cent proof. It is probably poisoned, deformed beyond all recognition.

I tell myself the test result must be wrong. That mine was the one per cent inaccurate test. Someone's has to be. I swish my mouth out and go into the kitchen and drink three glasses of water straight down. I pace around the flat for a bit, giving it time to work, trying to stop myself shaking.

When I can wait no longer I go back to the bathroom and take out the second stick from the box on the floor. I repeat the test, sure it will be different this time, brazenly daring the blue line to appear before me as I watch. When it does I throw it in the bin with the other one and slide off the toilet into a quivering heap on the floor. I am crying again now, safe in the knowledge I have messed up big time. There is no mistake. This is my penance, sent by whoever it is that stands in judgement, who has watched my selfish behaviour and felt repulsed by it.

Eventually, I haul myself up off the floor, stagger into the main room and collapse on my bed in a giddy mixture of nausea, hysteria and panic. The invite is still on the table, the gold embossed lettering glinting in the sunshine. Mr and Mrs Jenkinson request the pleasure of my company at the wedding of their daughter Amanda Jane to Mr Nicholas Hardwick. It is taunting me from across the room. I hear the congregation laughing at me as they wait for the main event. I am the warm-up act, the funny girl who screwed up. Would it have made any difference to Nick if he'd known? Probably he'd have thought it was a ploy, a trap to snare him. That is what the other woman does, isn't it? Get pregnant 'by accident' in a desperate bid to win her man. He might not have, though. He might have seen that I was mortified by this. That genuine mistakes do happen.

I glance at the clock. Eleven-thirty. He should be on his way to church by now. Perhaps he is there already. Waiting nervously inside. Realising that this is it, there is no going back now. It is too late.

Or is it? Maybe there is still time. Maybe if I told him it would prompt a last-minute change of heart. Make him realise he is doing the wrong thing, marrying the wrong woman. He has a right to know. It is his. This baby growing inside me.

I gather myself up off the bed, gripped by a desire for a dramatic final scene instead of seeing things ebb away privately, quietly, without a struggle. I run to the bathroom and splash water over my tear-stained face, the shock hitting my skin first then seeping through beneath, jolting my body into action. I will wear my wedding outfit. I am a guest, after all. Even if I am out to spoil the party. I dash back into the room, take my top off and grab my dress from the wardrobe, pulling it over my head as I wriggle out of my jeans, letting it slither down, finding its way over the curves, settling into place. I slip on my black slingbacks, grab my hat from the top of the wardrobe, pick up my handbag and clatter downstairs.

My hand is shaking so much I struggle to open the car

door. I throw my hat on to the passenger seat, jump inside and start the engine, pulling the seat belt on as I drive off. My heart sinks as I see the traffic crawling along the main road into town. I wind down the window; the heat is stifling. I tap my fingers on the steering wheel, the tapping getting louder as the minutes tick by. I decide to take a different route and turn left, accelerating between the speed humps and hitting each one hard. I have written stories about people who do this, interviewed the residents who complained, the same ones who will be twitching behind the curtains now, threatening to ring that woman at the paper again. I turn left and right and right again, only to find myself staring at a queue of cars in front, people who all had the same idea as me and are now wishing they hadn't bothered. I notice there are traffic cones along the side of the main road and barriers further down towards the town centre. Families are milling around, small children with looks of anticipation on their faces. The carnival. Despite everything I have written about it, I have forgotten the bloody carnival.

It all comes back now. The town centre is going to be closed to traffic from midday. I am not going to make it. I am going to be sitting in a car, pregnant, watching the carnival procession go by when Nick marries someone else. I pull out of the queue of traffic, perform an unconventional three-point turn and park on the other side of the road. I am on double yellows, I will get a ticket but I don't care. I have more important things to worry about. I put my hat on, lock the door and start to run, aware that people are watching me. I weave in and out of the gathering crowd. At first I say 'excuse me', after a while I don't bother. I can hear the tutting and complaining as I push past, children staring, mothers explaining that the woman is in a hurry and that is why she is being rude. I raise my wrist to look at my watch, only to realise that I didn't put it on. The policeman up ahead is turning the traffic away now, so I guess it must be gone twelve. I still have more

than a mile to go. It is not easy to run in my slingbacks.
I wish I'd put my trainers on; it wouldn't have mattered.
It is getting there which is important. I stumble over a
cracked paving stone and come crashing to my knees.
The pain sears through me, bringing tears to my eyes. A
small crowd gathers, an elderly woman asks if I am OK.

'Yes,' I say, 'fine, thanks.'

I am used to telling lies. I am very good at it. A man
hands me my hat which is slightly crumpled but otherwise unscathed. I pick myself up; my left knee is bleed-
ing. I reach down and dab it with my hand, brushing dirt
into it in the process. A St John Ambulance woman is
walking towards me. Fucking busybody Elastoplast
brigade. I have no time for tea or sympathy, for antiseptic
lotions or kissing it better. I put my hat back on and start
off again towards the town centre, walking at first until
I feel steady enough to run again. My eyes are still
watering. That is how I explain the rivulets of hot, salty
liquid running down my cheeks. I run under the railway
bridge, past the park gates, familiar places passing by in
a blur. I give up pushing through the people on the
pavements, scramble through a gap in the barriers and
take to running in the gutter. The best place for me.

'I love you,' I whisper in gasping breaths, 'I love you, I
love you.'

The crowd is denser now. I am joined in the gutter by
a man dressed in a lion suit brandishing a collecting
bucket.

'Have you lost your float, love?' he says as I push past.
I want to tell him to fuck off but I don't have the breath
left. Someone throws twenty pence at the lion's bucket; it
misses and hits me on the arm. The first floats are
approaching from behind. I can hear the soft growl of a
lorry engine and the distant beat of a drum. I squeeze
through a gap in the barriers back into the crowd, ready
to cut down the next corner, away from the procession
route towards the church.

'I love you, I love you.'

I am wheezing now. I have no idea how I am managing to keep my legs moving. I round the corner, and can see St Andrew's church, set back in a shady recess behind the cast-iron railings. I look up at the church clock, twelve forty. I want to climb up and haul the hands back to twelve but I can't. The energy has sapped from my body. I slow to a trot, sure I am too late but drawn to go closer. Perhaps he was late as usual, or she was. Caught up in the traffic. Perhaps there is still a chance.

The wedding car is outside, a silver Rolls-Royce with a white ribbon, the chauffeur mopping his brow with a handkerchief. I walk past it, up to the railings. The front doors are open. I think I can hear music drifting across from inside but it is hard to tell with all the noise from the carnival behind.

'I love you, I love you.'

I stand and brace myself for what I am about to do. There is nothing for it but to go in, to see where they are in the ceremony, to find out if it is legal yet. To do what I have to do.

As I start down the path I see a vision in white drifting towards me from the darkness inside. I dart back out of sight behind the railings as the happy couple emerge on the church steps to a flurry of activity from the photographer. She is radiant, her hair piled elegantly on top of her head, the smile on her face tearing me in two. Hail the victor, who won without even knowing she was in a battle. Beside her Nick is smiling too. Beaming, in fact. Like he is genuinely happy and I have been kidding myself all this time to think he loved me more than her. The shutter clicks. Their happiness captured for ever on film. He is hers now. My gaze drifts down to his left hand. The ring is in place: the circle is complete, unbreakable. Unlike me.

'I hate you,' I whisper under my breath. 'I hate you.'

Fourteen

It was like old times again. Not eating at lunchtime. Pretending all day that there was nothing going on. Striking that fine balance between not ignoring Nick and fraternising with him too much. And the guilt eating away at me from the inside.

Cayte guessed, of course. She was tuned into it now. Took great delight in studying our every move. I wouldn't have been surprised if she was making notes somewhere, taking down times and places when looks were exchanged across the desk.

'You're shagging him tonight, aren't you?' she whispered after Nick had left for an afternoon council meeting. I stopped typing and looked at her sternly.

'I've been invited round for dinner.'

'Same thing.'

'No, it's not. We're only going to talk.'

'That's what you said last time, isn't it?'

I didn't reply. She was right, of course. I was well aware of that. I was walking a tightrope, an exceptionally narrow one at that. I didn't know which way I would fall. All I knew is that I would fall. And there was no safety net.

'Is it that obvious?' I said to Cayte. 'Me and Nick, I mean.'

'Only to my educated ears and eyes.'

'Has anybody else said anything?'

'One or two. But as rumours go it's dying a bit of a

death. Seems everyone thinks you're too nice to cheat on Jonathan. And that Nick wouldn't go for a woman like you.'

I was embarrassed by the first part and took offence at the last. Wondering what kind of woman I was seen as. Whether it was the sensible shoes that did it and if I should invest in some leopard-skin stilettos, simply to give the rumour a longer lease of life.

'God, you make me sound like the Ann Widdecombe of the newsroom. I'm not that bad, am I?'

'I hate to break it to you but you didn't make it on to the guys' office totty top ten list.'

'I didn't know there was such a thing.'

'Afraid so. There's a top ten mingers list as well. Though if it's any consolation you weren't on that either.'

I wasn't sure whether I should feel offended or relieved at Cayte's last comment.

'Where did you come?' I asked.

'Number five,' said Cayte. 'On the totty list. I think I was the token New Age weirdo. I guess I was marked up for wearing short skirts.'

'So who won it?'

'Lisa, of course. Big tits, tight tops, lots of giggles and obviously up for it. The judging criteria aren't exactly sophisticated.'

I shook my head and turned back to my computer screen.

'Talking of marks out of ten,' said Cayte, 'you still haven't told me.'

'Told you what?'

'Is Nick any good in bed?'

I gave Cayte the look she deserved and started typing.

'Come on, you can tell me.'

'I could but I'm not going to.'

'He said you were pretty hot.'

I spun round. Cayte had a huge grin on her face. I couldn't believe I'd fallen for it.

'Piss off,' I said. 'And don't go stirring up the rumours. I don't want this getting out. I feel bad enough as it is.'

'Calm down,' said Cayte. 'You're going to do yourself in if you carry on like this. Why don't you come to my yoga class tomorrow night? We're looking for some new people to join and you could do with chilling out.'

'I'm not sure,' I said. 'I don't fancy chanting "om" with a bunch of New Age weirdos.'

'We're not that bad. At least give it a try. I think you would benefit from some alternate nostril breathing right now.'

I had no idea what she was talking about but figured it was worth a try.

'OK,' I said. 'I'll come. Is it all right if I ask Najma too? I remember her saying she used to do yoga.'

'Yeah, of course.'

'Not a word to Najma, though. About Nick, I mean. She thinks I'm a nice girl.'

'I did,' said Cayte. 'Until yesterday.'

I ignored her and started typing again.

I hung about at work as long as I could. I didn't want to go home before going out again. It would make me too edgy. Jonathan's forlorn face from this morning was a distant memory. I didn't want to refresh it, to give him the chance to make me feel bad. Or to have to repeat the lie about having a late job.

I popped in to see Terry who was doing some heavy duty staring into space.

'Hi,' I said. 'I'll give you a penny for them.'

Terry looked up. It took a moment for him to twig.

'Hello, Sarah. I was wondering if I should take redundancy.'

'They're not offering it to you.'

'I know. But they might do if I ask.'

I sighed and sat down. Wondering if I should charge by the hour.

'You don't want to leave this place.'

'Nor do any of the others. I've got less than seven years left. Some of them have only just started work. Maybe it's time for me to go.'

'What, and leave the way open for Keith to seize power in a military coup? He'd have us all wearing combat gear and holding MOD-style debriefings instead of editorial meetings.'

Terry snorted a laugh. 'I hadn't thought of that.'

'We need you to stay put. Can't have the captain deserting the sinking ship.'

Terry frowned and scratched his head. 'When's your ballot?'

'Tomorrow.'

'How do you think it will go?'

'I don't know, to be honest. People are angry but they might get cold feet when it comes to the vote. Most of them have got mortgages and kids to think about.'

Terry nodded solemnly.

'Anyway, I'm out of here,' I said, standing up and moving towards the door. 'See you tomorrow.'

'Yeah,' said Terry, showing no sign of making a move himself. Sometimes I wondered if he actually went home at all. Or whether he watched the sun rise and set each day from his goldfish bowl.

Nick opened his front door to let me in. The mere sight of him was enough to set the emotion sensor off inside me, causing the alarm in my head to start ringing again, warning me to be careful not to step too near the edge. I wasn't sure if I should give him a proper kiss, peck him on the cheek or just say hello. Neither was he. We made a hash of it and clashed heads, leaving us both grinning awkwardly. And reminding me of how different this was from the old days.

I followed him through to the main room. The toys had been tidied up, put away somewhere discreet. Only the photo of Jess remained. I sat on the sofa facing away from it. The image remained firmly in my head, though. Nestling alongside the one of Jonathan.

I handed Nick the bottle of wine I'd brought.

'Thanks,' he said. 'Have you got my sock?'

'Can't find it. I've looked everywhere. I think it's disappeared into that odd-sock version of the Bermuda Triangle.'

Nick smiled momentarily before his face fell serious again.

'Does Jonathan suspect anything?' he asked.

I shook my head. 'Doesn't seem to. He said what a nice guy you were after you left.'

Nick shut his eyes for a second.

'I felt awful,' he said. 'Lying to him like that.'

'Not half as awful as I did,' I said, staring at a purple stain on the carpet which I suspected had been caused by Jess and a spilt cup of Ribena. Nick put the wine bottle down on the table and walked to the far end of the room.

'So why are you here?' he said.

I looked up at the ceiling while I decided what to say.

'Because sometimes you can't help yourself, no matter how bad it makes you feel. You of all people know that.'

The hurt registered in Nick's eyes. 'Yeah, but I was weak and impulsive. You've got no excuse.'

'Because I'm so together and sensible, you mean?'

'So I'm told. Though the people who say that don't know you. All they know is the image you want to project. They're not looking behind the spin.'

'You make me sound like Alastair Campbell.'

'You've done a pretty good job of keeping them away from the real story.'

'Which is?'

'You and me.'

I looked down at my hands, twiddling my thumbs round each other while listening to the thumping of my heart.

'At least it stopped the gossip at work,' I said. 'Seems no one believed the author of the Writing Wrongs column would cheat on her boyfriend. Or that you'd be interested in a woman in sensible shoes like me.'

Nick snorted. 'Who told you that?'

'Cayte. Apparently I didn't even make the office totty top ten list.'

Nick started laughing.

'Don't tell me you were involved in that,' I said.

'I voted, that's all.'

'Who for?'

'Cayte, actually. Thought it would boost her spirits.'

'Oh.' I looked at the stain on the carpet again.

'I didn't think you'd approve of something like that,' said Nick.

'I don't. But I did hope I might have got one vote.'

Nick shook his head and walked across the room towards the patio doors.

'I'd have voted for the Sarah I used to know,' he said. 'But she wasn't on the list. It was the one everyone else at work knows. The sensible, sorted one. Who doesn't laugh and throw her hair back, who wouldn't dream of going camel racing and who no longer lights up the office with her smile when she arrives in the morning.'

I sat on the sofa, his words raining down on me. Saddened by the way he said them. And how uncomfortable they made me feel.

'I'm sorry I'm not the life and soul of the office,' I said. 'I'm the chief reporter and I've got union members to represent. I can't spend my time pissing about laughing. I'm there to do a job, not to provide entertainment.'

'You find time to provide a counselling service,' said Nick.

'Don't worry, I'm withdrawing that. Apparently my advice is not always welcome.'

'Who said that?'

'Cayte. Reckons I get off on telling other people what to do.'

'She's right. Part of the image though, isn't it? If you're busy sorting everyone else's problems out it doesn't leave you any time to face up to your own.'

I frowned at him. I wasn't going to ask what my problems were. I didn't want to hear.

'What is this? Am I on the psychiatrist's couch, or something?'

'Uncomfortable, isn't it?'

'How would you know? You seem to spend all your time analysing me.'

Nick fell silent. He walked over and sat down next to me, the tension fizzing as he did so.

'I had some counselling,' he said, after a long pause.

'When?'

'After my marriage broke up and Amanda and Jess left.'

'Oh.' I went back to twiddling my thumbs.

'I needed to figure out how I'd screwed my life up so badly,' said Nick. 'Why I let people down. How I've managed to hurt the only three people I've ever loved.'

It was Nick's turn to look at the stain on the carpet, his face crumpled, his shoulders hunched and shaking. I reached out and squeezed his left thigh, leaving my hand there.

'For what it's worth,' I said, 'I forgave you. I wouldn't be here if I hadn't.' He looked up at me. 'I wasn't talking about you. The third person was my mother.'

My cheeks reddened for a second before I noticed him trying not to laugh. I took a cushion from the sofa and hit him with it in the chest.

'No it wasn't, you lying git. You can't stand your mother.'

'Had you worried for a second, though. Didn't I?'

He leant over and nuzzled my face. His hands on my shoulders, hair falling into mine. I was right about it not being like the old days at all. It was deeper, richer. Altogether more grown-up. I loved him at that moment. Loved him more than I ever had. But I couldn't let it happen again. Couldn't twist the knife in Jonathan's back. I pulled away.

'Anyway,' I said, 'am I going to get something to eat or not?'

Nick looked at me, unable to hide his disappointment.

'Sure,' he said quietly. He disappeared into the kitchen, telling me to put a CD on and make myself at home. It wasn't my home, though. I was all too painfully aware of that. I wandered over to the coffee table and picked up the photo of Jess, studying it more closely than I had allowed myself to previously. I noticed the light freckles on her nose. She had Nick's hair and eyes but Amanda's nose. It hurt. Wondering what might have been. Who might have been staring out of that photo frame, if things had been different. If I'd got there in time. If I hadn't been so unbearably cruel.

I sighed and walked over to the CD rack, tilting my head to one side as I scanned the contents. Some familiar favourites, ones I had maybe touched myself many years ago. Most of the more recent additions predictable. Though I noticed a Style Council CD in there amongst the newer Paul Weller offerings. Nick used to hate the Style Council. But then again he used to hate Tony Blair. I plumped for *Badly Drawn Boy* in the end. It seemed safe, neutral. Unconnected with the past.

Nick returned a few minutes later carrying two pizzas and a bowl of salad.

'Dinner is served, courtesy of Marks & Spencer,' he said, pulling the chair out for me as I sat down. 'Sorry it's not much. I will cook you a proper meal one day.'

He wouldn't, of course. Because he would be leaving in a few weeks. And I'd already decided not to come again. He fetched some Perrier and poured a glass for me and some red wine for himself. He ate his pizza with his knife and fork this time. But as I watched I remembered how he'd eaten it on election night, seven years ago. With his fingers, licking them as he went. I managed about half of my pizza before putting my knife and fork down and pushing back my plate.

'You're not full already?' said Nick. 'I've got ice cream in the freezer.'

'I should go,' I said.

Nick stared at me as he finished chewing a mouthful of pizza.

'Why?'

'You know why,' I said, pushing my chair back.

'You can't keep doing this, Sarah. Starting things and not finishing them.'

'It's only a pizza.'

'You know what I mean.'

He took another sip of wine. I stood up, feeling my legs trembling, my pulse racing.

'You're right. I can't keep doing this. So I'm going to end it here.'

Nick's jaw dropped open as he put his glass down with a clatter. 'But we haven't talked yet. Not properly.'

'We could talk for ever, Nick, but it won't change anything. There's another person involved here. And he's not going to go away.'

I moved towards the door, picking up my coat and bag.

'Please don't do this,' said Nick, standing up and taking a tentative step towards me.

'I have to,' I said. 'It's the only way. I'm sorry.'

I hurried to the door and let myself out. Not even turning to wave goodbye. In case the look on his face made me change my mind again. I was doing the right thing. I was sure of it. It was simply that it would take a while for my heart to believe it.

Fifteen

I opened my eyes. Jonathan was lying next to me, smiling.

'What?' I said.

'Just you. I like looking at you when you wake up. Reminds me how lucky I am.'

I reached over and stroked his head. The way you would an old Labrador. They weren't so bad, Labradors. Loyal, dependable, adoring. And safe. I kissed him on the forehead. Relieved he hadn't been hurt by my selfish behaviour. And desperate to make it up to him.

'Have you got time for a couple of hours off, tonight?' I asked.

'I guess so. If I get the marking out of the way as soon as I get home. Why, what have you got planned?'

'We should spend some time together,' I said. 'I'm going to a yoga class with Cayte and Najma straight after work. I'll get a takeaway and a video on the way home. Nice quiet night in, curled up together on the sofa. We haven't done that for ages.'

Jonathan smiled. Enough for his dimples to show. 'You're on,' he said.

I'd almost forgotten how nice he looked when he smiled like that.

I slunk into the office and past Nick's desk. His head, which was staring straight at the screen, didn't move an inch. Neither of us offered any word of greeting or recognition.

Cayte, who served as a useful physical buffer between us, looked at Nick then at me and mouthed, 'What happened?'

I sent an e-mail by way of explanation.

SUBJECT: You know what

It's over, for good. We had pizza, nothing happened, nor will it from now on. I've decided to make a go of it with Jonathan. No more questions. Don't let on to him that you know.

PS At least one of your votes in the top totty thing was a sympathy one.

She devoured it hungrily, her facial expressions changing as she read. I could almost hear the sound effects, the aahhs and groans from the audience. This is what my life had been reduced to. A daytime soap opera for Cayte's entertainment.

The reply was predictable.

SUBJECT: Re: You know what

Hope you know what you're doing, and that it's not just because Jonathan's a better cook. Don't like to ask this while you're still obviously upset but what would be an acceptable amount of time before I can make a pass at him?

PS Only trying to cheer you up. Will give you a hug later.

As I finished reading the e-mail Nick stood up and left the office without a word, a pile of council agendas under his arm, the weight of the world seemingly resting on his shoulders.

'Poor guy,' said Cayte. 'You could have let him down gently.'

'There's no such thing,' I said. Worried she was right. If it had all been a bit sudden. But it was too late

now. There was no going back. I decided to change the
subject.

'How are things with Jazz?'

Cayte shrugged. 'OK, I guess. He's been around a bit
more this week. And we're going to a gig together on
Saturday. I want to get him tickets for the Chili Peppers
at the NEC next summer but that's probably risking it. I
expect he'll have dumped me by then.'

'Hey, come on, think positively,' I said. 'You two can
still make a go of it. And something local might come up.'

Cayte shrugged. 'Well, if not I've got an interview with
the *Shetland Times*. Came this morning.'

'Oh,' I said, unsure whether I should congratulate her
or offer my commiserations. Before I could decide my
phone rang. The female caller introduced herself as
Imogen something double-barrelled, from the Ikon art
gallery.

'I'm calling about the photos you published the other
day, taken by the *Big Issue* seller.'

'Oh yes,' I said.

'We wondered if he'd taken any more?'

'Yeah, a couple of rolls, all of them good enough to
publish.'

'I am glad,' she said. 'We were wondering if Mr Leake
would allow us to exhibit them.'

I wasn't sure I'd heard right. 'An exhibition? Of Colin's
photos?'

Cayte turned to look at me, the surprise and delight on
her face mirroring mine.

'That's right,' said Imogen. 'We've got a last-minute
slot to fill, just before Christmas. It's a small gallery but I
think they'd work amazingly well in there.'

'He'd be delighted,' I said. 'You'd be making his
Christmas.'

'Wonderful,' said Imogen. 'Here's what we'd like to do.'

She spoke in an excited babble, using phrases like
'punchy perspective' and 'politically challenging

imagery'. I wrote it all down so I could remember it to tell Colin later.

'So who was it?' said Cayte, when I put the phone down a few minutes later.

'Only the bloody Ikon. They want to put on an exhibition of Colin's work before Christmas.'

'That's fantastic. That's his dream.'

'I know,' I said, warming inside at the thought of it. 'He's coming in this afternoon. He'll be so chuffed.'

We held the strike ballot at lunchtime. It was all done secretly, each member casting their vote in a sealed box in photographic. I was hoping Nick would come back from the Council House to take part. He didn't, though. I guessed he'd decided that, for once, not voting was the right thing to do. I knew what the result was going to be from the expressions on people's faces as they filed out. People who had been angry last week now seemed resigned to their fate. Sad that they couldn't afford to go on strike, sorry they were working for a company which wouldn't have given a toss if they had. As it turned out, the motion was only lost by a handful of votes. But that was enough. The resistance had come to nothing. I felt deflated. And that I'd let everyone down. People trooped back to work, aware that this was the beginning of the end.

When I got back to my desk Cayte was giving me one of her looks.

'What's up?' I said.

'That woman from the art gallery just rang back,' she said.

'Imogen? Why didn't you call me?'

'She didn't want you. She wanted to speak to Nick.'

'Oh.'

'Left a message for him saying thanks for the tip-off about the photos and for suggesting the exhibition.'

I stared at Cayte, unsure how to react.

'I always said Nick was a nice guy,' said Cayte.

I sat down and started leafing through my notebook. Knowing she was right.

Colin arrived at three that afternoon for his visit. I went downstairs to reception to greet him. He stood a few steps back from the counter, jacket collar turned up, woolly hat pulled down firmly over his forehead, glasses steaming up rapidly.

'Mr Leake, I presume,' I said, peering at what I could make out of his face.

'It's a bit warmer in here than it is outside,' he said.

'I thought you'd taken to going incognito. All this adulation must be getting a bit tiresome for you.'

Colin managed a grin. 'I've had a few comments. My regulars thought it was great.'

'They'll be even more impressed when they hear you've got an exhibition on,' I said, as we climbed the stairs to the newsroom.

Colin stopped where he was and looked at me. 'Are they going to put my pictures in the front window downstairs?'

'Oh, I think we can do a bit better than that,' I said. 'How about the Ikon? I know it's not the Tate but you've got to start somewhere.'

'You're having me on.'

'Nope. This is the woman you need to call,' I handed him Imogen's number. 'I told her I was sure you'd go for it but you need to have a chat with her. Sort out all the arty farty details I know nothing about. You need to do it today as well. She wants to put it on very quickly to fill a gap they've got before Christmas.'

Colin still didn't move. Now that the steam had cleared from his glasses I could see his eyes bulging at me.

'I don't know what to say. Was this your idea?'

'No. It was, um, Nick's, actually.'

'I can't believe they'd want to exhibit my photos.'

'Well, you'd better get used to it. And you'd better take good care of the camera Roger's dug out for you. No sticking it up Razor's nose this time.'

'No problem there. He's sweet now. Ever since you got him those pictures we've been getting along fine. I was talking to him the other day, actually. He was telling me he used to be in the psychiatric unit you're doing that story on. You know, the Rupert Bear place. Reckons it was even worse than he says.'

'Really? Would he be willing to talk to me about it?'

'Yep, all sorted out for next Wednesday afternoon. Two-thirty at the hostel. I've even negotiated a price for you. Photos of Raquel fucking Welch. That's what he says he wants.'

'No problem.' I laughed. 'Tell him it's a done deal.'

We reached the newsroom, Colin looked around.

'Is Nick in?' he said. 'I'd like to thank him.'

'No, he's at the council,' I said. 'I'll pass on the message, though. Now, let me introduce you to Roger.'

I watched Colin and Roger go off to the darkroom together, the pair of them bouncing up and down like kids in a toyshop. I stopped off at Terry's office on the way back to my desk to tell him the result of the ballot.

'We're not going on strike,' I said, hovering in the doorway.

'Right,' he said without looking up. He was watching the fish but rather than the usual blank look the cogs were turning this time, I could hear them. Somehow it was even more worrying. I shut the door and sat down opposite him.

'I thought you'd be pleased,' I said.

'Yeah, I am. What do you reckon they think about, Sarah?' he asked, still staring into the tank.

'Are we talking about the fish?'

'Yeah. Swimming round in circles all day. There must be something going on in there.'

'Probably wondering who the poor bastard is who sits

watching them all the time when he's got a million and one better things to do.'

Terry chuckled, his shoulders shaking. 'Jealous of them, I am. Life must be pretty simple in there.'

'Well, yeah, if you like swimming and fish food. I can stick a hosepipe in here, fill it up and chuck you some crumbs through the roof every now and then if you fancy giving it a go.'

'No complications, no relationships to break down, no bickering families. More hassle than they're worth, relationships, families, all that stuff.'

'What's brought this on? Apart from sharing your home with your wife's live-in lover.'

Terry ignored my less than subtle dig. 'Nick came to see me this morning. Have you seen him today? Looks like he's been kicked in the balls.'

I decided not to tell Terry that the foot in question belonged to me.

'What did he want?' I asked, trying to fake indifference.

'Asked for the morning off, a week on Tuesday. It's his daughter's nativity play at school. Apparently her mum's just announced they're moving to Germany with her new bloke after Christmas. Doesn't look like he's got any say in the matter. Poor bastard.'

I felt a low kick to the stomach. Fully deserved for my vanity in thinking Nick's crushed demeanour had been down to me.

'Oh, I hope you said yes.'

'Of course. I told him to take the whole day off, spend some time with her. No skin off my nose.'

'What about the leaving do?'

The nine who were being made redundant were supposed to be having a joint leaving do on the Tuesday evening, before people started drifting off for Christmas.

'He said no one would miss him. And that seeing his daughter was more important. I know you don't like the guy but I really felt for him. It was all he could do to hold himself together while he was in here.'

I mumbled something to Terry about having to go and backed out of the office. Nick would be in pieces. I knew that. I wanted to go to him, to hold him. Be there for him when he needed me. But I couldn't because I had ended it. I had given up that right.

I pulled into the car park at the community centre in King's Heath after work that evening with my head full to overflowing. Thoughts I didn't want there, flying around. Refusing to let go. Najma waved to me through the windscreen of her Ford Fiesta. I locked the car and hurried over to greet her.

'Hi,' I said. 'Glad you could make it. This was Cayte's idea so if it's awful we can sneak out halfway through and blame her.'

Najma smiled. 'No, I'm looking forward to it. I haven't been to a yoga class for years. And I could do with unwinding.'

She seemed a little subdued. I put it down to her having had a bad day at work.

Cayte was waiting for us in the foyer, sporting a pair of fuchsia pink leggings teamed with an orange and pink flowery top, no doubt picked up from the Oxfam shop on the High Street, like most of her wardrobe.

'Hiya,' she said, grinning at us both. 'Welcome to our little oasis of calm. Please leave your troubles at the front door, this is a stress-free zone.'

'Steady on,' I said. 'You're making it sound like some kind of cult.'

'Didn't I tell you?' said Cayte. 'When we've finished the chanting and ritual burning of incense sticks we'll begin the brainwashing. You'll both leave here believing in the power of om.'

I shook my head and groaned as Cayte led us into the draughty hall. The teacher was suitably toned, willowy and away with the fairies-looking. The regulars arranged their yoga mats in a semicircle in front of her. Najma and I put our blankets on the floor towards the back of the room and lay down as instructed.

'Allow your body to settle and your mind to empty.' She said it as if it was a two-minute job. If I lay there until Christmas I didn't think I'd be able to accomplish it. 'If any thoughts come into your head, imagine they are balloons and simply allow them to float away.'

The thoughts in my head were beating the inside of my skull with hammers. I could hardly hear her for the clamour they were making. They were telling me I had made a mistake. To go to Nick. That he would be hurting. Needing me. I tried popping the balloons rather than allowing them to float away. Piercing them with giant knitting needles so they exploded loudly in my head. I was feeling more stressed than when I started. Clearly I wasn't very good at this visualisation lark.

'And simply allow your eyelids to close.'

Mine stubbornly resisted. I was always sceptical of people who asked me to close my eyes. Ever since Robert Bradshaw at school had asked me to do so before depositing a slug in my outstretched palm. I glanced at the teacher through my half-shut eyelids. She was a picture of serenity. I envied her at that moment. Would have done anything to swap my head for that nice, calm, empty one.

'Breathe in deeply, allowing your tummy to rise like a balloon.'

There was no room in my tummy for anything like air. The knots were taking up too much room. You were supposed to breathe out for a count of eight. I only had enough breath to make it to three. I was glad when the relaxation was over and the postures began. I wasn't very good at them but at least it gave me something else to think about other than emptying my head of balloons.

'Did you enjoy it?' Cayte asked as she rolled up her purple yoga mat afterwards.

'Kind of,' I said. 'Although I discovered my brain doesn't have an off switch and I'm not half as supple as you and Najma.'

Najma smiled.

'I was surprised I could still do some of those postures,' she said. 'It's been a good few years.'

'You and Cayte have got age on your side,' I said. 'Trust me, when you hit thirty you won't even be able to touch your toes any more.'

We said goodbye to Cayte and walked across to the car park together. Najma seemed quiet. She'd made no mention of Paul tonight. Normally she couldn't stop talking about him.

'Are you OK?' I said. 'Only you seem a bit distracted.'

'I'm fine,' she said. 'Just got a few things on my mind.'

'Such as?'

'I don't want to burden you with it, Sarah,' she said, her eyes moist and heavy.

'Hey,' I said. 'I'm an experienced agony aunt looking for new clients. Why don't you give me a try?'

Najma smiled.

'If you're sure,' she said.

'Positive. Get in my car, it's too cold to talk out here.'

As soon as she sat in the passenger seat, Najma's bottom lip started to tremble.

'Is it Paul?' I said, reaching in my bag and passing her a tissue in time to catch the first tear. 'Has something happened?'

Najma dabbed at the corners of her eyes.

'Sort of,' she said. 'My brother Surrinder spotted me and Paul holding hands in the cinema queue.'

She blew out as she said it. I knew very little about her family. She'd only left home a year ago but she didn't talk about them much.

'They didn't know?' I said.

She shook her head. 'My parents are devout Muslims, very traditional. They had expressly forbidden me to date any non-Muslims.'

'Oh, Najma, I had no idea.'

'They're very private people, my family. It's not the sort of thing I talk about.'

All those times we'd chatted about stuff and nonsense, the way you do with neighbours who become friends. I'd thought I knew her. She probably thought she knew me. But neither of us had scratched the surface. Had any inkling of the darkness lurking beneath.

'So what's happened? What have they said?'

She fiddled with the soggy tissue in her hand. 'My parents are refusing to meet or speak to me. They sent Surrinder round instead. He told me I'd brought shame on the family. That my mother was inconsolable and my father was dreading the moment when someone at the mosque finds out.'

'Did you tell him that you're happy? That Paul treats you really well?'

'I tried to but he didn't want to hear it. Said I knew the score. That I must choose between the family and Paul. And that if I chose Paul the family would disown me. For good.'

'Oh, God. You poor thing. Is there no way you can reason with them? Get them to meet Paul so they can find out for themselves what he's like?'

'No,' she said. 'It doesn't work like that. You have to stick to the rules.'

I nodded slowly, realising how little I understood.

'What does Paul say?'

Najma pulled a face.

'I haven't told him yet. I don't know how to. I've been making excuses about why he hasn't met my parents yet. Said they'd been away with family in Pakistan. I'm worried he might end it if I tell him the truth.'

Her voice faltered as she brushed away another tear. I leant over and gave her a hug.

'Oh, Sarah. I'm in such a state,' she said. 'I just don't know what to do for the best.'

'I think you should tell Paul, for starters,' I said. 'You're going to need his support. I know it's not going to be easy but I guess you'll find out what he's made of. And that might actually help you make a decision.'

Najma looked up at me. 'You think I should choose him, don't you?'

'It's difficult for me to say. I'm not close to my family, like you are. It wouldn't be such a big wrench for me.'

'I don't want to lose them but I do love Paul. Really love him.'

'Then talk to him. Let him know what you're going through.'

She nodded. 'Thanks, Sarah. You've been a great help. You always seem to know the right thing to do.'

I smiled at her. It was easy when it came to other people. It was only my own life I struggled with.

I stopped off at the video shop on the way home. Choosing a film which would meet with Jonathan's approval wasn't easy, which was why I usually left it to him. Eventually I plumped for something by Ken Loach which I couldn't remember seeing, knowing it would be acceptable even if it turned out we had watched it before.

I walked up to the counter and handed the membership card over to the young woman serving. She swiped it and waited for the details to come up on screen before asking me to confirm our address.

'And your memorable name?' she asked.

I looked at her blankly.

'You have to give the memorable name for security purposes.'

Jonathan had taken the membership out; he usually got the videos. I had no idea.

'Er, Sarah?' I suggested hopefully.

The girl shook her head, her ponytail exaggerating the refusal.

'Sorry,' she said, 'I do need it to let you take the film out.'

'Hang on,' I said. 'I need to ring someone.'

I got out my mobile and called Jonathan. 'Hi,' I said. 'I'm at the video shop. What's the password name thing I have to give?'

'Oh, that,' said Jonathan. 'It's Aung San Suu Kyi.'

I paused for a moment, waiting for him to say it was a joke. He said nothing.

'Of course,' I said. 'I should have guessed.'

I hung up and repeated the name back to the girl, who clearly wasn't well versed on the political opposition in Burma.

'I'm not surprised you couldn't remember it,' she said. 'I've never heard of her. Who is she?'

I hesitated. 'A porn star,' I said. 'A Thai porn star. My boyfriend's seen all her films. Ask him about her next time he comes in.'

I took the video from her and walked out of the shop, heading for the Indian to pick up our chickpea curry. Our quiet night in no longer seemed quite so appealing.

Saturday 19 July 1997

I pull my hat down over my face and slip into the shadows behind the church railings where they can't see my tears, or hear me choking on their happiness. I can hear them, though. Her laughing, the photographer barking instructions, Nick obliging by giving her a kiss, prompting a cheer from the guests.

My heart is beating double time to the steel drums from the carnival float at the top of the street. A gust of wind blows a handful of confetti over me. It catches in my hair. I try to flick it out but it falls down the back of my dress. Torn fragments of something that was once much bigger, clinging to me, not wanting to let go. I could stay and watch, wave them off in the car, offer my congratulations. But there is only so much a person can take – or fake.

I walk away, past the wedding car, the chauffeur now with his cap on standing to attention, ready to whisk the happy couple on their way. Would it have made a difference if I'd got there in time? If I'd told him? It doesn't matter either way now. He is lost to me.

I arrive back on the main road. The carnival is in full flow. The children from the Catholic school are dressed as leprechauns. They are waving and rattling buckets, a huge Irish tricolour draped over the back of the float. Nick suspects the head teacher is a paedophile but what does Nick know? I push my way along the back of the crowd of spectators lining the pavements, hoping Karen

320

and Ted, who drew the short straw of covering the carnival, haven't spotted me making a spectacle of myself. Or slinking away now to lick my wounds. When I get to my car there is a parking ticket on the windscreen. I do not care.

I stop at the off licence on my way home, the sound of the steel band still ringing in my ears. Music, laughter, happy sounds. I have to get rid of them, drown them out. I buy two bottles of Absolut vodka. It never hurts to have a spare one in. The woman serving gives me a look, somewhere between pity and scorn. I realise I must look a state: sweaty body, tear-stained face, bloodied knee. I am thankful I did not have time to apply any make-up. My mascara would have run. I would have looked like one of the clowns from the carnival; people would probably start singing the Smokey Robinson song. She puts the bottles in a carrier bag and I hobble back to the car.

The flat feels emptier than it has ever felt before. The bathroom is still strewn with debris from this morning, the smell of vomit lingering in the carpet, seeping into the grouting between the tiles.

They will probably be on to the speeches by now. I should get a mention really. Somewhere between the bridesmaids and the best man. 'And thanks to Sarah, whom I was shagging up to a few weeks ago but who has had the good grace not to show her face today. Or to bother me with the details of her pregnancy.'

Except he wouldn't say that last bit because he doesn't know. And he won't, not ever. I'll make sure of that. What would be the point? Why spoil everything when he has managed to extricate himself from such a potentially messy situation without any spillages? Any blood on the carpet. No, it is my problem now. I must deal with it on my own. The only way I know how. I take one of the vodka bottles from the bag, the sheer weight of it feeling good in my hand. I open it, loving the sound of the seal breaking as the cap tears away from the metal collar on the neck. I do not bother with a glass. I put my mouth to the rim and swig it back, feeling the soothing medicine flow down my throat, entering my bloodstream where it is needed. I have no desire for drugs; for pills, powders and needles. I have alcohol.

'To the bride and groom,' I say, holding the bottle aloft, hearing the clink of their champagne glasses, seeing the reflection of their smiling faces in the bottle, smelling their happiness. 'Bastard.'

For the first time ever I want him to be hurting. Want him to feel some twinge of remorse. I wonder if he has even thought of me today. I suspect he has. But only for a fleeting moment, some brief pause in the celebrations. Only to hope I wouldn't turn up and make it difficult for him. He has no idea how close I came to making it enormously difficult. No idea that a part of him is growing inside me. A part I do not want. If he could have left me a digit, a little finger perhaps, I could have kept it in a bottle of formaldehyde above the fireplace for sentimental reasons. But this, this part of him, is not pure. It has been contaminated by me and turned bad. Like everything I touch.

I toast the happy couple again. And again and again. I do not want to have to think about what they are doing for the rest of the day. What he will say about her in his speech, what song they will have for their first dance, where they will spend their honeymoon night. I want to obliterate everything from now onwards. To erase the future in a way I can't erase the past. Only that will be difficult when the future is growing inside me. Has embedded itself, feeding on me like a leech, sucking me dry. It is a future that scares me rigid. A future I am not strong enough to cope with. Not on my own.

I tip the bottle back and feel my throat as I swallow, counting each glug. I am sitting on the floor, propped up against the bed. Without it I am not sure I would be able to support myself. The vodka is starting to work its magic. I can't even remember what her dress looked like. That was this afternoon. That was a long time ago.

At some point much later I realise the bottle is empty. I feel sad, a sense of loss. And then I remember the second one, in the carrier bag in the corner of the room. I start crawling on my hands and knees towards it. Just one more and I will feel better. It will all go away.

It is dark when I wake, early-hours-of-the-morning dark. I am slumped on the carpet. As I wait for my eyes to adjust I am conscious of a variety of sensations. I have a crick in my neck. I am cold. I have no feeling in my right calf. It is still there because I can reach out and touch it but it is bent up under me at an odd angle. My dress is damp, a mixture of sweat from earlier and – judging by the smell – alcohol. I reach out into the darkness, patting the floor around me. The first thing I come across is a small patch of wetness. I put my hand to my nose and sniff. It is sick. I am surprised it doesn't smell much but then it is mainly liquid. I carry on feeling. Eventually I locate an empty vodka bottle and a few seconds later another. My head is pounding, the steel drums continuing to beat out their carnival rhythm. I can't work out whether I feel sick or hungry, probably a mixture of both. And I have a cramping pain low down in my belly. Like a period pain but different, sharper somehow.

I try to sit up, everything hurts, the darkness spins. I give myself a few minutes and try again, managing to hoist myself up on to my elbows this time. I stay there for a moment, daring myself to go further, before pushing down with my hands and shifting so that I am propped up against the bed. When I put my hand back down I find another wet patch. At the same time I realise I am desperate for a pee. I feel the seat of my dress: it seems I have wet myself already. I appear to have lost control of my bodily functions. I push myself up using the bed, and the cramping pain causes me to double up. I sit on the edge a moment, waiting for the pain to ease and my head to stop spinning. Neither seems to happen but the urge to pee gets worse. I stand up and stagger towards the bathroom, clawing my way along the walls and any furniture I can reach. I can feel liquid trickling down my thigh. A grown woman should not allow herself to get in this state. Somehow I reach the bathroom and manage to hitch my dress up and lower myself on to the toilet seat. The relief is instant. The cramping pain remains, though; if anything it gets worse. For a second I wonder if it is a period pain, if both tests could have been wrong after all. But although I have only known for a matter of hours, I feel pregnant now. I am sure of it. I decide it must be the alcohol, twisting my gut. I stand up and head back to the doorway, not being in a state to flush or wash my hands. I realise liquid is still trickling down my thigh. I do not understand. I fumble for the light cord and pull it. The first thing I see is the streaks of red on my hand. I think it is the drink playing tricks on me. Until I see the trail of red spots and confetti leading back to the lavatory. There is blood on the carpet. I hurry over to look into the pan, and a violent palette of red greets me. A sharp intake of breath: I want to scream but no sound comes out. The cramping pain tightens. I lift my skirt again and pull down my knickers to be confronted by a clot of something, darker red, a tiny lump of fibrous tissue – human tissue. The scream emerges, shrill and ragged. I frantically pull off my knickers and throw them into the bath. I don't want to examine the evidence; I know what I have done. I sit down heavily on the toilet seat, breathing fast and shallow between sobs. My body is shaking, my head seems suddenly clear, but I have no idea what to do. I screw my face up as the cramping comes again and the realisation hits me in the same wave as the pain. I have killed Nick's baby, the baby he didn't even know he had. I have poisoned it, flushed it out of my body. I may as well have drowned it in the bath at birth. Baby killer. That is what I am.

My body continues contorting, squeezing the life from me. I have no idea how much blood I have lost or how much more there is to go. I cannot face looking in the bowl again in case I see more clots, more tissue, a heart which has stopped beating.

In one day I have lost everything: the only man I have ever loved and the only thing I had left of him. I want it back now, but it is too late. I should have thought of that before I pulled the trigger. Because I did. My baby's blood is on my hands. Literally. The sobbing becomes hysterical. I sit and rock back and forth on the toilet seat, trying to calm myself, to soothe the pain away.

'I'm sorry,' I say in the direction of the bath. 'I'm so sorry.'

Sixteen

It was Sunday morning before I found an excuse to get out of the flat. I told Jonathan I was going round to Cayte's to help with her CV. Actually Cayte's CV was a triumph of creative writing which needed no input from me or anyone else with an eye for factual accuracy.

I pulled up across the road from Nick's flat and sat quietly for a moment. Despite lying awake most of the night I still hadn't worked out what I was going to say. All I knew was that I wanted to be there for him. I took a deep breath and opened the door. I was about to get out when I heard another car approach. It was a red Peugeot. The female driver parked on the other side of the road from me, directly outside Nick's. It was only as she stepped out that I recognised her. She was older, of course, and not quite as glamorous, her hair pinned up on top of her head. But she still had that air of sophistication about her. Was still unmistakably Amanda. I shut the car door quickly and ducked down in the driver's seat, hoping she hadn't noticed me. I watched as she walked up the path and rang Nick's doorbell. I was in shock, my brain not functioning properly. It wasn't until the front door opened that I realised why she was here. Nick emerged squinting in the bright morning sunshine, cuddling a little girl with dark curly hair and a familiar smile in his arms.

'Mummy,' Jess squealed. She still had her arms draped round Nick's neck, clearly reluctant to let go while at the same time eager to greet her mother.

'Big hug,' I heard Nick say as he kissed Jess goodbye, the pain visible in his eyes even from my distant vantage point. He passed her across into Amanda's arms, kissing her again on the forehead as he did so. Then stepped back into the shade of the doorway as Amanda fastened Jess into her seat. I was sinking lower and lower in mine, worried Nick would spot me at any moment. I needn't have bothered, though. He only had eyes for Jess. That much was clear. He waved as Amanda pulled away, Jess's tiny hand just visible at the bottom of the window, and shut the door the second they had slipped from view.

I closed my eyes, my head resting on the steering wheel. The pain clawing inside. Jess was beautiful. She was Nick's little girl. She was what could have been. I sat there for a long time. Probably an hour. Seeing it all again in my head, the images still vividly real. The hurt as deep as if it was yesterday. I waited until I had regained some kind of composure before I stepped slowly from the car and made my way up the path to knock on the door.

Nick opened it and stared at me.

'Sarah,' he said, clearly startled.

'I wanted to see you. To talk.'

'I thought you'd said all you wanted to on Thursday?'

'Terry told me. About Jess.'

Nick's eyes were dark and heavy, threatening rain.

'Oh,' he said.

'I'm sorry, Nick. I had no idea.'

'Nor did I till Amanda rang me half an hour after you'd left. It was a good night, Thursday. One of the best.'

The sarcasm didn't suit him today. It spat instead of fizzed.

'Can I come in?' I said. Nick shrugged and left the door open. I followed him into the living room. The floor was littered with Jess's toys.

'She's not long gone,' said Nick, by way of explanation. I nodded, not wanting to admit that I had seen her.

'So what did Amanda say?' I asked. Nick started pacing the room, his sneakers squeaking on the floorboards as he walked.

'Just that they were going. It had all happened very quickly, something to do with Robert's firm getting a big new contract in Frankfurt. She said it was the opportunity of a lifetime.'

'When do they leave?'

'January the second. Great New Year I'm going to have.'

'What about Jess?' I said softly.

'Oh, she can't wait. Spent the whole day yesterday jabbering on about it. They've sold it to her as some sort of extended holiday. She's too young to understand what it means.'

'Don't you have any rights?'

Nick snorted and shook his head. 'Amanda said I can go over to visit one weekend a month. Big of her, I know. Oh, and that when they come over to see her parents they'll try to pop in and see me, depending on where I'm living by then.'

I hadn't asked him whether he'd applied for any jobs yet. Because I didn't want to know. Nick thumped his fist on the patio doors and stared out into the garden.

'I can't deal with this,' he said. 'I can take one part of my life falling apart, Sarah. But not everything at once.'

He looked at me as his voice trailed off and swallowed hard.

I felt the blow. I was part of this. Part of the pain he was feeling. I wanted to tell him it was OK. That I would be here for him, even if we couldn't be together. But I knew that wasn't true. It was all or nothing. That was the only way it could be. I walked over to him and reached out a hand. He turned to stop me.

'Don't,' he said. 'You'll only make it worse.'

I drew my hand back and joined him in staring out into the garden, as if the answer lay buried deep beneath the turf. Neither of us said anything for a while. I searched desperately for something comforting, something worth saying.

'Did she say how long the contract's for? It might only be a short-term thing. A year or two maybe. People often move abroad for a new life. I blame Channel Four, puts all these stupid ideas in their heads. Then when they get there they realise it's not as great as they'd thought. It still rains, the people talk a foreign language, they can't buy Marmite at the local shop, that sort of thing. They could be back before next Christmas.'

Nick shook his head. 'Amanda said it was a permanent move. Robert already speaks fluent German. She said it would be great that Jess would grow up bilingual. Fantastic, isn't it? I'm going to have a German-speaking daughter whom I'll get to see a dozen times a year if I'm lucky. I won't even be her dad any more. Robert will be. He'll be the one living with her, kissing her goodnight, telling her off when she's naughty. Some uptight fucking banker bringing up my daughter.'

He banged his fist on the window again and let his head rest there, his eyes shut for a second. I scrabbled around for the right words, desperate to make things better.

'Hey, come on,' I said. 'It's up to you to make sure she can't forget who her dad is. You can still ring her. Give her a few years and you'll be able to text and e-mail her as well. Maybe by then she can come over and stay with you on her own.'

I knew instantly that it had come out all wrong. Sounding like the sort of advice Cayte had been talking about. The unwanted, sanctimonious, 'never mind, pull yourself together' crap that spilled out of my mouth sometimes. Nick looked at me, obviously having drawn much the same conclusion.

'Thanks for the pep talk, Sarah. You're absolutely right, mustn't let these little things get me down.'

'I'm sorry. I didn't mean it like that. I was trying to say that I understand how you must be feeling.'

Nick shook his head. 'You can't possibly. You're not a parent. You've got no idea what it's like to love your own child, the only child you've ever had and probably ever will have. And then to face losing them.'

I bit my lip as the knife twisted inside, trying not to let the pain show. To reveal more than I wanted to. But the pressure was too great; the tears seeped out, sharp and bitter on my face.

Nick frowned at me.

'Sarah? What's the matter,' he said.

'It's nothing,' I said, blinking hard. 'I'm fine.'

'You're not. Is it something I said?'

A sob forced its way out. My face screwed up in agony. 'I saw her, Nick. I saw your beautiful Jess.'

Nick pulled me to him, stroking the back of my head. 'What? Just now?'

I nodded without looking up.

'Is that what's upset you? I don't understand.'

'You never saw *my* baby.' I screamed the last bit out, the only way to get it past the protective layers which had kept it hidden away for so long. I started shaking violently. Nick squeezed me harder, trying to get me to stop.

'Sarah, talk to me, please. You're scaring me.'

'You don't want to know,' I said.

'I do,' he said. 'I want you to tell me, whatever it is.'

'I never meant for it to come out like this. I never meant for it to come out at all.'

'For what to come out?' Nick's voice was pleading with me. I couldn't deny him any longer.

'When you got married,' I said, and paused for breath. 'I was pregnant.'

I heard the words ricocheting between us. Nick unable to absorb them, me unwilling to let them back in having finally unleashed their full force. Nick stood silently for a long time before he spoke.

'I don't understand. I thought you were on the pill?'

'I was but I'd been sick a few times, with the stress and everything. It can stop it working.'

The frown on Nick's face deepened. His hand was shaking on my arm.

'Why didn't you tell me?' he said.

'I only found out on the morning of your wedding. I went to the church but I was too late.'

He nodded slowly, started to say something then stopped himself. I could hear the question spinning around in his head before he was able to voice it.

'What happened? Did you have an abortion?'

I shook my head. 'I lost it. The next morning.'

The tears came again, drawn from a well deep inside which I hadn't known existed. Nick held me tighter still, allowing himself to be a human tissue, a giant piece of blotting paper for my gaping wound.

'I'm so sorry,' he said. 'I had no idea.'

'I'm the one who should be apologising.'

'What on earth for?'

'Losing your baby,' I said, wiping my eyes with the back of my hand.

'It wasn't your fault.'

'It was. I'd been drinking.'

Nick shrugged. 'Loads of women drink when they're pregnant.'

'Not two bottles of vodka in one night.'

Nick pulled away enough to look at my face. 'Is that what you had?'

I nodded, averting my eyes.

'Why?'

'Because I'd lost you. Because I was scared. Because I couldn't cope with having a baby on my own.'

Nick shut his eyes and lowered his face. He hated me. I knew that. I should never have told him.

'So that's why you ran away.'

'I couldn't face seeing you. Not after what I'd done.'

'Sarah, it wasn't your fault.'

I didn't want him to be understanding. I deserved a public flogging. Or a verbal tirade at the very least. I walked to the far end of the room before turning to face him.

'You don't have to put on a show for me, you know. Why don't you say what you're really thinking?'

Nick shrugged. 'I wish I'd known at the time. Wish you hadn't lost it. Wish we didn't have to keep saying "it".'

'And you'd have wanted *it*, would you? Would have welcomed us both into your family? I'm sure Amanda would have been delighted, me and you going shopping for prams together.'

'We could have worked something out.'

'Bullshit. You'd have told me to get an abortion. You should be grateful I saved you the money. A lot cheaper, these do-it-yourself jobs.'

'Don't talk like that, Sarah.'

'Why not? That's the truth. I killed your baby. So the least you can do is be honest about how you feel instead of coming out with all this sympathetic new man crap.'

'Sarah, listen to me . . .'

I was already striding towards the front door, reaching for the handle.

'It's OK, I'm going to save you the job of throwing me out. And don't worry, this time I won't be coming back.'

I slammed the door behind me, ran to my car, started the engine and put the windscreen wipers on before I realised it wasn't the rain which was blurring my vision. I let the tears fall. Silent and hot on to my trembling hands.

Seventeen

Nick was off sick the next day. Some kind of stomach bug. Probably only a twenty-four-hour thing. That's what he told Doreen when he rang in. Sure enough he was back at work on Tuesday. He'd left for the Council House before I got in but not before he'd sent me an e-mail.

'Meet me at Starbucks midday. Nick.'

I read it and deleted it instantly, as if destroying evidence of espionage. I knew I would go; I felt obliged to take whatever abuse he wanted to throw at me.

I left the office at half eleven. Earlier than I needed to but I didn't want to keep him waiting. I walked briskly through the subway and out the other end, watching my warm breath hit the cold air and rise like an Indian smoke signal warning of my impending arrival. When I reached Starbucks Nick was waiting outside.

'Thanks for coming,' he said.

I followed him inside, refusing his offer of lunch and buying my own. I let him lead the way downstairs, aware of the rattling of my coffee cup, grateful to be able to put the tray down on a table, to hide my shaking hands down the side of the chair. It was quiet, still early for the lunchtime brigade. I was relieved there was no one within earshot for whatever it was Nick was going to say. I watched as he scooped the froth off the top of his cappuccino into his mouth, taking his time, letting me sweat it out for a little longer while he savoured the taste.

'I'm sorry,' he said eventually.

'What for?'

'Seven years ago. I was a complete bastard to you. I've only just got round to acknowledging it though, even to myself. That was one of the reasons I started looking for you. I wanted to apologise.'

I shrugged.

'You didn't commit a crime,' I said. 'Unlike me.'

Nick lowered his voice. 'I brought you here so you would have to listen to me. You didn't kill our baby, Sarah. You had a miscarriage.'

'Yeah, because I poisoned it with alcohol.'

Nick shook his head firmly. 'About one in six pregnancies end in miscarriage. They don't know why. There isn't always a reason. And drinking doesn't make the risk any greater, not after the first couple of weeks.'

'You sound like you've looked it up on the Internet.'

Nick blushed and took a sip of his cappuccino followed by a bite of his tuna wrap. I figured it was an admission.

'I can't imagine two bottles of vodka did it any good,' I said.

'Nor did the stress I caused you. I behaved like a complete shit. The only difference is I haven't beaten myself up about it all these years.'

'I did a bad thing. I can't simply forget about it, pretend it didn't happen.'

'But you could stop punishing yourself for something that wasn't your fault. And for everything else you seem to blame yourself for.'

'Such as?'

'Colin's problems, for one.'

It was my turn to take a sip of coffee. To move the salad around on my plate.

'I've been meaning to thank you,' I said. 'For ringing the Ikon gallery, I mean. They've offered him an exhibition.'

'Good. Debt repaid.'

'I owe him more than that.'

'And what do you owe yourself?'

'Me?'

'Yeah. How about a bit of happiness? Or is that against the New Sarah religion?'

'What do you mean?'

'You're not the Sarah I used to know. All the fun's gone out of you.'

'It's not surprising, is it? Considering what happened.'

'You can't stop doing everything you used to enjoy because of that. It's like throwing the baby out with the bath water.'

He realised as soon as he said it. It was too late though. The tears welled in my eyes. He reached out across the table and touched my hand.

'I'm sorry, Sarah. I didn't think.'

'It's OK,' I said, breathing hard. 'I guess I'm a bit raw at the moment. It's kind of brought everything back, talking about it.'

Nick gripped my hand tighter. 'You've been through a horrible time. But what I'm trying to say is it hasn't got to go on being horrible for ever.'

'My happiness only seems to come at a cost to other people.'

'Is that what Jonathan says? That you must share in the suffering of the great unwashed? Mustn't have joy or a widescreen TV while others have neither?'

'It's about making sure other people don't suffer because of your actions.'

'Bollocks it is. It's about being pious and going to bed at night feeling smug because the guy who picked your coffee beans was paid a few pennies more for his efforts. It's not exactly going to change the world, is it?'

'You've got to start somewhere.'

'So start with yourself. Leave Jonathan and come and live with me. I can't guarantee you Fairtrade coffee and you might have to pay the rent until I get some work but at least I can give you a chance of happiness.'

I stared at him. Stabbing desperately at a piece of lettuce. Wanting him to repeat the offer to make sure I heard it right. To put it in writing so I could study it in private later, have it checked over by a team of lawyers to ensure I hadn't missed some crucial catch.

'You don't mean that.'

'I do. I spent a lot of time thinking yesterday. And I've realised that there's still one thing left worth salvaging out of this mess. Me and you.'

'I can't leave Jonathan.'

'Can't or won't?'

I couldn't answer. I managed to get a sliver of cucumber from the plate to my mouth. I couldn't seem to chew or swallow so it stayed there, rendering me speechless.

'At least think about it,' said Nick, filling in the silence. 'I know it's a big decision. I won't hassle you but I want you to come over to my place a week tonight and tell me your answer. Around seven-thirty. It's a kind of alternative leaving do.'

'Who's invited?' I asked, the cucumber having finally submitted and freed my tongue in the process.

'Just you.'

'What if I don't turn up?' I said, avoiding his gaze.

'Then it's just me. And I'll have to eat a meal for two myself again, like I did last time.'

'Jonathan's a good man, Nick. He loves me. Never done anything to hurt me.' My throat was tight, the words came out squeaky.

'And I'm a flawed, domestically challenged former love cheat who messed up big time and is trying to put things right,' he said, almost choking on the honesty. 'The choice is yours.'

He stood up and left me to finish my salad in peace. Not that it was peaceful inside my head. Some kind of epic battle between good and evil worthy of *The Lord of the Rings* was going on. I followed each thwarted attack with an air of detachment. I'd seen the films, all of them. They'd kind of merged into one in my head. All I knew was that the good guys always won.

I made a detour to see Colin on the way back to work, keen for news of any developments.

'Hi, Sarah. Nick was right, then.'

'Sorry?' I said.

'He was here a few minutes ago. I gave him his envelope and I was going to give him yours but he said you'd probably be along soon.'

'What are you talking about, Colin?'

He fished inside his jacket pocket before handing me two envelopes, one addressed to Mr Roger Photographer and the other to Ms Sarah Roberts and guest.

'What are they?'

'Open yours and see.'

I slid my finger under the corner and tore it open. Inside was a stiff piece of white card with one of Colin's photos printed on it under the words 'Homeless at Christmas. Invitation to the opening of a photographic exhibition by Colin Leake at the Ikon Gallery. Tuesday 21 December, 6.30 p.m.' The date hit me before anything else.

'Oh, a week tonight,' I said.

'Yeah,' said Colin. 'Bit of a rush job but I'm not complaining. You will come, won't you? It would mean a lot to me to have you there.'

'Of course,' I said. 'Wouldn't miss it for the world.'

'Great,' said Colin. 'Nick's coming too. He said to give you a message. Something about the leaving do being put back till eight-thirty. Does that make sense?'

I nodded. Clearly I wasn't going to get out of it that easily.

'Is Razor all set for the interview tomorrow?' I said.

'Yeah. Do you want me to be there with you?'

'No, I'll be fine, thanks.'

'He wants payment in porn, mind.'

'Hey, I don't supply porn. It's called art. The Raquel lookalike is almost tasteful.'

Colin chuckled and shook his head. I walked slowly back to the office, my head spinning.

When I got back, a strange noise was emanating from the darkroom. A noise never before associated with photographic. I couldn't be sure at first so I put my ear to the door and listened again. Whistling. It was definitely whistling. From Roger on a miserable Tuesday afternoon.

I slipped my head round the door and called out into the gloom. 'Are you OK?'

'Never been better,' came the chirpy reply. 'Come on in.'

Roger was hovering over the trays of chemicals, dancing between them, shaking and tipping, whistling something from one of the musicals that I vaguely recognised but couldn't name. I peered over his shoulder as one of the prints emerged. It was like watching a child colour over that magic paper to reveal the hidden image. The photo was good. Different good, not what I'd expected. Taken from somewhere down in the canal basin on a frosty morning. A couple of narrow boats in the foreground, the Birmingham skyline rising behind, a challenging mixture of old and new, sun glinting on glass and cobblestones.

'I like that,' I said.

'Good,' said Roger. 'So do I. Took it this morning before I came into work.'

'Are you sure you're OK?' I said.

'Yep. Like I said, raring to go.'

'Go where?'

'Out of this place.'

I didn't take any notice. I'd heard the record so many times before. 'Got an invite for you,' I said, handing over the envelope. 'Colin's exhibition, opens on Tuesday evening.'

'Good on him,' he said. 'Tell him I'll be there.' Roger looked at me. 'You don't believe me, do you?' he said.

'Yeah. I know you'll be there.'

'Not about that, about me leaving.'

'Roger, you could have taken redundancy but you didn't.'

'I have now, though.'

One glance at Roger's face confirmed he was telling the truth.

'But the deadline for redundancies has gone.'

'I know. Terry said he'd wangle it with the people upstairs that I could still take it, as long as I didn't mind having two weeks' notice. Suits me fine. The sooner I'm out of here the better.'

'What changed your mind?' I asked.

'Your mate Colin, actually. Seeing his work, hearing him talk about photography like it genuinely meant something. It made me want to rediscover how that felt.'

'So what are you going to do? Have you got another job?'

'Nope. I'm going freelance. Doing my own thing. Good stuff, proper stuff, work I can be proud of instead of the shit we shovel out here every day. I've got enough contacts in this city, plenty of irons in the fire. I'm sure things will work out.'

I stared at Roger, delighted but at the same time unnerved by the way he was talking. The shackles had fallen off his wrists and ankles; he looked as if he might rise up off the ground at any moment. I walked across to hug him, my ball and chain dragging along the floor.

'That's fantastic,' I said. 'I'm so pleased for you. You won't regret it.'

'I know,' he said. 'You only regret the things you don't do.'

I chose to ignore the last comment.

'Is it official?' I asked. 'Can I tell Cayte? You know this means she can stay.'

'Yep, be my guest. It's nice to be able to spread a bit of good news about the place for a change.'

I hurried back out to the newsroom to find Terry had beaten me to it. Cayte was in there with him, brandishing an imbecilic grin. I waited by the door for her to come out.

'You know the downside of this, don't you?' she said to me as she opened the door.

'What?' I said.

'Instead of listening to sheep-shagging court cases in the Shetland Islands, I've got to put up with hearing your bloody advice for God knows how long.'

I gave her a hug, feeling her chest rise and fall with the exhalation.

'I'm glad you're staying,' I said. 'It wouldn't be the same without you. It would be quieter and I'd no doubt have an easier life but it wouldn't be the same.'

Cayte sauntered back to her desk, careful not to make too much of a scene in front of those still on redundancy row. She picked up the phone and dialled, a hushed conversation with more pauses than words. When she put the receiver down she turned and hissed in my direction.

'Jazz said he's relieved. So relieved he's not going to the band rehearsal tonight. He's taking me out instead.'

'You'd better get on the phone for those Chili Pepper tickets then,' I said. 'I think somebody might be getting an extra special Christmas present.'

Cayte smiled as she got out her credit card. We both knew Jazz would never have made the Shetland Islands. In Birmingham, the two of them stood a chance.

Dinner was on the table when I got home. I ate quickly, relating the day's events between mouthfuls. Not all of them, of course. I kind of skipped-over lunch, concentrating instead on Cayte's last-minute reprieve.

'Oh, and we've got an invite,' I said. 'For the opening of Colin's exhibition at the Ikon. Next Tuesday.'

Jonathan put his fork down. 'The twenty-first?' he asked.

'Yeah. Six-thirty. I said we'd go.'

'We can't. Have you forgotten?'

I stared at him blankly, trying to remember whatever it was that had slipped my mind while chewing a mouthful of lasagne, but it stubbornly refused to come to me.

'My Freedom for Tibet talk,' he said with a sigh. 'Seven o'clock at the library. You wrote a bloody press release on it.'

I'd also read through his speech for him, and listened to one of his many practice sessions. Nothing short of the Dalai Lama popping round for tea should have made me forget.

'Shit, sorry,' I said.

'You'll have to send our apologies to Colin. Tell him we'll go another night.'

My skin prickled. 'And you speak for me now, do you?'

Jonathan looked taken aback. 'Don't be silly. It's just that you agreed to come to this ages ago.'

'I know, but this is a big thing for Colin.'

'And what about me?'

'This could change Colin's life. What's your talk going to do? Force the Chinese out of Tibet by Christmas?'

Jonathan fell silent, his face crumpled. He put his knife and fork down. 'It's a big thing for me too, Sarah. Mum left a message today: she can't make it. I'm relying on you to be there for me. I need your support.'

His voice was shaky. My resentment was confronted with the dual forces of a wave of remorse coupled with a severe pang of guilt. I pushed my plate away and leant over to stroke his arm.

'Hey, I'm sorry. I didn't realise it was such a big deal.'

'Just going into work every day is a big deal right now. I've seen the way they look at me, the other teachers. Ever since the whole Daniel thing. They think I'm unprofessional. They think I did the wrong thing. And do you know what? They're right.'

'Nobody's said that.'

'They don't need to. I know it. And that's what's doing me in. I screwed up, I let one of the kids down. They used to respect me, the other teachers. Thought I was a bit special. But not now. They think I'm lucky to still have a job.'

I got up from my chair and went to hold him, resting his head against my chest, stroking his hair, letting him stroke me back. Eventually he raised his head.

'This talk,' he said. 'It's a chance for me to get back on my feet. To do something worthwhile. And I need you there, Sarah. Because I don't think I can do it without you.'

I kissed his forehead. Feeling the brittleness within.

'I'm sorry,' I said. 'I should have realised. I guess I've been wrapped up in things at work. All these redundancies and that. Of course I'll come. I'll tell Colin we'll go Wednesday night instead.'

Jonathan nodded.

'Thank you,' he said. 'I know I haven't been much fun to be around lately. I'm hoping this will help me turn the corner.'

'Yeah,' I said. 'Maybe I'll come home and find you listening to Ozzy again one of these days. Or even catch you with that air guitar.'

Jonathan smiled. We finished our lasagne in silence as I tried to work out how to split myself in two.

Saturday 9 August 1997

I sit in the chair staring at the woman who faces me in the mirror. She repulses me. So much so that I cannot bear to look at her any more. I am getting rid of her. She is rotten. All the badness needs to be cut away.

The hairdresser is standing behind me. Jane her name is. I don't know her; I have never been here before. The salon was picked at random from the Yellow Pages. I don't want chit-chat, questions about whether I'm going out tonight or have any holiday plans. I want the job doing quickly and properly. No questions asked.

She is combing through my long, wet hair, the water flicking off the ends of my curls on to my gown. She puts the comb down and picks up the scissors.

'Are you sure about this?' she says, looking at me in the mirror. 'Only sometimes people get cold feet at the last minute. I'd rather you change your mind now than when it's too late.'

I fix her a look. I do not need this.

'Short, please. Like I said.'

She starts cutting. The snip of the scissors gathers pace, the cold steel blades tickling the back of my neck. I watch my long, wild curls fall silently on to the floor. There is no place for such frivolity in my life now. I repent. I am going straight.

Already my head feels lighter, my shoulders less burdened. It will be a long time before I can hold my head up high, perhaps never. But it is a start. I watch the emergence of the new Sarah in the mirror. It suits her, short hair. She looks serious, businesslike. Someone not to be messed with.

Jane finishes off and shows me the back of my head in the mirror. I nod approvingly. The remnants of the old Sarah lie lifeless on the floor around me. She is dead now. Dead and buried. Jane seems sad about this. She brushes some stray hairs from my gown, sweeps up the considerable pile of dark curls on the floor and pushes them out of the way. I am not sad. It is long overdue, this parting of the ways. I want everything swept under the carpet. I want to start anew.

I walk out into the street. People look at me differently. In fact, most of them don't look at me at all. Which is good, it's what I want: a cloak of anonymity I can hide behind. I catch the bus back to my flat. My car is gone. Sold to a woman from Brownsover who wanted something fun to ferry the kids around in. I didn't tell her the real reason I was selling it. That Nick had been in it once, that I could still see him sitting there in the passenger seat, smell him on the upholstery. Just said I was going away. That I needed the cash.

I let myself into the flat and immediately recheck my hair in the hallway mirror. She stares back at me, the new Sarah. Not smiling, of course. It is too soon for that. But at least she can look me in the eye. If the Labour party can reinvent itself successfully then so can I. The new Sarah is different. Not just on the surface but inside as well. She is good. Sensible. Serious. Her head rules her heart. She doesn't do bad things. She will not hurt others, or get hurt. She is tough. She has to be to survive.

I go through to the main room. A small pile of my belongings sits in the corner. A large suitcase of clothes, a holdall of books, CDs and newspaper cuttings and a rucksack crammed full of my remaining possessions: CD player, camera, a pair of walking boots which wouldn't fit

in my suitcase, that sort of thing. I have left the side
pockets empty for the last-minute bits and pieces I need to
pack in the morning, but essentially that is it. All my
worldly goods. They do not amount to much. But it is all
I am taking with me. The furniture came with the flat. I
never got round to buying a TV. There is some crockery,
of course, and silly things like pedal bins and washing-up
bowls but I am leaving those for the next tenant. I do not
want anything which reminds me of this place or which
Nick has touched. Which is why I am not taking the
bedding. The pillows we kissed on, the sheet we had sex
on, the duvet we draped our deceit in. They are contaminated. Soiled. And no amount of washing will remove
it. I will buy a fresh set when I get there. It will be worth
it to feel clean again.

What I am looking forward to most is having a bath. I
have not been able to bring myself to have one here since.
As far as I'm concerned I no longer have a bathroom at
all: it is a crime scene. I see it in my head cordoned off
with orange police tape, the guys from forensics dusting
the surfaces, ripping out the pipes and delving into the
murky depths for evidence.

I wish I never had to go in there. But unfortunately I
still have to use the loo. Like I do now. I walk up and
down, trying to put it off as long as possible. Waiting
until desperation overrides the dread. I turn the handle
and dash inside, unzipping my jeans as I go. I shut my
eyes as I near the toilet, still unable to look into the pan,
instead feeling for the seat with my outstretched hand.
When I reach it I turn round, drop my trousers and hover
over it as I pee. I keep my eyes on the far wall, not daring
to look down. I bought a long rug to cover the bloodstains
on the carpet. But it is purely cosmetic. I know what lies
beneath. I zip myself up, wash my hands and march out,
pulling the door shut tight behind me as I breathe out. It
is all over for a few more hours. If I don't drink much I
might make it until bedtime without having to go again.

And tomorrow is Sunday. Tomorrow I shall be leaving and never coming back.

The bell in my flat rings. The cab is ten minutes early which is good. I am ready to go. I do not want to wait any longer. The suitcase and rucksack are already downstairs in the hall. I pick up the holdall and take one last look round. I see Nick lying on the bed, the same expression on his face I always see. The one he used to wear just before he said it was time to go. Only it is his turn to be on the receiving end this time. Because although he doesn't know it yet, I am leaving him.

I sling the holdall over my shoulder and walk briskly out of the room. As I pass the closed bathroom door I feel my stomach tighten, the tears prick at my eyes again. For the first time since, I actually want to go inside, to say my farewells. I won't though. I will let it rest in peace. And I will flee the scene of the crime.

I tell the cab driver to go the long way to Rugby station. The route that takes us past the *Chronicle* offices. I want to ensure I have left every part of me behind. That I will not be carrying excess baggage. We swing round the corner, I glance up to the first floor, see the window above Nick's desk. He is not there, of course. He is on his way back from honeymoon. Somewhere over the Atlantic. Bronzed and beaming, his new wife by his side. But when he arrives at work tomorrow he will find me gone. I haven't left him a note, I don't have the words. The others will have to tell him. That I handed my notice in two days after his wedding. Before I'd had the interview at Scarborough, let alone been offered the job. But that it is official now. I am taking the last week of my notice period as holiday. I have left. And I won't be coming back.

The cab pulls up outside the station. The driver takes my luggage out of the boot as I rummage in my purse for some change.

'Off somewhere nice, are you?' he says.

'Yes,' I say. 'Away from here.'

I hoist the rucksack on to my back, pick up the holdall and inch the suitcase towards the ticket booth with my foot.

'Single to Scarborough, please,' I say.

'You'll have to change at Birmingham New Street, then again at York,' the small man behind the glass says. I nod. It's not a problem. Change is good.

I take my ticket and drag my suitcase through the tunnel to platform one. It is Sunday morning quiet. A few students on their way back to university, a few Saturday-night stragglers heading home. The train arrives on time. I struggle on board, suitcase first, me laden with the rucksack and holdall behind. I sit in a forward-facing seat. I want to see the future, not the past I am leaving behind. But as we are about to set off I catch sight of her standing on the platform. The old Sarah. Her long curls blowing in the breeze, tears streaming down her face. She is clutching Nick's denim jacket and wearing a blood-soaked skirt. She is waving to me, calling out my name. I pretend I do not recognise her and do not wave back. The train pulls slowly away.

Eighteen

I was still in my dressing gown when I heard the knock on the door. Jonathan had already gone to work. I'd have to answer it myself. I brushed the toast crumbs from my lips and padded in my bare feet down the hallway. I opened the door a crack to see Najma standing there.

'Hi, come in,' I said. 'Is everything all right?'

'Sorry to call so early,' she said, stepping inside and following me through to the lounge. 'I wanted to catch you before work.'

She sat down on the sofa, clutching her hands together in her lap. Her face was closed, hiding whatever it was she was about to tell me.

'I told Paul,' she said. 'Last Friday night, after I'd spoken to you.'

'And?'

'He was shocked at first. And cross with me for not telling him before. Said he needed some time to think about it, decide what to do for the best.'

'Oh God, that sounds heavy. Are you OK?'

'I am now,' she said. 'He came to see me last night, took me for a meal. And gave me this.'

She unfurled her left hand, revealing a diamond engagement ring, big enough to be impressive, small enough to be tasteful. Najma was beaming, her eyes dancing, reflecting the warm glow from her face.

'Congratulations,' I said, throwing my arms round her. 'I take it you did say yes?'

Najma nodded. 'I know it's a bit quick, what with us only being together for a few months. But you know what it's like when something feels so right. When you know you're meant to be together no matter what obstacles are in the way.'

'Yeah,' I said, biting my lip. 'I know.'

'Hey, you soppy thing,' said Najma. 'Don't start crying, you'll set me off as well.'

I hadn't realised I was until she said it. I dabbed quickly at the corner of my eye with my dressing gown sleeve.

'I'm so pleased for you, Naj. So glad Paul's come through for you. You'll need his strength. I know it won't be easy for you.'

She looked down, her face clouding over for a moment. 'It'll be harder the longer it goes on, I think. Wondering how my family are, what they're doing. And around Eid, and times like that, when I know they'll all be together.'

'You never know,' I said, 'maybe as time passes and they miss you, they might get in touch.'

'Maybe,' said Najma, 'but I won't be holding my breath. And I'm determined not to let it spoil things for me and Paul.'

'Good for you,' I said.

Najma glanced at her watch. 'Anyway, I'd better go and let you get dressed. Just wanted you to be the first to know.' She stood up and walked towards the door.

'Thanks,' I said. 'You've got my day off to a cracking start.'

Najma smiled. 'And thank you for your advice. You were right, you know. I shall use your counselling service again.'

I drove to work in a daze, seeing Najma's dancing eyes and huge grin reflected in my rear-view mirror. And my own face, still and lifeless as I pondered my own big decision.

*

'You did well with that one. I have to say I thought he was a nutter.'

Coming from Terry, this was praise indeed. I looked at the first edition of the *Gazette*. 'Scandal of Patient Abuse' screamed the headline. It was the nearest I would probably ever get to my own *One Flew Over the Cuckoo's Nest* moment. Rupert Bear had turned out to be telling the truth. The internal investigation had upheld most of his complaints, other former patients, including my top source Razor (whose real name, rather disappointingly, had turned out to be Adrian Jones), had spilled the beans to me, the staff in charge had been suspended and Clare Short was calling for heads to roll. A picture of a stern-faced Mr Bear appeared on the front page. You could just make out Shirley Bassey's left ear in the background.

'Nutter or not, he didn't deserve to be treated like that.'

'You could have got a quote from old Shirl, mind. She might have promised to dedicate her next album to him.'

'Stop taking the piss. He's got you a big front page today. We'll get some good follow-ups out of it as well.'

'As long as you don't mind running the nutter hotline. And if Noddy and Big Ears call, it might be a wind-up.'

Terry chuckled to himself, the well-worn creases on his face falling into an unfamiliar pattern. Even his eyebrows appeared lighter than usual, his shoulders not sagging as much.

'What's up with you today?' I said. 'You seem a bit perkier than usual.'

He smiled, a knowing smile. 'I did it. I did what you said. Threw them both out. Him and Sylvia.'

His revelation was accompanied by corresponding hand actions, as if he needed them to illustrate his words. I stared at him, seeing only an X-ray vision of his backbone, the vertebrae standing strong and proud like a Roman pillar.

'Bloody hell,' I uttered finally.

'I know,' he said. 'Can't quite believe it myself. And do

you know the strange thing? I thought I'd be as miserable as sin but I've never felt better in my life.' He chuckled again as he said it, just to prove the point.

'So what happened?' I said. 'Did they go quietly?'

'I put bolts on the doors while they were out, left all their stuff in bin bags and suitcases in the front garden. Sylvia was pretty hysterical when they got back, but she soon shut up when the curtains started twitching and she realised all the neighbours were watching her instead of the box.'

I shook my head, imagining the impact of such a commotion on the quiet cul-de-sac in Solihull. Terry was in full flow now. Obviously enjoying relating the story.

'Derek packed everything into his car. He seemed rather resigned to it; I almost felt sorry for him. Only almost, mind. Then he got in, waited for her to quit shrieking, and when she finally did she had no option. She had to get in and he drove off. That was eight-thirty last night. Haven't heard from them since.' Terry looked around as if expecting a round of applause.

'What about the boys?' I said. 'Were they upset?'

'Didn't seem to be. Came down to ask what was going on, I told them, they nodded, said it was about fucking time and went back upstairs. Paul even made me a mug of tea this morning. And Darren smiled at me. Never been known before.'

'So what made you do it?' I asked. 'Was it something she said?'

'No, it was Nick who started me thinking. Him walking around looking so miserable made me realise that unlike him I had the power to change things. And when I woke up yesterday I decided I'd had enough of it. That it was now or never.'

I glanced out of Terry's window at Nick, who did indeed look miserable. I suspected the news that his misery had spurred Terry into such decisive action would offer little consolation.

'And what if Sylvia comes back?' I asked. 'Rings you up and begs forgiveness. What are you going to do then?'

'Tell her where she can stick it,' said Terry. 'I've got the taste for this no-nonsense stuff now. You were right, Sarah. But then again you always are.'

I forced a smile, managed a mumbled 'good on you' and slunk out of the office. The trouble with everyone taking my advice was becoming all too apparent. I had nobody else's life left to sort out. Apart from my own.

I shut down my computer at four-thirty sharp. I'd decided to tell Nick before I left. I didn't want him buying food for tomorrow night when I wouldn't be going.

I hovered over Nick's desk. He looked up at me with an enquiring raise of the eyebrows. I found myself suddenly rendered speechless, unable to offer any kind of satisfactory explanation. So I simply shook my head, my gaze lingering long enough to see the bullet hit him square between the eyes, before I hurried, head down, out of the office.

The wind whipped at my coat, forcing me to button it tightly closed as I battled my way to the car. It stung my face too, bringing beads of moisture to the corners of my eyes. I was aware of people hurrying past, eager to beat the rush hour home. They might mistake my watering eyes for tears. They would be wrong, though. Sarah Roberts didn't do weak, I reminded myself.

I reached the car, pulling the door to quickly behind me. Nick's car was parked a few rows along. I thought of pinning a note to the windscreen, trying to find the words to explain how I couldn't undo everything I'd built over the past seven years. Couldn't open myself up again, in case I didn't go back together next time. But I knew that an explanation wouldn't make it any easier for him. It was a straight yes or no he'd needed. It was simply that my answer had been the wrong one.

At least with Colin I could soften the blow. Tell him I'd

be coming to his exhibition Wednesday night instead of tomorrow. And if I sat there long enough I knew I could muster the strength to tell him something else. Something I should have told him a long time ago.

The Ikon gallery appeared quiet from the outside, only the lights from within the neo-Gothic building giving a hint of the activity going on inside. Colin had told me he would be here this evening, watching them put the finishing touches to the exhibition, making sure everything was ready for his big night tomorrow.

The front door was open. I climbed the stairs to the first floor where two women dressed entirely in black with matching short, spiky haircuts were running around positioning, adjusting and repositioning. Colin was standing in the centre of the room, rotating slowly to get a view of everything taking shape around him. I watched from the doorway as a couple of times he opened his mouth to say something, raised his arm and then thought better of it. It was a whole new world to him; clearly he didn't feel part of it yet. But they were unmistakably his photographs, his grainy black and white images adorning the expanse of white walls, looking every inch the part.

'And here's the star of the show,' I said, my footsteps echoing on the polished wooden floor.

Colin turned to greet me with a grin on his face.

'You're a day early,' he said. 'Unless we've lost track of time.'

'I know, don't panic. I'm here to get a sneak preview and to offer my apologies.'

Colin's face visibly dipped. 'You are coming, aren't you?'

I shook my head. 'Not tomorrow, I'm afraid. I'm really sorry but Jonathan's giving a talk for Amnesty at the library. I'd forgotten all about it but it's a big thing for him and I don't want to let him down.'

'It's OK,' said Colin, 'I understand. I didn't mean to put

pressure on you. I should have realised other people have got their own commitments and stuff.'

He laughed, a polite tinkle of a laugh. I could tell he was putting on a brave face.

'We're going to come Wednesday night instead,' I told him. 'We'll come early, be your first paying guests. Not that you'll need it. They'll be flocking in, I bet. We gave it a good plug in tonight's paper.' It was my turn to let out an effort of a laugh to try to hide my discomfort.

'I know, I saw it. Thanks for that. And thanks for everything you've done for me, Sarah. I wouldn't be here tonight if it wasn't for you and Nick. I owe you both so much.'

I shifted awkwardly, trying to deflect the praise which rested so uneasily on me. It was time to put my hand up. To come clean, to risk Colin's wrath, even if it meant that in a few minutes he would be taking back those words.

'The thing is, Colin. You don't owe me anything. I owe you.'

Colin was looking at me warily, his tiny eyes peering at me from behind his glasses. 'I don't understand.'

'I didn't vote for you, Colin. You lost the general election because of me. I was going to, had every intention, but something unexpected came up. I was with Nick, you see. I shouldn't have been but I was. I'm really sorry and I'll understand if you never want to speak to me or see me again.'

I paused for breath but before I could carry on I heard Colin laugh. Not a polite or anxious laugh this time but a full-throated guffaw, enough to make the two gallery women stop what they were doing and turn round to look. Colin was doubled up with laughter. I stared at him blankly, unsure how to react.

'Sorry,' said Colin, gasping for breath, 'I know it's cruel to laugh; you obviously feel bad about this. It's just that, well, there's no need. No need at all.'

'What do you mean?' I said.

'I know someone else who didn't vote.'

'Who?'

'Me.'

I stared at Colin some more, waiting for an explanation.

'I was so busy leafleting on the day, all that door-to-door stuff, I never actually made it to the polling station. I kept thinking I'll go in a minute and of course I never did. It was only when I got to the count and things were looking a bit tight that I realised what a plonker I'd been.'

'You're making this up to make me feel better.'

'I wish I was. But I was truly that stupid. I lost it myself. It's not your fault or anyone else's. Honestly, if I had a pound for everyone who came up to me afterwards and admitted they didn't vote for me not only would I be a very rich man I'd have won by a landslide. At least you had a good excuse, at least you were enjoying yourself. One bloke I knew said he hadn't been able to get to the polling station because of an ingrowing toenail.'

Colin started chuckling again. Within a few seconds I joined in, letting the relief ooze out of me.

'So you're not mad at me?' I said.

'Of course not. I just think you're a silly bugger for letting it eat away at you all this time. Confession cleanses the soul, that's what my old mum used to say.'

'I know. I guess I'm one of those who prefers the burial option.'

'Well, now you've exorcised that one, don't feel bad about tomorrow night. Go and enjoy yourself at this talk and I'll see you on Wednesday.'

'Thanks,' I said, as I walked towards the door. 'The photos look fantastic, by the way. Your friend Mr Salgado would be well impressed.'

I drove home feeling washed out, seven years of guilt about Colin seeping out of me. Though no sooner had it gone, leaving behind a void, than the remaining guilt came rushing in, expanding to fill the available space. And hard as I tried to visualise Colin's face, hear his laughter, it was Nick I kept seeing. Whose pain I felt tearing me apart inside.

My legs were heavy as I walked up the garden path. I put the key in the front door. The silence hit me as soon as I stepped inside. No music, no cooking sounds, no movement inside. Something had happened, I knew straight away. All I could think of was Daniel. That he'd been beaten up again. Or worse. I hurried past the open door of the empty kitchen and went straight through to the lounge. Jonathan was sitting on the sofa, his face pale and gaunt, staring at the coffee table on which lay a black sock. Nick's sock.

Shit. My eyelids fell down like a theatre curtain. But when I hoisted them back up a second later there was no scene change. Everything was as it had been. I was on stage and the spotlight was on me.

Jonathan said nothing. Just continued staring at the sock. I wondered for a second if I could bluff my way out of it. Play dumb, deny ever having seen it before or even try to pass it off as mine. But it was clear from Jonathan's demeanour that he not only knew whose sock it was but also had a clear idea of when and how it got there. That was my starting point. The cue for my opening line.

'Where did you find it?'

'In Nelson's basket, under his blanket. I was cleaning it out.'

I nodded, cursing the bloody cat for betraying me.

'It's not what you think, Jonathan.'

'How do you know what I'm thinking?'

'I've got a rough idea. I know it doesn't look good.'

'You're right there. What happened that night, Sarah? Did you sleep with him?'

I closed my eyes and shook my head. I'd never felt so bad telling the truth.

'So why was his sock in Nelson's basket? Tell me, Sarah.'

I looked up at the ceiling. Knowing I had to make a confession. A partial one at least.

'We, we kissed. That's all. He got a bit carried away, thought we were going to, well, you know . . .'

Jonathan turned and stared at me.

'You kissed him?' he said.

I nodded. I heard the disappointment in his voice. Saw the hurt scrawled across his face.

'And you would have slept with him if I hadn't come home early.'

'No,' I said firmly. 'I'd already told him to stop. Told him I didn't want to.'

'So why did you lie to me? Pretend nothing was going on? Why did he come out with that stupid thing about Beckham only wearing one sock?'

I shrugged. 'We panicked, I guess. I knew it looked bad. I wasn't sure if you'd believe me if I told you the truth.'

'You could have tried me. I'm a pretty trusting guy, Sarah. I came home early, found you alone with a good-looking guy you work with and I accepted it, didn't I? Made him a bloody coffee, if I remember rightly.'

'I know. I didn't want a big scene, that was all. Telling you what had happened in front of Nick. It was embarrassing enough as it was.'

A long silence followed. Jonathan reverted to staring at the sock. I tried to stop my hands from shaking, to still my beating heart, to slow down the thoughts that were whizzing through my head.

'Why did you kiss him, Sarah?'

I sighed deeply and shut my eyes again. It was time to tell him. About seven years ago, at least.

'Me and Nick have a history, Jonathan. We had a thing going on, when I worked with him before.'

Jonathan shook his head in disbelief. 'This just gets better. First you forgot to tell me you used to work with the guy. Now it turns out you not only knew him, you shagged him as well. You'll be telling me you were fucking married to him next.'

Jonathan shouted the last bit, the words stinging my skin. He had no idea, of course. How much that hurt. And I wasn't going to tell him. Because it was nothing compared to how much I'd hurt him.

'I'm sorry. I didn't want to say anything because it all ended horribly and I wanted to keep the whole thing buried in the past. Where it belonged.'

'But you lied to me, Sarah.' Jonathan's voice was on the edge of breaking.

'Only to protect you. I know how insecure you can get. I figured it would be better all round if I didn't mention it.'

'Well, you figured wrong, didn't you?'

'I know that now. But I did what I thought was right at the time. I messed up. I'm sorry.'

Jonathan ran his fingers through his hair. 'Did you love him?'

'What's that got to do with it?'

'I need to know.'

I hesitated. Unsure of the best thing to say.

'Yes,' I said in the end. 'I did. But it was a long time ago.'

'And now?'

I shook my head. Somehow it didn't seem as bad as lying to him verbally.

'And I suppose you're going to tell me that he's backed off since you told him to. That nothing's happened since.'

I was relieved he'd said it like that. Made it so I didn't have to lie again.

'Yes,' I said. 'Because it hasn't.'

'The trouble is,' said Jonathan, 'I don't know if I believe you, or trust you. Not after this. I don't feel I know you any more.'

I sat down on the sofa next to him. He moved a couple of inches away.

'I'm going to need some time alone,' he said. 'To get my head round this. Think the whole thing through.'

'OK,' I said. 'Do you want me to go?'

Jonathan nodded. I went into the bedroom and quickly packed an overnight bag.

'I'll be at Cayte's,' I said. 'If you want to talk.'

He nodded again. And sat staring at the sock as I walked towards the front door.

 Nineteen

'Did you get any sleep?' asked Cayte, putting a mug of steaming coffee down next to the sofa.

'Not much,' I said, sitting up still cocooned in her sleeping bag.

'I take it you're not going to work.'

It was almost eight. Cayte was already dressed, ready to leave. I shook my head.

'Do you want me to say anything?'

'No. I'll give Doreen a ring in a few minutes. And don't let on to Nick that you've seen me. I'd rather he didn't know.'

Cayte nodded. 'Will you be OK on your own?'

'I'll be fine. I'll grab a shower, get a bite to eat. Maybe even watch a daytime talk show. See if anybody out there has screwed up worse than me.'

'Hey, I told you. It'll be fine. You just need to give Jonathan some space. He'll come round.'

I wasn't so sure. I'd betrayed him. A kiss was a big thing. And lied to him about my past. I didn't know whether Jonathan would be able to forgive that. All I did know was that if I'd confessed the full truth, about sleeping with Nick, we would already have been over.

Cayte bent down and gave me a hug. 'Ring me if you need to talk, OK.'

'Sure,' I said. 'And thanks for last night. Putting up with all my blubbing and that.'

'No problem,' she said. 'Just don't make a habit of it.

I'm not after your agony aunt crown, you know.'

She grinned and pulled the door to behind her. I let out a long sigh. Hating the mess I'd got myself into. It was like being a teenager again, running to your best mate and sobbing your heart out after a row with your boyfriend. Only I was thirty-one years old.

I hadn't expected this. Jonathan was the one constant, the one person I could always rely upon. I thought I'd got away with it without hurting him. I shouldn't have been so complacent. I'd let him down. Taken advantage of his trusting nature. He deserved better. I knew that.

But at the same time I knew Nick was hurting. And that I had the power to take part of that hurt away. Only I'd turned him down. Blown him out. So at the point where I thought I was going to have to choose between them, it looked like I had no one left to choose.

I arrived at the Ikon just after six. I had no reason to let Colin down now. I hadn't heard from Jonathan all day. I presumed my presence at his Tibet talk was no longer required.

Colin was standing in the centre of the room, looking surprisingly dapper in the black polo-neck I'd bought him from Oxfam, his glasses cleaned especially for the occasion, a glass of white wine in his hand. Quite unrecognisable as the *Big Issue* seller who usually stood on the corner of New Street in a tatty waterproof. He saw me straight away, his face lighting up. The most welcome expression I'd seen for days.

'I thought you weren't coming?' he said.

'Last minute change of plan.'

'That's a relief. At least I have one guest, now. I was beginning to worry no one would turn up.'

I noticed the glass in his hand was shaking.

'Hey, don't worry, they'll be flocking in soon, you'll see.'

Colin nodded, seeming reassured. 'Is Jonathan coming?'

'Er, no, he's doing his Tibet talk at the library.'

'Wasn't that where you were supposed to be?'

I gazed out across the gallery. 'Yeah. But I'm no longer needed. Anyway, this looks fantastic, Colin. You must be so pleased.'

Colin nodded as he admired his photographs on the walls, the lights reflecting in his glasses, an unmistakable glint of pride in his eyes. This was a whole new world to him. He was doing what he had always wanted to do. It had just been a very roundabout way of getting there.

A few more guests arrived, and Colin seemed to relax a little. An elegant woman in black came over and introduced herself as Imogen, assistant director of the gallery. She spoke in gushing terms about Colin's work, enough to make him blush, before whisking him off to do some mingling.

I stood on my own, admiring one of Colin's photos. Knowing that any time now Nick was going to walk in. And I was going to have to be strong again. I heard his footsteps first. Before I smelt his aftershave. And felt his presence at my side.

'Hi,' Nick said. 'I wasn't sure if you'd be here. Are you feeling better?'

My stomach lurched, my skin tingled. I was still unable to stop the chemical reaction in my body his arrival had always prompted. But I could at least mask the outward signs. I turned to face him. He looked tired and sad and broken. I hesitated before answering. Deciding I couldn't bring myself to lie to him.

'I wasn't ill,' I said.

Nick's eyebrows raised enquiringly. 'I didn't think you threw sickies.'

He was right, of course. I never had done. Until today.

'Jonathan found your sock in the cat's basket.' I blurted it out, mainly because I couldn't think of any other way of saying it. I saw the information register on

Nick's face, watched as he took it in and processed it, blowing out deeply as he realised the implications.

'Oh shit. I'm sorry,' he said.

'It's not your fault.'

'It was my bloody sock.'

'And my stupid idea to invite you back in the first place.'

Nick looked hurt. I realised he probably thought I meant stupid to invite him. Not stupid for not realising we could get caught.

'What did you tell him?' asked Nick.

'That we'd kissed but I'd stopped it going any further.'

Nick pulled an agonised face. Before he had the chance to say anything else Colin waved across the gallery and hurried over.

'Hello, Nick, thanks for coming,' he said, shaking him enthusiastically by the hand.

'Honoured to be here,' said Nick, switching instantly to cheery guest mode. 'Congratulations. Your photos look great.'

Colin grinned, his cheeks rosy due to a glass or two of wine.

'Well, it's all thanks to you two,' he said. 'Whatever it was you were up to seven years ago, you're officially forgiven.' He winked and went off to mingle with his other guests.

Nick stared at me. 'You finally told him?'

'Yeah, it was my big confession day yesterday. Jonathan knows as well. Not about the voting thing, but that we have a past.'

Nick whistled and raised his eyebrows. 'So how did he take it all?'

'Not well,' I said, pushing my hair back behind my ears. 'I don't know if he even believed me. He said he needed some time on his own to think things through. I stayed at Cayte's last night.'

'Sorry,' said Nick again. I pursed my lips, trying hard

to hold myself together. A woman from the gallery came over and offered us both a glass of wine. Nick took a red, I politely declined. Nick looked at me, something inside his head having obviously clicked.

'That's why you don't drink. Because of the . . .' He stopped himself from saying baby. 'Because of what happened.'

I dug my fingernails into the palms of my hands.

'How long are you going to go on punishing yourself, Sarah?'

'I'm trying to make sure I don't hurt anyone else,' I said, my voice cracking with emotion.

'Apart from yourself, you mean,' said Nick.

I shifted my feet. He was getting close now. Uncomfortably so.

'My offer's still open,' he said softly. 'If you want to reconsider.'

'Nothing's changed, Nick.'

'It has. Jonathan's thrown you out.'

'It was my idea to stay at Cayte's.'

'You know what I mean.'

He was getting frustrated. But I was determined not to be blown off track.

'I'm hoping we can patch things up,' I said. 'Make a go of it.'

'Why?'

'Because that's what I want.'

'Is it? Or is it because you think it's what you should do?'

'I've made my decision, Nick.'

'It doesn't have to be your final answer.'

I rolled my eyes. Not sure how much more pressure I could withstand. 'This isn't a quiz show, you know. It's my life.'

I glanced round as I heard a commotion at the entrance. The group of guests clustered about the front door parted and a man came striding towards us. His jaw set, his eyes fixed straight ahead. I blinked hard, hoping I had imagined it. But no. It was Jonathan.

I shut my eyes and groaned. Not wanting to believe this was happening. I didn't want a scene. But I had been cast in the starring role in some massive final act to be played out in front of an audience. And the worst thing about it, the terrible thing, was that I still wasn't sure who the hero was. Or who was the bad guy.

Jonathan stopped right in front of us. He looked from me to Nick and back again

'What's he doing here?' he said, gesturing towards Nick.

'Colin invited him,' I said. 'It's nothing to do with me.'

'Haven't you done enough damage?' said Jonathan, jabbing his finger in Nick's face.

'We were only talking,' said Nick.

'Yeah, like you were only having a fucking coffee.' Jonathan's voice was loud, his tone bitter. I cringed inside, aware that other people were looking at us. That at any moment it could spill over into a public brawl. Old Sarah in the red corner, jumping up and down excitedly, cheering on her man. And new Sarah, lurking anxiously in the blue corner, ready to throw in the towel before either of them got hurt. I looked over my shoulder. Colin was at the other end of the room, blissfully unaware of what was going on. I prayed it would stay that way.

'I'm sorry,' Nick said to Jonathan. 'It was my fault. I made the first move. Sarah stopped me. She couldn't bear to hurt you. I thought you should know that.' His voice faltered for a moment. 'You're a very lucky man to have her.'

I stared at Nick. He'd had no need to say that. He could have boasted of his conquest, picked a fight with Jonathan, roughed him up a bit. He hadn't, though. He'd made a noble sacrifice on my behalf. The old Sarah was hailing her gallant hero. The new Sarah standing silently by, taking no pleasure in her man's victory.

Nick's eyes met mine. Revealing the hurt he'd suffered in defeat. Urging me to soothe his pain away. He waited long enough to know I wasn't going to. Then he turned and walked away.

Jonathan appeared surprised that he had seen off the enemy so easily. Though not half as surprised as I was.

'That was quite a speech,' he said.

I shrugged, unable to make eye contact for fear of revealing too much.

'Why did you come here, Jonathan?' I said, looking down at my feet.

'To ask you to come back with me,' he said hesitantly. 'To the talk.'

'Oh. I didn't think you wanted me there.'

Jonathan fiddled with the buttons on his jacket. I noticed for the first time that his hands were shaking.

'I've been doing a lot of thinking,' he said. 'I'm not going to pretend you haven't hurt me. But I believe you, about what happened. I want to try to put it behind us. To move on.'

I had not expected to be forgiven. I was used to being punished for my sins.

'Thank you,' I said to Jonathan. Knowing it was the right thing to say.

'You have to promise me one thing, though,' Jonathan continued, his eyes big and earnest, his voice on the point of breaking. 'Promise that you won't ever lie to me again. Not even to protect me. I don't want to be protected from the truth.'

'OK,' I said. 'I promise.'

A smile appeared on Jonathan's face for the first time since he entered the room. 'You'll come back to the talk with me, then?'

'Yes. Yes, of course.'

'Thanks,' he said. 'We'd better get a move on, we haven't got much time.'

'Sure. Just let me say goodbye.'

I threaded my way to the other end of the room with Jonathan in tow. Colin was talking to the leader of the city council. No doubt reminiscing about his former life. I coughed quietly.

'Sorry to interrupt,' I said. Colin turned round, surprised to see Jonathan standing behind me.

'Hello,' he said to him. 'I thought you were giving a talk?'

'I am,' said Jonathan. 'It's a flying visit, I'm afraid.'

'Sorry, Colin,' I said. 'We've got to dash now. There's been another change of plan.'

'Oh, sure,' said Colin, looking suitably confused. 'Thanks for coming.'

'We'll come again tomorrow,' I said. 'See the whole thing properly. Good luck tonight. You're a star.'

I gave him a peck on the cheek and followed Jonathan towards the exit, scanning the room for Nick as I went. It was only as I neared the door that I saw him. Standing in a corner on his own. I caught his eye and mouthed 'thank you'. He mouthed back. I was good at lip reading. 'I love you,' he said.

Jonathan was holding the door open for me. I stood for a moment, my legs heavy. My heart too. Before summoning the strength to walk through. Without looking back.

I shivered as I stepped on to the pavement outside, pulling my coat collar up round my ears. Jonathan was hovering anxiously next to me. I realised he must have come on his bike.

'Can I give you a lift?' I asked.

'Thanks,' he said, rubbing his hands together. 'But it'll probably be quicker to cycle, by the time you've parked and that. I'll see you in there.'

I turned to walk away, hating the awkwardness between us. Knowing it would take a long time to repair the damage I had caused.

'Sarah,' Jonathan called.

I spun round, hoping for something to cling to. A dimpled grin perhaps.

'I've forgotten the milk for the refreshment stall,' he said. 'You couldn't pop and get some on the way, could you?'

I nodded slowly and walked back to my car.

The atmosphere at the Central Library was predictably earnest, posters advertising Jonathan's talk placed with precision on every available surface along the route to the lecture theatre.

Rachel and Richard were already there, surrounded by an array of colourful banners, posters and Amnesty merchandise which they had arranged with military (or whatever the non-violent equivalent was) precision on and around a long trestle table.

'Hi, Sarah,' Rachel said. 'Jonathan said you'd be along in a minute, he's just checking everything's ready to go in the hall. I like your hair like that, by the way. Are you growing it?'

I hadn't realised there was anything different about my hair.

'Oh, thanks. I haven't had a chance to get it cut lately, that's all.'

'I've got a favour to ask you,' she continued. 'Pam's been struck down with flu, can't make it tonight. So we're short of someone to run the refreshment stall. I was wondering if you'd mind.'

I realised now why she'd paid me the compliment. Unfortunately I couldn't think of an excuse within the necessary time.

'I guess not,' I said.

'Thanks, Sarah. I'll be over in a minute with the cakes. You know the ropes.'

I squeezed behind the table on the other side of the lecture theatre doors. An empty plastic ice cream tub had been left for me to collect the money, together with a bag of small change for the float, a stack of polystyrene cups and the tea and coffee urns. I wondered what Nick was doing. If he'd left yet. If he was eating a takeout on his own.

'I see Rachel's got you working.' It was Jonathan, standing in front of me, his Free Tibet badges jostling for space on his Amnesty T-shirt.

'Yeah,' I said, without the required enthusiasm. 'Are you all set?'

'I think so. I'll be all right as long as I don't get a computer glitch with the Powerpoint.'

I nodded. Rachel trotted over and handed me two homemade fruit cakes, already cut into the correct-sized portions. She was about to walk away when she stopped and gave me a strange look.

'Where's your Amnesty T-shirt, Sarah?' she said. I felt like a schoolkid being reprimanded for not wearing the correct uniform. I looked to Jonathan for support. He said nothing.

'At home. I was in a rush.'

'Here,' she said, handing me a T-shirt from the stall. 'Can't miss a chance to wear the merchandise when you're meeting and greeting the public.'

I stared at her hard. I was an advertising billboard now, as well as a human vending machine.

'I'll watch the stall while you go and get changed,' volunteered Jonathan. 'Don't be long, mind. It's only twenty minutes to kick-off time.'

I started to say something but stopped myself when I noticed Jonathan's trembling hand. Clearly the big night nerves were getting to him.

I disappeared into the ladies' loos to replace my offensive plum-coloured shirt. I caught sight of my reflection in the mirror as I entered. Rachel was right. My hair had grown, flicking up at the ends, brushing past my collar. A few definite kinks, if not yet curls. But my face was lifeless, my eyes flat, my skin sallow. Something

had died inside me. I tried to remember when Sarah
Roberts's spirit had departed her body, leaving behind an
outer shell, hard and resilient but hollow-sounding.

I made my way back to the refreshment stall, pushing
past the members of the public who were now milling
around in the corridor. Jonathan was about to serve a
grey-haired lady. He was looking agitated.

'The milk, Sarah,' he said. 'Did you remember the
milk?'

'Yeah, don't worry,' I said. 'I stopped off at the petrol
station. It's in my bag, there, on the floor.'

Jonathan was staring at me.

'Which petrol station?' he said.

'The Shell garage on the corner.'

'You bought milk for my Tibet talk from a company
which has invested millions in an oil pipeline in China?
How do you think the Dalai Lama would feel about that?'

I looked at him, unable to believe what he'd just said.
Angry that he was doing this again. Making me feel bad.
Something inside me snapped.

'I don't expect he'd give a fuck, and nor do I.'

Jonathan stared at me as a hush descended on the
corridor.

'Sarah. What on earth's got into you?'

'Nothing,' I said. 'I stopped at the first place I came to
for the milk. All so I could get here sooner and offer you
the support you said you needed. And this is what I get
in return.'

Jonathan looked down at his feet. 'I didn't mean to
have a go. I'm just surprised at you, that's all.'

I shook my head. He was sounding like his mother
again. I wasn't sure how much more I could take.

'There are more important things in life to worry
about, Jonathan, than where a bloody pint of milk came
from.'

'What's more important than upholding our
principles?'

I slapped my hand to my forehead in disbelief. He wasn't listening. Wasn't understanding what I was getting at. Nor was he ever going to.

'Us, Jonathan. Me and you. At least it should be.'

I pulled the Amnesty T-shirt over my head and dropped it on the fruit cake, not caring about the stares and gasps that greeted the appearance of my Wonderbra. Jonathan's jaw dropped open, his eyes bulged wide in horror.

'Sarah,' he shrieked.

'I'm sorry, Jonathan, but I'm not going to pretend to be the person you want me to be any more. I'm going to start being me again.'

'Is this about Nick?' said Jonathan.

'No, it's about me. You asked me not to lie to you. But my whole life is a lie. And I don't want to live like that any more.'

'I don't understand.'

'I know,' I said. 'And that's the problem.'

Jonathan's face crumpled. He looked small and fragile now he had climbed off his soapbox.

'I don't love you, Jonathan. Not the way I should do. You've been incredibly good to me and I'll always be grateful for that. But it's over.'

'No, Sarah, please . . .'

I looked down, aware from his quivering voice that he was close to tears.

'You'll be fine without me,' I said softly. 'You're stronger than you think. And I'm really sorry for messing up your talk.'

I strode off up the corridor, hurriedly pulling my shirt from my bag and doing it up as I went. Knowing I had hurt him. But freed myself in the process.

I stood on Nick's doorstep, bulging suitcase in one hand, a trembling, tingling sensation in the other. I reached out and rang the bell. I heard the TV being turned down and footsteps approaching. Nick opened the door, a ten pound note in one hand. He stared at me for a long time without saying anything.

'What did you order?' I asked.

'A medium-sized thin and crispy marinara.'

'Happy with what you've got instead?'

Nick nodded. Unable to speak.

'Good, then put your money away and let me dump this case in your hall because I'm taking you out for a meal to celebrate me moving in with you.'

A big smile drifted over Nick's face.

'Which Sarah is it who's moving in?' he said.

I hesitated as I shivered on the doorstep.

'The old one,' I said. 'High mileage, a bit of rust, some crash damage that will need sorting out. But she has at least got a reconditioned engine. And bags of character.'

'Fantastic,' he said, taking the case from me with a huge grin. 'That's exactly who I've been looking for.'

Now you can buy any of these other bestselling
books by from your bookshop
or *direct from the publisher*.

FREE P&P AND UK DELIVERY
(Overseas and Ireland £3.50 per book)

The Island	Victoria Hislop	£7.99
Left Bank	Kate Muir	£6.99
Wicked	Gregory Maguire	£7.99
Cuban Heels	Emily Barr	£7.99
The Distance Between Us	Maggie O'Farrell	£7.99
Blue Water	Manette Ansay	£6.99
Sparkles	Louise Bagshawe	£6.99
Come and Tell me Some Lies	Raffaella Barker	£7.99
The Lost Art of Keeping Secrets	Eva Rice	£6.99
The Godmother	Carrie Adams	£6.99

TO ORDER SIMPLY CALL THIS NUMBER

01235 400 414

or visit our website: www.madaboutbooks.com

Prices and availability subject to change without notice.